PIRATE: FREEBOOTER

TIM SEVERIN

PIRATE

VOLUME FIVE
FREEBOOTER

MACMILLAN

First published 2017 by Macmillan
an imprint of Pan Macmillan
20 New Wharf Road, London N1 9RR
Associated companies throughout the world
www.panmacmillan.com

ISBN 978-1-4472-6225-1 HB

1 3 5 7 9 8 6 4 2

A CIP catalogue record for this book is available from the British Library.

Map artwork by Neil Gower
Typeset by Ellipsis Digital Limited, Glasgow
Printed and bound by CPI Group (UK) Ltd, Croydon, CR0 4YY

Visit *www.panmacmillan.com* to read more about all our books
and to buy them. You will also find features, author interviews and
news of any author events, and you can sign up for e-newsletters
so that you're always first to hear about our new releases.

PIRATE: FREEBOOTER

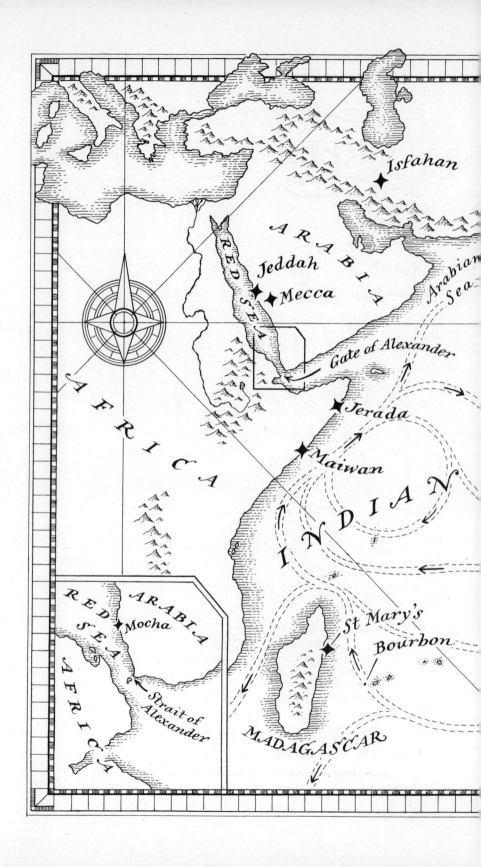

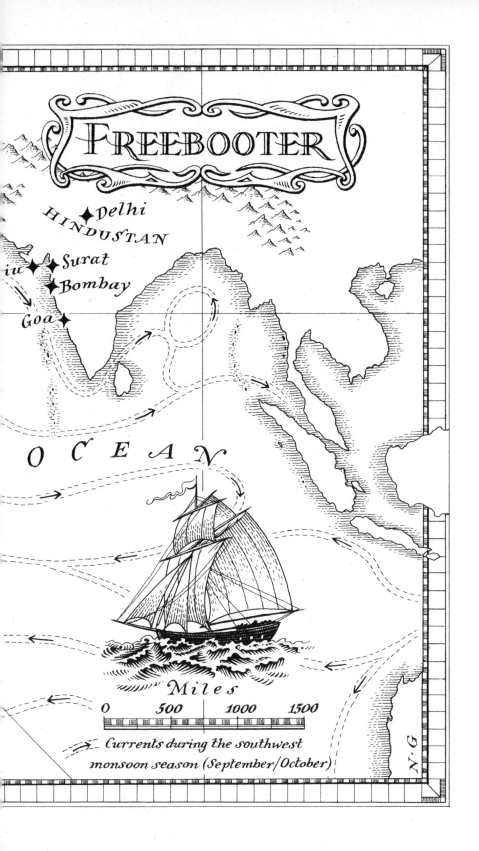

FREEBOOTER

Delhi

HINDUSTAN

Surat

Bombay

Goa

OCEAN

Miles

| 0 | 500 | 1000 | 1500 |

Currents during the southwest
monsoon season (September/October)

N·G

ONE

THE SHARP, FLAT CRACK of a single cannon shot brought Hector Lynch to a halt. Turning, he looked back along the path through the forest. He had been walking uphill for half an hour and a gap in the trees gave him a clear view down into St Mary's shallow harbour, where half a dozen small vessels lay at anchor. Experience told him that the sound came from a 'murderer', a giant musket classed by artillerymen as a falconet. The gun was light enough to have been carried ashore from one of the ships, then mounted on wheels. His eyes searched for the telltale puff of smoke but it was difficult to pinpoint exactly where the sound had come from. It was less than an hour after sunrise on another swelteringly hot day, and a thin haze of smoke from the morning cooking fires still lingered over the palm-thatch roofs of the settlement. He presumed the falconet had been fired from the open space normally used as a marketplace. He could see that a small crowd was already assembling there.

'How many more, would you guess?' Hector asked his companion.

Before he answered, Jacques Bourdon pulled the grubby handkerchief off his close-cropped head and used the cloth to dab the sweat from his face. The letters GAL branded into his right cheek were barely noticeable beneath the beard stubble.

They marked him as someone who had served as a convict oarsman on King Louis's galleys, a legacy from his days as a Parisian pickpocket and housebreaker. After more than ten years of seafaring alongside Jacques, Hector no longer noticed the faint scars, nor his friend's crooked nose, broken long before the two men had met in a Marseilles holding cell.

'Why don't we make a bet on it?' suggested the Frenchman.

'I've learned not to wager with you,' replied Hector.

'Then I'll make it easy. Anything less than thirty and you win.'

Another cannon shot echoed around the low green hills over-looking the settlement.

'He'd never have lasted beyond thirty, not the way he lived,' Jacques coaxed.

About my own age when he died, thought Hector. What was the motto that such people lived by? That was it: 'A short life and a merry one'. The firing of the falconet was to salute the passing of one of St Mary's wilder characters. A boisterous man and a heavy drinker, he had been unruly to the point of being a danger to himself, and generous with his money, of which he had acquired a fair sum by dubious means. Already well liked, he had added to his popularity by announcing as he lay dying of the bloody flux that one tenth of his fortune was to be spent on free drink for the townsfolk. The remainder of his worldly goods was to be shared equally among his former shipmates on condition that they buried him with his pistols and cutlass. After they had tamped down the earth over his coffin, they were to fire a minute gun over his grave, one shot for every year of his life.

'Not what we had been led to expect,' observed Jacques, re-knotting his head cloth back in place. Like Hector, he was wearing only a loose cotton shirt and breeches suited to the sultry and oppressive climate, and on his feet were the lightest pair of boots that he had been able to find. He would have preferred to go barefoot but the soft mud of the path concealed an occasional sharp twig that could cause nasty cuts that were likely to fester.

Worse, he had seen for himself the revolting worms that could enter through the sole of the bare foot and burrow upward: thin and pale as a candle wick, their heads later erupted out through a man's skin, usually at his foot or leg below the knee. The creatures had to be extracted slowly and painfully, inch by inch, by being wound around a thin stick. The longest such parasite he had watched as it was teased out had measured more than a yard.

Hector was too distracted to reply. He was staring out at the disappointment that was St Mary's: an untidy straggle of shacks and large sheds newly erected around a notch in the rocky coast. To the west, across the narrow channel, loomed the bulk of Madagascar, shadowed that morning under a lowering cloud-bank. From there the warring native tribes paddled their dugout canoes to bring their prisoners for sale to the slave traders in St Mary's. All around him the vegetation was smothering the land with a suffocating green carpet. Trees, shrubs and climbing vines thrived in the warm, moist conditions that made Jacques and him pour with sweat. The palms, bamboos and mangroves down by the shoreline were familiar. He had seen them in other countries during his voyages, but some grotesques were new to him, with broad fleshy leaves or clusters of exposed roots like bundles of huge parsnips. Thankfully the forest did not seem to harbour snakes or other dangers, though the gnats and mosquitoes and other flying insects were a trial. It was the emptiness, the sense of untamed, rampant wilderness, that he found so overwhelming and depressing. As Jacques had said, this was not what he had expected eighteen months ago.

Libertalia was the name he had heard back then: a new, distant country on the farthest rim of Africa, founded by free-minded people who rejected the notions of class and privilege. They held that all men were born equal and elected their own council to make their laws. They had no interest in amassing wealth, abhorred slavery and had devised their own language: in Libertalia the citizens spoke a mixture of the tongues of all those who chose to live there, and no longer considered themselves to be English or Scots or Irish, or French or Dutch or African. They simply called themselves Liberi. The fertile soil and pleasant climate allowed a man to support his family by his own labour with crops grown on smallholdings. Everything was held in common, so hedges and fences were unknown.

The thought of moving to live in Libertalia had cast a spell on Hector. He was yearning to set up a secure, permanent home with Maria, the woman with whom he intended to share the rest of his life, and to raise a family. In the four years he had known her, he doubted they had been together for more than a third of that time. Their days as a couple had been a struggle, constantly on the move, frequently disrupted. In the beginning it was because she was of Spanish descent and he was half-Irish, half-Galician and a subject of the King of England, and their respective sovereigns were at war. More recently, the governments of both countries had been pursuing him, laying charges of piracy against him. A great earthquake in Jamaica had saved him from the hangman, when the shaking ground and tidal waves had collapsed the prison where he was being held, wrecked the courthouse and other government buildings and swept away all semblance of order. In the chaos, he and Maria, together with Jacques, had slipped away to Bermuda, where the corrupt governor was known to turn a blind eye to men on the run. There he had talked with a merchant captain of a ship chartered to deliver a cargo halfway around the world, to St Mary's. According to what he had heard, St Mary's was either Libertalia itself or very close to where it was to be found. So he had spent the last of his money to buy passages there for himself and Maria; and Jacques, attracted to the idea of a country where his criminal past would be ignored, had accompanied them.

Now, as Hector looked out over the dispiriting sight of the settlement, he feared that he had made a disastrous error. He had yet to meet anyone in St Mary's who believed in the sharing of worldly goods or in the equality of man. Quite the opposite.

People came there with the sole intention of making themselves rich as quickly as possible, by fair means or foul, and the slave trade flourished.

Hector knew that St Mary's could never provide them with the sanctuary they sought.

His gloomy thoughts were interrupted by an ill-tempered shout, ordering him and Jacques to stand aside. A short, stocky man of middle age richly dressed in a fine lace shirt, pale grey silk breeches and stockings and expensive black leather pumps on his feet was coming down the track towards them, striding confidently towards the settlement. To make his meaning clear, he made a couple of sideways swings with a polished ebony cane as if sweeping aside weeds. A respectful few steps behind him followed two heavily muscled black men dressed in cast-off European clothes. One carried an umbrella and the other a portable stool. Hector had no difficulty in recognizing them as household slaves. Bringing up the rear of the little group was a handsome young woman of about sixteen years old. She too was dressed in European clothes, a loose gown of some gauzy material tightly belted to show off her generous figure, yellow satin slippers now splashed with mud and a matching broad-brimmed bonnet that set off her natural colouring. Her perfect skin was a dark coffee brown and marked her out as locally born.

Hector and Jacques both stepped off the path and into the undergrowth and waited to let them pass. As the man with the cane drew level, he gave them a sharp glance and came to an abrupt stop.

'Do I know you? You seem familiar,' he demanded rudely, staring into Hector's face.

'I don't think so. We only landed a week ago,' Hector replied.

The man turned toward Jacques, and must have noticed the faint galérien's brand, for he pointed at it with his cane and announced in a sour rasping voice with a faint trace of a Scots accent, 'Don't think you can bring your misbegotten ideas here, Frenchie.'

The tip of the cane was quivering within inches of Jacques's face and the Frenchman reached out a hand to push it aside. Instantly the nearest black slave dropped the umbrella, lunged forward and grabbed his arm, clamping it tight.

'Here, let me see that hand,' growled the stocky man.

The slave twisted Jacques's wrist, forcing him to splay his fingers. The skin between thumb and forefinger was tattooed with the letter V for voleur.

'So a thief as well as fugitive,' observed the stocky man. 'I could have you locked up until the next French ship calls by, and then hand you over. But I'll be generous. You've got ten days to get out of St Mary's, and when you meet your false prophet, tell him that if he ever sets foot here I'll stuff that white flag up his backside.'

He nodded at his slave to release Jacques's arm and strode onward, stabbing angrily at the mud with his cane. Hector heard him mutter, 'I'll give them "God and Liberty".'

Jacques waited until the little group had disappeared around a bend in the path.

'What was all that about?' he asked, opening and closing his hand to flex his fingers. 'If I find him without those two brutes, I'll punch him in the mouth.'

'Not a good idea,' Hector told him. 'That must have been Adam Baldridge.'

'Stuck-up bastard.' Jacques spat into the bushes.

Hector did not need to explain who Baldridge was. His admirers were only half-joking when they called him 'the King of St Mary's' and many were in awe of him, as well as envious. Baldridge had founded St Mary's, setting up an isolated trading station at great personal risk. He had dealt with the chiefs of the local tribes, supplying them with liquor and weapons. He bought slaves from them for shipment to the Americas, and taken a chieftain's daughter as a wife. Within a couple of years his success was attracting others to his settlement. He now owned a major share in most of its businesses, especially the lucrative drinking shops.

The largest building in the settlement was his warehouse, stocked with goods that supply ships regularly brought from Europe and the American colonies. Recently he had built himself a mansion on the hill overlooking the harbour, and lived there with a retinue of servants and a small harem of native women. But he had made enemies as well. Those whom he had bullied or cheated would not hesitate to stick a knife between his ribs. For that reason Baldridge, whenever he ventured into town, took along his body-guards.

'At least he knew about the white flag. So he's heard of Libertalia. Maybe it's somewhere else farther along the coast,' said Hector, trying to sound more optimistic than he felt. A white flag with 'God and Liberty' written on it was said to be the flag of Libertalia.

'It would help if we could find someone who sailed on the *Victoire*,' said Jacques. From what he had heard, Libertalia had been founded by one of his countrymen, a certain Misson, captain of the French privateer *Victoire*, just as Baldridge had established St Mary's.

'There's tavern talk that Misson went farther north. Maybe that's where we should search,' Hector suggested. He looked up at the sky as he felt a single fat drop of rain land on his shoulder. Away to the east a line of clouds was moving in from the sea, their underbellies dark and swollen. A moment later the first warning roll of thunder reached them, punctuated by another sharp report from the minute gun.

'We'd better turn back,' he said to Jacques. The two of them began to retrace their steps and were still well short of St Mary's when the deluge hit them. The rain cascaded down, spattering up little sprays of the mud as it hit the ground, turning the path into a braid of rivulets. Jacques and Hector took shelter under a tree and listened to the drumming of the torrential rain on its broad leaves. Very soon the drips were finding their way onto them and they were as wet as if they had stayed in the open.

'Should have made that bet with me,' said Jacques. The sounds of the funeral salute from the falconet had stopped. 'They never got beyond ten. Wouldn't risk getting their powder soaked.'

'Maybe they'll start up again once the sun comes out,' Hector answered him. The island's heavy showers rarely lasted for more than ten or fifteen minutes.

'I doubt it. The gunners will have gone off to the tavern to help their shipmates drink up the dead man's legacy. They'll soon be too fuddled to remember what they were meant to be doing, or to keep count.'

A sudden quick movement on a nearby branch caught Hector's eye. A tiny frog, scarcely larger than a grape, had jumped across from the main trunk and was clinging on, watching him suspiciously. It was at head level and not more than a yard away, close enough for him to see the large black pupils in the bulging eyes. The body was extraordinarily beautiful, a glistening emerald green as a background to bold black stripes edged with white. He wanted to reach out and coax the creature to jump to his hand but knew that the moment he moved it would leap away.

'I wonder where she's from?' Jacques's question interrupted his thoughts. The Frenchman had spotted a vessel just coming into view from behind the islet in the mouth to St Mary's anchorage. She was a slender, black-hulled sloop with an unusually long, slanting bowsprit that gave her a rakish air, quite unlike the square-built, sturdy ships from New England bringing Baldridge the rum, gunpowder and other stores that he sold on at three times their cost. The sloop was neatly handled. Hector watched as her two headsails came down, and then the mainsail swung over as she tacked and lined up for the final approach. In less than five minutes, she would be gliding past the land battery of four cannon that Baldridge had installed to protect his investment. Hector's spirits rose. Perhaps the sloop's captain was only making a brief stopover in St Mary's to take on water and supplies, then continuing farther north. He and Jacques should go in that direction if they hoped to find Libertalia.

'Let's get down to the harbour,' he said, 'before anyone else asks the captain if he's taking on extra crew.'

TWO

THE TWO OF THEM hurried down the track, avoiding treacherous patches of slippery wet leaf mould and stepping across the little gulleys carved by the run-off. By the time they passed the first of St Mary's outlying houses, the rain had ceased, leaving the humid air heavy with the smells of woodsmoke, cooking, mould and wet thatch. They skirted around the small marketplace where a scavenging dog was guzzling on the entrails of a slaughtered goat among the litter of rotten fruit, broken baskets, chicken feathers, fish guts and other rubbish. The earlier crowd had dispersed, leaving several small native boys to take it in turns to peep under the old canvas sail that covered an odd-looking shape standing in the middle of the open space – the abandoned falconet.

Hector and Jacques reached the dockside to see that the newly arrived sloop had dropped anchor some distance away and already lowered a small boat. The rain clouds had moved on out to sea and towards the Madagascar highlands and Hector had to squint into the sun's glare reflected off the pale blue water of the harbour. A sailor was climbing down a rope ladder. Once in the boat, he set his oars in place and waited for a second man to take his seat in the stern before he began to row towards the shore. The oarsman was a giant. Even with his back towards him, the broad shoulders and the way he moved, pulling a long, powerful stroke, was familiar.

Jacques let out a grunt of surprise. 'Surely that's Jezreel. I thought he'd gone home to London. I wonder what made him change his mind.'

'Maybe that murder charge is still held against him,' said Hector. Both men knew that Jezreel Hall, their former shipmate, had once made his living as a prize-fighter. He had specialized in the vicious contests where he and his opponent stood toe-to-toe and cut and parried, using blunt backswords. The accidental death of one of his opponents in the London ring had obliged Jezreel to flee the city, and he had set up as a logwood cutter on the Caribbean's wild Campeche coast where Hector had first met him.

The two men made their way cautiously out along the loose planks laid on top of the bamboo scaffolding that served as the jetty. As they stood watching the skiff come closer, Hector had an uncomfortable feeling that the past was catching up on him. He, Jacques and Jezreel had been on several voyages together, and he was aware that the others had come to look to him as their natural leader. He did not relish the role. There had been times when the responsibility had weighed very heavily on him. When Jezreel had announced after the Jamaican earthquake that he was returning to England it had seemed that at least some of the burden was lifting. Now Hector was ashamed to find himself hoping that it was a coincidence that Jezreel should be here in St Mary's. In his bones, however, he knew that was unlikely.

The skiff was soon close enough for him to look down and see the pattern of scars on Jezreel's scalp, a legacy from his days as a prize-fighter. The big man was still facing over the stern of the skiff as he rowed, unaware of the presence of his friends so close by. Only when the skiff bumped against the jetty and Jezreel put down his oars, turned, picked up a rope and got ready to throw it, did he look up and saw his two friends waiting there. They had been expecting a smile, but instead saw an expression of relief. 'Thank God, you're here!' he called up, then threw the rope for them to catch.

There was a pause while the skiff was made fast and Jezreel held the little boat steady against the bamboo pilings so that the man in the stern could clamber up onto the dock. Hector presumed he was the sloop's captain and looked at him with interest. He saw a handsome, athletic man in his early forties who wore his long dark hair tied back at the nape of his neck with a black silk ribbon. A short moustache was carefully trimmed and combed, and his beard came to a neat point. The well-cut frock coat of deep blue broadcloth had silver buttons and its fashionably long pocket flaps were edged in silver lace. Slightly sea-stained white stockings and breeches, buckled shoes, and a rapier hanging from an embossed leather baldric completed his dress. Hector, aware that a rapier was far less use aboard ship than a cutlass, wondered why the newcomer had chosen to create such a swashbuckling impression.

The newcomer nodded politely as he stepped round them and began walking briskly into the settlement. It was evident that he knew his way.

'Greetings, you great ox!' Jacques exclaimed, slapping Jezreel on the back as he heaved himself up on the jetty. 'Chased away from England again! What was the reason this time? Your missus asking why you'd abandoned her for so long?'

Jezreel shook his head, his brief grin of pleasure replaced by a more earnest look. Addressing Hector, he asked, 'Is there somewhere we can talk privately?'

'Of course. We can go to the house where we have our lodgings.'

St Mary's only street was the unpaved track that traced the curve of the foreshore. On one side was the gently sloping beach where a dozen native dugout canoes were drawn up on the sand. Opposite, a ragged line of mismatched buildings looked as though they had been thrown up wherever someone had chosen to cut back the encroaching vegetation. The only large and substantial structure was Baldridge's warehouse strategically placed nearest to the bamboo jetty. Its walls were built of stone blocks cut from the coral reef, and there were imported tiles on the roof. The other buildings were constructed in the native style with mud brick walls and roofs of pandanus leaves. Most were little more than shacks that served as shops, storehouses or dwellings, or – more likely – as all three at the same time. Only the several barnlike taverns stood out. They were larger and noisier and had front porches where, that morning, their customers were raucously celebrating the generosity of the dead man in his grave. Dishevelled and disorderly, the drinkers were typical of the drifters, mavericks and adventurers that pitched up in St Mary's. Some had the raw sun-scorched complexions of northerners, others were almost as dark-skinned as the native Africans, and there was every shade in between. Their dress was equally varied: red pantaloons of standard shipboard issue were popular; others wore grubby white cotton trousers cut short to make loose breeches. Most garments were ragged and patched, and among the smocks and shirts, some wore only a waistcoat or went bare-chested in the heat. Hats, caps and head cloths were of different styles and colours, and many heads were shaved bare and glistening with sweat. The majority of the drinkers were in their twenties or early thirties though Hector noticed one grizzled veteran wearing what must once have been a military buff coat from which he had cut away the sleeves.

There was no sign of the sloop's captain.

Jacques's light-hearted banter trailed away as soon as he realized that Jezreel was ill at ease and anxious. The three men walked in silence to where Hector had rented a room at the shabbiest and cheapest of the taverns. Here, too, the funeral celebrations were in full swing, and they were bombarded with drunken invitations to join the merrymaking before they managed to find themselves a quiet spot where benches and tables had been left out under a palm tree.

'Is Maria here with you?' demanded Jezreel abruptly as soon as they had sat down.

The bluntness of his question took Hector aback. In Bermuda, he had explained to his comrades that he felt his life had reached the stage where he should give priority to his future with Maria. He had spoken at length about his plans to establish a new home in Libertalia, and they had respected his wishes. If he ever needed their help, they told him, it would be given. Now, judging by Jezreel's anxious tone of voice, it seemed that something was not quite right.

'Maria will join me after I've settled in Libertalia,' he answered defensively. 'On the voyage here we learned that she is with child. Luckily, our ship stopped in the Canaries, where she has some distant cousins in Tenerife. She'll stay with them until the baby's born, then she'll follow on.'

He broke off as a sudden quarrel erupted among the drinkers in the tavern's porch. Two men were in a furious shouting match. Hector turned to see what was going on. One of the revellers ran out into the open and began to mince up and down, wiggling his hips suggestively while his colleagues looked on, hooting with laughter and making lewd comments. Hector gathered that the quarrel was about who should inherit the dead man's woman. Moments later the quarrel turned ugly. One claimant to the woman leaped forward, got his hands around his rival's throat and tried to throttle him. There were whoops of encouragement as their drunken comrades gathered round to watch the fight. The two men swayed back and forth, then tripped and fell to the ground, and were lost from view. There was more excited baying, followed by a pistol shot, and when the crowd parted it was to leave space for the wounded victim to be carried away by his friends.

When the hubbub had settled, Jacques could contain his curiosity no longer. 'Jezreel, what made you change your mind about returning to London?'

'I got as far as New York and was looking for a ship to take me to England when I came across the captain of that sloop.'

Jacques frowned. 'Quite a coxcomb, by the look of him.'

'That's Thomas Tew.'

The mention of the name made Hector sit up straight. 'Tew! Jacques and I have trying to track him down. It's said that Misson has put him in charge of all Libertalia's ships. Tew can tell us how to get to Libertalia—'

The stony look on Jezreel's face made him hesitate.

'Have you heard different?' Hector finished on a slightly puzzled note.

Jezreel chose his words carefully. 'I heard the exactly same rumour in New York: that Tew is teamed up with Misson in his Libertalia project. So when I learned that Tew's ship was in port and due to sail for Madagascar, I went aboard to ask him if he could help you and Maria when he got here.'

Hector sensed that Jezreel was holding something back. 'What made you come all the way here yourself? Tew would have put in a good word with Misson after you had spoken with him.'

Jezreel pressed his lips together like someone considering how to deliver an unpleasant message with the least hurt. 'Hector, I have to tell you that Thomas Tew has heard about Libertalia. But he has no idea how the rumour got started that he has anything to do with Misson. I asked him straight out.'

Hector was unwilling to be put off. 'But when Tew came ashore just now, he looked as if he knew his way about. He must have been in St Mary's before?'

Jezreel nodded. 'He has. But he told me that he's never been to any country by the name of Libertalia nor has he ever met with Misson . . .' He paused, before adding in an unhappy voice, 'If such a person really exists.'

Hector could not believe what he was hearing. 'But that's impossible! Who else could have founded Libertalia?'

Jezreel's silence was unnerving. When he next spoke, his

voice was full of apology. 'I only know what I've heard from Thomas Tew, and he had no reason to lie to me. So I decided I had to get here and warn you before you and Maria blundered into real trouble. It's lucky that I caught up with you when you had got no farther than St Mary's. Thankfully, Maria isn't here.'

Hector gazed in shock at the big man. Jezreel had called into question everything that he and Jacques had hoped for and planned. If neither Misson nor Libertalia existed, then by raising her false hopes he'd failed Maria just as he had failed the Frenchman.

Jacques provided a brief moment of support. 'You're wrong there, Jezreel,' he said. 'This morning we ran into the chief man of this place. Right bastard by the name of Baldridge. He believes in Misson, even told me to clear off before I brought any of Misson's ideas into St Mary's.'

Jezreel opened his mouth, but nothing came out, then he sighed and stated with a tone of calm finality: 'There is no such place as Libertalia. It's a fancy tale, invented to attract people to come out here. I wish it was otherwise.'

There was a long silence. Finally, Jacques asked quietly, 'Just supposing that you're right, Jezreel, what do you suggest we do now?'

Hector knew that the question had really been addressed to him, not Jezreel. He was all too aware that Jacques had followed his example when deciding to seek a new life in Libertalia.

'I suppose we could head back to Bermuda, or Jamaica,' he heard himself say. 'Pick up where we left off. I could send word for Maria to join me, with the baby.'

He tried to force brightness into his voice though he was numbed by the collapse of his dream. He knew that what he was proposing was an act of desperation, full of risk. Eventually the authorities in Jamaica would receive from London their official copies of the various charges of piracy against him. Then the machinery of justice could grind back into action. If he returned to the Caribbean with Maria and the baby, he – and his friends as well – would probably finish up in prison or on the gallows. He felt slightly sick as he recalled that he was virtually penniless. He did not even have enough money to live on while he came up with a new way of providing for Maria and the baby.

Jacques must have guessed what he was thinking. 'Don't worry about me, Hector. I'll wait for a ship heading out of here and offer to work my passage before that whoreson Baldridge makes good his threat to put me aboard a ship bound for France. I don't expect much of a welcome there.'

When Jezreel next spoke, he was not looking directly at his friends but down at his hands. They were big and calloused, the knuckles marked with the scars from backsword cuts. In a hoarse voice that was just above a whisper, he said, 'There is a way we can make enough money to start all over again, sufficient to buy ourselves new identities, or purchase pardons from a willing judge who'll pocket a juicy bribe to make the past disappear.'

Hector felt an awful tightness gathering in his chest. He knew what Jezreel was going to propose. He had been hiding the truth from himself ever since he had come to St Mary's. He had seen the ne'er-do-wells in the taverns, and the occasional glimpse of unlikely wealth: a rough-and-ready sailor wearing a gold brocade sash to hold up his pantaloons and paying for a round of drinks in the tavern with an unfamiliar silver coin. Then there had been the exotic items, including a magnificent feather fan on a six-foot gilded shaft, that were carried from the jetty into Baldridge's warehouse. They were not items obtained by legitimate commerce, not even in the slave trade. They were loot from the sea. Baldridge, and others like him in St Mary's, were dealers in stolen goods, the proceeds of piracy.

Jezreel spoke again. 'On the voyage here I got friendly with the crew on Tew's ship. Most of them have sailed with him before, and they say this is their final trip. There's a great prize to be had – they would not tell me what it is. But it's enough to set them up for life.'

'You mean, we go back to piracy,' said Hector in a stiff voice.

'It won't be the same,' Jezreel insisted, speaking more firmly now. 'We're on the far side of Africa. The authorities in London or the Caribbean could not care what happens here. Even if they do find out, it'll be far too late. We'll have gone our own ways.'

'You're forgetting about the ship-owners,' Hector told him. 'If they're hurt, they'll insist we're hunted down and hung.' He was thinking of the powerful trading companies – English, French and Dutch – whose vessels sailed the eastern routes. These would be the most likely targets for men like Tew.

'Tew's not so rash as to interfere with them. From what I learned from his crew, it's foreigners who'll be losing their riches – and there are other raiders coming to join him. There'll be a whole squadron of freebooters.'

Hector stared glumly out towards where Tew's sloop was at anchor. From the moment he had seen the vessel entering harbour, he had known she had no merchandise in her hold. Her sleek hull was never designed for cargo, and she gave off an air of menace.

Jacques leaned forward and laid a hand on his arm. 'Hector, if we do as Jezreel suggests, maybe we'll stumble across Misson or even Libertalia on the way to wherever it is these freebooters are going. There's nothing here for us in St Mary's. I'm prepared to take the chance.'

The atmosphere hung heavily between the three friends as Hector struggled with his conscience, unwilling to take the next step.

'Very well,' he said at last and with a heavy heart. 'But just for this one venture, and if there's any risk to my future with Maria, I'll back out.'

He rose to his feet. 'Let's join the others in the tavern. At least we can celebrate Jezreel's arrival.'

That evening Hector drank himself into a stupor. Maria had

trusted him to shape a law-abiding future for them to share. The thought that he had now chosen to put her faith in him at risk was difficult to bear.

THREE

ANOTHER CANNON SHOT woke him, this time a very different sound – a deep heavy thud followed immediately by two similar detonations in quick succession. They were so close at hand that the air shook, and a sharp jab of pain lanced through his skull. He forced open his gummy eyelids. He was lying on the earth floor of their rented room and could not remember how he had got there. The inside of his mouth tasted foul, his tongue swollen and rough. He closed his eyes and waited for the throbbing pain in his head to subside, but he was desperately thirsty and needed to empty his bladder.

He was summoning up the strength to get to his feet when he became aware of people outside, cursing and calling out in alarm. He heard someone yell that St Mary's was under attack. Groggily he hauled himself to his feet, shambled to the door, and looked out. To his astonishment, he saw that a large and heavily armed three-masted ship was already halfway along the approach channel. Very soon she would be safely past the shore battery that defended St Mary's and the settlement would be at the mercy of her broadsides. Hector hung on to the doorpost to steady himself. It was mid-morning and the bright sunlight hurt his eyes. This newcomer was truly formidable. He judged her to be close to 400 tons, more than three times the size of Tew's sloop.

Laboriously he counted the guns facing him on the port side – twenty-three of them arranged in two tiers, some on the upper deck, and the muzzles of the others poking out through gun ports cut in the hull. Those he could see clearly were demi-culverins that fired a nine-pound ball. Two or three well-placed shots would reduce even Baldridge's well-built warehouse to rubble. He winced, and gripped the doorpost more firmly as one of the stranger's deck cannon fired and the blast ripped across the calm water of the harbour. A flock of gulls circling over the mangroves dipped and swerved away. 'Shit! That's a king's ship!' exclaimed a man standing nearby in the tavern's porch. He sounded as though he had a bad case of the jitters, and judging by the grey haggard look on his face, he must have been one of the revellers on the previous day.

'Why didn't the shore battery stop her?' complained his companion, who looked equally worse for wear.

'Gunners too drunk or sleeping it off, no doubt. Lazy swine.' The unknown vessel was taking in her sails and turning up into the wind. 'She's coming to anchor. We better shift ourselves before the shore party gets here.'

Hector looked for an ensign flying at the mainmast or the vessel's broad stern. There was nothing to identify her nationality. If this was a king's ship, he could understand the near-panic among the observers. Many of them would be wanted by the law.

Jezreel sauntered round the corner, a half-eaten loaf of bread in his hand and his mouth full. He must have been having breakfast in the front room of the tavern. He appeared to be remarkably relaxed.

'What do you make of her?' Hector asked him.

Jezreel chewed and swallowed before answering. 'English-built by the look of her. As I said last evening, there are other captains coming to join Tew. This one's prepared to waste some gunpowder by the sound of it.'

The consternation outside the tavern was beginning to subside as the onlookers realized that the strange vessel had been firing a salute, not bombarding the settlement. Jezreel offered Hector the rest of the loaf. 'Here, have a bite of this. You look dreadful. Something in your stomach will help.'

Hector shook his head and went to relieve himself behind the bushes before re-joining Jezreel. The big man had taken a seat on the same bench as the previous evening, and was calmly watching the scene unfold. The newly arrived ship dominated the small harbour. Her hull was painted black with a broad white stripe just above the waterline that ran full length from bow to stern. Some sort of carved figurehead decorated her stem, though it was too far for Hector to make out what the image represented. There were still no national colours at her stern or the mainmast and Hector allowed himself to imagine the white ensign of Libertalia hoisted there. He was beginning to recover from Jezreel's disastrous news, and deep down, he clung to the notion that Libertalia or a sanctuary like it would eventually materialize.

After a while, an oared boat came into view from the far side of the vessel. Unlike the little skiff in which Jezreel had rowed Tew ashore, this was a pinnace manned by six oarsmen. A single figure sat in the stern.

'I'm curious to see who that is,' said Jezreel.

'Where's Jacques?' Hector asked.

'Gone to the market to buy some fresh coconuts. Said that you'd find that coconut water is a great tonic after too much rum.' He stood up and gave Hector a quizzical glance. 'A walk to the landing place would also do you good.'

'Let me clear my head first,' Hector answered. He went to the rainwater butt at the side of the tavern, doused his head and took several sips of water from his cupped hands before accompanying Jezreel to the jetty. Sixty or seventy men, the greater part of St Mary's roving population, were already gathered there. Nearly all of them looked to be suffering from the effects of the previous day's heavy drinking session, and there was an undercurrent of curiosity mingled with apprehension. He overheard someone claim that he recognized the vessel: 'She's the *Charles*, a man of war. Saw her on the Thames two years ago. I heard she was hired by the government and fitting out for the Caribbean.'

'Then they took a wrong turn. Should string up their navigator,' said someone else, and there was a spatter of laughter.

Hector had slept in his clothes and he was aware that he stank of sweat and booze. A wave of nausea came over him as he stood among the crowd, waiting for the pinnace to discharge its passenger. He was wishing that he had stayed lying flat on the floor of the rented room.

Close by him someone announced in disbelief, 'That's Long Ben sitting on his arse, being rowed. What's he doing in command? I sailed with him three years ago and he was no more than junior master's mate.'

Hector craned his neck to see whom the speaker meant, but the wall of spectators blocked his view until the crowd moved back to allow the crew of the pinnace and their commander to climb up on the jetty. Hector found himself jostled to one side. A loose plank wobbled under his feet, and if Jezreel had not reached out and grabbed him, he would have fallen into the water. By the time he had regained his balance, the new arrivals were already shouldering their way through the press of onlookers. He scanned their faces, trying to pick out their leader. He was curious to learn what sort of man could make the dizzy ascent in just three years from junior master's mate to captain of a government warship.

The same speaker who claimed to know 'Long Ben' called out, 'You've done well for yourself since Beachy Head! Any chance I can have a share?'

The man who responded could have been anything between thirty and fifty years old, and everything else about him was characterless and unremarkable. His slightly chubby face was clean-shaven so that his cheeks showed ruddy patches where the sun had burned his fair skin. His hair was a nondescript mousey brown, growing thin on top, and he wore the same ordinary seaman's clothes as his companions. With his bland features, he would not have stood out in a crowd, and even his height was nothing unusual. Jezreel was a head taller, and Hector wondered how the warship's commander had got his nickname of Long Ben. Yet clearly he was the leader of the little group. He had a leather folder clamped under his arm, some sort of chart case.

'You can have your share if you're willing to earn it. That's why *Fancy*'s here,' he called back. 'After I've paid my respects to Mr Baldridge, I'll speak with volunteers.'

The stranger's deep, husky voice was his distinguishing feature: it carried complete self-assurance. It was the sort of voice that persuaded the listener that the speaker had given full and careful consideration to what he was saying and that he knew exactly what he was talking about. Hector had never heard anything like it before, and he concluded that the secret of Long Ben's authority was a rare ability to make men pay close attention to whatever he had to say and accept his way of thinking.

'What's on offer?' shouted another onlooker, his words slurred.

'I'll tell you when you're sober,' came the riposte.

There was laughter and a ripple of excitement as people turned to one another and began to speculate what might be involved.

'Now if someone could show me where I can find Mr Baldridge . . .' prompted Long Ben, looking around.

'This way, Captain!' A small, bow-legged ruffian darted forward. Despite the heat, he was wearing a sailor's thrum cap. The cap's shaggy surface of loose woollen threads made it look as if he had some strange furry animal on his head. 'You'll find Mr Baldridge in his warehouse . . .' and he led the *Fancy*'s captain off the jetty.

One of the pinnace's oarsmen approached Jezreel. 'Where's the nearest place I can get decent fuddle?' he asked brightly. He had wide-set blue eyes in a pleasant freckled face and curly reddish hair. He clipped his words short, speaking with a chirpy accent.

The big prize-fighter pointed to the tavern immediately next to Baldridge's warehouse. 'That's the closest place but not the cheapest. You'll be paying over the odds.'

'I've plenty of chink,' said the man. 'Care to join me? I'm John Dann, coxswain of the *Fancy*.'

'If my friend here can come along as well. His name's Hector and I'm Jezreel. It would be good to hear the news from London.'

'By all means,' said the stranger.

More strong drink was the last thing that Hector wanted and he was finding the newcomer's rapid-fire speech difficult to follow. But in the faint hope that the newcomer might know something about Libertalia, he tagged along as John Dann led them briskly in the direction of the tavern. The sailor's rolling gait spoke of many weeks spent on a swaying deck before setting foot on solid land.

'How did you know he's from London?' Hector asked his friend in a low voice.

'By his accent, and because he uses London cant. "Chink" means money in your pocket.'

Dann must have overheard for he glanced back over his shoulder and added, 'Born and bred in Clerkenwell, though Rochester is now my home. Moved there to be near the navy yard.'

Hector quickened his pace to draw level with the coxswain. 'Have you ever come across a ship called the *Victoire*, under a captain by the name of Misson?'

'Sounds French. She could have been at Beachy Head.'

Hector's hope flickered into life. 'When was that?' he asked eagerly. 'What happened at Beachy Head?'

Dann gave a dismissive snort. 'The French fleet swaddled both us and the cheese-heads.'

Hector had heard the Dutch called cheese-heads, and guessed that 'swaddled' meant giving someone a thrashing. 'And you were there?'

'So was Henry Avery, though I wasn't his coxswain, nor was he the captain.'

John Dann's sharp Cockney accent was making Hector's headache worse. 'Then Long Ben's real name is Henry Avery?'

The coxswain smirked. 'Only when it suits him.'

They reached the tavern, finding the place deserted except for a handful of listless customers seated at the tables. The Londoner lost no time in calling out for drinks, a large brandy punch for himself, and whatever his companions wanted. Wisely, Hector settled for lime juice and water while Jezreel chose strong beer mixed with rum. Waiting for his drink, Hector looked around. It was evident that the tavern's customers were able to pay for the very best. Makeshift shelves displayed ranks of Rhenish and Madeira wine in bottles, and the coxswain's rum punch was ladled from a large silver bowl that Hector imagined had a temporary home in the drinking den until the landlord, presumably Baldridge, shipped it onward for sale elsewhere.

John Dann took his first long sip and let out a sigh of satisfaction. 'So,' he said, waving his tankard in Jezreel's direction, 'would you think of joining the *Fancy*? We need big strong cullies like you.'

It was clear that he too was on a recruiting mission for his vessel.

Jezreel considered for a moment. 'I'd need to know about her captain.' He waited until Dann had again buried his face in his tankard before catching Hector's eye. It was evident that the prize-fighter had his suspicions about the *Fancy*.

Dann puffed up his chest. 'You won't find a more cunning cove than Henry Avery. He's a sly fellow, a real dry boots.'

'And what about his officers?'

Dann allowed himself a self-satisfied smile. 'There aren't any.' His tongue flicked over his lips, as he savoured the taste of the rum. 'We've a quartermaster, a bosun and a first-rate gunner, but it's only by the say-so of the ship's company.'

The message was clear. *Fancy* was not a king's ship. She was not even a privateer, cruising with a government licence to provide legal cover for her activities. She was a vessel outside the law. Her crew were outright pirates and the ship was theirs – a freebooter.

Jezreel raised his bushy eyebrows questioningly, and Hector knew what was going through his mind. A forty-six-gun man-of-war belonged in a royal navy or, at very least, was the property of a rich and powerful trading company. How the *Fancy* came to be in the hands of a roving gang of sea robbers was intriguing.

John Dann sensed their quickening interest. 'It's thanks to Henry Avery. He was first mate of the *Charles*, as she was then. We were with the fleet bound for the Caribbees but got stuck in Corunna port. Swinging on the anchor for more than half a year, no one paid, and everyone bored out of their minds and unhappy. Rumour got about that we were to be sold to the Spaniards. It was Avery suggested we take the matter into our own hands.'

'Didn't your officers intervene?' asked Hector.

'The admiral was ashore most of the time, wining and dining with the locals. One captain dead, another so dozy he never noticed that Avery was chatting with the lads. Rowed round the fleet, giving them ideas.'

The coxswain smiled at the memory. 'Picked his moment, too. Admiral was away, and that same evening the captain of the *Charles* retired to bed early, weeping drunk. As soon as it was dark Avery got together a bunch of us, cut the cable and we put to sea.'

'You stole the ship?' said Hector amazed.

Dann grinned. 'As neat as kiss your hand! As we were sailing out, the captain of the frigate anchored next to us calls out that he heard there was a mutiny brewing. Avery shouts back, "Indeed that's true!", bold as brass. Then we were gone.'

'And what happened next?' Hector enquired.

'Avery was very fair. Next morning he offers command of the ship back to the *Charles*'s captain. When he turned it down, we put him ashore with the men loyal to him. The rest of us voted to serve under Avery. We renamed our ship as the *Fancy* and set course for the Guinea coast. There we heard about your Mr Baldridge and how this is the place for the real rum quids.'

For a moment, Hector thought that the coxswain was referring to the contents of his tankard, then realized that rum quids must mean booty in London cant.

Dann drained the last of his punch, and gestured for a refill. 'We heard tell that a lucky crew made a rich haul north of here. Sloop by the name of *Amity* under Thomas Tew.'

'That was last season,' said Jezreel. 'I'm with Tew's company this voyage.'

'Are you indeed?' said the coxswain looking at Jezreel with interest.

It was becoming clear to Hector that this was Dann's first trip to Madagascar and he was unlikely to have any information about Libertalia.

He tried one last approach. 'Who told you about St Mary's?'

'First mate of a slave ship we took when we were off the Guinea coast.' Hector noted the outright admission of piracy. 'He said he'd done business with Baldridge in the past and still had his charts and logbooks. He could bring us here to re-supply, and afterwards show us where to make our fortunes.'

The coxswain coughed, then wiped the back of his hand across his mouth. 'But he was already taken with the Guinea fever.' He gave a quick grin. 'Don't worry. There's been no sickness on the *Fancy* since we tipped his corpse into the sea, along with twenty of our company, and that was before we rounded the Cape.'

'What happened to those charts and notes?' Hector asked. The dead man's logbooks might have contained some reference to Libertalia.

'Avery has them. They're all a muddle: loose pages torn from notebooks, sketches of the coastline, scraps of paper with foreign writing on them, a few unfinished charts with no clue where they're from. He's gone to ask Baldridge if he can make sense of them.'

Hector stifled a sour-tasting belch. His stomach was in such turmoil that he thought he might have to leave the tavern and find a place to throw up. 'Maybe I could help if I took a look,' he managed to murmur.

Dann looked at him doubtfully. 'Are you a navigator?'

Fortunately Jezreel came to the rescue. 'He can read an almanac as quick as you and I could judge a hand of cards . . . and equally good with charts.' He launched into a tale of how Hector had located a passage through a coral reef in the Caribbean and succeeded in luring aground a warship that had been chasing them.

When he finished, Dann leaned forward and clapped Hector on the shoulder enthusiastically. 'Then I must bring you to meet the captain. No time like the present.'

He beckoned to the tavern keeper. 'Cancel that second drink,' he told him. 'What's the best kill-devil you have? I'll take a bottle of it back to the ship with me.'

While the coxswain was shown the selection of bottled rums, Hector had a chance to speak with Jezreel on his own.

'Thanks for your support. Maybe I'll turn up something about Libertalia.'

'I doubt it,' said Jezreel. 'But I'm hoping Avery will offer you a berth aboard the *Fancy*. When he hears that you are a navigator, he may agree to take on Jacques as well.'

'I thought we'd be joining you on the *Amity*?'

'Tew's already got a full crew. Besides, I wouldn't trust the *Amity* to last out her next voyage. She's in poor condition and badly shook.'

He fell silent. Dann was coming back towards them, a swarthy fist wrapped around a flask.

'Let's go!' said the Londoner, ushering them outdoors with the confidence of someone who had spent weeks, not hours, in the settlement.

*

HE WAS EQUALLY self-assured in dealing with the two brawny men posted in front of the solid double doors of Baldridge's warehouse. Hector recognized them as the native bodyguards who had been with Baldridge on the forest path the previous morning. They eyed him suspiciously but made no effort to stop the coxswain leading him and Jezreel inside. This was Hector's first time to enter the warehouse because the building was closed to visitors unless they had business with Baldridge or his store men. His first impression was of a well-provisioned and orderly stockroom. Shafts of light entered through tall narrow openings in the thick walls to illuminate a cavernous interior some forty paces long and twenty wide. To his right were heaps of shovels and axes, barrels of nails, woven baskets overflowing with carpenter's adzes, hammers and saws, all the tools and material needed for the clearing and maintenance of an isolated settlement like St Mary's. There was even a blacksmith's anvil. An open crate held bundles of long-stemmed clay pipes tied together with twine. To his left was the wet store: pyramids of barrels neatly stacked by size, from large hogsheads to firkins, many of them exuding a hint of their contents. The air was rich with the smell of rum, brandy and tobacco. Somewhere in the darker recesses, Hector guessed, would be the crates and boxes with the wines that Baldridge imported and on which, according to rumour, he charged a mark-up of nine hundred per cent.

As the visitors moved deeper into the storehouse in search of the *Fancy*'s captain, they came across rack after rack of muskets, piles of small boxes containing gun flints and lead shot, and – beyond a low stone barrier that served as a firebreak – yet more barrels. Unlike the wine and spirit barrels stacked on their sides, these were stored upright and Hector knew that they were gunpowder kegs. The building was both an armoury and a magazine.

'Pull the trigger on one of those and it'd blow your noddle off,' commented Dann as they passed a stack of antiquated carbines. Hector guessed that the obsolete muskets were traded to native warlords in exchange for slaves. By contrast several racks contained muskets of the most recent design, more suited for sea combat, and he had a hunch that they were destined for the arms chests of vessels such as Tew's pirate sloop.

The farthest end of the warehouse was screened off with a length of heavy canvas hung from a rope. He would have liked to have looked behind the curtain. This was likely to be where Baldridge kept the inbound goods he did not want any visitor to see: the looted items that his customers had bartered in exchange for their munitions.

A sudden loud gulp followed by a high-pitched cackle made them jump. 'Christ's bones! What's that!' exclaimed Dann, swivelling round in surprise. The weird sounds had come from above, and Hector looked up to see an odd-looking creature clinging to the rope that held up the curtain. The size of a small dog, it had grey fur and a very long bushy tail with bold black and white rings. It was peering down at them with very round eyes that were a startling orange-yellow.

'The local people call it a *maki*,' he said. 'It's harmless.'

The creature jumped nimbly down from its perch, landed on the top of a barrel and scampered off down the floor of the warehouse, the ringed tail held high.

'Half squirrel, half cat and all monkey,' muttered the Londoner. The creature raced to a wooden partition that divided off what appeared to be a storekeeper's cubicle. It gave a great leap, scrabbled for purchase and dropped out of view on the far side.

Moments later a door in the partition swung open and Baldridge looked out, scowling. 'What is it?' he snapped, seeing the visitors.

'I need a word with the captain,' said Dann, not the least abashed.

'Very well,' said Baldridge and moved aside to let them troop into an office so small that they had to squeeze together to find standing room. Henry Avery sat at a small table, pen in hand and a wine glass at his elbow. He was wearing mariner's spectacles. The two round eyepieces set in leather frames were held against

his face with a ribbon tied behind his head. He was using them
while making notes on a loose sheet of paper and in front of him
lay the leather document case, its flap open. A half-empty
decanter and a wine glass marked where Baldridge had been sitting though his chair was now occupied by the *maki*. The animal
was glaring at the intruders, making an alarmed chattering noise.

'What is it, Dann?' asked Avery.

'Thought you should meet these men here,' said the coxswain
bluntly, indicating Jezreel and Hector with his thumb. 'This is
Hector Lynch, captain. He's a navigator who can also draw
maps.'

Avery removed his spectacles, and studied Hector for a long
moment before finally saying, 'Tell me what you make of this.'
He reached into the document case and took out the topmost
item, a single large sheet of paper, spotted with mildew and with
a large tear across one corner. He smoothed it flat and pushed it
across the table.

The movement frightened the *maki*. With a sudden bound it
jumped from the chair onto the table, knocking over the empty
wine glass, then sprang into Baldridge's arms. Stroking his pet,
the trader looked on as Hector examined the paper in front of
him. It was a roughly sketched nautical chart. A long coastline
was drawn in brown ink, several towns were indicated with a
house symbol and a series of straight lines were labelled with
letters of the alphabet. He presumed that these lines provided
compass bearings to certain coastal features listed elsewhere,
probably in a logbook. One end of the coastline bent sharply,
more than a right angle, creating a headland. Some distance away,
facing this headland, was another coastline. He was looking at
the entrance to a broad strait. In the lower right hand corner
of the page was inset a much more detailed chart. It depicted a
crab-shaped island with what could be an anchorage between
the claws. Small crosses marked outlying rocks, and there were
several ill-defined reefs. Neither chart had anything to show scale
nor a compass rose for the cardinal points.

'Any details that you recognize?' asked Avery.

Hector shook his head.

'Nothing you can tell me?'

'Never sailed there,' he admitted. 'Nor heard of those towns.'

A quick light of interest gleamed in Avery's eyes. 'What towns?'

Hector bent to take a closer look. 'Jerada, Maiwan, Failak, Mayyun, though the last is probably a cape or an island, not a town. Beside it are the words "the gate of Alexander".'

'You're sure?'

'That's what written.'

'So you can read Moorish script?' Avery commented.

Hector had scarcely noticed. As a young man he had learned his first principles of navigation when secretary-slave to a Turkish corsair in Algiers. He read Arab letters as naturally as Roman ones.

'Do you speak the language as well?' asked Avery.

'A little.' His hangover was receding but he still felt bilious and out of sorts.

Baldridge, still cradling the *maki* in his arms, leaned in to take a quick look at the chart. 'My guess is that's a drawing of the mainland coast a good way north of here,' he said.

Despite his headache, Hector looked down again at the chart, scanning it more closely this time and searching to see if there was any mention of Libertalia. To his chagrin, there was nothing.

'I have a vacancy for a good navigator aboard the *Fancy*. Would you be interested?' said Avery.

Hector hesitated. The interview was going exactly as Jezreel would have wished, yet it was clear to him that Avery and his men were intending to cruise for plunder, and he was uncomfortable with the notion of joining them. 'I came to St Mary's for a different purpose,' he said.

'And what was that?'

'To locate Captain Misson and his colony at Libertalia.'

Beside him Baldridge made a derisive noise through his nose.

Avery, however, was attentive and polite. 'In Corunna some of the men talked about the place, though I have no knowledge of it,' he said in a serious voice as he took a long careful look at the chart in front of him as though he too was prepared to believe that he might find Libertalia written there.

'I wish to settle there, with my wife,' Hector told him.

Avery put down his pen, leaned back in his chair, and steepled his fingers together. 'In that case, I'll strike a bargain with you: come aboard *Fancy* as navigator, and if we should find this Libertalia on our voyage, you will be free to leave the ship and stay there.'

He looked directly at Hector, holding his gaze. 'Jezreel here can accompany you. He has the appearance of someone capable of handling himself in a tight situation.'

Hector was beginning to feel trapped. 'Thank you, but I made a promise to my wife. I've been in some difficulties with the authorities and I swore to her that I would stay away from anything that might result in further trouble.'

'I understand your position. Indeed I sympathize.' Avery cast a quick glance at his coxswain. 'Dann may have mentioned that *Fancy* cruises for the benefit of her company.' He smiled encouragingly and reached forward to extract another sheet of paper from the document case. 'But we are scrupulous. You might like to read this.'

It was an open letter over Avery's signature addressed to the captains of all Dutch and English ships. Should they encounter the warship at sea, they were to signal by furling their mizzen sail and hoisting a balled-up flag to the masthead. Then *Fancy* would ignore them and allow them to go on their way.

'If you join my company, you'll help me write several copies of that letter,' said Avery. 'They will be left at every port we visit and given to every ship we encounter. It will make our peaceful intentions clear.'

Hector handed back the letter. He was mystified how Avery proposed to make a profit from *Fancy*'s voyage without molesting

English or Dutch ships. It was common knowledge that these nations profited most from the trade to India and beyond.

Jezreel spoke up. He had made up his own mind. 'I'm ready to volunteer for *Fancy* and there's another of my shipmates who will likely do the same.'

'His name?' asked Avery settling his spectacles back on his nose and picking up a pen.

'Jacques Bourdon.'

Avery paused, pen poised. 'French?' he sounded uncertain. Hector recalled that in his navy days Avery had fought against the French at the battle off Beachy Head.

'Yes, and a prime hand.'

The pen still hovered. 'What skills does he have?'

'He's an excellent cook.' Jezreel evidently saw no need to mention that Jacques was also expert at picking locks, cheating at cards and could tell the difference between paste jewellery and the genuine article, and its discounted value when sold to a fence.

'Splendid,' said Avery, scratching down the name.

All of a sudden, Baldridge let out a curse and glanced down at his silk shirt front. A pale yellow stain was spreading where the *maki* had sprayed him. 'If you want to continue your discussion you'll have to do it elsewhere,' the trader growled.

'I think we've finished here. Thank you for your hospitality,' said Avery urbanely. He slid all the documents back inside the case and stood up. 'If you do decide to join *Fancy*, let Dann know,' he told Hector. 'But don't leave it too long. From what I saw on the jetty I have the impression that there will be plenty of volunteers lining up to take part in our venture.'

They followed Baldridge out of the warehouse and the trader supervised his bodyguards as they bolted and padlocked the storehouse doors. Dann and Avery then set off to make a round of the drinking dens, to interview volunteers. Jezreel, sensing that Hector wished to be alone, went in search of Jacques.

Hector walked back to the jetty, deserted now. For a long time he stood, gazing out at the ships in the anchorage, thinking.

Henry Avery had made a very good impression on him. It was clear that Long Ben was astute and meticulous, a natural leader. If he was as competent as he seemed, *Fancy*'s venture – whatever it was – stood a good chance of succeeding. It was also significant that John Dann, who knew Avery well, held his captain in high regard. Nevertheless, Hector felt faint stirrings of unease. He could not put his finger on the exact reason but he had a vague suspicion that something lay hidden behind Avery's polite, thoughtful exterior. Hector wondered whether Avery was playing some sort of double game and, if so, whether joining him would bring in enough money to set up a new life with Maria.

His thoughts turned to the sketch map that Avery had showed him. Judging by Avery's eagerness to offer him the task of navigator, Avery was convinced the chart contained valuable intelligence that would result in a highly profitable cruise for the *Fancy* and her company. Hector was confident he had the skill and experience to make the best use of the sketch if he went aboard as navigator.

Without knowing it, Hector was drifting towards a decision. He had told Avery that he did not recognize anything on the map, but that was not entirely true. There was something familiar about the profile of the coastline where it formed the entry to a wide strait. He had seen it before, but he could not remember where. Doubtless it would come to him, and when it did, he would keep the information to himself. If Avery was keeping secrets from his company, then he would do the same.

Hector sucked in several deep, slow breaths, trying to rid himself of the lingering effects of his over-indulgence. Then he began to trudge back towards his lodgings, already composing in his mind the letter that he would write to Maria. He would explain what a disappointment St Mary's had proved to be, and that by sailing with Avery he was able to search farther afield for Libertalia. Naturally he had to mention that the *Fancy* was a freebooter but he would reassure Maria that he had been given a promise that the vessel would not molest friendly shipping.

Before going aboard *Fancy* with Jezreel and Jacques, he would search out which of the ships in St Mary's harbour was next due to sail for the Atlantic and ask for the letter to be handed on. But where he would be when Maria received and read that letter, he had no idea.

FOUR

HECTOR WAS ON LOOKOUT duty. He sat on stony ground at the highest point of the crab-shaped island of the sketch map that Avery had shown him in Baldridge's office. The noonday heat reflecting from the sun-baked stones around him was making the skin on his cheekbones feel scorched and drawn. The island, he was thinking, was one of the most desolate places on the face of the earth. All rock and grey-black gravel, there was no water, little vegetation and no signs of life. Below and in front of him a myriad of small whitecaps flecked the glittering surface of the Small Channel. They were whipped up by the breeze that regularly rose one or two hours after dawn as the sun climbed in the sky, hotter and hotter. If he turned around, he had a view of *Fancy* where she lay at anchor in the bay between the claws of the crab, an old mainsail spread as an awning to keep the blistering sun off her deck. The warship looked very different from when he had first laid eyes on her. The carpenters had taken their axes and saws to the higher parts at bow and stern, removed the fore and after decks, knocked away the cabins, and removed all top hamper. Even the carved figurehead – a gilded lion holding the royal arms in its paws, as it turned out – had been cut away and dumped, a sacrifice to lessen weight. The purpose was to lower the profile of the ship so that she sailed closer to the wind and was easier to handle, and to give the deck guns more working space. Now *Fancy* was leaner and lighter, and any seafarer could see that she was very evidently a predator poised for action.

All this under Henry Avery's direction. Long Ben was intent on robbing the richest, slowest convoy in all these seas. He intended to waylay the fleet of the Great Mogul himself and plunder his ships bringing pilgrims back from Mecca. The plan was breathtakingly audacious and full of risks. If successful it could make very wealthy men of everyone, from captain to deck-hand, who played an active part in the enterprise.

Hector's misgivings about his captain had faded during the four months it had taken to reach the island. On the voyage northward he had seen qualities in Long Ben that were rare in a freebooter: *Fancy*'s captain took few risks, planned carefully and made it his business to see that every task was done properly. He had also kept his word about issuing letters telling Dutch or English ships that they had nothing to fear from *Fancy*. At the various ports of call along the African coast he had sent Hector ashore to leave copies of the letter, and this had given him ample opportunity to pursue his enquiries about where to find Libertalia. The result, Hector thought gloomily to himself, had been disappointing. No one could provide a clear answer, and he was on the point of accepting that Jezreel had been right: Libertalia was a fantasy. Worse, he was beginning to question if Captain Misson really existed. Many had heard his name, but he had yet to talk with anyone who had actually met the mysterious French captain.

The clatter of loose stones slithering underfoot broke into his thoughts. Glancing over his shoulder, he saw Jacques toiling up the slope to join him, a full water skin slung over his shoulder.

'Move over,' said the Frenchman as he eased himself on the ground, panting from the heat. He dumped the water skin between them, and the sloshing sound reminded Hector just how thirsty he was.

Jacques screwed up his eyes, squinting into the distance,

checking the horizon to the north-west. 'No sighting?' he asked.

'Nothing,' Hector croaked. He reached for the water skin and took a mouthful, swirling it around his mouth before swallowing. He replaced the bung and set the water skin down carefully. It would have to last another three hours before his replacement arrived to take up the watch.

'Maybe we've missed them,' said Jacques. He gave Hector a sideways glance. 'You've lived among them, what do you think?'

'It's possible. Their holy month finished with first new moon early in July, and now we're into September.' The previous evening he had double-checked the lunar calendar in *Fancy*'s navigation almanac.

'More than enough time to pass by and get home,' said Jacques, 'unless the pilgrimage was delayed.'

Hector shook his head. 'The hajj always takes place in the twelfth month by their reckoning.'

Jacques was finding the sharp-edged rocks uncomfortable beneath him and shifted his position. 'What does Avery think? Has he talked to you about it?'

'Avery's prepared to wait,' said Hector. Avery, he had noted, had the patience to play the long game while men like Thomas Tew were always in a hurry, rushing about, responding to every sniff of gold.

'He can't wait for ever. The others are getting restless.' Jacques gestured towards the ships anchored close to *Fancy* and dwarfed by the warship. There were five of them, all sloops including Tew's *Amity*, drawn by the same rumour of great riches to be had. They reminded Hector of wolves assembling around the leader of the pack.

'They elected Avery to overall command. They'll follow his lead.'

'Only as long as their supplies last. Then they'll go their own ways.'

And what if this ambush is successful? Hector asked himself. If the loot is even a fraction of what is rumoured, it will be too much of a temptation. He felt a slight prick of anxiety as he wondered how the plunder was to be divided among crews of the wolf pack without fighting breaking out.

He took another long look to the north, the direction from which Avery's hoped-for victims should approach. The sea was empty. There was still no sight of approaching sails.

Hector smiled wryly as he recalled John Dann's describing his captain as a real 'dry boots', a cunning fellow. It had been clever of Avery to show him the letter informing the captains of Dutch and English vessels that they had nothing to fear from the warship. At the time it had allayed his misgivings about joining *Fancy*. Only later had he realized that Avery's real reason for this apparent forbearance had been to avoid the word spreading that *Fancy* was on the prowl. He wanted his intended prey to know nothing of the approaching menace. Then he could strike and take them unawares.

'I've been offered odds of four to one that the Moors will avoid the Small Channel,' said Jacques.

'Who by?'

'Hathaway. He reckons it is too narrow and dangerous for their ships. He thinks they'll be passing to the west, using the Big Channel.'

Hathaway was *Fancy*'s quartermaster, a hard-faced, quick-tempered bull of a man. The crew had elected Hathaway to represent them, and by the unwritten laws of freebooter custom the quartermaster was second only to the captain in authority aboard ship. Hector tried to have as little as possible to do with the man. He found Hathaway to be pugnacious and self-important.

'Hathaway's ill informed,' Hector said. 'The Big Channel has a bad reputation. The locals call it "The Straits of Grief".'

'Who told you that?'

'A trader in the last port we visited. The Small Channel is known as the Strait of Alexander because it's believed that Alexander came this way returning from his invasion of India.'

'Then he must have had damned good pilots to get through,'

Jacques said. He swivelled round and pointed. 'See where the whitecaps clash together in the middle. There must be a powerful swirl or counter-current running.'

Hector had leaned forward, concentrating. To the north where the sky met the sea everything was distorted through the heat haze. Within the quivering band of the horizon he thought he glimpsed a lighter, brighter patch. He stared until his eyes hurt, then touched Jacques on the arm. 'There! Do you see?'

Jacques gazed in the same direction for a full minute. 'Could be sails, several of them.' He gave a sigh of satisfaction. 'If so, it can only be them. It's the pilgrim fleet, at last.'

'They're a long way off yet. We'll wait to see what course they intend,' said Hector. 'Then report to Avery.'

The two men watched for a full hour before Hector finally stood up on the skyline and waved his arms, signalling for a boat to collect them. They made their way down the side of the ridge and by the time they reached the landing place they could see that the other ships had spotted his signal. Small boats were converging on the *Fancy*, carrying the freebooter captains.

The air was tense with expectation as Hector and Jacques climbed aboard. The ship's company clustered along the rail, shouting down at them and demanding to know the news. Hector ignored them and headed for Avery standing with the other captains. He recognized most of them from the conference held aboard *Fancy* when they had elected Avery as their overall leader. Thomas Tew of the *Amity* was in shirtsleeves and still wearing his rapier. Joseph Faro of the *Portsmouth Adventure* was chatting with Thomas Wake of the *Susanna*, while the big black-bearded man was Richard Want. His vessel, *Dolphin*, was a small and sluggish sloop whose rigging was so wispy and badly frayed that the sailors had dubbed her the 'hay wain'. The final member of the group was a squat, heavy-set man with narrow, watchful eyes. Hector presumed that he was William Mayes, captain of the *Pearl*. His ship had only arrived in the anchorage the previous evening and, at 200 tons, was the second largest vessel in the squadron, though comparatively toothless as she mounted only sixteen guns.

All six captains were regarding him with close interest, waiting to hear his report. Behind him the *Fancy*'s company edged forward, close enough to listen in.

'Sails to north.' Hector spoke directly to Avery.

'How many?' Tew interrupted harshly. He was finding it difficult to contain his eagerness, shifting his weight from one foot to the other. He had one hand on his baldric and kept adjusting it, sliding it back and forward, across his shoulder.

'Difficult to say at this distance,' Hector answered. 'Between twenty and twenty-five sail.'

'How long before they get here?' Joseph Faro wanted to know. Like Tew he spoke with the nasal accent that marked him as being from the New England colonies.

'Jacques and I observed for an hour and we estimate that they'll be off the island in another four or five hours if the wind holds.'

'And what course are they following?' This time it was Avery who asked. As always, he was calm and matter-of-fact, though his was the crucial question.

Hector paused for a moment before answering. 'They appear to be sailing along the coast, keeping a couple of miles off shore. That would take them into the Small Channel.'

Tew let go of his baldric and smacked a fist into the palm of his hand. 'Then we've got them!' he burst out. 'They won't get here until dusk and they can't risk passing through the channel in the dark. They'll shorten sail and wait until daylight when they can see where they are going.'

A broad smile split Richard Want's black beard. 'I propose we remain here, out of sight so as not to scare them off. On the morning breeze we weigh anchor and emerge from behind the island just as they are entering the channel. They'll be unable to turn back and will drop into our hands like over-ripe fruit. We won't even have to shake the branch.'

He beamed at Avery. 'Long Ben, it seems like your luck is holding. I'll send two of my own lads up on that ridge to stay overnight. They'll signal us when the fleet is well and truly committed into the channel.'

Tew made a sucking noise through his teeth, expressing his disagreement. 'Better if we left the anchorage as soon as it is too dark for the Moors to see us. There's no moon tonight and we can loiter in position. That way they'd run right into us.'

Avery turned to Joseph Faro, seeking his opinion. The captain of the *Portsmouth Adventure* was the oldest of the group, a seasoned campaigner with a reputation for always calculating the odds before he committed himself and his vessel. 'There are too many rocks and reefs. In the dark someone could easily come to grief,' he said.

Tew nodded at Hector. 'He's been doing his homework. We ought to be able to stay clear of trouble.'

Avery looked across at Hector and raised an eyebrow, inviting him to comment. Hector hesitated, uncertain what to say. Twice in the past fortnight he had rowed out in a small boat with Jacques and Jezreel to make notes on the position of rocks and other dangers in the mouth of the bay. Tew must have seen them at work.

'Well . . . ?' Tew prompted.

Out of the corner of his eye Hector saw Avery give a very slight, almost imperceptible shake of his head.

Hector raised his voice so that all could hear. 'With the sun high the water is clear enough so that the rocks show up well against the sandy bottom. But it would be a very different matter in the dark.'

Tew's gaze swept across his fellow captains as he sought their support for his proposal. When none was forthcoming, he shrugged, pulled his rapier a couple of inches from its scabbard and slammed it back again irritably. 'Just one more point,' he added, 'plunder is to be shared only between those vessels that take an active part in a capture. Nothing for those who hang back. That's our custom.'

Avery checked with the other captains. 'Are we agreed?'

Richard Want gave a reluctant nod.

'Good. Then that's settled. We return to our ships and prepare for tomorrow. There's much to do.'

The meeting broke up, and Hector and Jacques went to join Jezreel in the crowd of onlookers.

'Sorry now that you didn't stay on *Amity*?' Jacques asked the big man mischievously as the three of them made their way to a quiet spot near the bow. They knew exactly why Tew had spoken up. *Amity* was the swiftest vessel in the squadron. When the ambush was sprung, his ship would be first on the scene, and have the choice of the richest prize in the pilgrim fleet. If she succeeded in capturing her chosen victim, without help from another vessel in the squadron, all the loot from that ship would be for the *Amity*'s company alone. That was freebooter law.

'Tew's too bold for my liking,' said Jezreel. 'I've seen the like of him in the ring. Goes charging in recklessly and finishes up flat on his back, with a dent in his skull. Besides, how's he to tell which is the richest vessel in the pilgrim fleet?'

'A good question,' said Jacques looking at Hector. 'Why would pilgrims be carrying anything worth plundering?'

Hector rubbed his sore eyes with the back of his hand. It made him see spots. 'The hajj is more than just a pilgrimage. It's a chance to combine piety with profit. Everyone who can afford to do so takes some trade goods with them when they set out for their holy places. There they spend their spare time in buying and selling, and now they'll be bringing home their acquisitions.'

He stepped to one side as *Fancy*'s gunner came past with two of his assistants. They were checking the demi-culverins, one by one, lifting the small lead apron covering the vent hole, removing the plug of greased oakum, and poking in a thin wire to make sure that there was no obstruction when the touch powder was ignited and the fire reached the main powder charge.

'Then there are the merchants who travel with the convoy. They reserve cargo space, often a year in advance.'

'What about escort ships? Will there be any?' Jacques asked.

'I don't know,' Hector told him. 'We can't be the only ones who've thought about robbing the fleet.'

'Perhaps they're relying on safety in numbers,' Jezreel suggested.

'Or on the prestige and power of the Great Mogul. He's a very devout Muslim. You can imagine how he will react to an attack on pilgrims from Mecca. He'd consider it sacrilege.'

Jacques pulled a face. 'Then we'd better make sure to disappear afterwards. I wouldn't like to be on bad terms with the Emperor of India as well as with the King of France.'

FIVE

AVERY, WITH HIS customary thoroughness, set the crew to preparing the ship for action. *Fancy*'s sun awning was taken down and stowed. Men climbed out on the spars, checking on the furling of the sails, tying each one in place with twine. In the morning a strong tug on the sheets would snap the twine, allowing the sails to fall free and catch the wind and ensure a quick departure from the bay. The support boats – the larger pinnace and two skiffs – had been lifted aboard and placed on their chocks amidships. The heavy thick anchor cable was brought up short, ready to be hoisted in, and the last of the chain shot left over from the warship's original navy stores distributed among the top-deck demi-culverins. These guns had the clearest field of fire and were most likely to bring down the target's masts and rigging. Avery's plan was to cripple, not sink, *Fancy*'s chosen victims, then get close enough to put boarding parties on them. As the light faded Quartermaster Hathaway and his team of assistants opened the arms chests and handed out muskets, half-pikes, pistols and cutlasses. The ship's company spread along the full length of the deck, a hundred and fifty men busying themselves with preparing cartridges, filling powder horns and replacing flints. Once that was done, there was nothing to do but wait. As a precaution the master gunner had not yet issued powder for the cannon, and as night fell, the flare and glow of dozens of clay pipes punctuated the darkness. There was not a breath of wind so the smoke and smell of burning tobacco hung in the night air. The general feeling on board was of pent-up anticipation tinged with nervous uncertainty as to whether the long voyage to stalk their prey would finally produce its reward. Many of the men formed small groups to gamble away the hours with cards and dice. Others dug out the bottles of rum and brandy they had been hoarding.

'I wonder where Dan is at this moment,' said Jezreel. He had cleared himself enough deck space to stretch out between two of the demi-culverins and was lying on his back, staring up at the sky where a thin veil of cloud was moving in from the south and beginning to dim the stars. Dan had been the fourth member of their tight-knit little group. A Miskito Indian from the coastal swamps of the western Caribbean, he had gone back to his homeland shortly before the great Jamaica earthquake.

'If we had a few more like him aboard I wouldn't have to listen to your stomach rumbling,' Jacques muttered. Miskito Indians were renowned as hunters and fishermen, and it was claimed that four Miskito Indians were enough to keep a ship's crew supplied with fresh food. With the ship's stores almost exhausted, meals on *Fancy* had become very meagre.

'Somehow I don't think Dan stayed at home. He's not one to settle down,' observed Hector from where he was sitting, his back against a gun carriage. A sudden outburst of swearing made him look round. Without a moon, there was no longer enough starlight for the gamblers to see their cards and dice clearly. It sounded as if someone had already staked and lost the plunder he confidently expected to win the next morning, and he wanted the game to continue. The winner was refusing.

'Things could get out of hand tomorrow over the division of the plunder.' Hector took care to keep his voice down.

'And Hathaway needs to be watched. He never stops grumbling that there was no vote before we joined up,' added Jezreel. It was the quartermaster's role to share out the spoil between the crew, and it was a time-honoured rule that a freebooter's company only accepted new crew members after agreement among themselves. Each additional recruit meant a smaller portion of the plunder when it was divided. Deliberately or not, Avery had bypassed this custom when he added Hector and his friends to *Fancy*'s complement.

'Well, it's too late to do anything about that now,' said Jacques. 'Without Hector to make sense of that sketch map, *Fancy* might not have got here at all.'

Hector was grateful for what had been left unsaid. Hathaway's initial resentment had been greatly sharpened by the way Avery had favoured his new navigator. In front of the crew Avery had complimented Hector on his skill in bringing *Fancy* into harbour past the dangerous reefs that ringed the island. The quartermaster's dissatisfaction had spread to his circle of cronies, and they made their hostility towards him and his friends very plain.

Aboard one of the sloops anchored nearby, someone began plucking the strings of an out-of-tune guitar, playing the same few notes over and over again until a rough voice called out for him to stop his racket. Hector glanced towards the stern, hoping to catch a glimpse of Avery where he had last seen him beside the foot of the mizzenmast. But the captain was nowhere in sight. Picking up one of the shot wads that had been placed in readiness, he used it as a pillow, leaning his head back against the breech of the gun. He closed his eyes and focused his mind on Maria. Their baby had been due in late May, and now it was early September. Whether it was a boy or a girl was unimportant, only that Maria and the child were healthy and well looked after. He longed for the next twenty-four hours to be over and for the ambush to have been a success. It would mean that the *Fancy* could set course back to St Mary's, where Baldridge would be waiting to acquire the spoils and forward them to his contacts in Europe and New England. It should be possible to find a ship that was due to call in at Tenerife en route. Hector made a mental calculation. By the time he next saw Maria, their child would be crawling, maybe even learning to stand. He wanted very badly to be there where the toddler took its first few steps.

*

HECTOR AWOKE with a start. It was still very dark and someone had tripped over his outstretched foot. He heard a sigh of relief, then the sound of a thin jet of water striking the surface of the bay. Whoever had trodden on him was at the ship's rail and pissing over the side. He reached behind him and used the demi-culverin's barrel to pull himself upright. The metal was still slightly warm from yesterday's sun, though this was the coolest hour, shortly before sunrise. Jezreel was snoring softly, still lying on the deck, and he couldn't see where Jacques had got to. The thin layer of cloud was dissolving into streaks. A few late stars were showing through, enough to reveal the dark outline of the island ridge to the north. He could picture the two lookouts from *Dolphin* up there on their vantage point, watching over the channel, waiting for the first tinge of daylight to reveal the position of the pilgrim fleet.

Jacques appeared, an indistinct shape in the darkness. 'A little treat from the ship's stores,' he said quietly. Avery had assigned the Frenchman to help the *Fancy*'s cooks, and Hector imagined his friend had stolen some ship's biscuit. It would make a pleasant change from the gritty flat discs of unleaven bread made from local grain. Instead, there was a gurgling sound and Jacques thrust a small metal cup into his hand. He took a sip. It had the tangy, slightly sweet taste of small beer. Hector drank slowly, savouring every drop.

'That's the last of it,' the Frenchman murmured. Since arriving at the waterless island, the crew of *Fancy* had been drinking vile-tasting cloudy water from barrels filled a month earlier on the African coast. It was wise not to look too closely into one's cup, as there would be tiny worms wriggling in the bottom of it.

Jacques stirred Jezreel with his foot. 'Time to wake up, you great lunk.'

The big man sat up, yawned noisily, gave a deep gassy belch and stretched. Jacques passed him the refilled cup. 'Maybe that will settle your guts,' he said. Bad water, as everyone knew, caused the flux.

Hector peered up at the masts. He could make out the tracery of rigging and the pennants hanging limp at the mast tops. It was still too early for the first hint of wind that would carry the squadron out from the bay. They would have to wait at least another hour until the rising sun warmed the mainland and sucked in the onshore breeze.

All around the anchorage, as the light strengthened, the smaller ships were preparing for the ambush. He could hear the squeal of ropes in blocks, the calling of commands and the rub of timber on timber as the spars were hauled into place. On board *Fancy* there was a general stir. Men were getting to their feet, hawking up phlegm and spitting over the side, breaking wind noisily and deliberately, groaning and stretching. Someone tossed a bucket on a rope over the side and hauled it up, the contents slopping loudly. He heard coxswain Dann's sharp tones telling the laggards to move away from the guns so that the gunner's assistants could set out the gunpowder charges. Jezreel, who was still sitting on deck, was chivvied out of the way.

There was so much bustle and activity that the faint cries from the land could have been mistaken for the calls of a seabird.

When he next looked towards the island, he could just make out two figures. They were running down the side of the ridge towards the anchorage. As he watched, the lead runner lost his footing and fell. His companion tripped over him and both men slithered down the steep slope for several yards before coming to a halt. When they got back up again and began to run downhill once more, he realized that the cries had come from them.

'They must be the two lookouts sent by Richard Want,' he said to Jacques.

'Worried that they'll miss out on the plunder if they don't get back on *Dolphin* before she sails.'

Hector saw the two lookouts reach the landing place and scramble on to the little skiff that they had left beached there. Instead of heading back to *Dolphin*, they set course for *Fancy*, rowing frantically. Every few seconds one of them glanced over his shoulder and shouted, but the distance was too great to make out the words.

'What's going on?' asked a gunner's assistant who had been checking the gun tackles.

'I don't know,' Hector told him. One of the rowers missed the water with his oar stroke and fell off his seat. His companion stood up, turned and shouted at *Fancy* through his cupped hands.

'Drunk, both of them,' observed Jacques sourly.

Aboard *Fancy* several men gathered at the rail, peering out into the half-darkness.

'What's he yelling about?' asked someone.

'Something about the Moors,' said his colleague.

'Lynch! Report aft!' called a voice. It was Avery standing beside the helm. Leaving his friends, Hector hurried along the deck, pushing past the late risers who were grumbling and demanding to know what all the excitement was about, their voices petulant.

Arriving in front of Avery, Hector was relieved to see that the *Fancy*'s captain was unperturbed. He was standing astride, hands on his hips and bending his body from side to side, exercising to ease his back muscles. It occurred to Hector that Avery had spent the night sleeping on deck like all his crew as there was no longer a captain's cabin now that the poop deck had been cut away.

'I have a feeling that we are about to adapt our plans, Lynch,' he murmured as he straightened up.

There was a clatter of oars being dropped and a slight scraping sound as the rowing boat came alongside, and then the two lookouts appeared. They half-ran, half-stumbled to where Avery stood. Both men were out of breath and the light of early dawn was enough to show their nervousness and the guilty looks on their faces.

'What is it?' Avery asked, a slight hint of irritation in his voice.

'The Moors, sir,' blurted one of the men. He was a gangling specimen, with spindly arms and legs, his hair sticking out at all angles.

'What about the Moors?' asked Avery.

'They're through the Channel already, well through.'

Avery put up his hand to stroke the bristles on his chin, calmly delaying the moment before asking casually, 'What do you mean "well through"?'

'That's it, sir. They went through the Small Channel during the night.' Even from two yards away Hector could smell the rum on the man's breath.

Avery turned to Hector. 'Is that possible, Lynch?'

'If they had really good pilots, I suppose so.'

Avery pressed his lips together in a tight line and raised an eyebrow. 'In a flat calm, like we had for most of last night?'

Hector remembered Jacques pointing out the strong current running in the strait. 'They could have taken advantage of the current to carry them through.'

'Skilfully done then,' said Avery drily. He turned his attention back to the sailor. 'And where's the fleet now?'

'Near out of sight, sir,' the man confessed. 'Well to the south.'

Avery gave a deep sigh as if to emphasize that he felt surrounded by fools and incompetents. Looking past the two shame-faced lookouts, he raised his voice. 'It seems we've missed the fleet.' His voice carried well.

There was a chorus of groans, oaths and angry shouts from those of the crew who had wandered aft, curious to find out what was happening. Someone shouted, 'Shit! All this way for nothing!'

Avery was unperturbed. 'We will give chase and overhaul them. This gives give us more time to pick our targets.'

The mood on *Fancy* was turning ugly. Frustration and anger swept through the onlookers. Quartermaster Hathaway stepped up, grabbed the thin man by the collar, twisted the cloth so his victim nearly choked and hauled him away. The other man looked around nervously and sidled off to one side, trying to avoid notice.

Avery called for silence. 'We won't have a sailing breeze for another hour at least. We'll tow *Fancy* out of the bay.'

He turned to his coxswain. 'Dann, lower our boats, put your best men into the pinnace.'

It was a shrewd move, Hector thought as he watched Dann cuff and push the men to their duty. Giving them some work to do would distract the men from their immediate disappointment.

Avery took Hector by the elbow and drew him aside. 'It seems you were right about the Small Channel. What course do you think the Moors will now take?'

'Depends where they're headed,' Hector answered. As usual, *Fancy*'s captain was thinking clearly, calmly assessing what should be done next. 'My guess is that they'll keep following the coast, staying within sight of land.'

Men were calling across to the nearby ships, relaying the bad news. All around the squadron there were more baffled shouts, howls of rage.

'I told you we should have been in position earlier!' It was Captain Tew. *Amity* was anchored no more than fifty yards away and he had a speaking trumpet to his lips. 'I've had enough of this dithering and hesitation,' he bellowed. He spun on his heel and stalked away across his sloop's deck, giving orders. There was a flurry of activity and his crew began bringing up their anchor, though there was still no sign of the morning breeze.

'The cheating bastard,' growled Dann. *Amity* was sprouting long thin legs, three on each side of the long, black hull, like some water insect. They were sweeps, the long oars for moving a boat when becalmed or manoeuvring in harbour. *Fancy* was too large and heavy to be moved in this way, but *Amity* was light and nimble enough for them to be effective.

Hector checked the other vessels. News of the Moors' escape had reached them, and it seemed that none of them carried sweeps like *Amity*. Instead they were beginning to copy *Fancy*'s example, lowering their boats and preparing for the long laborious tow that would bring them out of the anchorage.

In less time than it took for coxswain Dann to get his pinnace into position and rig a towline to his own vessel, *Amity* was on the move, steering to pass very close under *Fancy*'s stern. Several of Avery's crew gathered there and yelled across, asking if *Amity* wanted any volunteers to help with the sweeps. Their requests were met by jeers from Tew's men. 'Go shares with you lot, not likely! Get stuffed!' one them crowed.

Tew raised his speaking trumpet again. He was close enough to be looking up to where Avery stood at the warship's rail. 'A pilot would be helpful. Send me Lynch.'

Avery turned to Hector. 'Your choice,' he said, then lowering his voice he added, 'It could be to our advantage.'

Hector thought furiously. He did not want to abandon his friends. Tew's sloop would be well away from the island by the time the other ships towed clear. With *Amity*'s superior speed under sail, there was no chance that he could get back aboard *Fancy* for many hours.

Avery was calling back to the other captain. 'I'll send Lynch to you if you agree to get ahead of the Moors and turn them back toward the rest of us. You'll still have the pick of them.'

'It'll be like driving sheep!' Tew gave a confident laugh.

'Lynch, I rely on you to see he keeps his word,' Avery said in a quiet aside.

Hector came to his decision. He flung one leg over the rail and climbed halfway down the rope ladder that *Dolphin*'s drunken lookouts had used to come aboard. He hung there, dangling against the warship's hull as Tew shouted for the starboard-side sweeps to be taken in. The sloop glided past less than an arm's length away and Hector timed his jump. As he landed sprawling on the sloop's deck, he heard Jacques call from above him, 'Save some plunder for us.'

SIX

TEW GRASPED HIM by the shoulder as he got to his feet. 'Those pilgrim ships will be waddling along. With a stiff breeze on her quarter, *Amity* can catch them before they know what's happening.' He pointed to the two low headlands on each side of the entrance to the anchorage. 'The moment we're clear of those, I want to steer south-south-west.'

The sloop's captain was dressed in the same long blue coat that he had worn when he came ashore in St Mary's. His eyes gleamed with excitement. Hector judged that the thrill of the chase exhilarated Tew as much as the prospect of plunder.

'It would be safer if we took the same route we used when we entered the anchorage . . .' Hector began.

'I know that,' Tew smiled wolfishly, 'but the best place to find the wind at this time of day is three or four miles offshore. Now get up on the bowsprit and show us where to go. I'll watch for your signals.'

Hector made his way forward. It was the first time he had been on *Amity* and, just as Jezreel had told him back in St Mary's, the sloop was old and evidently the worse for wear. Her deck boards were scarred and warped, the seams in need of caulking. Thick layers of black paint failed to cover up major repairs to her bulwarks, and the top section of her tall, raked mast was held in place with wooden splints and a tourniquet of heavy rope. He counted only sixteen guns; all of them were sakers that fired a ball less than six pounds in weight, barely a quarter the weight of *Fancy*'s main armament. Everything about the vessel looked to be in need of replacement or strengthening – except the ship's company. The six-man teams on the sweeps were driving the sloop through the water expertly. No one was shouting orders or urging them to keep rhythm. *Amity* had a first-class crew, a good match for her fire-eating captain.

Grasping a forestay to stop himself falling into the water, Hector edged out on the sloop's long, slanting bowsprit as far as he dared. A quick glance over his shoulder showed that the other freebooter ships had yet to move. It would be another hour before they emerged from the anchorage, towed by their boats. Even then they might still have to wait for the breeze. By that time, if Tew was correct, *Amity* would be almost out of sight, overhauling the pilgrim fleet.

He turned his attention to the sea directly ahead. He could already see several white patches where the swell, barely perceptible in the dawn calm, lifted and broke lazily over submerged rocks. Those dangers were easily avoided. Elsewhere the sea was a shifting pattern of deceptive shadows. With the sun not yet over the horizon, he would have to judge whether a darker patch was a danger to the ship or nothing more than a misleading illusion. During his reconnaissance with Jezreel and Jacques he had plotted the positions of many of the outlying rocks, but not all of them and he had left his notes where they belonged, with *Fancy*'s charts. It was now a question of using his judgement. He took a deep breath and began to concentrate. *Amity* was gliding along at two or three knots, and the only sounds were the regular splash of sweep blades, the grunt and shuffle of the oarsmen as they took up the strain and the faint mutter of water sliding along the sloop's black-painted hull.

Time passed. Whenever he saw a hazard, he raised an arm and pointed. Tew, standing close to the mainmast, immediately called out an instruction to the men at the sweeps. Obediently they eased the stroke on one side or stopped altogether, or they pulled harder on the other side so that the vessel changed direction. Slowly, very slowly, the sloop progressed, leaving the anchorage behind, then weaving her way between the underwater hazards that ringed the island. After a while the sun rose and the slanting rays penetrated the clear water, making it easier to distinguish the dark mass of solid rock from the shadow cast by a strand of cloud or a raft of seaweed floating half-submerged. Eventually, after more than half an hour of intense concentration, Hector became aware of a slight lift and fall of the hull as the sloop entered deeper, safer water. He decided that his vigilance was no longer required. He was inching his way back along the bowsprit when Tew gave the order to the oarsmen for the sweeps to be brought inboard and stowed. There was an immediate flurry of activity as men ran to throw off the securing lines and haul on the lift that raised the sloop's main yard. Tew found time to give Hector a quick nod of thanks, then looked away to the north. There, a quarter of a mile away and rapidly coming towards them, was a catspaw, a ripple on the flat surface of the sea, the first sign of the morning breeze. Above Hector's head, the rising mainsail shivered, flapped and then flapped again. The sail was far larger than he had expected, its worn canvas faded to a greyish-brown. Some areas were so threadbare that pinpricks of sunlight showed through the thin fabric. Patches of newer material had been sewn on to strengthen the weakest areas and repair various splits and tears. Scarcely had the mainsail been fully set than the rigging gave a low creaking groan as it took up the pressure of the first puff of wind. The crew were already hurrying forward to hoist the sloop's two headsails. By the time they had finished, *Amity*'s deck had taken on a slant beneath his feet. Tew's pride in his vessel was vindicated: the sloop gathered pace, surging forward, the water now swirling past,

Hector chose his moment. He waited until everything had settled down on board, each sail adjusted to precisely the right angle, the falls of the ropes coiled down neatly, lookouts posted. Only then did he approach Tew, who had taken up his position by the windward rail. The flamboyant captain was hatless, and the rapidly strengthening breeze occasionally flicked his long dark hair across his eyes.

'What speed's she doing?' Hector asked.

Tew glanced over the stern at the sloop's bubbling wake. 'Seven or eight knots.'

'A fine vessel.'

Tew laid a hand on the worn timber beside him. '*Amity* may be old, but given the right breeze on the quarter she can outrun many a new-built ship.'

'I was wondering about her name – *Amity* meaning "friendship"?'

Tew showed his teeth in a thin smile. 'You're thinking that it's a strange name for a vessel that rarely displays any friendship to others.'

Hector judged his next words carefully. 'But a good name for a vessel of Libertalia, where men live in harmony. I understand that Captain Misson asked you to take charge of their ships.'

Tew scowled angrily. 'I'd like to know where that rumour got started,' he snapped testily. 'There's no truth in it. I'm part owner of *Amity*, along with investors in New York. *Amity* is the name her builders gave her at the very start. They were Puritans and over-pious, but they knew how to make a fine ship.'

Hector hid his disappointment. The reason he had decided to transfer from *Fancy* to the sloop was the chance it gave him to question Tew in person about Libertalia. He decided to risk Tew's ill temper with one last approach. 'I'm hoping to settle in Libertalia with my wife, but I haven't been able to learn where Captain Misson is to be found.'

The wind was increasing to a stiff breeze, the first white-tipped waves forming. *Amity* thrust her bow into one, throwing up a burst of spray that came rattling on board. The helmsman braced himself at the tiller, feet apart, to keep the sloop on her course.

Luckily Tew was quick to regain his good humour, and the flush of anger that had risen to his face faded. He was relishing the way his ship was responding to sailing conditions that suited her so perfectly. 'What I know about Misson is only what I've heard: that he was a serving officer in the French navy when he fell in with a renegade Italian priest who preached the merits of liberty and equality. They stole a warship and set out for Mada- gascar . . .' He paused and gave Hector a meaningful glance. 'Does that sound familiar to you?'

'Apart from the bit about the Italian priest, Captain Avery did the same. I hadn't thought of that before,' Hector admitted.

'Exactly.' Tew gave a sardonic laugh. 'Though I've never heard Long Ben talk about liberty and equality. More often he talks about plunder.'

'So there's been a mix-up, some sort of mistaken identity.'

'Perhaps.' Tew shrugged. He looked up again at the perfect set of the sloop's straining sails. 'I have a vague recollection of meeting someone with the name of Misson. It might have been on my last trip. Somewhere along the Madagascar coast. But he wasn't a sea captain, least of all in command of a warship. Other- wise I'd have remembered more clearly . . .'

'I'd be grateful for any more details, if you do recall them,' said Hector. He was unable to keep a note of despondency from his voice. *Amity*'s captain had been his last remaining hope for information.

Tew sensed his gloomy mood. 'Lynch, put Misson out of your mind—' He broke off as an excited cry of 'Sails ahead!' came from one of the lookouts posted on the foredeck. 'Where away?' he shouted back.

'On the starboard bow!'

Men were rushing to the starboard rail, gazing forward eagerly. Several swung themselves up into the main shrouds to get a better view, their expressions hungry and impatient.

Tew hurried along the deck to join the lookouts, then beckoned to Hector to join him. 'Just two ships, large ones. What do you make of them, Lynch? And where's the main fleet?'

The sails were not where Hector had expected to find the pilgrim fleet: well out to sea. 'Perhaps they took the Big Channel last night because their pilots considered them too unwieldy to go safely through the Small Channel using the current,' he suggested.

Tew chewed his lip, staring towards the unknown ships. Hector could see that he was strongly tempted to investigate a possible new prey.

'Long Ben is relying on *Amity* to get ahead of the pilgrim fleet and turn it back towards *Fancy* and the others,' he reminded Tew.

Tew ignored him, frowning as he weighed up his options. For several minutes the only noises were the sound of the wind in the rigging and sails, the rhythmic creaking as the sloop flexed to the motion of the sea and the regular swash of the waves against her hull. Finally, Tew came to a decision. 'We'll go after them!' he called out to his crew.

There was an outbreak of whooping and cheering, accompanied by the stamping of feet on deck. People were slapping one another on the back, and someone began to clang the ship's bell vigorously. Amid the hubbub there was a shout of 'Let's drink to that!' and very soon bottles and tankards were being passed around as the jubilant crew toasted their coming good fortune and made wild guesses on how much plunder they would win.

When Hector next looked towards the stern, he saw that someone had gone aft to set an unusual flag on *Amity*'s ensign staff. He presumed it was Tew's personal banner. White on black, it showed a man's arm brandishing a broad-bladed cutlass.

SEVEN

AMITY RACED ON. The weather was perfect for the chase. In bright sunshine the breeze strengthened, lifting the crests off the waves in brief flashes of white foam whose contrast gave the sea an even deeper, richer blue. By mid-morning it was clear that the two unknown ships had not attempted to spread more sail in an attempt to outrun the pursuit but were deliberately holding their course. They kept ploughing sedately forward even though the sloop was in full view and catching up fast. Aboard *Amity* the crew's initial confidence slowly changed to a puzzled, more thoughtful caution. The noisy chatter died away as the men looked towards the two vessels, calculating the odds. They were formidable ships, much larger than anyone had anticipated. Hector judged that the smaller of the two was the same size as Avery's powerful *Fancy* and, like her, appeared to be a warship though of an unusual type. Her two huge triangular sails reminded him of his days aboard a Turkish galley. The second vessel was immense, the largest vessel that he had ever encountered. He could see a resemblance to a Spanish galleon though this ship was more spectacular. Fully 800 tons, she was a floating castle, with a high forecastle, three masts and a great towering stern. Hector counted four decks, perhaps five, from sea level to her poop. But what struck his eye most of all was the exuberance of decoration. Riotously bright colours had been applied every-where: red, blue, purple and gold – they dazzled and gleamed in the sun. The stern was wide enough to have a span of five glazed windows and was richly carved with geometric shapes, each one painted and gilded to bring out the pattern. The same motifs were repeated all along the sides and carried right forward to the massive bows. Coloured streamers, some almost as long as the vessel herself, and cloths and pennants of every shape and size fluttered at the yardarms and mastheads, while a huge yellow ensign flew from a gilded flagstaff at the stern. The effect was of a sumptuous pageant at sea.

Tew paced back and forth by the helm, occasionally pausing to shield his eyes against the sun's glare as he reviewed the pro-gress of his prey, or glancing up to check the set of *Amity*'s sails. There was no need for him to supervise his crew. All sixteen sakers had been charged, loaded with round shot and primed. The sloop's bulwarks were padded with thick bundles of bedding and rolled-up sails to provide extra protection from enemy fire. Muskets and pistols had been handed out in plenty of time for checks that they were in working order. Each man had half a dozen dry cartridges in a bag at his waist, and twice that number of lead musket balls. Now the ship's company idled on deck, dividing their attention between their captain as they waited for his instructions, and the formidable sight of their intended targets less than a mile ahead.

No one took any notice of Hector. He was growing increas-ingly uneasy as the gap between the vessels narrowed. The big ships were certain to be well armed and there was no way of knowing how many cannon they carried, or of what calibre. It was virtually certain that their guns would outrange *Amity*'s and the freebooters would be obliged to run the gauntlet of their gun-fire long before she came to grips with them. Even then the outcome was likely to be disastrous. He could count no more than sixty men aboard *Amity*, while each of the large ships must carry at least six or seven times that number, more than enough to repel any boarding party, however ferocious. He thought about suggesting to Tew that *Amity* delay her attack and wait for *Fancy* and the other ships to catch up, but knew that he would be wasting his breath. The sloop's crew had no intention of sharing the spoils, and Hector recalled Jezreel's description of *Amity*'s captain as foolhardy and hot-headed.

'Hold this course?' the helmsman was asking Tew. There was a tremor of excitement in his voice, elation too, making Hector wonder how many members of Tew's crew were as reckless as their commander.

'Bear away a little,' Tew answered. He pulled a black silk ribbon from a pocket and tied back his long dark hair. Then he adjusted his coat across his shoulders and patted down the lapels. When he was satisfied with his appearance he picked up his speaking trumpet and addressed his men, speaking slowly and clearly and with complete certainty. 'We take the farther vessel, the one that looks like a fairground show,' he called. 'To get at her, we'll run past that warship, then turn hard to starboard, close under her bows.'

Hector looked across to the two great ships. They were less than a thousand yards away now, and one of them – the warship – was finally reacting to the sloop's close approach. She was turning towards *Amity*, placing herself between the sloop and the second vessel. The manoeuvre was slow and ponderous but with a twist of fear in his stomach he saw the gun ports along the warship's hull start to swing up in a ragged sequence, and the barrels of her cannon poke out. He understood what Tew had in mind: he would use *Amity*'s superior speed to overtake the warship, then suddenly cut across her bows where she would mount fewest guns, and fall upon the larger vessel that was following along behind. With luck and if the wind held, *Amity* would be exposed to the warship's gunfire for perhaps ten or fifteen minutes. Much would depend on the accuracy of the warship's gunners and the range of their cannon.

'You'll be needing these, captain.' A heavy-set, hard-faced

seaman with streaks of grey in his beard, older than most of the crew, was holding out Tew's baldric with its sheathed rapier and a long-barrelled pistol. Hector guessed he was the quartermaster. Tew laid down the speaking trumpet and took the weapons, slipped the baldric over his head and adjusted the rapier at his right hip. He slid the pistol into the deep pocket of his blue coat so that the butt protruded close to his left hand. It seemed that the captain of the *Amity* was left-handed. The quartermaster treated Hector to a flat disapproving stare, making it clear that he was not considered a proper member of the ship's company and would have to look after himself. He did not attempt to provide Hector with a weapon though the helmsman, not a yard away, had already been issued with a blunderbuss that lay on the deck beside him.

Hector stepped forward and stooped to pick up the speaking trumpet. The attack was now inevitable, and it would be vital for *Amity*'s outnumbered crew to hear and follow orders that might be missed in the noise, smoke and confusion. If he made himself useful, the quartermaster might decide on giving him a share of plunder, however small.

'I'll watch out for your signals, then relay them to the crew,' he told Tew. 'Where do you want me?'

Tew responded with a crooked smile. 'The foredeck would be as good a place as any. I'll lead the boarding party myself.'

The oncoming warship fired her first gun. The ball went wide, skipping three times across the sea before plunging into the water – but Hector caught the look that passed between Tew and the quartermaster. The warship had opened fire at well over eight hundred yards, much more than the range of *Amity*'s smaller guns. The sloop would have to run the gauntlet for longer than had been expected. The ship's company, grasping their weapons, were already moving into shelter. Some crouched behind the padded bulwarks, others lay down flat on the deck. Wasting no time, Hector ran forward at a crouch, and joined the lookouts on the foredeck where they were stretched out on their bellies, peering over the bow. Everyone knew the danger they faced.

Another bang from a cannon, and this time a hole appeared in the sloop's mainsail. The warship's gunners were beginning to find their aim.

The sailor lying next to Hector could not have been more than eighteen years old. He was ash-blond and fresh-faced with great red patches where the sunburned skin had peeled away. He winced the next time the warship fired, two shots in quick succession. The second one must have struck the sloop for a tremor ran through the foredeck. His knuckles went white as he tightened his grip on the wooden shaft of a short boarding pike, and he turned his face towards Hector. 'Useless marksmanship,' he managed to say, though his voice was unsteady.

'Not long to go now,' Hector assured him. 'As soon as we cross her bows, she won't be able to bring her main guns to bear.'

'Captain Tew took a thirty-gun ship last season, near as big as that one.' The young sailor's eyes were stretched in fear and he was talking fast, almost babbling, to keep up his courage. 'My cousin was aboard that voyage. Brought back enough plunder to retire from the sea.'

'Did your cousin get you your berth on *Amity*?' Hector asked.

The sailor nodded, a short nervous movement. 'Recommended me to the captain. He picked me ahead of a dozen other volunteers.'

More cannon blasts, at least five of them at irregular intervals. A crash from somewhere amidships near the waterline made the sloop shudder again. An acrid whiff of gunsmoke came drifting down on the wind. *Amity* must now be level with the warship.

Hector wriggled around so he could look aft. Tew and the helmsman were the only two men still standing. All the rest of the crew were huddled in shelter though it would do little good if the next cannon ball scored a direct hit. Hector had seen the appalling wounds of men struck by flying splinters.

He turned back and raised his head over the low cap rail of

the foredeck to risk a glance forward. The ordeal was coming to an end. *Amity* had sailed beyond the warship. Soon she would be able to turn and cut across the warship's bows, and that would bring the sloop close enough for her sakers to be within range. A minute later he felt the slope of the deck suddenly change beneath him as the sloop straightened up and came on a level keel. There was a clatter of canvas, a thumping sound as the great mainsail swung across, and a sudden burst of activity as the sail-handlers jumped to their feet and hauled on the sheets that controlled the headsails, before flinging themselves back on deck. Now the sloop was heeling over on the opposite tack, already slicing her way past the warship's bows. It had been neatly done.

Again he glanced back over his shoulder. Tew in his long blue coat was standing by the stern rail. He had drawn his rapier and was waving it defiantly at the warship. *Amity*'s gun crews had scuttled into their positions and were frantically preparing to fire their cannon. The range was point-blank, and there was no need for them to adjust their aim. To loud cheers from their comrades they fired each gun as soon as it came to bear on target. Hector watched the results. A section of the warship's forward rail abruptly vanished, smashed to matchwood. Two holes appeared in the great triangular foresail. One cannon ball struck the side of the warship and bounced off, falling uselessly into the sea.

Already the gap between the two vessels was widening as *Amity*'s helmsman brought the sloop on a course that would place the sloop directly into the path of the larger ship, still wallowing slowly onward, the huge hull rising and falling on the swell. More than ever, the vessel looked like a floating pageant. It had not fired a shot.

Aboard the warship the gunners were re-loading and firing single shots aimed at the stern of the sloop as she sailed away at speed. *Amity*'s men were back on their feet, coughing to clear the smoke from their lungs, grinning at one another in the knowledge that the worst was past. A man who Hector supposed was the ship's carpenter clambered down a hatchway, presumably to check if there had been any damage to *Amity*'s hull. Hector stood up on the foredeck, still holding Tew's speaking trumpet, and rested a hand on a forestay to maintain his balance. His knees were trembling from relief, though he would not have admitted this to the young sailor who gave him a cheerful punch on the shoulder. 'Now for the prize,' the young man crowed.

At that moment Hector felt the forestay suddenly go slack under his hand, then snap taut. Alarmed, he looked up at the masthead. It was swaying from side to side, a yard or so in each direction. An upper section of the starboard main shrouds was hanging loose, severed by a lucky shot from the warship. A grating sound, loud enough to be heard over the noise of the waves and wind, brought his attention down to the spot where the mast had been repaired with wooden splints bound with heavy rope. There, thirty feet above the deck, the rope was bulging under the strain. Raising the speaking trumpet he bellowed at Tew to attract his attention, pointed at the damaged rigging, and shouted a warning. Tew turned, his glance flicking upward. But it was too late. There was no time to reduce sail and relieve the pressure on the weakened mast. Men on deck scattered as the top section of the mast began to buckle, leaning farther sideways each time the sloop rolled. The young sailor beside Hector gave a yelp of fear, and jumped off the foredeck in case the mast snapped and fell.

At the stern Tew reacted strangely to the crisis. He sheathed his rapier, and climbed up on the sloop's rail, his coat tails flapping. He grabbed hold of the ensign staff with his right hand and pulled himself upright, balancing to face the warship. His black flag with its arm-and-cutlass emblem rippled and curled around his torso as he drew the pistol from his pocket. He raised his left arm and took careful aim though the range was far too great. In a flash of understanding Hector realized that Tew knew that his luck had run out. This was his final gesture of bravado.

Tew's hand jerked up as he pulled the pistol's trigger. There was a small puff of white smoke. Tew had not yet returned the empty pistol to his pocket when another cannon ball from the warship fell short, skipped off the surface of the sea and took him full in the stomach. He was hurled backwards, his blue-coated corpse tumbling across the deck until it came to rest by the helm.

Then the mast snapped. Hector heard a great rending creak, a shadow passed over him and the flogging headsail as it descended dealt him a glancing blow on the side of the head. It swept him overboard. He hit the water backwards, arms flailing, and went under. Seawater rushed into his mouth and nose, and when he spluttered back to the surface, he found himself facing the sloop. He could see at once that *Amity* was crippled. Two-thirds of her mast still stood, enough to support the drooping mainsail on its spar so she was still moving slowly forward. But the two head-sails dragged in the sea beside her like an injured seabird with a broken wing.

Hector kicked off his shoes and trod water. He was unharmed apart from a painful scrape on his cheek and a numbness in his right ear where the sail had hit him. His first thought was to swim after the sloop and try to get back aboard. But it was soon obvi-ous that the sloop, even in her battered state, was moving too fast for him to catch up. Nor would she put back to collect him. *Amity* was no longer under control, and her captain was dead. Twisting round, he looked for the warship that had done the damage. He fully expected to see that the vessel had altered course and was closing in for the kill. To his amazement he saw that the warship was sailing calmly onward, making no attempt to finish off its helpless victim.

Something made him look to his right. Fifty yards away and bearing down on him was the huge flag-covered ship. Already she was close enough for him to see the broad green stripe of seaweed at her waterline each time she rolled.

He took a deep breath and began to swim to one side, fearing that he would be run down. He was a good swimmer but barely succeeded in getting far enough to avoid being swept under. As the great hull passed by him he was floundering within touching distance. He heard a faint shout from above. There was a splash in the water close to him and something hit him on the shoulder. It was a rope's end with a loop. The crew had thrown him a life-line. As he slipped the loop over his head, he had a sudden sharp memory of Captain Tew, making exactly the same gesture as he put on his baldric before his last fight. Then, with a jerk, the rope cut into his chest and under his arms and he was snatched out of the water. Dangling and spinning, he was hoisted yard by yard until unseen hands reached out to drag him over a broad wooden rail. Finally, he was lowered onto a sun-baked deck where he stayed on all fours like a dog, head down and his chest heaving as he gasped for breath.

EIGHT

HE BECAME AWARE of a circle of bare feet surrounding him. When he looked up, his eyes smarting from the salt water, he saw a ring of brown faces staring down at him. They were small, scrawny men, at least a dozen of them standing shoulder to shoulder. They wore sweat-stained head cloths, tattered shirts and a skirt-like cloth wrapped around their waists. Several had hitched the garment up between their skinny legs to give free movement. Hector presumed that they were the ordinary deck hands that worked the great ship. Their expressions were a blend of curiosity and surprise as if his rescuers were puzzling over what to make of such unlikely flotsam pulled from the sea.

Carefully he pushed himself to his feet, aware that his wet clothes were sticking to his body, and that the deck was uncomfortably hot. He felt strangely disoriented. There was none of the sea motion that he had experienced on the sloop. In its place was a ponderous fore and aft rocking, slow and gentle. Strangely, the effect was to throw him off balance. Around him, everything was eerily placid, almost serene after the clamour and confusion aboard *Amity* during the fight. He shook his head to clear the water from his ears. The loudest sound was the constant fluttering and snapping of dozens of flags and banners over his head. He could just detect the regular creak of rigging in the background and the faintest sigh of the wind. There was also a trace of a strange smell, something he could not identify. It reminded him of the inside of a church.

Looking over the heads of his rescuers, he was awed by the vast scale of the vessel on which he now found himself. He was in the waist of the ship, the lowest open area, and the deck was at least fifteen paces from rail to rail. The mainmast was so huge that two men would have had difficulty in encircling it with their outstretched arms. The smallest rope was as thick as his wrist, and the two companionways, fore and aft, that gave access to the higher decks were like stairways in a mansion. Equally unexpected were the piles of bales, boxes, cloth bundles and sacks that lay in untidy heaps everywhere. The owners of this clutter had to be the crowd of onlookers who sat or sprawled on their baggage and were staring at him with unconcealed fascination. Judging by their clothes – loose, open-necked cotton gowns like long shirts – they were men of modest means. He supposed they were ordinary ship's passengers on their way home after their pilgrimage. The majority were greybeards, but at least one traveller had brought his family with him. A cloth stretched between the barrels of two large deck cannon gave some shade for several half-naked toddlers and the veiled figure seated on deck whom Hector supposed to be their mother.

One of his diminutive rescuers was plucking at his sleeve and pointing toward the foot of the companionway leading aft, gesturing that he must go to an upper deck. The sailor accompanied him up the steps and as he climbed, he got a glimpse of *Amity* already half a mile astern. The crippled sloop was being left farther and farther behind. He doubted that her crew, however expert, would resume the chase. They would need at least a day to carry out repairs, jury-rig her mast top and make her seaworthy. The warship that had done all the damage was off on the port side, half a mile away and still keeping pace with her escort. *Amity*, it seemed, had been no more than a nuisance, easily brushed off.

At the top of the companionway a burly guard stepped into their path. His thick black beard and moustaches gleamed with oil and were caught up in a light net looped over his ears. He was dressed in tight-fitting trousers of white cotton, slippers with pointed toes and a splendid surcoat of coarse silk, broad across the shoulders, held in at the waist with a wide sash, and flaring out to knee-length skirts. The canary yellow of his turban, sash, and surcoat exactly matched the colour of the standard that Hector had earlier seen flying at the stern of the great ship.

Hector's rescuer cringed as the guard loomed over him and barked an angry question in a language that Hector did not recognize. The sailor shrank even further as he mumbled his reply, and the guard snapped an order that sent the deckhand scurrying back down the steps. The guard then turned his attention on Hector, looked him up and down several times, and placed a beefy hand flat on his chest, leaving him in no doubt that he was to stay where he was. Then the guard turned and strode off. While he waited, Hector examined his surroundings. To his left a screen of light muslin blocked his view, and the aft section of this upper deck had what appeared to be a number of cabins. To his right a number of well-dressed figures stood in the open air, chatting idly among themselves or gazing out over the sunlit sea. Most were in long flowing robes and turbans, others in bright waistcoats worn over shirts and loose white pantaloons. Among them were several men whose sashes or turbans were of the same yellow as the guard's livery.

One of these – a short, neat man in a brocade waistcoat and yellow sash – was strolling back with the guard as he returned. Hector supposed he was an officer.

'Who are you?' the newcomer asked, first in careful Spanish, then in English. He had a pleasant, open face, a head of black curly hair, and a trim beard. With his brown eyes and dark complexion he could have been taken for an Arab or an Easterner, but Hector recognized his Portuguese accent.

'My name is Hector Lynch,' Hector replied in Galician, the

tongue his mother had taught him. 'I fell overboard from that sloop that lost the top of its mast.'

The officer's eyes widened with surprise.

It dawned on Hector that the action of a few humble sailors had gone unnoticed from the higher decks. 'Your people rescued me,' he added.

'What possessed your captain to launch such a mad attack?'

'The hope of seizing a fortune.'

The officer grinned. 'Well, he wasn't wrong about that . . . welcome aboard *Ganj-i-Sawa'i* – it means "exceeding treasure" – and our ship lives up to her name if you count the value of her cargo. Also, as you may have guessed, she carries a most prestigious passenger.'

Noting Hector's blank look, he tapped his yellow sash. 'You don't recognize this? Or the ship's ensign?'

Hector shook his head.

'The royal colours. An older sister of the emperor travels with us. She returns from making the hajj.' The Portuguese man lifted a chin towards the accompanying warship. 'That's why *Fateh Muhammed* was assigned as escort, to see that we reach Surat safely.' He paused. 'By the way, what did you think of *Fateh*'s gunnery?'

'It cut our rigging, and killed our captain.'

The Portuguese looked pleased. 'That's good to hear. I trained her gunners myself. They are landsmen and this is their first time at sea.' He extended his hand to shake. 'My name is Jeronimo Tavares, and I am *hazari* – that's to say, captain – of artillery in the army of Aurangzeb Alamgir.'

Hector was warming to the easy self-confidence of the man. He knew that adventurers of all nations – French, Dutch, German and English – served as mercenaries in the armies of the Great Mogul, but he had not expected to find one of them so open and friendly towards a recent foe.

'Come with me,' said Tavares. 'I'll take you to meet our captain, *nakhoda* Ibrahim.'

They had to pass another burly guard in yellow livery before mounting another companionway up one more level to a half-deck open to the sky. On the port side a striped canopy had been stretched between light poles to provide an area of shade. Under it was spread a fine silk carpet, and a silver tray of sweetmeats, delicate coloured glassware and a porcelain flask had been placed on a low table. Seated among cushions behind the table was a tiny figure, who Hector presumed was the Great Mogul's sister. It was impossible to tell much about her because she was swathed from head to toe in a garment of shimmering moss-green silk edged with gold that left her face in deep shadow. The only clue was the hand that emerged briefly to draw the folds of the fabric even closer, making sure that her face was not visible. It was the bony hand of an older woman, the small fingers loaded with magnificent rings, while her thin wrist seemed barely able to support a broad, triple banded bracelet of pearls. On each side of her sat two female attendants, also wearing fine silks but showing enough of their faces for Hector to see the gold jewellery hung across their foreheads and the glitter of gold nose rings. Aware that he was staring and might give offence, Hector quickly dropped his eyes and allowed Tavares to conduct him to the opposite side of the deck.

'*Nakhoda*, here's someone you should meet,' said the Portuguese, addressing a small, wizened man in a plain white gown. 'He's from the Frankish ship that was driven off by *Fateh Muhammed*.'

Sharp, probing eyes took in Hector's bedraggled appearance. 'How does he come to be on my ship?' The captain of the *Ganj-i-Sawa'i* must have been at least sixty years old, though he appeared as alert and trim as a man of half his years. A snow-white beard was clipped very short, framing an intelligent fine-boned face.

Hector had been able to follow the conversation's blend of Arabic and Turkish, and decided it would be better if he spoke for himself. 'I was thrown into the water when the vessel's mast was damaged. Some of your crew pulled me from the sea.'

The *nakhoda* spoke quietly but his voice was loaded with contempt. 'Your captain is an uncivilized savage. Even a worthless pirate should respect those who travel peacefully, wishing only to perform their holy duty.'

'He paid the price,' Hector ventured to say. 'A cannon ball killed him.'

'No more than the brute deserved.' The comment came from a sleek, portly man who had drifted across to join them from where he had been standing by the ship's rail. Everything about him spoke of good living, from the comfortable paunch bulging under the embroidered shirt to the large gemstones in the cluster of rings on his chubby fingers. Hector took him to be one of the wealthy merchants who sailed aboard the pilgrim fleet.

Ibrahim tilted his head back so he could look Hector fully in the face. 'Can you think of any reason why I shouldn't have you thrown back into the sea where you came from?'

When Hector stayed silent, Tavares intervened on his behalf. '*Nakhoda*, this man could be useful if he is handed over to the foreign merchants in Surat. He would be living proof that their governments must do more to stamp out the pirates that sail here to do us damage.'

Ibrahim considered for a long moment, and Hector held his breath, his stomach knotted with anxiety, as he waited for the *nakhoda*'s verdict.

'Very well, *hazari*,' the captain of the *Ganj-i-Sawa'i* announced at last. 'The prisoner is your responsibility. Lock him in the small storeroom next to your own cabin. Arrange that he receives food and water and make sure that he causes no trouble.'

Listening in, the well-fed merchant gave a malicious smile. 'A sound decision: when we get to Surat, the foreign merchants can punish this man according to their own customs. They need to show respect for the terms of the Emperor's firman that allows them to trade in his domains.'

The artilleryman flashed Hector a cheery smile as the two of them walked back to the companionway. 'That was easier than I thought. Ibrahim's a decent old fellow at heart,' he said, switching back to Portuguese.

'Who was that fat man who talked about the foreign merchants and the emperor?'

'That's Manuj Doshi,' Tavares replied. 'He's a Surati merchant, one of several aboard, immensely rich as well as very devious. From what I know of Manuj and his associates they will make sure that everyone, especially Aurangzeb, gets to hear about the captured *ferangi* who made a piratical attack on a vessel carrying his sister.'

'He seemed to be gloating over it.'

'Manuj Doshi and his friends are constantly looking for ways to harm their business rivals in Surat, the European trading houses. The Moguls lump together all foreigners from Europe as *ferangi* – "Franks". Manuj will try to engineer it so that Aurangzeb expels all the representatives of the foreign trading houses in Surat, their factors, and seizes their warehouses and goods.

He gave Hector a sideways look. 'You speak excellent Galician, but I detect that you're not from Spain.'

'My mother was from Galicia, and my father from an English family settled in Ireland. That makes me a subject of the English king.' Hector allowed himself a bleak smile. 'But I came out to this part of the world hoping to settle in a free country, in Libertalia where every man is equal to his fellow.'

Tavares pulled a face. 'Never heard of the place. Sounds like Utopia, an unlikely paradise.'

'I'm beginning to wonder if it exists,' Hector admitted.

'And how did you finish up aboard a pirate sloop with a mad captain?'

'He asked me to help pilot his ship among the reefs in the Straits of Alexander.'

They had descended back to the middle deck where Tavares opened a door set in the bulkhead behind the companionway. It gave on to a short ill-lit passage. They entered and Hector was about to explain that he had joined the *Amity* only that morning when he caught a whiff of some sort of perfume.

'Am I imagining it, or do I smell roses?' he asked.

The artilleryman glanced back over his shoulder, a playful grin on his face. 'Your nose has detected the choicest of our "exceeding treasures": *Ganj-i-Sawa'i* carries thirty Turkish slave girls. They're a gift for Aurangzeb, though I don't know who from. They and their two chaperones occupy all the cabins on the left-hand side, except for the last one: that's the largest and reserved for Her Highness and her attendants. It is a Mogul custom that any room used by their womenfolk is sprinkled daily with attar of roses.'

Tavares stopped in front of a door a few paces on the right along the passageway. 'Annoyingly, we don't get to appreciate those beauties. They're only allowed out on deck for fresh air for a couple of hours each day. Even then they stay hidden behind that cloth screen that you may have noticed.'

He produced a ring of keys and searched for the right one. 'Manuj Doshi and the Surati merchants have been grumbling that the girls take up too much space. Normally the girls' cabins are where the most precious cargo is kept securely. The merchants don't like having their ivory, silks, spices and other valuables stowed down in the hold where the ordinary passengers might filch a few items.'

He chuckled. 'I must admit I enjoy watching Manuj and his colleagues puffing and panting as they climb up and down between decks two or three times a day as they venture into the bowels of the ship to check that nothing of their property has been stolen.'

He found the key he was looking for and fitted it into the lock. 'But they can't have it both ways. They waited in Jeddah until there was a suitably safe vessel to bring their goods and gold to Surat. With Aurangzeb's sister aboard, and *Fateh Muhammed* as an escort ship, they got what they wanted.'

He turned the key and pulled open the low door. 'This is where Ibrahim told me to put you.'

Hector peered into a windowless cubbyhole. His makeshift cell was a storage locker scarcely larger than a decent-size wardrobe.

'I'll arrange for one of the guards to bring you food and water once a day, and to accompany you to the privy,' Tavares told him. 'When there are not too many people about on deck, I'll come and fetch you myself so you can stretch your legs and we can talk further.'

Hector felt a great weariness settling over him. The day's events had drained him of energy and all he wanted to do was curl up and rest. Even the prospect of being shut in the small cubbyhole was appealing. 'Thank you for what you've done for me,' he said, 'without you, I would have been thrown to the fishes.'

Tavares waved a hand dismissively. 'No need to thank me. I'm looking forward to our chats together. It'll be good to talk in a language that reminds me of the mother country.' He paused, seeing the strain on Hector's face. 'Try to get some rest. You're in a different world to anything you will have known before: the world according to the Great Mogul. It's the exact opposite of that Libertalia you were seeking: every person has his proper place, from the Emperor down to the humblest street sweeper, and the hierarchy is strictly observed. On the other hand, when the Great Mogul smiles on you, nothing is impossible, and something may yet work out.'

Hector had to bend double to enter the tiny space. The door closed behind him, there was the sound of the key turning, and he was left in darkness. He groped his way into a corner where he found a piece of sacking to sit on, and tried to make himself comfortable. His first thought was of Jezreel and Jacques. If the freebooter squadron had kept to the original plan, his two friends would be with Avery aboard the *Fancy* chasing after the main pilgrim fleet. Unless the squadron came across the crippled

Amity – which was unlikely as Tew had changed course to attack *Ganj-i-Sawa'i* – his friends would presume that he was still with Tew. They would expect to meet up with him when the *Amity* had intercepted and turned back the pilgrim fleet. Instead, *Ganj-i-Sawa'i* was taking him to Surat, to hand him over to foreign merchants who would put him on trial for piracy. A guilty verdict and death sentence were inevitable, and the fat merchant Manuj and his associates would make sure that news of his crime and execution was spread far and wide. His heart sank at the thought that Maria might one day learn how he had died. She would be devastated, believing that the father of their child had ended his days as a vicious pirate who preyed on helpless pilgrims. As he drifted off into an exhausted sleep, he was overwhelmed by a cloud of such black despair that he wished the humble deckhands of the 'Exceeding Treasure' had not thrown him a rope. It would have been better if they had left him to drown, unknown.

NINE

Jeronimo Tavares kept his promise about coming to visit. The next day, shortly after Hector heard the faint echo of the midday call to prayer penetrate the wooden walls of his prison, the door to the cubbyhole swung open. 'Come and join me on deck,' said the artilleryman cheerfully, as Hector blinked up at him. 'It looks as though you could use some fresh air. Just promise me you won't try to jump overboard.'

Hector climbed stiffly out over the threshold and stretched to ease his cramped muscles. His chest and arms hurt where the rescue rope had left purple and blue bruises.

'I told the guards to see that you were fed. Have you been brought anything to eat?' asked the Portuguese. He seemed in remarkably good spirits and was obviously eager for conversation.

'Yes, thank you. A guard delivered a bowl of rice and dried fish and a jug of water earlier this morning,' said Hector. He knew that he looked scruffy in his soiled clothes and shoeless, while the artilleryman was wearing a freshly laundered white shirt under his brocade waistcoat.

'It's still too hot for most of our august passengers. They'll emerge once the air cools,' Tavares told him as he led Hector out on deck where the only other persons were the sentries guarding the companionways. Off the port beam the warship *Fateh Muhammed* was under full sail, more than two miles distant and apparently heading away on a different course.

'*Fateh Muhammed* is leaving to check on the rest of the fleet, to see that they're not being molested,' Tavares explained. 'She should be back with us late tomorrow.'

'How long until we get to Surat?'

Tavares reached inside his waistcoat to scratch his ribs. 'Difficult to say. Maybe another week. Ibrahim is in no hurry and even if he was, the *Ganj* is a real slug.'

He looked directly at Hector, holding his gaze, and when he spoke, his tone was serious. 'Hector, you should claim to be Portuguese. Your Galician is close enough to Portuguese for you to say that you grew up in the north of the country. It would mean that when we get to Surat, you would be handed over to the city's Portuguese merchants for your trial as a pirate. If I put in a good word, they might find a way of avoiding a harsh sentence.'

'What about Manuj and his friends? They wouldn't be pleased.'

'That's partly why I'm offering you my help.' Tavares's expression, normally amiable and engaging, hardened. 'My family had a thriving business in Surat not so long ago. We were independent traders, not like a big Dutch or English company operating from its own factory with warehousing, offices and living quarters. Our modest size made us vulnerable. Manuj and his cronies bankrupted us. They dishonoured contracts, delayed payments, bribed judges, pulled all the usual tricks. Instead of inheriting the business I was obliged to go to Portugal and join the artillery to learn about big guns.'

'What made you return to India?'

'It was always my intention. Promotion in the Portuguese army requires friends in high places. By contrast, when you work for the Moguls, you're rewarded with more than enough gold rupees to hire servants, rent comfortable lodgings and enjoy life to the full.'

Tavares' eyes had brightened with enthusiasm. 'You should think about getting a job with the Moguls instead of chasing after that fantasy of Libertalia. Do you have any professional qualification? In medicine, for example? Foreign doctors are much in demand in the Mogul court.'

'I was a loblolly boy for a ship's surgeon, but that scarcely qualifies me as a doctor.' Tactfully, Hector did not mention that the surgeon had been a member of a buccaneer raiding party.

The artilleryman gave a dismissive grin. 'Some of the so-called doctors at the Mogul court are complete charlatans. All mumbo-jumbo and dog Latin. They've been getting away with it for years. You know the old saying: a doctor buries his mistakes.'

'I'd rather not put my limited medical knowledge to the test.'

Tavares considered for a moment. 'How about offering your expertise as a navigator or a pilot? Aurangzeb doesn't have much of a fleet, but you could apply to the *mir-i-bahr*, the officer in charge of the navy.'

'I don't know these seas well enough to call myself a pilot.'

The good-natured artilleryman was not to be put off. 'Yesterday you told me that you were picking a way through coral reefs for the captain of that sloop.'

'That was what Tew asked me to do.'

Tavares rolled his eyes theatrically. 'Whatever happens, don't say that you sailed with Tew. He sacked a thirty-gun ship out of Surat only last year. His name would be known to the *mir-i-bahr* as a notorious pirate.'

'So I've been told,' said Hector. He wondered what had happened to the eager young sailor who had sheltered beside him on *Amity*'s foredeck. The young man's hopes of a quick fortune and swift return home under Tew's command had been dashed. 'But I wasn't involved. I was in the Caribbean at the time.'

He stopped short, thinking that he had as good as admitted his dubious background of piracy.

To his relief Tavares merely cocked an eyebrow. 'Whatever

you were up to in the Caribbean makes little difference to the supreme ruler, who calls himself "Seizer of the Universe".'

'Have you ever met Aurangzeb?' Hector asked.

'Not in person. But I've seen him close up dozens of times. The Moguls treat their big guns as symbols of status, so the artillery is attached to the imperial household and is separate from the Mogul army. Whenever the emperor goes on a journey, even in peacetime, he likes to take along his gun batteries. They're hauled by teams of elephants and shown off to his people.'

'You make it sound as if the guns are no practical use.'

The Portuguese shrugged. 'On the battlefield they scare the opponent's war elephants with the noise. The bigger the bangs the better. Come with me, and I'll show you what I mean.'

He strolled with Hector to the low, intricately carved wooden balustrade that overlooked the lower deck.

'See those big cannon down there,' said Tavares.

Hector found himself gazing down on the same place where he had been pulled from the sea. The scene had not changed: scores of pilgrims sprawled on untidy heaps of baggage that left little room to move. Tavares leaned over and pointed to the two large guns that still had a cloth spread between them to provide shade.

'Those two are 30-pounders, monsters, as big as anything I saw in the Portuguese army. It takes ten or twenty minutes between each shot, sometimes longer if the gunners are out of practice. I'd be careful about the amount of powder I'd stuff into them. They're made locally of cast iron, not bronze, and I wonder just how safe they are. On the other hand they make a magnificently loud noise when firing a salute.'

He straightened up and turned to Hector. 'They were already fitted to this vessel when I came aboard, and I'd be surprised if they've ever been fired in anger. They're all show and little substance.'

He gestured toward the yellow turbaned sentry who stood guard at the head of the companionway. 'The same goes for him and his lot. They're supposed to be crack troops, seasoned musketeers, but they were mostly picked for their size and swagger. They make an impressive sight when escorting the emperor's sister on land. But there are only a handful of them, and I very much doubt they've seen active service.'

Hector looked down again at the crowded lower deck. It did not take an expert to see that it would be nearly impossible to defend the great ship, either with cannon or muskets, until the clutter was cleared away. He wondered where all the pilgrims' mass of baggage could be stowed if, as Tavares said, the *Ganj-i-Sawa'i* was already overloaded.

He felt a discreet nudge on his elbow. 'Here they come to inspect their ill-gotten gains,' Tavares muttered. Manuj Dosi and three other merchants had emerged from their cabins and were making their way towards the companionway that led to the lower deck. The artilleryman steered Hector off to one side, well out of the way of the group who treated Hector to a hostile stare as they walked past. Tavares waited until they were well out of earshot before he confided with a chuckle, 'Rumour has it that when Tew ransacked that thirty-gun ship, a good part of the lost cargo belonged to Manuj. Of course he was safe in his counting house in Surat at the time.'

Hector scarcely heard him. His mind was racing ahead. He was sure that Maria would agree to him obtaining a post with the Mogul navy if it meant they were free from harassment from the authorities in London. She had already spent several years in Peru in the household of a Spanish colonial official so she knew what it was like to live in a foreign country. As for Jezreel and Jacques, they too could follow his example and work for the Moguls. It was certainly a better option than reverting to outright piracy. For the first time since coming aboard *Ganj-i-Sawa'i*, he saw a glimmer of hope for the future.

*

THAT EVENING, back in his makeshift cell, Hector sat in the dark, with his arms around his knees, his back pressed against a bulkhead. The more he considered Tavares' scheme, the more attractive it seemed. There were questions he needed to ask Tavares: was India a safe place to raise a child? And was it normal that Frankish officers were accompanied by their foreign wives? With so much to think about, it was difficult to relax. He tried to settle, shifting his position on the hard boards and unable to stretch out fully. The constant noises of the ship all around him made it difficult to do much more than doze in short spells. There were the different creaks from the various timbers as the ship moved on the swell, a scuttling sound that could have been a rat, footsteps on the deck overhead, cabin doors opening and closing. Once was he jerked wide awake by the sound of female voices. He leaned across and pressed his eye to the crack between the door and its frame. There was a momentary glimpse of candle-light and veiled figures as the Turkish slave girls moved about in the passageway. Eventually he must have fallen into a deeper sleep because he was only faintly conscious of the *fajr*, the pre-dawn call to prayer, and, a little while later, a distant thunderclap. After a few seconds the thunderclap was repeated, followed by a long interval, then twice more. He lifted his head and listened. It was not thunder he was hearing, but the thud of cannon fire from far away, the sound travelling a distance across water. He slowed his breathing and concentrated, but there was nothing more. His first thought was of the freebooter squadron led by Avery with the *Amity*. It was now the third day since he had left them, and there was no way of knowing where their ships had got to. The gunfire might be nothing to do with them. He told himself to be patient and wait for the guard to bring him his food or for Tavares to visit. Either man might be able to explain.

The hours dragged by, and the wait lengthened. From the unchanged, steady motion of the ship, he could tell that *Ganj-i-Sawa'i* was keeping her course, sailing on as before. The patter and scuff of bare feet on the deck above him could have been sail handlers at work, and that was nothing out of the ordinary. Further along the passageway the doors to the cabins occupied by the merchants opened and shut several times. He caught a snatch of conversation that sounded anxious though it was in an unknown language and meant nothing to him. From the women's cabins across the passageway there was neither sound nor movement, and no one – not even a guard to bring food – came to see him. Deep in his bones he sensed that something was amiss aboard the 'Exceeding Treasure'. It made no difference to his decision: he would do as Tavares had suggested. He would claim to be Portuguese and, if all went well and he survived a trial for piracy in Surat, he would seek employment with the Great Mogul.

It was long past midday when finally he heard the key turn in the lock. Tavares was standing in the open doorway, his expression grim. 'Hector, you're wanted on deck,' he said. There was a tense edge to his voice.

Hector followed the artilleryman along the passageway and out on deck where a dozen merchants clustered in an agitated group, talking amongst themselves in loud shrill voices and with much waving of hands. With a curt nod to the sentry at the foot of the companionway, Tavares hurried him up to the next deck, two steps at a time. There Hector's eyes had to adjust to the bright glare reflected from the sea. All should have been well. It was another perfect day, full of sunshine. Overhead the banners and pennants still fluttered and snapped in the breeze, and the *nakhoda* Ibrahim was standing by the rail, looking astern.

Hector saw at once why he had been summoned.

A couple of miles in distance, trailing in the wake of the 'Exceeding Treasure', were three ships. He knew them at once – *Fancy*, *Pearl* and the *Portsmouth Adventure* from the freebooter squadron.

'Friends of yours?' Ibrahim asked, turning, his voice as calm and soft as usual.

Hector stood silent, not knowing how to answer. He stole a quick sideways glance to the spot where Aurangzeb's sister had sat with her attendants. The canopy had been removed and the deck was bare. There was no sign of the emperor's sister.

The silence stretched, then Ibrahim gave a slight shrug. 'They will not overtake us until long after dark. So nothing will happen until tomorrow.'

Tavares, standing beside Hector, shifted uneasily. It was clear that he was troubled. 'My friend, if you do know anything about them, you should tell us,' he said.

Hector's mind whirled. He was torn between his loyalty to Jacques and Jezreel on the one hand and his new-found belief in Tavares. He trusted the artilleryman and needed his help if he – and his friends – were to enter Mogul employ.

'The large vessel is *Fancy*, commanded by Captain Henry Avery,' he said slowly, trying to gain time and see a way out of the trap in which he found himself.

'How many guns and what weight?' Tavares demanded sharply.

'Forty, I think, demi-culverins.'

Tavares made an unhappy clicking noise with his tongue. 'What about the other two ships?'

'The second vessel is the *Pearl*, but I don't know much about her.'

Ibrahim was pointing to the third and smallest ship. 'What about that little one?'

'*Portsmouth Adventure*. She mounts only eight guns and I believe they are small, only six-pounders,' Hector told him.

'Then *Fancy* is the only real danger,' Tavares summed up. 'My guess is that she already outmatched *Fateh Muhammed* and has overwhelmed her. That was the gunfire we heard this morning.'

Hector detected the fatalistic tone in the artilleryman's voice and recalled Tavares' description of the weakness of the great ship's defences – too few musketeers and unreliable cannon. All of a sudden he saw a solution to his dilemma.

'Henry Avery is a former officer in the English navy. He seeks only to plunder this ship. Not destroy her.'

Tavares looked at him stony-eyed. 'Are you hinting that we surrender?'

'Afterwards Avery would allow *Ganj-i-Sawa'i* to proceed on her way. Her pilgrims would reach Surat unharmed. No one would be hurt.' Also, he thought to himself, Tavares would take considerable satisfaction from the financial losses that Manuj Dosi and his merchant fellows would suffer.

'No surrender,' the *nakhoda* murmured in a tone of calm finality. There was something about the old man's expression that told Hector the veteran mariner was prepared to accept the consequences.

'With a member of the emperor's family on board, surrender would be treason,' Tavares added. His mouth curved down in a grimace of distaste. 'Also, Hector, you're forgetting the well-being of our other passengers. Even a captain of the English navy cannot guarantee that they reach the imperial court intact if we allow this ship to be pillaged.'

It took Hector a moment to understand that the Portuguese artilleryman was referring to the gift for Aurangzeb: the Turkish slave girls. He tried to form a response but his mouth was dry and his tongue felt thick and clumsy. Tavares was right. There was no chance whatever that Avery would be able to restrain the crew of *Fancy* once they boarded the vessel.

A sudden disturbance made all three of them turn. The merchants from the deck below had forced their way up the companionway. There were at least a dozen of them and they erupted on deck, angrily pushing the hapless guard ahead of them. They surged forward, their frightened voices rising in panic as they demanded to speak with the *nakhoda*. They gathered around Ibrahim, all shouting at once, wanting to know what he proposed to do to protect their lives and their goods. Their hysteria was palpable. Tavares pulled out a silver whistle hanging on a cord around his neck, and blew three loud blasts to summon more guards. Hector was pushed aside and, with Ibrahim struggling to make himself heard over the hubbub, no one took any notice of him until one of the merchants caught sight of him and began bawling that Hector was a spy, that he had wormed his way aboard so that he could signal his companions on the pursuing ships. Soon it was Hector who was at the centre of the frenzied mob. They pressed around him, shouting and threatening. Hands reached out to grab him. He had to duck as someone swung a blow at his head, and for a moment he thought he would be bundled to the ship's rail and heaved into the sea. Then the extra guards arrived, and began shoving back the merchants violently, making plain their dislike of them. Hector stepped off to one side, panting heavily, as order was restored.

Tavares came over to him, brushing down his jacket. 'For your own safety, Hector, I think we should return you to your cubbyhole. I'll place a guard outside.'

Hector nodded toward the three freebooter ships still shadowing *Ganj-i-Sawa'i*. Even in the bright afternoon sunshine there was something darkly sinister about the way they were closing the gap yard by yard. 'What do you propose to do about them?'

A stubborn look came into the artilleryman's brown eyes. 'I'll earn my gold rupees,' he said softly.

TEN

NEXT MORNING THE CRASH of an opening broadside obliterated the last fading echo of the *fajr*. It was the same sound Hector had heard all those months earlier when he first laid eyes on *Fancy* sailing into St Mary's and firing a salute. This time the blasts of the warship's demi-culverins were followed by several shuddering thumps as the iron cannon balls struck the enormous bulk of 'Exceeding Treasure'. There were wails of terror from the rooms across the passageway where the slave girls had their accommodation, and a single, piercing scream. Moments later and much closer to hand, a number of deeper, heavier cannon blasts signalled that Tavares' gunners were returning fire. Hector swore aloud in frustration. He turned around, braced himself against the bulkhead behind him, and kicked vigorously at the door with both feet, trying to break out from his prison and observe for himself what was going on. He discovered that the door – like the rest of 'Exceeding Treasure' – was stoutly built. The lock was not about to burst. So he concentrated his efforts on the weakest point, the lower corner furthest from the hinges. He kicked repeatedly until he succeeded in making a narrow gap between the door and the frame. He turned around, lay flat on the floor and squinted out into the corridor. It was deserted.

He had no fears for his own safety. The *Ganj-i-Sawa'i* was

built of massively thick timbers and his cubbyhole was deep inside the ship. During the brief exchange of fire between *Amity* and *Fateh Muhammed* he had seen how several of *Amity*'s six-pound shot had bounced off the hull of her opponent. *Fancy*'s demi-culverins threw a heavier, nine-pound ball, but he doubted they would penetrate the hull of 'Exceeding Treasure' except, possibly, at point-blank range. Besides, he knew that Avery and his men were trying to keep damage to a minimum. They wanted to capture *Ganj-i-Sawa'i* without risking any valuable cargo she might be carrying and they certainly did not intend to sink their target. They would be hoping that a brief but accurate cannonade – accompanied by bloodthirsty shouts and brandishing of weapons – would intimidate the defenders of 'Exceeding Treasure' into an early surrender.

He smiled grimly to himself. Avery was in for a disappointment if he thought that *Ganj-i-Sawa'i* would give up meekly. Ibrahim and Tavares would battle to the finish. Avery would have to get *Fancy* close enough for grappling irons to be thrown, and the two ships lashed together. Next, a boarding party armed with pistols, pikes and cutlasses would be faced with clambering up the towering sides of the great ship. And even when they reached *Ganj-i-Sawa'i*'s deck the outcome of a hand-to-hand fight was far from certain. Avery's men were likely to find themselves outnumbered.

Hector slumped back against the bulkhead. His main dread was that Jacques and Jezreel – or Tavares – might be killed or maimed. As for the hapless pilgrims crowded on the lower deck, he could only hope that they had managed to take refuge in the hold. They were innocent bystanders in the fight. So too were the men who had rescued him, the humble sailors who worked the great, lumbering ship. Unarmed, they were completely vulnerable as they went about their duties. He could imagine their terror when Avery's gunners began to concentrate their fire on the mast and sails of 'Exceeding Treasure', intending to cripple her and bring her to a halt.

The cannonade continued. In his head he began keeping a rough tally of the number of cannon shots, first from Avery's ship of war and then from Tavares' guns. But he abandoned the count when it became clear that *Fancy* was firing three or four times as often as the *Ganj-i-Sawa'i*. He recalled Tavares telling him that *Ganj*'s unwieldy cannon were difficult to load, and that his gunners were poorly trained.

Sometime later, in mid-morning, he heard scraping sounds from the next-door cabin and a voice, low and urgent, giving instructions. He pressed his eye against the crack and peeked out. A worried-looking merchant, a man he did not know, was standing in the corridor. He was supervising two servants who were dragging a small iron-bound chest out of the cabin. The chest was so heavy that it took both servants to lift the box between them. They staggered off, closely followed by their anxious master. Hector guessed that the merchants were removing their most valuable possessions from their cabins, taking the treasure down into the hold, below the waterline.

Hector was about to abandon his spyhole when the door to the furthest cabin opened quietly. It was the cabin reserved for the emperor's sister. Hector recognized the woman who stepped out as one of the attendants he had seen on deck seated beside her mistress. She had removed her gold jewellery and was now wearing a long piece of cotton cloth printed with a simple pattern wrapped around her. Draped over her head was a cheap shawl similar to those worn by the pilgrim women. She waited several moments, checking that the corridor was clear. Then the old lady and her second attendant emerged. Hector blinked in surprise. The small figure was unmistakably the emperor's sister. She barely came up to her companion's shoulder. Now that he could see her more clearly, Hector put her age at somewhere in her mid-sixties. She too was wearing a plain cotton wrap-around garment and with a similar shawl on her head. It was her taller companion who was dressed in costly silks. Treading softly, the three women came down the corridor, their slippered feet passing in front of Hector's nose, and out of his line of sight. They were, Hector was sure, on their way to mingle with the crowd of humble pilgrims on the lower decks.

Hector's neck and shoulders were aching from the awkward angle he had been forced to adopt. He wormed back to his former position in the corner, and rolled his head from side to side to ease his neck muscles. The acrid smell of gunpowder smoke was seeping into his cubbyhole, and he was thirsty and hungry. He did not expect anyone to bring him food or water. All Tavares' men would be too busy occupied with the fight. He closed his eyes and returned to his attempt to track the progress of the sea battle by its sounds. He listened out for the sounds of smaller, lighter cannon that indicated whether *Pearl* or *Portsmouth Adventure* had joined the fight. But there was nothing. He presumed that their captains were waiting for Avery with the much more powerful *Fancy* to overwhelm the defenders of 'Exceeding Treasure'.

As the day wore on it became evident that *Fancy* was gradually getting the upper hand. Her gunfire steadily came nearer. Eventually one of her broadsides resulted in a loud crash that shook the deck immediately above him. Something heavy had fallen on the upper deck. He guessed it was the spar that held up the mizzen sail. If it was shot away, *Ganj-i-Sawa'i* was half-crippled.

One of the bigger guns on the 'Exceeding Treasure' had a distinct booming blast, deeper and heavier than the others. He supposed that it was one of the huge thirty-pounders on the lower deck that Tavares had pointed out to him. Each time it fired, the tremor of the recoil came through the wooden floor beneath him. This gun fired so regularly – five times an hour was his guess – that he was able to anticipate its next shot. It was well into the afternoon when there was a longer delay than usual, and he began to wonder if Tavares's men were running out of suitably large cannon balls or the great quantity of gunpowder needed to charge such a giant weapon. Moments later came an immense explosion. It was unlike anything that had gone before, a huge detonation that nearly deafened him. 'Exceeding Treasure' quivered along her entire length. The floor of the cubbyhole bucked beneath him. He was certain the explosion had been what Tavares had most feared: the great gun had burst. In the stunned silence that followed aboard *Ganj-i-Sawa'i* he thought he detected faint cheering that could only have come from the crew of the *Fancy*.

The sound of running feet, heavy sandals this time, brought him back to where he could use the spy hole. Three yellow-clad musketeers were in the passageway outside, bundles of clothing in their arms. He watched as they hammered on the doors of the cabins where the slave girls still sheltered. The doors opened, there was a quick shouted exchange and the men tossed the clothes inside. The doors closed, two of the musketeers raced back out on deck, while the third stayed waiting in the corridor. Hector remained where he was, watching. He was expecting the slave girls to come out in disguise, dressed as pilgrims. When they did emerge a short time later, he blinked in astonishment. The slave girls were also wearing the yellow uniforms of musketeers. Immediately the soldier who had been waiting for them ushered them out towards the deck.

As the girls passed out of view, Hector knew the situation was now desperate. Tavares, or whoever was in charge of the defence, was trying to bluff that a large force of musketeers was ready to repel any attempt to put a boarding party onto 'Exceeding Treasure'. *Fancy* must be closing in for the kill. He began to hear, very faintly, the sounds of drums and blaring trumpets – the freebooters' way of unnerving their victims before the final assault.

He struggled to stay calm. The gentle rocking motion of the ship had ceased. 'Exceeding Treasure' was no longer moving forward, but lay dead in the water. Instead of cannon fire there was now the rattle of musket shots. A gentle thump, and *Ganj-i-Sawa'i* lurched sideways a fraction. He guessed that the hulls of the two ships had touched, and *Fancy* must now be alongside. There were more trumpet calls and the rattle of a drum: the signal for a boarding party to attack.

Hector could contain himself no longer. He yelled for someone to open up and again kicked at the door in desperation. But it had no effect. He heard more shots, pistols as well as muskets, and the distinctive hollow sound of a blunderbuss. A second slight jolt, from a different direction as if a second ship had come alongside. It seemed that Avery's boarding party had been reinforced by *Pearl* or *Portsmouth Adventure*. From the deck above him came the noises of hand-to-hand fighting, wild shouts and calls for help, thuds and the clash of metal. Eventually – and by then he was hoarse from shouting – the sounds of battle began to die away. The last few pistol shots were followed by an unnerving silence.

It was then that he recalled Tavares' warning about what would happen if the freebooters seized the ship.

*

IT BEGAN WITH coarse whoops of triumph mingled, as often as not, with the rush of feet, roars of ugly-sounding laughter, and the sounds of struggle. Then the screams started. Some cries were repeated again and again, others suddenly choked off. His imagination told him that the worst elements among the freebooters had gone on the rampage. Hard, violent men, they would satisfy their lust as a reward for the risks they had taken. No one would be able to rein them in.

Hector must have fallen asleep because the next thing he knew someone was wrenching violently at the door handle to the cubbyhole.

'Use the crowbar,' a voice suggested. The speaker had a Welsh accent. 'Doors only get locked when there's something valuable inside.'

Hector's shout came out as a dry rasp. 'Get me out of here!'

A moment of surprised silence. 'Who's in there?' demanded the Welshman suspiciously.

'Lynch, Hector Lynch . . . from Captain Avery's company.'

'Don't know about Avery's lot. We're from *Pearl*.'

'Just open the door.'

A series of jabbing crunches as the end of the crowbar was repeatedly rammed home, the splintering sound of the door frame splitting apart, and the door swung open. Hector climbed out shakily. He was faced with two looters. The Welshman was short and stocky with slightly bulging eyes. His companion, holding the crowbar, was taller, with narrow, crafty face and long greasy hair. From the way they were looking at him, the iron crowbar ready to wield as a club, Hector wondered if they were ransacking the ship on their own initiative, and not as part of its organized robbing.

'What have we got here, cullies?' A Londoner's accent this time and Hector felt a surge of relief. John Dann, Avery's coxswain, had stepped into the corridor.

'Says he belongs to your company,' said the first man sulkily.

Dann walked down the passageway and stared Hector in the face. He looked haggard and drawn.

'Lynch, isn't it?' said Dann. 'How in God's name did you get here?'

'Fell off the *Amity*.'

Dann grinned. 'Should have held on tight.' The grin vanished as Dann rounded on the two men. 'Anyone caught pinching on the quiet will get a basting . . . or worse.'

'I need a drink of water,' Hector croaked.

'Come along then.' Dann treated the men to a hard glare, and led Hector away.

The scene out on deck was a shambles. There were gaps where the ship's rail had been wrecked by cannon fire, streaks and patches of blood on the deck planks, tangles of fallen rigging. To reach the water butt at the foot of the mizzenmast, Hector had to clamber over the mizzen spar that lay where it had fallen, the sail draped across it. A group of exhausted-looking prisoners had been herded together in one corner and made to sit. Hector spotted *nakhoda* Ibrahim among them. The loss of his ship had diminished the old man. He appeared to have shrivelled up and was gazing straight in front of him, his expression blank. By contrast the half-dozen merchants around him were clearly terrified. They kept casting unhappy looks in all directions as if expecting something terrible to happen. As Hector stood at the water butt, sucking up a drink from the wooden dipper, he looked for Tavares. Eventually he saw him. He had missed him the first time though the artilleryman was only a few paces away, seated with his back against the bulwarks and his legs straight out in front of him. Hector could only identify him by the embroidered waistcoat. Most of Tavares' face was hidden by a bloody rag wrapped around his head.

Hector hurried over, the dipper of water in his hand. Tavares' mouth was barely visible below the bandage. He knelt down beside the artilleryman. 'Jeronimo,' he said in Galician. 'It's me, Hector Lynch. Here, drink.'

There was no reply. Hector tried again, louder this time. Still no reaction. He leaned forward and brought the wooden ladle up to Tavares' lips, and succeeded in dribbling a little water into the slack mouth. Tavares's clothes reeked of gunpowder and charred cloth. His chest, exposed where the shirt was torn, had great patches, cherry red at the edges and dark black in the centre, where the skin had burned off.

Hector raised the ladle again to tip more water between the blistered lips, then rose to his feet, and looked around for help. From his days as a loblolly boy he had some knowledge of how to deal with burns. Dann was nowhere to be seen, and a single guard armed with a musket watched over the prisoners. To his left, *Fancy* lay lashed alongside with the ropes and grappling irons thrown by the boarding party, and *Pearl* must have joined the attack for she was now made fast on *Ganj-i-Sawa'i*'s starboard beam. There was no sign of the *Portsmouth Adventure*. He crossed to the head of the companionway and when he looked down on the lower deck, the first thing that caught his eye was the shattered ruin of one of the great guns. Half the long barrel was missing, five feet of metal blown away. The remaining stub with its jagged rim was still attached to the gun carriage that lay on its side, toppled by the explosion that, Hector suspected, had caused Tavares such terrible injury. There was no sign of the pilgrims who had once gathered there, and their clutter of baggage had been pushed aside to clear a space. There, behind a plank-and-trestle table, stood Hathaway, *Fancy*'s quartermaster, and a thick-necked man with unruly grey hair whom Hector supposed was his opposite number from *Pearl*. They were supervising the collection of valuables from the captured ship. Already on the deck beside them were several elephant's teeth, rolled-up carpets, a heap of garments made from heavy silk or cloth of gold, and – laid out in a neat line – half a dozen strongboxes.

A giant of a man emerged from a hatchway that led deeper in the ship's hold. He was cradling in his arms a heavy chest very like the one that Hector had seen carried away from the merchant's cabin.

'Jezreel!' Hector called out. The prize-fighter looked up and his face broke into a huge smile, then he turned and shouted down the hatch, 'Jacques, come on up! There's someone you need to see.'

Hector hurried down the steps as Jacques, looking equally pleased, joined his friend.

'Thought we had lost you,' announced Jezreel, setting down the chest next to the others. 'Where did you spring from?'

'I'll tell you later. Right now I need to find the cooks' storeroom on this ship.'

'It's in the forecastle,' said Jacques promptly. 'I'll take you there.'

As he passed Hathaway, Hector glanced down at the table in front of the quartermaster. Here were being gathered the smaller, more portable items of high value that had been discovered:

flashy ornate daggers with jewelled handles, pearl necklaces, gold chains, belts studded with gems, silver tableware, bangles, brooches, rings, and pendants.

Jacques led Hector and Jezreel forward between decks, stooping beneath the beams. This part of the great ship was dark and airless, and once again he noticed the smell that reminded him of the inside of a church. Hundreds of pilgrims had taken shelter in this confined space, huddled together so tightly they could scarcely move. Most had been able to sit down on the deck, but others were forced to stand, awkwardly hunched over. All of them followed the progress of the three newcomers with frightened eyes. Hector saw only men, and wondered what had happened to their womenfolk, and the children he had seen earlier. He tried his best not to add to their unease as he and his two companions picked their way through the mass of bodies.

'Jacques never fired a shot during the entire battle,' Jezreel said, edging around the base of the foremast and at the same time trying not to step on an elderly pilgrim who had fallen into a doze, his head lolling forward on his chest. 'Avery kept him in the galley, insisting that the men had regular meals during the fight.'

'Shows what a wise captain he is,' said the Frenchman over his shoulder. 'Lets the lame brains do the fighting.'

'Where's Avery now?' Hector asked.

'Still aboard *Fancy*. Long Ben never left the ship. He directed the entire battle from the poop deck.'

'So who did he put in charge of the boarding party?' Hector asked.

The barest flicker of a pause. 'Hathaway.'

Hector knew that his friend was holding something back. 'How was he?'

'He led from the front, first across the gap between the two ships, yelling like a madman, and cut down anyone who got in his way. You'd have thought he was going to seize the ship single-handed.'

'And then?' Hector remembered the cries of pain and the screams after the boarding party had taken the ship.

Jezreel gave a short, bitter laugh. 'About what you would expect . . . it made matters worse that there were women dressed up as musketeers. It made it seem that they were defeated and should pay the price.'

'I heard.'

'Several of the girls threw themselves overboard rather than submit.'

Hector wanted to change the subject. But the big man had not finished. 'Hathaway's savage and dangerous. As long as he's quartermaster, I'm not happy about being on *Fancy*. We should think about getting off the ship as soon as possible.'

'Avery's the captain. He's the man in charge,' Hector said.

'I think Jezreel's right,' Jacques cut in. 'Hathaway is gathering more and more cronies around him. Soon there'll be enough for them to vote Avery out and Hathaway to replace him.'

'You make Hathaway out to be a monster,' Hector objected.

Jacques made a grimace of distaste. 'This morning he sent the rest of us off to search the ship for valuables while he organized a gang of his cronies to check up on all the passengers on the lower decks. Anyone who looked too wealthy to be down there has been hauled out on deck and brought before him. He asked where they had hidden their valuables. If they didn't cooperate, they got beaten up.'

That explained the terrified looks on the faces of the pilgrims, Hector thought to himself.

'One man was brought out because the searchers had noticed his soft pudgy hands and ring marks on his fingers, but no rings.'

Hector wondered if this unfortunate had been Manuj Dosi, and waited for Jacques to go on.

'Hathaway asked where he had hidden his rings, but the fellow kept on insisting that he never wore rings. In that case, Hathaway told him, he didn't need so many fingers. Hathaway pressed the man's hand down onto the table, and used his cutlass to chop off his little finger.'

They had reached the bows of the ship, where a low half-bulkhead divided off a storage area. In the near darkness Hector could make out rows of rice sacks, bundles of firewood and a dozen earthenware jars the size of beer kegs. There was also a pungent aroma of spices. He recognized clove and garlic. The others were exotic and unknown to him.

'What are you looking for?' Jezreel asked.

'Fresh cooking oil.'

Hector stepped over the divide and lifted the wooden lid to an earthenware jar. He dipped in his finger, and licked: coconut oil.

'This will do. We need to find a small container.'

'What's it for?'

'There's a Portuguese artilleryman on the mid-deck aft. He's very badly burned. I need to dress his wounds with something oily to prevent putrefaction and help them heal.'

'This might do a better job,' said Jacques. He had been poking around and was holding up a clay pot. 'Butter.'

'In this heat that'll be rancid,' said Jezreel.

'You stick to your backsword fights, the kitchen's my patch,' Jacques told him. 'Butter that's simmered and skimmed will last for months if kept in the dark.'

'Let's not waste time with cookery lessons,' said Hector sharply. 'We'll use the butter. Bring it along.'

On the way back to Tavares, Hector tried to recall the contents of the medicine chest that had been his responsibility when he was loblolly boy. He could still picture the surgeon's fine mahogany box, its interior divided into two dozen neat compartments. Inside the lid had been pasted a strip of paper listing the contents of each compartment, and how it should be used on its own or in conjunction with others. The surgeon's ornate slanting writing and some of the Latin words had so impressed his patients. Ointment was *Unguentum*, of course, and there had been at least two for treating burns – *unguentum aureum* and *unguentum nutritum.* Hector racked his brains for what they had contained. As they emerged on the open deck by the heap of plunder, it came to him.

'Find out if the passengers have been burning Arabian frankincense to make that smoky smell,' he said to Jacques. 'If it is, bring me a double handful.'

He took the pot of butter from the Frenchman. 'And a mortar and pestle. The cooks are sure to have some for grinding spices. I'll see you up on the aft deck.'

With Jezreel, he headed to the cabins where the Turkish slave girls had lived. Their rooms had been thoroughly ransacked. Clothes, cushions and bedding had been tossed about, as well as the trinkets that the looters judged to be valueless.

'Pick out anything that might be turned into bandages,' he told Jezreel, 'silk or cotton, it doesn't matter so long as it's clean. I'll see if I can find the girls' personal possessions.'

A few moments of searching produced a small box daintily inlaid with mother of pearl. It contained tweezers for plucking eyebrows, fine brushes for applying kohl and face powder, and scissors. He continued his hunt, sifting carefully through the chaos until he located what he had hoped to find: a small glass vial with a pale yellow liquid. He removed the stopper and sniffed: attar of roses. Mixed with water it had created the perfume he had smelled in the corridor. In the surgeon's list it had been described as *oleum rosarum* and recommended, when mixed into a salve, for the treatment of severe burns.

*

TAVARES SAT in exactly the same position as when Hector had left him, and for a moment Hector thought that the artilleryman had died. He knelt down to check that Tavares was still breathing, before starting to peel aside the scorched fabric of the shirt. Behind him, Jezreel give a hiss of dismay as he saw the extent of the wounds. Tavares groaned in pain, making Hector flinch. Burned skin and flesh were sticking to the cloth.

'Start cutting up the cloth to make dressings and bandages,' he said to Jezreel. 'When Jacques gets here, we'll prepare a salve and spread it on the dressings, and lay them on the wounds.'

When Jacques re-joined them, he brought a small stone mortar and pestle and a cotton bag filled with what looked like broken bits of hard yellow-brown gum. 'This is the stuff the passengers were burning in little clay pots. Reminded me of going to mass when I was a lad,' he said.

'Grind it to a fine powder, mix thoroughly into the butter, then add the attar of roses,' Hector instructed him.

'In what proportions?' the Frenchman asked.

'I have no idea. Just make sure the mixture remains easy to spread.'

With infinite care they dressed Tavares' wounds, laying on cotton pads thickly coated with the salve, and holding them in position with silk bandages wrapped right around his body. Treating the artilleryman's ravaged face was the most difficult part. The skin on the cheeks and forehead had melted or been stripped away, leaving a raw expanse, weeping red. Using the scissors, Jezreel prepared a mask of clean silk with holes for the eyes and nose, and a slit for the mouth. Jacques smeared it with the ointment and Hector tied it gently around Tavares' head, aware of the sharp reek of burned hair. All the while he tried speaking to his patient, to reassure him that he would survive. But there was no answer. It seemed that the gun's explosion had damaged the artilleryman's hearing. Tavares was deaf.

Hector finished tying the mask in and sat back on his heels. Tavares now looked like a ghost, his body and head wrapped in white silk.

He felt a light touch on his elbow. All his attention had been concentrated on Tavares, and he had not noticed that one of the merchants held prisoner nearby had left the group and quietly come across to squat beside him. A man of middle age, the merchant was round-faced and plump, his dark liquid eyes full of sympathy. He was offering a small lacquer container, the lid open. Inside were a dozen dark brown pellets, the size of a thumbnail.

'To take away the pain,' he said,

Hector took one of the pellets from the box, and pressed it between finger and thumb. Slightly sticky, it reminded him of a fresh sheep dropping.

'It can be dissolved in warm water and given as a drink,' the man added.

All of a sudden Hector was aware that someone was watching. He twisted round and saw that Quartermaster Hathaway had appeared on deck.

'You're wasting time. He'll die anyway,' Hathaway commented maliciously, a cold look on his face.

Hector deliberately turned his back on him. 'Will you give my friend your medicine when he is able to swallow?' he said, handing the pellet back to the merchant. He had heard of opium but never seen it before. 'And make sure that he is looked after when we've gone? Bring him down into a cabin where he'll be in shelter. I'll leave you the rest of the ointment.'

Behind him Hathaway was telling Jacques and Jezreel to get themselves down to the lower deck if they wanted a share of the booty.

'Lynch!' the quartermaster called out. 'No need for you to come. You can carry on chatting with your new cronies. You played no part in the fight so you'll get no portion.'

The merchant leaned in very close. 'Perhaps it is your turn to be careful,' he whispered and his eyes flicked to where Hathaway was standing.

ELEVEN

BOTH CREWS, FROM *Fancy* and from *Pearl*, had assembled in the open space of *Ganj-i-Sawa'i*'s lower deck. A crowd of almost a hundred men jostled in front of the two quartermasters, trying to get a closer look at the display of plunder. Many still had smears of gunpowder on their faces. Several wore bandages, and one man was hobbling on a crutch. Their clothes were dirty and sweat-stained, and there was a babble of excited talk, oaths and coarse laughter. Leaving Jacques and Jezreel to join them, Hector seated himself on a step halfway down the companionway where he could see and hear what was going on. The deep mistrust that lurked beneath the greed of the freebooters was immediately obvious. Men who had fought side by side a few hours earlier now eyed one another with suspicion, determined to receive their due and not be cheated.

Hathaway brought some sort of order by banging the table in front of him with the flat of a cutlass blade and bellowing for silence.

'Spread out! So all of you can see what is going on! *Fancy*'s company to my right; *Pearl*'s company over there, behind your Quartermaster Gibson.'

He gestured with the cutlass and, reluctantly, the throng of onlookers fell back to form a half circle. Some of the men climbed up on the piles of pilgrim baggage to get a clear view. Others came and sat on the steps in front of Hector. Looking on, he noted that *Fancy*'s men greatly outnumbered the crew from *Pearl*. Also, *Fancy*'s contingent showed many more signs of having been through a hard-fought battle.

Hathaway rapped on the table again. 'Division will follow custom,' he bawled. 'Captains will receive two and a half portions; carpenters, gunners, coxswains and other skilled men one and a half portions. All others one portion.'

He paused and cleared his throat. 'Only those who fought, of course.' His gaze swept over the crowd, and Hector detected that just for a second his glance lingered on him.

Hathaway held up some sheets of paper. 'This is *Fancy*'s muster list. Quartermaster Gibson has the same for *Pearl*. When his name is called out, each man comes forward to receive his fair share.'

'What's fair about that?' came a harsh shout. It was one of *Fancy*'s men, a mean-looking fellow, tall and bony, with one arm in a grimy sling made from a strip of sailcloth.

'*Fancy* did all the hard work,' the man shouted, his voice sharp and clear. 'We engaged for eight hours, cannon and musket, long before *Pearl* joined in, which was only after we had boarded.'

There was a growl of agreement from his companions. Hector caught the words 'shitten cowards' and 'tell them to fuck off'.

From across the circle the men from *Pearl* glared back and one of them yelled, 'What about the plunder you lifted from that ship you took two days back? Where's our portion of that? All agreed to share equally in this venture.'

A slight movement, high up and from the forecastle deck opposite, made Hector glance in that direction. A number of *Ganj-i-Sawa'i*'s sailors, the men who worked the great ship, had crept out of their hiding places and taken up positions at the rail overlooking the lower deck. They were gazing down on the squabble; their faces spoke of curiosity and distaste for the spectacle below them, and fear.

The quarrel on the lower deck was getting uglier with catcalls from both sides, accompanied by insults and lewd gestures. One of *Fancy*'s company shouted out, 'Three to one would be a fairer deal,' and his companions quickly took up the refrain, and started stamping and shouting, 'One to them, three for us!' Their shipmates who still had their muskets and boarding pikes beat out the rhythm, thumping the butts of the weapons on the deck boards.

It was several minutes before they realized that someone seated directly on the steps in front of Hector had risen to his feet, and was standing, waiting to be noticed. It was *Fancy*'s captain – Henry Avery.

The hubbub died away and Avery addressed the meeting in his quiet, persuasive voice. 'I know that a captain has no authority in this assembly. Division of the plunder is a matter for the ship's company under the direction of the quartermaster. But may I make a suggestion?'

He gestured towards the piles of loot and the strong boxes in front of the two quartermasters. 'Open one of the strong boxes now and share out whatever is in it. Every man, whether he is from *Fancy* or *Pearl*, receives his portion as a payment in advance. Afterwards each ship's company chooses three members for a joint committee to establish the total value of the remaining plunder, and decide on its fair distribution.'

Avery was being clever once again, Hector thought. Cash in hand would take the edge off the hostility between the two crews and prevent their quarrel from exploding into violence.

'Which strong box?' demanded someone from among *Pearl*'s company, his suspicion evident.

Avery turned towards where William Mayes was standing in the front rank of his men. 'Why not leave the choice to *Pearl*'s captain?'

Mayes's eyes darted from Avery, to the strong boxes, and across to the hostile glare of the men from *Fancy*.

It was another shrewd suggestion, Hector decided: if Mayes chose the strong box, there was no reason for anyone to suspect that Long Ben was pulling some sort of trick.

After a moment's thought Mayes nodded and pointed to the largest and stoutest of the strong boxes. Hector had a feeling that it was the same that he had seen carried from the adjacent cabin when he was a prisoner in his cubbyhole. It was too heavy for one man to lift on his own, and after they had cleared a space on the table, Gibson helped Hathaway heave it up. The weight made the thick planks sag.

'You'll need a hammer and chisel to get into that,' someone shouted.

Hathaway flourished a selection of keys strung on a loop of cord. 'These were placed in my safe keeping. One of them should do the job.'

There was a knowing chuckle from several of his cronies.

Hathaway found the right key on the second attempt, unlocked the strong box and swung back the lid. With Gibson's help he tipped the box on its side so its contents spilled across the table. Dozens of sausage-shaped, greyish cloth bags tumbled out. There was a low groan of disappointment from those in the crowd. They had expected to see a torrent of precious stones or pearls. Hathaway picked up one of the bags. Six inches long and tightly packed, it was marked with symbols in indigo-blue ink. He turned it over in his hand, searching for a drawstring, but it had been stitched closed. With the edge of his cutlass he slit one end, then held it up in the air to shake out the contents. A cascade of gold coins, each the width of a man's thumbnail, clattered down on the table.

There was a moment of awed silence. One or two men gave whistles of astonishment. Everyone glanced at the pile of unopened bags trying to gauge how many more there were.

Hathaway picked up a second bag and repeated the process. Another rivulet of gold coins. A third bag disgorged more coins, this time silver.

'Give me a bite!' someone shouted.

Hathaway picked up a silver coin and flipped it through the air. 'Catch!'

The man who caught the coin placed it between his teeth, and bit down to test the quality of the metal. 'Better than anything from the galley,' he shouted to a general guffaw of laughter as he tossed the coin back.

Gibson and Hathaway were busy slicing open the rest of the pouches. When they had finished, there were two heaps of money on the table before them: one of silver, the other of gold and slightly larger.

A ripple of anticipation passed through the crowd as Hathaway addressed his audience. 'There's enough here for each man to start with twenty coins, fourteen of gold and six of silver. Anything that's left over we'll keep back for the committee to decide on.' He looked across at Gibson. 'Agreed?'

Pearl's quartermaster nodded.

'Come forward when I read out your name. Gibson will make the payment. Then put your mark on this paper where I show you.'

It was a slow process. Each freebooter collected the twenty coins that Gibson had stacked for him, signed his mark, and then returned to stand among his company. Hector felt tiredness creeping over him as he watched. Apart from a few sips of water, he had not had anything to eat or drink all day, and he was exhausted. The distribution of the plunder had nearly reached its conclusion, with Jacques and Jezreel among the handful of men still unpaid, when he remembered that neither of their names was on *Fancy*'s muster list. He wondered if Hathaway would ignore them.

The next name to be called out was John Dann's. *Fancy*'s coxswain was due a share and a half and Gibson had already laid out his coins. Dann came forward, swept them up, turned as if to sign the muster sheet, then spun round and grabbed *Pearl*'s quartermaster by the wrist. Gibson tried to pull away but Dann had him in a tight grip. Their tussle attracted the attention of the free-booters who had already received their money. One of *Pearl*'s men moved to intervene, but Jezreel stepped forward and blocked his path.

'Open your hand,' Dann ordered, loud enough to be heard by his shipmates from *Fancy*.

The quartermaster opened his fingers, and a gold coin dropped onto the table.

Without a word, Dann laid one of his own coins on top of it, then slid both in front of Hathaway. 'Well?' he demanded.

Hathaway looked down, and his eyes narrowed. He rounded on Gibson. 'You cheating turd!' he snarled.

Dann turned to face the crowd. 'I've been watching our friend here,' he told them. 'He palms the good coins and makes sure that if a coin is clipped or counterfeit, then it goes to men from *Fancy*.'

A roar of anger spread through *Fancy*'s company as its members realized the swindle. They surged forward, intent on attacking Gibson and the men from *Pearl*. Knives appeared, and the first punches were thrown.

'Hold hard!' bellowed Hathaway over the fighting. 'Let them keep what coin they have because that's all they'll get. Clear them off the ship.'

Jezreel and Jacques dodged their way through the mob to re-join Hector as the enraged freebooters from *Fancy* used their weight of numbers to hustle the men from *Pearl* back. In the brawl Gibson took a fist in the face which knocked him down. He was given a heavy kicking before being manhandled roughly towards the ship's side and back onto *Pearl*.

'Gibson needs to sharpen up his hocus pocus,' said Jacques smugly, taking a seat on the step beside Hector.

'And you can show him how, I suppose,' Jezreel murmured.

Jacques gave a sly grin. 'That's right.' He shook his closed fist, and there was a soft clink of coins.

Below them the last of *Pearl*'s men were being bundled over the side and down a rope ladder back to their vessel. One man lingered, clinging on to the rail and protesting that he had not known about Gibson's sharp practice. He let go with a howl of pain as the butt of a musket mashed down on his fingers. Finally only Captain Mayes remained, guarded by a member of Hathaway's gang, armed with a blunderbuss.

Henry Avery had stood aside from the turmoil. Now he sauntered across to have a quiet word with Hathaway. Then the quartermaster raised his voice to address his crew.

'Captain wants us to clear the area in case other ships show up and want a share. We'll load all the plunder aboard *Fancy* and finish the division later. Does anyone object?'

When there was no answer, he looked straight at Hector and called out, 'You there, Lynch! I've unfinished business with you.'

Hector stood up and waited for him to go on. Hathaway looked around at the men from *Fancy* until he had their full attention.

'That man has no place in our company,' he announced harshly, pointing a finger.

'What's he done?' Avery asked, frowning.

'He's in thick with an officer from this ship, one of their wounded. I don't know what information he was passing on because it was in a foreign language. But I saw him speaking to the officer on the quiet. If that officer lives, he'll hold witness against us.'

Avery looked at Hector. 'Is this true?'

'I was telling him not to give up, that he would survive his injuries,' Hector told him.

Hathaway cut in angrily. 'Lynch was never voted on to our muster. For all we know he fought against us yesterday.' He appealed to the men within hearing. 'This is our chance to be rid of him. What do you say?'

There was a general murmur of agreement. The only voice Hector heard in opposition was Dann's with his London accent.

Hathaway turned his attention to Mayes. 'You can have him as a present. He's handy with charts.'

Pearl's captain scowled. 'Not sure I want a turncoat. Who was he being friendly with?'

Hector decided it was time he spoke for himself. 'Jeronimo Tavares, a Portuguese artillery officer in the Mogul's service. He treated me decently when this ship rescued me from the sea after a fight with Captain Tew and *Amity*.'

Mayes gave a grim smile. 'I heard that *Amity* came off worst. Tew should have known better than to race off, leaving the rest of us in the lurch.' Addressing Avery, he asked, 'Do you vouch for him as a navigator?'

'He's a good one, and can read a Moorish chart,' Avery answered.

Mayes scratched at his heavy beard, thinking over his reply. Hector detected a gleam of interest in the deep-set eyes. 'Then I'll take him.'

'I will be coming along as well. So too will my big friend here,' said Jacques, jerking his thumb at Jezreel. 'The three of us stick together.'

Mayes looked the two men up and down, then shrugged. 'As you wish. Collect your belongings and be quick about it. But don't expect to be made welcome by my quartermaster or the rest of the ship's company.'

Hector crossed the deck with his friends to pick up their bedding rolls and possessions from *Fancy*. As he passed within an arm's length of Avery, it seemed to him that the captain gave him a slight nod. Hector had no idea what private message Long Ben wished to convey and he dismissed it from his mind. His immediate concern was with the captain of *Pearl*. He sensed that Mayes' reason for taking him aboard *Pearl* had little to do with his skill with maps. It was something that Mayes had just heard or seen and everyone else missed. Whatever it was, he was sure that as soon as the captain of *Pearl* had no further use for him, Mayes would get rid of him and his friends without a qualm.

TWELVE

THE DIVISION OF the plunder had taken up the entire afternoon, and now the sun was low on the horizon. Clutching their belongings, Hector and his two friends climbed down the rope ladder and stepped aboard *Pearl*. Mayes ignored them. He was stalking up and down the deck, bawling orders to his men to cast off the grappling lines. He showed no sign that he had just lost his share of a great fortune though his crew were sullen and bitter. A slovenly lot, they grumbled and cast black looks at the three new arrivals, as well as shouting obscenities back at the men from *Fancy* who lined *Ganj-i-Sawa'i*'s side, jeering. One of Mayes' men, a shambling loutish fellow, was slow in obeying his captain's command. Mayes marched over, grabbed the man by the front of his shirt and flung him violently against the gunwale.

Hector took in his new surroundings. It was evident that *Pearl* would have been no match for *Fancy* if it had come to a fight. Much smaller than Avery's formidable ship of war, she had all the appearance of a workaday merchant vessel now used for piracy. He counted only sixteen small cannon and found it difficult to imagine how her crew ever expected to overwhelm any prey that put up a decent resistance.

Jacques interrupted his thoughts. 'You haven't yet told Jezreel and me what happened after you went off with Tew to pilot

Amity through the reefs, nor about that Portuguese officer we treated for his burns.'

Hector related all that had happened to him from the moment he had been knocked overboard from *Amity* until his decision to follow up on Tavares's suggestion and take service with the Great Mogul.

'Of course, everything changed when Avery attacked *Ganj-i-Sawa'i*,' he said. 'And now, because of me, all three of us are back where we were more than a year ago in St Mary's when we decided to join up under Avery. Except we are on a vessel with less than half *Fancy*'s armament and a captain who is a bully . . . and you two have walked away from your share of plunder.'

'Hathaway would never have allowed Jezreel and me to have our proper shares,' Jacques assured him. 'Getting rid of the two of us meant more for everyone else. Most of *Fancy*'s crew will be glad to have seen the back of us.'

Jezreel tilted his head back to look up at the side of *Ganj-i-Sawa'i* still towering over them. 'I've a feeling that Long Ben may have overstepped the mark by pirating that ship. If she's as rich a prize as she seems, the authorities will come after him in earnest, and it won't be difficult to trace his crew. With so much money to spend, they'll soon draw attention to themselves.' He turned to glance towards Mayes, who had taken up his stance beside the helm and was glowering down the length of the ship at the grudging efforts of his men. 'Maybe entering the service of the Great Mogul would be a good option for all three of us . . . if somehow we can get clear of this scruffy lot.'

'They'll tip us overboard given half a chance, especially that crook Gibson,' Jacques put in.

Jezreel grinned and clapped Hector on the shoulder. 'Don't look so down in the mouth, Hector. By the look of you, a rest would do you good. Things will sort themselves in the morning. We'll stay just where we are for the moment and take it in turns to keep watch.'

With barely enough wind for *Pearl* to get underway, the gap between the ships was widening slowly. Hector spread his bedding roll on the deck boards and lay down, but fierce pangs of hunger kept him from falling asleep. He could not banish from his mind the sight of Tavares' terrible burns and he hoped that the drug offered by the kindly merchant was dulling the pain. He was reasonably confident that the salve he had concocted would prevent infection. If 'Exceeding Treasure' continued on to her planned destination as soon as Avery let her go, there was a chance that the artilleryman would survive to reach his family home in Surat. Hector found himself wondering whether the Great Mogul paid pensions to officers in his service if they were badly hurt. When he eventually nodded off, he was still waiting for the stars to come out and tell him on which course Mayes was taking *Pearl*. He needed a clue as to what the hardened captain planned to do next.

*

HE AWOKE WITH A START. Dawn was just breaking, and Jezreel and Jacques had let him sleep through the night. His two friends were leaning on the ship's rail close by, and gazing out over a calm sea.

'Going to be another fine day,' observed Jezreel, glancing back over his shoulder.

'You should have woken me when it was my turn to go on watch,' Hector muttered as he got to his feet. He tried not to sound crotchety, but there was no need for his friends to mollycoddle him.

'No point. Everything was quiet and we've been heading on the same course all night: north-east,' Jezreel assured him.

Hector looked around the horizon. There was not another vessel in sight, and *Pearl* was under plain sail, easing forward over a gentle swell. Only the helmsman and a couple of deck hands were awake to mind the ship. The rest of her company lay scattered around the deck, still fast asleep.

'Time we got ourselves something to eat,' Jezreel suggested.

The three of them made their way to *Pearl*'s galley where both the ship's cooks were still snoring beside the hearth. They quietly helped themselves to stale bread, a dipper of water and some dried fish.

They returned to their place, carrying their food and ignoring hostile glances from those of *Pearl*'s crew who were just beginning to wake up.

'Captain's up and about,' muttered Jacques. Mayes had emerged from the cabin under the low stern deck and was heading in their direction. In the dawn light his heavy tread and hulking manner only added to his forbidding appearance.

'Lynch, come with me,' he rasped. He turned and began making his way towards the helm, kicking at sleeping figures and telling them to get up.

Hector followed him to the helm where Mayes began to clang the ship's bell as loudly as he could, a jarring, insistent rhythm. *Pearl*'s surly company responded sluggishly. Grumbling, they roused themselves and assembled, bleary eyed, scratching themselves, hawking and spitting. Hector decided he had seldom seen a less attractive group. They were very near to mutiny, and he understood what lay behind Mayes' bullying manner: without the threat of physical violence, he risked losing control of his crew.

Mayes' sour gaze swept over his men. 'Long Ben is not as clever as he likes to think,' he announced. His harsh, gruff voice carried well.

'How's that?' came back an unhappy shout. 'He and his men have run off with our rightful prize.'

'*Pearl*'s not strong enough to take on *Fancy* and get it back,' called a man with a face heavily pitted with the smallpox scars. 'We'd be slaughtered.'

'I'm not talking about getting even with those bastards on *Fancy*, however much I'd like to,' Mayes retorted. 'Instead we're going after the Moors' ship a second time.'

'But we stripped their ship bare. Nothing left.' Quartermaster Gibson standing in the front rank raised the objection.

Mayes treated the quartermaster to a withering glare, then looked out over the crowd. 'Didn't anyone notice something very unusual about that vessel?'

'Only that the musketeers had tits!' came a voice. There was a smatter of feeble laughter.

Mayes did not join in. He scowled at his men. 'What about the great big yellow ensign flying at the stern? I don't suppose you remember what it looked like?'

There was silence. His audience had no idea why the flag was of such interest to their captain.

Mayes beckoned to the helmsman. 'I need one of those coins that Gibson gave you.'

The man pulled out his shirt tail and unknotted the cloth where he had stowed his meagre plunder. He gave a coin to Mayes who handed it on to Hector.

'Tell the company what is written on it,' he ordered.

Hector inspected the coin. It was silver money, newly minted, the inscriptions barely worn, easy to read. 'It is stamped with the place and year where it was minted.'

'And on the other side?' Mayes prompted. 'Speak up so all can hear.'

Hector turned the coin over and read out in a loud voice, 'The blessed coin of Muhammad Aurangzeb Bahadur Alamgir Badshah Ghazi.' He looked up at Mayes. 'That must be how the Great Mogul styles himself.'

Mayes plucked the coin from his fingers and held it up to show the crowd. 'And some of the marks on the coin – that foreign writing – are found again on this.' With his other hand he tugged from his pocket a length of yellow silk and held it up. It was one of the banners that had fluttered in the rigging of *Ganj-i-Sawa'i*. 'What do you think it signifies?'

His gaze swept the crowd. He was met with blank looks. Some men frowned as they tried to puzzle out their captain's meaning. Others looked away, bored.

Mayes answered his own question. 'No ordinary merchant

ship carries flags and banners written with the titles of the Great Mogul himself.' He jerked his head towards Hector. 'And I've heard this man say there was a royal officer aboard.'

He lowered his arms, then spoke again, his voice hard and assertive. 'That was a royal ship, and those musketeers were there as guards. You don't hire musketeers in smart yellow uniforms to stand over merchandise. Their job is to escort people of import-ance. So who were they guarding? My guess is that they were guarding members of the Great Mogul's own family.'

He paused a moment, waiting for the slowest of his listeners to catch up with what he was saying. Then he announced flatly, 'I intend to turn *Pearl* around and go back to sniff over that floating fairground. Somewhere aboard that ship there's a person or per-sons who will fetch a royal ransom, and I intend that we share it!'

His words were followed by several moments of silence as his audience thought about his proposal.

'How do we find the right person?' demanded someone from the back of the crowd.

Mayes allowed himself a dangerous grin. He draped a burly arm across Hector's shoulders and drew him close. Hector could smell the rank sweat on the captain's shirt. 'This man has a friend among the Moors. I'm sure that together they can identify for us the person we are seeking.'

Hector's stomach dropped. He had underestimated Mayes. Behind the scowling brutish exterior was a cunning brain, and a shrewd observer. Mayes was sharp enough to have noted the identical pattern of script on the coins and the flags, and he was ruthless. He was prepared to try extorting a ransom from the Great Mogul himself. Hector shivered at the risks involved. Rob-bery at sea was one thing, but to be involved in planned kidnap and ransom was quite another.

A murmur of excitement spread through Mayes's audience as the ship's company savoured the possible change in their for-tunes. As each man decided he was pleased with their captain's plan, his approval turned in a grin of hungry anticipation. All disappointment forgotten, Pearl's crew dispersed to tend the sheets and braces and reverse the ship on to her new course, heading back towards her prey.

Hector was left where he stood, filled with a sense of foreboding. He was trapped, so too were his friends. Mayes would show no mercy if he refused to take part in the captain's dangerously reckless scheme, and *Pearl*'s crew would gladly follow his orders if he decided to dispense with the three of them. And that still left Tavares: Hector dreaded to think what methods the captain would use on the badly wounded artilleryman to force him to identify the royal passenger aboard *Ganj-i-Sawa'i*.

THREE DAYS LATER, at daybreak, *Pearl*'s lookout called down from the masthead that he had the Mogul's vessel in sight, and by noon *Pearl* was within cannon range. Mayes fired a gun, aiming wide, and the great ship meekly dropped her sail and hove to. The once-proud 'Exceeding Treasure' was a sad, bedraggled spectacle. Battered and half-crippled, she still lacked a mizzen sail, and her mainsail was tattered and full of shot holes. All the jaunty flags and pennants were gone. The only signs of life were a handful of the native sailors securing the lowered mainsail, and a small group on the topmost deck.

'Hurry up, Lynch! Time to make yourself useful,' Mayes called to Hector. *Pearl* was putting a boat into the water and her captain was ready to be rowed across. With him were half a dozen freebooters armed with pistols and cutlasses.

As the oarsmen ferried the boarding party towards *Ganj-i-Sawa'i*'s cliff-like side, Hector recalled being hauled up it like a gasping fish, then the curious stares of his rescuers as they looked down at him on all fours on the deck. This time as he stepped out on the identical spot, he could almost smell the fear. The same brown-skinned sailors were waiting, but their thin features were drawn and strained, their eyes ringed in shadow. The crowd of pilgrim passengers that once thronged that part of the ship had disappeared, leaving behind their untidy piles of baggage. He caught glimpses of frightened faces peering out from the dark recesses of half-closed hatches. There was an ominous quiet as if every living soul was holding his breath, waiting for the worst.

Mayes led the way as if he owned the ship. He mounted the companionways, two steps at a time, to where *nakhoda* Ibrahim stood, his face a mask of resignation.

'What do your people want now?' the old man asked, treating Hector to a cold look full of disdain.

Over the *nakhoda*'s shoulder, Hector could see the Surati merchants standing in a terrified cluster. Manuj Dosi was among them, his hand heavily bandaged. He was glaring at Hector with unconcealed loathing.

'Lynch, tell him that we've come to collect his royal passengers,' Mayes prompted.

Hector translated the request and Ibrahim's face set like stone. 'I don't know what you are talking about,' he answered.

'No need to translate that reply,' Mayes growled. 'We'll find what we want for ourselves.' He turned to his men and told them to search the ship. 'Look for anyone who seems out of place, a pearl among swine.' He gave a coarse laugh.

'May I go to check on my friend Tavares?' Hector asked.

'Of course.' Mayes was expansive. 'We'll call on your help when we need it.'

Hector went down to the deck where he had been locked in the cupboard. As he had requested, someone had moved Tavares into one of the cabins that the Turkish girls had occupied. Tavares was lying on a mattress in one corner, propped up with cushions at his back, legs outstretched. His head was still swathed in white silk bandages, but his eyes were visible. They watched Hector approach and squat down beside him.

'I hadn't expected to see you again, at least not until the Mogul's court,' Tavares murmured. His voice was little more than a breathy whisper through the slit left for his mouth.

'I'm with a boarding party from one of the freebooter vessels.

They're searching for members of the Great Mogul's family,' Hector told him, keeping his voice low. 'The intention is to hold them to ransom. These men are cruel and ruthless, so please cooperate.'

'I cannot.' The eyes blinked.

Hector recalled the artilleryman's fierce loyalty to his hire. 'I'll do what I can to keep them away from you,' he said, 'but if they do come to question you, please re-consider.'

The grotesque white sphere of a head made a small movement from side to side. Then, with an effort that must have caused him great pain, Tavares reached out and touched Hector on the knee. 'We'll find a way to protect the old woman. For my sake, and perhaps for your own.' Then his hand dropped away.

Hector had only just got back on his feet when he heard voices in the corridor outside. A moment later Mayes walked in followed by the men he had sent to search the ship.

'Dead easy,' one of the sailors gloated. He stood aside to allow his companions to bring forward three women. 'Found this lot among the pilgrims in the main hold. Everyone else was packed like herrings in a barrel. But these had their own space. Seems it's disrespectful for the common herd to come too close. They had draped themselves with sacking to hide their clothes.'

He pushed forward the two taller women. Both were heavily veiled. One wore a full-length silk robe dyed a deep yellow and embroidered with patterns of tiny flowers in silver thread. The other was dressed more simply in a gown of plain ivory-coloured cotton. They were the same women he had seen leaving the royal cabin during the sea battle with Avery's *Fancy*, attendants for the Great Mogul's sister.

'Couldn't shake off this old hag, though. She's a right pain in the arse,' the sailor added. The third woman in the group was Aurangzeb's sister. She was dressed in the simple clothes of a pilgrim, a dark shawl partially covering her features. Her grey hair was scraped back, emphasizing the sharp nose and tight mouth, and her expression managed to be both imperious and indignant.

When Hector caught her eye, she gave him a brittle glance that reminded him of a hawk about to launch itself on its quarry.

'Just wanted to check that we've got the right ones,' said Mayes from the doorway. He addressed Tavares lying on the floor. 'Are these the women you were guarding?' There was an edge of menace in his question.

When there was no reply he walked across and prodded Tavares firmly in his bandaged ribs with the toe of his boot. The pain must have been agonizing.

The wounded artilleryman stayed silent.

'We'll find out from someone else, if you're stubborn,' Mayes said coldly. 'I repeat: are these the women you were escorting?'

This time there was a slight nod from the bandaged head.

'Thank you. That's all I wanted to know.' Mayes turned on his heel, and ordered his men to take away the two women.

Aurangzeb's sister gave an angry shriek and stepped in their path, preventing them from leaving. Hector listened to her stream of instructions mingled with abuse. Quivering with rage, she was demanding that her servants be set free at once, or she would see to it that her brother's executioners put the foreign bandits to death by the most painful means known. The *feringhee* scum, as she called Mayes and his men, should know who they were dealing with.

'What's the matter with her?' demanded Mayes, glancing at Hector.

Hector hesitated, unsure how to answer. The simple deception practised by the three women was unlikely to survive for long. If he failed to reveal their true identities now, and Mayes found out later that he had been duped, the consequences would be disastrous for himself and his two friends. He looked across the cabin at Tavares on his mattress, and felt sick. If Mayes learned that Tavares had just lied to him, the sadistic captain would also take it out on the injured man.

Yet if he told Mayes that the 'old hag' was the right person to be taken hostage, there was no turning back. He would have committed himself to the rash attempt at extracting a ransom from the Aurangzeb, and his chance, however slim, of a new life in the service of the Great Mogul would have vanished.

Just at that moment the taller of the two women, the one dressed in her silk finery, caught his attention. She raised a hand to adjust the scarf she held across her face. For just a second her eyes were revealed and she was looking directly at Hector. There was a message of pleading.

He understood.

'The old woman is a former nurse in the imperial household, now retired,' he invented. 'She helped raise the princess you are taking away. She does not wish to be separated from her former charge and demands to accompany her.'

'I'd sooner ship a scorpion,' Mayes scoffed. He nodded to one of his men to bundle the protesting woman aside.

As the little group left the cabin, taking the two taller women with them, Hector had time for one final look over his shoulder. Tavares still lay propped up on his pillows, his ghostly white head turned toward him. It was impossible to read any expression in the narrow gap in the bandages that had been left for his eyes. Aurangzeb's sister was hunched in a corner where she had been thrust so unceremoniously. There was an odd look on her wizened face, a blend of contempt and calculation.

✳

'Lynch, tell the women that I'm giving up my cabin for them and the door will be kept locked for their own protection,' Mayes announced as soon as they were back aboard *Pearl*. He allowed himself a malicious chuckle. 'Can't have them trying to jump into the sea like some of those pretty musketeers.'

As Hector relayed the message to the two veiled captives, he looked across at the huge ship they had just left. There was very little sign of activity aboard *Ganj-i-Sawa'i*. Her dispirited crew had not even begun to hoist the great mainsail to proceed on their way, bringing news of their catastrophic voyage to the outside world. He wondered what Mayes would do next now that he had in his grasp the woman he believed to be a member of the imperial family. No doubt *Pearl*'s captain had already devised a plan to set about extorting a ransom from the Great Mogul. But whatever his scheme was, he would have to put it into effect very quickly if he was to retain the initiative. Mayes would know that seizing the hostage had been the easy part. Prising a satisfactory ransom from the Mogul treasury was going to be far more difficult and dangerous.

*

MAYES LOST NO TIME in giving orders for a canvas shelter to be rigged under the break of the poop deck to serve as his temporary accommodation. 'Come over here, Lynch, your job's not yet over,' he called out when his personal belongings had been moved into its shade. As Hector made his way across, he saw that Mayes had a sea chart spread on the lid of his sea chest. Gibson the quartermaster had also been summoned.

'By my calculation this is approximately where we are now,' said Mayes, laying a thick finger on the map as the two men joined him. The chart was a general sketch of the seas between Africa and India. In some places the surrounding coastline was drawn clearly in ink, elsewhere it was left vague and uncertain. 'This is where the Moors will be heading.' The finger slid eastward across the map to one of the few places marked with confidence – Surat.

'It will take them at least a week to reach her home port,' Mayes went on. 'We can get there a couple of days ahead of her, make contact with the English merchants, and ask them to inform the authorities that we hold a member of the imperial family, and expect a reward for her safe return.'

He gave a wolfish grin. 'But I don't trust those money-grabbing bastards. They depend on the goodwill of the Great Mogul for permission to carry on their business so they'll try to double-cross us.'

He flicked aside a small insect that was crawling slowly across the map.

'So *Pearl* heads here instead.' The captain's finger moved to where the coastline was marked with very few details, and tapped on the name of the only port shown. Hector read the name written beside it in faded lettering: Diu.

Mayes looked up at Hector from under heavy black eyebrows. His gaze was far from friendly. 'And this is where you make yourself useful once again.'

Hector frowned down at the map. He racked his brains trying to recall what he had heard of Diu. It was not much. At one time the place had been a major port for foreign ships trading with India. Now it was bypassed and little used. He tried to remember why it had gone into decline, and – all of a sudden – it dawned on him why Diu was part of Mayes' plan.

'So I'm to be your negotiator,' he said.

'Well done!' said Mayes, his tone laced with sarcasm. 'I'll be setting you ashore in Diu with Quartermaster Gibson and a couple of trusted men. Your job will be to get word to the Great Mogul about what we expect by way of payment for safe delivery of our important passenger.'

Gibson gave a grunt of approval. 'And *Pearl* waits offshore until we get a reply?'

Mayes nodded. 'To show that we're not bluffing, you'll take Her Highness's attendant ashore with you as proof of whom we hold aboard.'

Mayes's attention returned to Hector and his face hardened. 'Don't imagine that this is a chance for you to disappear, Lynch. I'll be allowing you to land, but your two friends stay on *Pearl*.'

*

'WHY YOU?' demanded Jezreel when Hector re-joined his two friends.

'Because the Portuguese control Diu. They've a fort and governor there, and Mayes has seen me get on well with their compatriots, men like Tavares. My guess is that he thinks the Portuguese will be more likely to cooperate in his scheme than the English in Surat. He may even offer them a cut of the ransom.' He gave a rueful smile. 'What our captain doesn't know is that neither of his hostages is in fact a member of the emperor's immediate family.'

Jacques rolled his eyes. 'Hector, you'd better tell Jezreel and me exactly what's going on.'

Hector explained the deception that had taken place on 'Exceeding Treasure'. 'So when *Pearl* gets to Diu – if not before – Mayes is going to learn that he's been made a fool of, and then things are going to turn very ugly indeed. It's possible that I'll be ashore at the time, but you and Jezreel will still be on *Pearl* and will suffer.'

There was a moment of uncomfortable silence, and then Jezreel spoke up. 'As I see it, there's nothing we can do to change the situation until we reach Diu. So let's hope that those two women manage to keep up their disguise until then.' He looked around at the slovenly appearance of the ship. Most of her company were gathered in small groups to talk among themselves or play cards and dice. Some were stretched out on the planks, dozing in the sun. Three men were at the stern rail, trailing fishing lines in the water. 'This lot aren't up to much. It shouldn't be too difficult to get away from them if the chance presents itself. Then Captain Mayes can go hang.'

THIRTEEN

DIU'S FORT WAS NOT what Hector had expected. He had no idea that it would be so huge and imposing – much more of a castle than a fort. Mayes seemed equally impressed by the distant grey hump that first appeared on the low, featureless coastline, then gradually resolved itself into a massive military structure. He ordered sail to be reduced. Very cautiously *Pearl* crept closer until he gave the order to anchor while his ship was still out of range of even the largest cannon. The distance from land caused a good deal of discontent and grumbling among the sailors whom he ordered to row the landing party ashore in the ship's boat. Mayes had to threaten and curse until they obeyed his instructions. Eventually Hector climbed down the rope ladder with the two sailors who had volunteered for the mission, quartermaster Gibson and the veiled figure of the woman whom Mayes still believed to be the attendant to the emperor's sister. Neither she nor her companion had spoken a word to their captors from the day they had set foot on *Pearl*.

It took more than an hour for the sullen oarsmen to row to land, and Hector had ample time to study Diu's defences. Facing the sea was an immense curtain wall made of thousands upon thousands of honey-coloured bricks. It had a central bastion and multiple embrasures for cannon. A large donjon tower commanded the harbour mouth with twin platforms for gun batteries, and the Portuguese had fortified a small island in the middle of the entrance, sealing it completely against hostile ships. With its watch turrets and signal masts, Diu castle could anticipate an attack and then withstand a major siege. Yet he sensed something was missing. Only in the last hundred yards did he realize what it was: the vast fortification should have been swarming with soldiers. But as he gazed up at the towering walls, he saw only a few heads peering out between the merlons and a solitary figure high on the lookout platform where the Portuguese flag on its pole flapped languidly in the sultry afternoon breeze.

Gibson, as quartermaster, was at the rudder. He steered for the landing slip close to the foot of the donjon. As the keel touched the worn stones, a postern gate swung open and half a dozen soldiers emerged in loose formation. They were led by an under-officer wearing what Hector took to be the uniform of Portugal's colonial troops — knee-length green coat with the cuffs and lapels turned back to show a buff lining, white gaiters and black shoes, and a broad-brimmed black hat with a black feather. By contrast his men were dressed in a motley selection of jackets and smocks of different colours under cross-belts festooned with old-fashioned wooden cartridge cases that made a gentle rattling sound as they shuffled into a line to face the visitors. Their muskets, Hector noted, were older models than those that he had seen in Adam Baldridge's warehouse back in St Mary's.

'Papers and state your business!' barked the under-officer in Portuguese, then repeated the instruction in English and Dutch at Gibson. He had climbed out of the boat and walked up the slipway with Hector close behind him. The under-officer was short and bandy-legged, with hard, untrusting eyes and his left cheek was puckered with a star-shaped scar that looked like the wound left by a pistol ball. Hector guessed he was a veteran who had been sent to the colonies on an easy final posting before his retirement.

'I'm quartermaster of the ship *Pearl*, with a message from Captain Thomas Mayes for the governor,' said Gibson.

'The governor is not here,' answered the under-officer. Behind him his men were openly gawping at the newcomers, particularly at the veiled figure of the woman still huddled in the stern of the boat. Hector assumed they were locally recruited troops. Their complexions were dark and, though none of them wore beards, every one of them sported a glossy black moustache that seemed to be a local fashion. One or two, he noted, were barefoot.

'Perhaps we could speak with the governor's deputy,' Hector suggested tactfully, speaking in Galician.

The under-officer flashed him a quick, surprised look of relief. Then his air of professional suspicion returned.

'What was your last port of call?' he demanded in Portuguese.

For an alarmed moment Hector thought that news of the attack on the pilgrim fleet had already reached Diu. Then he realized that it was a routine question, to check whether there was a risk of importing foreign disease and, if so, the need for quarantine.

'We called at the Cape to take on water and provisions from the Dutch at De Kaapsche Vlek,' he lied.

The under-officer seemed satisfied. 'Very well, you may come with me. But your boat and its crew must return to the ship.'

'With your permission, may two of our sailors and the woman also come ashore?'

After a moment's hesitation, the under-officer nodded and Hector returned down the slipway. He held out his hand to the woman to help her climb out of the boat, but she shrank back, refusing to touch him, and insisted on climbing over the gunwale unaided. Wrapping her shawl and gown tight around her, she followed the rest of the landing party as it was escorted through the postern gate.

Inside, they turned to their left and entered the ground floor of the donjon through an arched doorway. A short corridor led into a guard room with a high vaulted ceiling, a floor of broad grey flagstones and high narrow windows in the walls that were three foot thick. Here the under-officer ordered them to wait with their escort while he stamped up a flight of wooden stairs to an upper floor. Looking around him, Hector calculated that the guardroom had been designed to accommodate at least fifty men. Judging by the empty weapon racks on the walls and the handful of chairs and benches, it currently housed less than a quarter that number. There was also a slight musty smell in the air. He could only conclude that Diu's garrison was badly under-strength and the castle was largely deserted.

Half an hour passed before the under-officer returned. Gibson and Hector were to follow him to be interviewed, the others to remain where they were.

'Don't try any tricks now. I might not speak the language but I can pick up the general idea of what's being said,' warned Gibson out of the side of his mouth, as the two of them mounted the stairs, their footsteps echoing on the wooden treads.

On the upper floor the under-officer rapped on one of several doors that led off the landing. A voice called on him to enter and he threw open the door, stepped inside and gave a smart salute. 'These are the visitors who asked to speak with the governor, sir,' he reported, then gestured for Hector and Gibson to come forward. He closed the door behind them, joining them in the interview room.

A small, compact man with a neat pointed beard and an alert, clever face was seated behind a desk. His hair was tied back in a queue and he was dressed informally in a loose white shirt open at the neck to reveal a small cross hanging from a gold chain. Hector put his age at close to forty.

'I'm afraid that the governor is unavailable. My name is Pedro Vieira, his deputy. How may I help you?' he enquired politely. He did not invite his visitors to sit.

Gibson, encouraged by the deputy governor's slow, careful

English, answered, 'We're from *Pearl*, anchored offshore. Captain Mayes would be obliged if you could send a message to the Great Mogul to tell him that among our passengers is his close relative, returning from the pilgrimage to Mecca.'

Vieira's face betrayed no emotion. 'I'm sure that the emperor will be pleased to hear the news. A lookout reported the presence of your vessel to me earlier today.' He paused. 'Is there a reason why your captain has chosen to anchor at such a distance? If he is worried about dangers in the approach channel to our harbour, I could send a pilot.'

Hector sensed an ironic undertone in the question. Gibson, however, was oblivious. 'Captain Mayes needs to make sure that everything is prepared for the reception of Her Highness, if I may call her that,' he said.

'Her Highness?' Vieira raised an eyebrow. 'The Mogul's relative aboard your ship is a woman?'

'A sister, or maybe his aunt,' said Gibson uncertainly, then darted a sideways glance at Hector, who gave a slight nod of encouragement. He had been looking around Vieira's office while the two men had been talking. It was sparsely furnished with only Vieira's desk and half a dozen chairs – all heavy pieces in the Portuguese style – and a large wooden cross prominently displayed on one wall. There were no pictures or carpets or any decoration. He had the impression that the deputy governor's office, like the guardroom, had seen busier times.

'And how is it that a member of the imperial family travels aboard your ship after the pilgrimage?' Vieira asked quietly. 'It is my understanding that the authorities in Jeddah license only vessels of their co-religionists to carry pilgrims.'

'Let me put it this way,' said Gibson, treating his listener to a knowing look. 'During her voyage Her Highness accepted our invitation to transfer to *Pearl*.'

Watching the deputy governor closely, Hector had no doubt that Pedro Vieira grasped what Gibson was implying. But the quartermaster was disappointed if he expected to lead Vieira into a discussion of a ransom.

Vieira merely nodded. 'I'm told that a woman has landed with you.'

'One of Her Highness's attendants,' Gibson answered. 'She will confirm that her mistress remains under our care.'

Vieira remained impassive. 'As you must be aware, it would be most improper for this aristocratic lady to remain in male company now that she has come ashore.' He looked past Hector's shoulder to the under-officer. 'See to it that she is taken to the women's quarters.'

Gibson shifted uneasily, clearly unhappy about the direction the interview was taking. Hector decided it was time to speak up. 'It has been a long voyage for all of us.'

He saw a flicker of understanding in Vieira's eyes as the deputy governor took the hint. 'You must both be looking forward to getting some rest. I'll arrange rooms for you overnight so we can continue this conversation tomorrow when you are refreshed. A clerk and an interpreter will be on hand to write down precisely what message you wish to send to Emperor Aurangzeb.'

He did not trouble to rise to his feet though it was clear the meeting was over. Hector took Gibson by the elbow and steered him toward the door. He could tell that the quartermaster was furious and frustrated.

'It's a mistake to let that woman be taken away from us,' he growled at Hector as they returned down the stairs to the guard-room. 'She's our only proof that we're got someone from the emperor's family on *Pearl*.'

'Nothing has changed,' Hector assured him. 'Vieira will speak with her and she'll confirm that we are holding a hostage.'

'You're the one who's supposed to get on well with the Portu-guese,' Gibson snapped angrily. 'You better make sure that Vieira knows we are serious.'

The quartermaster remained surly throughout the meal set

out for them at a table in the guardroom. They and the two sail-ors from *Pearl* ate under the gaze of the soldiers who now acted more like prison warders. Afterwards they were taken to what must once have been sleeping quarters for the garrison officers. Each was shown into a cell-like room, and locked in.

*

HECTOR LAY DOWN on the cot and listened to the croaking calls from unknown birds coming in through the small open window. The smells of spiced cooking drifted up from the fires of the gar-rison troops. There were occasional snatches of their conversation in a guttural language he could not understand. Soon afterwards, and to his surprise, he also heard the sound of church bells, quite close by. He got up and looked out of the window. By craning his neck he could see over the castle's outer wall to a white-painted spire. The Christian townsfolk of Diu were being called to evening prayer. When the chimes ended, he returned to the cot and lay down again, hands clasped behind his head, and stared up at the whitewashed ceiling mottled with specks of mould. The familiar sound of the bells had caused a surge of nostalgia. His thoughts turned to Maria in the Canaries with her baby and wait-ing to hear from him about their plans for the future. The meeting with Pedro Vieira had given him much to think about. He felt that the deputy governor of Diu was someone whom he should ask for advice on how, or whether, to follow up on Pedro Tav-ares's suggestion that he take service with the Great Mogul. But first he needed to devise some way to get Jacques and Jezreel off *Pearl*.

*

THE SOFT CLICK of the door lock roused him some time after midnight. He could just make out the figure of a native servant standing in the open doorway. He had been half-expecting the summons and was already dressed. Treading softly past the doors to the other rooms, he followed his guide back along the corridors to the office of the deputy governor. Except for the light from a candelabrum set on Vieira's desk, the room was in darkness. The windows were open to the warm night air and the buzzing and scratching sounds of myriads of nocturnal insects. The deputy governor was seated in the shadows just beyond the pool of yellow light which fell on a single chair placed in front of his desk.

'Take a seat, and tell me who you really are. Then explain what you are doing with that gang of criminals and outlaws,' Vieira began. His voice, flat and emotionless, gave no hint of his mood.

'My name is Hector Lynch, and I've been on *Pearl* for less than a week.'

'Long enough to be involved in an ugly plot to kidnap and ransom a member of the emperor's family. Am I right?'

'That's correct,' Hector admitted. 'Captain Mayes devised the scheme and I've gone along with it because it gave me a chance to get off his ship.'

'I've spoken with the lady whom you brought ashore, and she confirms that Mayes forcibly removed her and a companion from *Ganj-i-Sawa'i* on a voyage from Jeddah to Surat.' The deputy governor leaned forward and his eyes glittered in the candlelight. 'They were travelling in attendance to Her Highness Gaucharara Begum.'

'I didn't know the exact identity of their mistress, only that she is a sister of the Great Mogul,' Hector protested.

'A full sister,' Vieira informed him coldly. 'She's the daughter of Shah Jahan, the previous emperor and his favourite wife, Mumtaz Mahal.'

'Her Highness remains aboard *Ganj-i-Sawa'i*. Captain Mayes was duped into kidnapping the wrong person. So no harm was done.'

Vieira treated Hector to a withering look. 'That is only partially true.'

'I don't know what you mean,' Hector countered. 'The officer in charge of their escort was involved in the deception ... a countryman of yours by the name of Tavares.'

'Jeronimo Tavares?'

'Yes, Jeronimo. The two of us tricked Mayes into selecting the wrong victims. That was also what Her Highness's attendants wanted, as it turned out.'

Mention of Tavares' name brought about a softening in Vieira's tone. 'I think you'd better tell me the full story of what happened,' he said quietly.

Hector took a deep breath and began to explain how he had sailed from St Mary's with Avery aboard *Fancy*, the ambush of the pilgrim fleet, the sacking of 'Exceeding Treasure' and how Mayes had seen a chance to kidnap a member of the Mogul's family and demand a ransom.

Vieira listened without comment. When Hector finished, there was a troubled look on the deputy governor's face.

'I'm distressed to hear that Jeronimo Tavares is so badly hurt. It sounds as though he'll be cruelly disfigured for the rest of his life. Jeronimo is my cousin on my mother's side.' He allowed himself a hint of a nostalgic smile. 'When he came to Portugal for artillery training, the two of us had many good times together – making the rounds of taverns and chasing girls. He always claimed he was more successful because he was the better looking.'

The candlelight cast deep shadows under his eyes as he paused to gather his thoughts. Then his voice took on a firm, decisive edge. 'There is one thing in this whole hostage affair that you have overlooked.'

Hector waited for him to continue.

'Those two women whom you describe as being "attendants" on Gaucharara Begum are not ordinary serving maids. They come from the very best Mogul families.'

Hector was puzzled. 'But they did not give that impression.'

'Nor would they. In Portugal, we would describe them as court ladies-in-waiting. They were accompanying the emperor's sister while she was undertaking the most important pilgrimage of her life. In that situation their mistress is required to be humble, lacking in pretension, a simple pilgrim.' Unthinking, he had raised his hand to the little cross hanging against his chest from the gold chain. Hector suspected that Vieira had made a pilgrimage himself to a Christian shrine.

'By the standards of the Mogul court a journey made with only two ladies-in-waiting is the equivalent of wearing a hair shirt,' Vieira continued. 'Under normal circumstances Gaucharara Begum would be attended by a staff of at least forty women ranging from wardrobe minders to hair dressers and those whose sole function is to blend the exact perfume she wishes to wear that day.'

He gave Hector a bleak look. 'To be chosen to accompany the emperor's sister on the pilgrimage, and as one of her only two ladies-in-waiting, is a remarkable honour, bestowed only on highest-born aristocrats.'

'So Mayes still holds a very important captive.'

'Correct, a prisoner who must be restored to her family as quickly as possible. Otherwise there will be serious repercussions for anyone even remotely involved in her captivity, and that,' he added heavily, 'includes my own people here in Diu.'

'But they had nothing to do with the kidnap,' Hector objected.

Vieira's mouth turned down in a sardonic smile. 'Lynch, you need to understand the atmosphere of deep suspicion that pervades the Mogul court. The Moguls are outsiders in Hindustan, almost as much as we Europeans are. They are a tiny ruling minority, constantly on their guard for any attempt to topple them. They also conspire amongst themselves to gain a larger slice of power and riches, so do not trust one another. Naturally, they expect others to be doing the same. The moment they hear about this kidnap they will think that it was cooked up between Captain Mayes and me, or my superiors.'

Hector felt a twinge of guilt as he recalled this was exactly what had crossed his mind when Mayes had first suggested taking the hostages to Diu: he had wondered if Mayes would offer the

Portuguese a cut of the ransom price. 'So there's no point in trying to get the hostage back by paying a lesser ransom, after you've informed Mayes that his hostage is not as valuable as he thinks?'

Vieira shook his head. 'Even with a reduced ransom, the Moguls will still suspect me of collusion with Mayes. It'll be a case of two untrustworthy foreigners plotting together. Family honour is also involved. There is enough shame for a Mogul family that foreign infidels hold captive a daughter or wife. To get her back by giving in to the kidnappers' demand and paying a ransom adds to the disgrace.'

Hector saw the direction that Vieira's thoughts were taking and his next words confirmed it. 'We have to find a way of getting the lady off *Pearl*.'

They sat in silence. Hector had noted the use of 'we' and he had a proposal to make to the deputy governor. A scheme had occurred to him just as he was dropping off to sleep in his locked room, a scheme that required a certain amount of luck to be successful. Above all, it required Vieira's active participation. He eyed the deputy governor seated at his desk. The Portuguese showed no signs of softness. He looked tough and wiry as if he could handle himself in a tense situation.

'*Pearl*'s company is a slovenly lot,' Hector began. 'If taken by surprise, they would be slow to react.'

'And what sort of surprise do you propose we spring on them?'

'I have two friends aboard *Pearl*. Both men are competent and quick-witted. Mayes is holding them hostage against my return to his ship.'

'Hostage-holding seems to be the man's style,' Vieira grunted.

'With their help I think we can get the lady off the vessel.'

Vieira leaned forward; his face was alert with curiosity. 'Set out the details.'

*

NEXT DAY IT WAS well into the afternoon when Hector and Vieira finally came within hailing distance of *Pearl*, lying at her anchor. It had taken them the best part of two hours of tedious progress across a flat oily calm in what the deputy governor called a *thoni*, a local working boat rowed by scrawny native oarsmen. The day was hot and muggy, and each man labouring at the crude-looking oars wore no more than a loincloth and a cotton rag around his head to keep the sweat out of his eyes. By contrast, the deputy governor was magnificent in his formal dress: a coat of peacock blue embroidered with silver thread, a brocade waistcoat, cream-coloured breeches, silk stockings, and polished black shoes with silver buckles and two-inch heels. White lace frothed at his cuffs and throat, and he wore a neatly curled wig under his broad-brimmed velvet hat.

'Do we know the lady's name?' Hector asked under his breath as the *thoni* crept within pistol shot of Mayes' ship.

'Salima. Her uncle is Abdul Ghafar, a member of Aurang-zeb's *diwan*, his inner circle of ministers,' the deputy governor answered. Drops of sweat were oozing from under his wig, trickling down his cheeks and leaving tracks in the light coating of face powder to add to his dandified look.

Hector checked the *thoni*'s crew one last time. They were an ill-assorted lot. Two were in their late teens, one gangling fellow was old enough to be their father and several faces bore the marks of childhood smallpox. The only similarity between them was that they all had moustaches and looked too scraggy to pull an oar. There was nothing that Hector could see that identified them as soldiers. Vieira had assured him that every one of them was handpicked, came from a fishing family and was an excellent boatman. Their muskets lay hidden in the bottom of the boat, covered by palm fronds.

He could see Mayes's burly frame among the sailors lining *Pearl*'s rail. They had been observing the *thoni*'s slow approach for the past half-hour, and Hector was close enough to see one of them was armed with a blunderbuss while several others carried muskets. He was relieved to note that *Pearl*'s crew had been too lazy to shift their boat after returning from shore the day before. It was still tied to the foot of the rope ladder left dangling over the ship's side.

He stood up, cupped his hands and called, 'Captain Mayes! I've brought the governor of Diu. He's ready to listen to your proposal, but wants to meet the lady first.'

Beside him in the boat Vieira got to his feet and, wobbling slightly on his high heels, showed himself in his official costume, his hands held out from his side to make it clear that he carried no weapons.

'The governor may come aboard,' Mayes shouted back. 'Where are Gibson and the two men I sent with you?'

'They stayed to enjoy the town,' Hector called up. The truth was that Gibson and the two sailors were still shut in their rooms.

The *thoni*'s crew brought their craft to where Hector could push *Pearl*'s boat out of the way, grab hold of the ship's ladder and scramble up. Vieira followed, awkward in his finery, and tripped and nearly fell as he set foot on *Pearl*'s deck where Mayes was waiting. The smug look on the freebooter captain's face had replaced his usual scowl though his eyes remained hard and calculating. His ship's company clustered behind him, pressing forward and eager to follow what was going on.

'Captain, may I introduce the Governor of Diu – Pedro Vieira,' Hector began.

'Deputy Governor,' Vieira corrected him in his slow careful English and offering out a limp hand for Mayes to shake.

Mayes ignored it and came straight to the point. 'A lady of the imperial family is aboard *Pearl* and I need to be paid before I set her ashore. It will be a considerable sum. If you can assist, I will reward you for your help.'

'Mr Lynch has explained the situation to me,' Vieira murmured, reaching into an inside pocket of his splendid coat, pulling out a large handkerchief of fine white lawn and languidly mopping his face. 'Naturally I would like to see this passenger for myself. A formality of course.'

Mayes turned to two of his men and ordered them to bring the passenger from her cabin. Hector positioned himself a little to one side and glanced casually around the crowd of onlookers. Jezreel was standing in the rear, towering over those near him. Jacques presumably would be close by.

After a short delay, the crowd parted and Salima, as Hector now thought of her, came toward them. She was wrapped in the same long gown of yellow silk embroidered with patterns of tiny silver flowers that she had been wearing when she was taken from *Ganj-i-Sawa'i*. A fine shawl covered her head and shoulders, and she had drawn the free end across her face to conceal her features. Only her feet were bare, and as she advanced across the deck with small, neat steps, Hector noticed that she wore silver toe rings and anklets studded with tiny diamonds.

'You can see that she is unharmed and in good health,' Mayes said as Salima halted a few paces away. Hector detected a faint trembling and guessed that Salima was frightened to be on her own, without her companion, yet was managing to hold her nerve.

'Yes indeed,' Vieira agreed, again mopping his brow. He looked around anxiously. 'Perhaps I could have a little space? The air is very close.' Mayes glared at his men, and gestured at them to fall back.

Vieira mopped his brow again, and returned the handkerchief to the pocket in the lining of the resplendent coat. When his hand reappeared, he was holding a small short-barrelled pistol. In two quick strides he stepped close to Mayes and pressed the muzzle of the gun against the captain's ribs. 'Tell your men to stand aside, captain,' he ordered, his voice now sharp and clear. All trace of clumsiness was gone.

Mayes froze. Stunned that he had been taken unawares so easily, his face set into a stiff, enraged mask.

'I will not hesitate to pull the trigger. So do exactly what I tell you, captain,' ordered Vieira calmly. 'You will accompany me ashore where I will arrange for you to meet a representative of Emperor Aurangzeb.'

While *Pearl*'s company were still recovering their wits, Hector darted forward to the man holding the blunderbuss and took the weapon. 'Jezreel! Jacques!' he called. 'Get over here!'

His two friends shouldered their way through the crowd. Jacques was grinning. He had snatched a musket from a sailor and Jezreel had got hold of a cutlass.

'Jezreel, quick as you can. Get the woman over the side and into our boat,' Hector told him.

Everything was going exactly as he had agreed earlier with Vieira. If they moved swiftly, they should be able to get clear before Mayes' men could stop them. He kept a careful eye on the front rank of the crowd in case anyone was about to reach for a weapon. Fortunately the press of men on the confines of the deck meant that those at the back could barely see what was going on, still less do anything to intervene.

Jezreel shifted the cutlass to his left hand and reached out with his right arm. He intended to scoop up Salima, carry her to the rail and down into the boat. But the sudden movement panicked her. She started back, then she spun on her heel and fled in terror. Before anyone could stop her, she had run across the deck to the ship's rail. There she clambered up, balanced for a brief moment and threw herself into the sea.

It was Hector's turn to be shocked. He stood appalled. Salima's leap had taken her overboard nowhere near the *thoni*, tied alongside.

Jacques was the first to recover. 'No one move!' he shouted, bringing his musket up to his shoulder and aiming at the thick of the crowd.

But Mayes had seen his chance. He knocked aside the pistol that Vieira was holding to his ribs, and swung a savage blow at the deputy governor's head that sent the Portuguese reeling. Glancing round for the nearest weapon, Mayes decided on taking

Jezreel's cutlass. He lunged, grabbed Jezreel by the wrist and twisted savagely. Mayes was squat and powerful, accustomed to using brute strength to make his victims submit. But he had not dealt with someone who had spent years as a prize-fighter. Jezreel brought his free hand across and clamped down on the captain's grip. Taking hold of a middle finger, he deliberately bent it back. Mayes gave an agonized gasp and found himself being forced down on his knees.

Hector's mind was in a whirl. He swung the blunderbuss from side to side, menacing the crowd with its bell-shaped muzzle. In front of him, a ginger-haired sailor, braver or more stupid than his fellows, reached for the knife in his belt. There was a popping sound from Hector's right, and the sailor clutched his shoulder. Hector flicked a sideways glance to see Vieira lowering his pocket pistol. He had fired its single shot.

'Back to our boat! We can pick her up from the sea,' Hector shouted and watched as Vieira threw aside his empty weapon, kicked off his high-heeled shoes and ran in his stockinged feet to the ship's rail. A moment later his feathered hat was disappearing from sight as he went down the rope ladder.

Suddenly Jacques was beside Hector. Shoulder to shoulder they began to back away from the crowd towards the safety of the ladder, still aiming their weapons at the crowd.

'Time to go,' Jacques called to Jezreel. The big man bent Mayes's finger farther back until it dislocated, then kicked *Pearl*'s captain hard in the chest, knocking him over backwards.

In the scramble to get off the ship, Hector was first down the ladder with Jacques close behind. Jezreel remained still on deck, roaring and making great sweeps with his cutlass to discourage any of the freebooters from coming closer. Jacques's head was still showing above the rail when the Frenchman called down for Hector to pass him up the blunderbuss. Knives and blades had appeared in the crowd of sailors and in another moment they would surge forward. 'Stand aside, Jezreel!' Jacques called. He placed the blunderbuss on the rail, and pulled the trigger. There was a loud report, a cloud of black smoke and the gun's load of small shot spewed into the crowd. Two men fell and the crowd hesitated. Jezreel, cutlass in hand, vaulted the rail, and together he and Jacques tumbled in a heap into the waiting *thoni*.

Hector grabbed the cutlass from Jezreel and hacked through the rope that held *Pearl*'s boat. He gave it a shove with his foot and it floated away. If the *thoni* could get clear, no pursuit was possible.

Vieira, incongruous in his finery, was down on his hands and knees in the bilges of the boat scrabbling at the palm fronds that concealed the weapons. Above them heads began to appear at *Pearl*'s rail, and the first musket barrels. It was point-blank range and the sailors could hardly miss.

Vieira was just in time. He twisted round holding a loaded musket and fired upward. It was a lucky shot. The crack of his musket was followed by a splash as one of the freebooter marksmen dropped his weapon into the sea.

The crew of the *thoni* were using their oars to fend off from *Pearl*, and as soon as they had enough room to row, each man jabbed his oar blade into the water. He half rose from his seat, then threw himself backward as he heaved on the handle. The crew who earlier had seemed so lethargic and feeble now sent the boat surging forward as they set themselves a quick, short stroke.

Hector heard the whizz of musket balls overhead, and the surface of the sea around the *thoni* puckered with sudden water spouts. They were near misses from *Pearl*'s musketeers. Several sharp knocks sounded whenever the bullets struck the *thoni*, and one of the native oarsmen gave a thin cough. He slumped sideways, leaving his oar trailing alongside. 'Here, take over!' Vieira shouted in Hector's ear, thrust a musket into his grasp, then scrambled forward into the bows. Some thirty yards away a patch of yellow on the sea marked where Salima was managing to keep her head above water, her gown floating up around her. Hector knelt in the stern of the *thoni*, faced aft and braced himself as he tried to hold the sights on a sailor with a musket who had climbed into *Pearl*'s lower shrouds. The boat underneath him was rocking with each surging stroke from the crew, and a steady aim was impossible. He held his fire, aware that the *thoni* was slowing down, then felt a slight tilt. He presumed that Salima was being hauled aboard. He kept his attention on his target, waiting for the right moment, then pulled the trigger. He missed.

'Here's the next one. Priming's checked.' Jacques had moved up beside him and was handing him another loaded musket. Again he aimed and fired. The butt kicked against his shoulder. His eyes watered as the smoke drifted back in his face and the air reeked of gunpowder.

He was amazed at how quickly the native oarsmen were moving the boat. They had picked up their rhythm again, grunting with effort. Another minute or two and the *thoni* would be out of accurate musket range. It would take *Pearl* too long to load her cannon, and with his ship caught at anchor in a flat calm, Mayes was unable to hoist sail in pursuit.

'Here's the last of them, might as well use it,' said Jacques, passing Hector the final loaded musket. But the gunpowder and flint were damp, and there was nothing but a click and a tiny spark when he pulled the trigger. He laid down the weapon, his hands shaking as a sense of relief washed through him. The plan to rescue Salima had so nearly failed.

He took several deep breaths to calm himself, then got up from where he had been crouching. Next to him Jacques was peeling back the bloodstained sleeve of his shirt to examine a cut where a flying splinter must have nicked him. Jezreel sat among the native oarsmen. He had gone forward and taken the place of the man who had been shot. For a moment Hector could not see where Vieira had got to, and then he saw him upright in the bows. The deputy governor had lost his hat and wig, and no longer wore his magnificent peacock-blue coat. Trails of sweat had streaked and blotched the white powder on his face and made it look as if he had been crying, so too did his haggard expression.

Then Hector saw the coat. It was rolled up and being used as a cushion for Salima's head. She lay propped against the *thoni*'s hull, and blood was seeping through her yellow gown.

FOURTEEN

'SHE WILL HAVE BEEN buried already,' Vieira stated gloomily. 'In an unmarked grave within twenty-four hours, that's the custom. Her body was taken away by men sent by the local raja. He's a prince who's tributary to Aurangzeb.'

'So what happens now?' asked Hector. It was mid-morning on the second day after the bungled rescue and the deputy governor had asked him to call at his office. The air in the room was muggy and still, and Hector could feel his sweat-soaked shirt sticking to the back of the chair where he sat in front of Vieira's desk.

Vieira got up from his own seat, walked across to a window and stood there, staring out. Hector had an uneasy feeling that the deputy governor was avoiding looking him in the eye.

After a long moment the deputy governor spoke, and there was embarrassment as well as finality in his tone. 'I'm sending you and your companions to Delhi, to the Great Mogul's court, to give an account of what happened to the hajj fleet and to Salima.'

Hector shifted uncomfortably, unsure what to make of this turn of events. It seemed a poor reward for the attempt to rescue Salima.

'I haven't a choice,' Vieira said, his voice now full of regret as

148

he turned to face Hector. 'Aurangzeb is very devout. His own brother nicknamed him "the fanatic" and it's still spoken behind his back. When he hears that a pilgrim convoy was attacked while coming back from the hajj, he'll be enraged. I cannot afford to risk his wrath.'

'But you had nothing to do with what happened at the Gates of Alexander.'

'That doesn't matter. If the Mogul thinks that I am sheltering someone who took part in the assault on the pilgrims, he'll send an army against Diu.' He sighed and took a moment to wipe the sweat from his forehead with a handkerchief he drew from the sleeve of his loose cotton shirt. 'Hector, you've seen for yourself that Diu is a hollow shell, impressive from the outside but the garrison is far too small to resist a serious attack. A Mogul army would take no more than a week to batter down our defences and break in. We'd be crushed, and I'm responsible for the security of the people of the surrounding town.'

'But Aurangzeb's sister is safe. When *Ganj-i-Sawa'i* reaches Surat with Gaucharara Begum on board, Aurangzeb will learn that she has come to no harm.'

'I know that.' The deputy governor spread his hands in a gesture of helplessness. 'But there's Salima's death to consider. Her uncle Abdul Ghafar oversees the collection of taxes for Aurangzeb. You might say that he is the minister in charge of imperial revenue. Here in Diu we have a special tax concession that dates to the early days when we Portuguese established ourselves on these shores: we pay no import duties on goods from abroad. It's the single advantage that lets us compete with larger, more successful ports like Surat. Remove that concession – as Salima's uncle can arrange – and Diu will die a slow death, her commerce will dry up.'

He walked back to his desk, his face lined with concern. 'Hector, please believe me when I say that I have no choice but to send you and your companions to Delhi. You must appear before whomever Aurangzeb appoints to enquire into the assault on the pilgrim fleet, and give an account of what happened. Make the case that you and your friends should not be blamed.'

He picked up a document lying on his desk, the ink still wet in the muggy air. 'I've written an official report, very favourable to you of course. It is addressed to an *omrah* in Delhi who has helped me in the past. He's not as influential as Salima's uncle, but he is a senior figure at court, and may be able to assist you.'

'An *omrah*?' Hector said. 'What sort of person is that?'

'A grandee, a high noble,' Vieira explained. 'The Great Mogul surrounds himself with men to whom he gives titles and rank, gifts and salaries – his *omrahs*. They come from the same families as himself, descendants of the Persian invaders who over-ran Hindustan. They run his empire for him . . . just as long as he approves their actions.'

'And this raja who took away Salima's body? You described him as a prince.'

'The Mogul allows the outlying provinces of his empire to be ruled by their long-established princely dynasties on condition that they pay him tribute. Most of them go by the title of raja. However, if a raja makes trouble, he can expect to be overthrown by the forces sent from Delhi.'

'So I'm to go to Aurangzeb's capital to answer for what happened at the Straits of Alexander and aboard *Ganj-i-Sawa'i*. At the same time I'm to make it clear that Diu cannot be held responsible for Salima's death?' Hector asked sourly. He knew he was sounding aggrieved and bitter.

'I only expect you to tell the truth,' said Vieira wearily. 'We Portuguese have been in Hindustan much longer than the other European nations. We have learned to bend to the will of those far more powerful than ourselves.'

'And what will happen to me and my friends? What sort of punishment can we expect?'

The deputy governor was clearly distressed by the situation in which he found himself. He came across to where Hector sat, and laid a hand on his shoulder. 'You are resourceful and astute.

I saw that for myself aboard *Pearl*,' he said. 'I'm sending my most trusted assistant to accompany you. He's young, but he's very clever and he has lived in Delhi. He speaks several languages and with his help you may be able to navigate the whirlpools of court politics.'

'So you're not prepared to come to Delhi yourself?'

Vieira shook his head. 'Impossible. I have to stay here in Diu looking after my people. The government in Portugal would never forgive me if I left my post.'

Hector was feeling too resentful to respond at once.

'What's to stop me and my two companions quietly disappearing while we are on our way to Delhi?' he said after a while. 'Then slipping out of the country?'

'Because the raja is equally interested in seeing that you appear in Delhi to account for yourself and your friends. It's a chance to ingratiate himself with the Great Mogul. He's assigned one of his officials to escort you there under guard. He should be here by now.'

Hector let Vieira lead him down the stairs to the guardroom where a thin, dark-complexioned man with a long narrow face and hooded eyes was already waiting. He was austerely dressed in a plain white gown and turban. Loitering in the background were half a dozen natives armed with spears and short swords who Hector supposed were his retinue. Vieira introduced him as a *fawjdar* by the name of Darshan, in the service of the raja.

'Darshan's duties are similar to those of a senior magistrate,' Vieira explained. 'His men are what you might call his constables.'

The *fawjdar* said something in his own language and the deputy governor beckoned to a young man hovering nearby. 'Luis, I need your help,'

The young man came forward. He was a handsome lad in his late teens, with light brown skin, fine regular features, long straight jet-black hair, and long eyelashes to match. Hector guessed that he was part Portuguese and part native. There was something vaguely familiar about him.

'This is Luis,' Vieira said to Hector. 'He'll be travelling to Delhi with you. He speaks Arabic, Persian, and English much better than I do, as well as Portuguese and the local language, Gujerati.' He turned to the young man. 'Perhaps you would assist us by translating for the *fawjdar.*'

Luis listened as Darshan repeated what he had just said, then told Vieira that the *fawjdar* wanted to inspect all six prisoners he had been instructed to deliver to Delhi.

'The others have already been sent for,' said Vieira and indicated Hector, 'but this man is not to be treated as a prisoner, merely to be escorted to Delhi.'

Quartermaster Gibson and the two sailors from *Pearl* were the first to arrive. Clearly Gibson was in a foul mood.

'What's going on, Lynch?' he demanded angrily, though Hector caught a trace of fear beneath the bluster. 'I've been kept locked in my room these past two days. And who's this?' He nodded towards the *fawjdar.*

'He's taking us to Delhi to explain to the authorities what happened aboard *Ganj-i-Sawa'i*,' Hector told him. So much had happened in the past couple of days that Hector had given little thought to him and his two colleagues.

'What about Captain Mayes?' Gibson retorted. 'If we don't get back to *Pearl*, he'll make sure that Her Highness never sees her family again.'

'There is no member of the Great Mogul's family on *Pearl*, and never was,' Hector explained. 'It was a case of mistaken identity.'

Gibson's mouth fell open, then the look of pure hatred that flashed into his eyes warned Hector to step back. 'You double-crossing shit,' he snarled and sprang at Hector, reaching for his throat with both hands.

Two of the *fawjdar*'s men darted forward and grabbed Gibson by the arms. A third – a burly individual with a wrestler's physique – clasped the quartermaster around the waist and dragged him backward. At the same time, their colleagues quickly moved to surround the two sailors and levelled their spears. It was clear to Hector that the *fawjdar*'s men were well practised in dealing with troublemakers.

Gibson, his face flushed with anger, was still struggling to break free of his captors when Jacques and Jezreel strolled into the room. The quartermaster glared at them. 'I knew you were trouble,' he hissed.

Darshan had watched the scuffle calmly. He gave an order, and his men produced lengths of leather thong with which they quickly lashed together Gibson's wrists. They then searched him for hidden weapons, finding a short knife in his belt, and knotted a hobble between his ankles. They did the same for the two sailors, stood back, and waited for further instructions.

'Luis, tell the *fawjdar* that these men,' said Vieira, pointing out Jezreel and Jacques, 'helped in the attempt to rescue Salima and should not be tied.'

The *fawjdar* shot him a cold glance. 'He says that is for him to judge,' Luis translated.

'If he asks the lady we brought ashore earlier,' Hector cut in, 'she'll confirm that neither Jacques nor Jezreel had a hand in kidnapping Her Highness Gaucharara Begum.'

Darshan regarded Hector impassively while he listened to Luis's translation. 'I have already spoken with the lady,' came the *fawjdar*'s stiff reply. 'She says that you and a *hazari* of artillery were the only *feringhee* who gave any help to her and her highness. All the others are criminals who deserve to be put to death.'

He nodded to his constables and they closed in on Jezreel and Jacques.

Hector turned to the young interpreter. 'Luis, please explain that Jezreel and Jacques are my close friends, and that I give my word that neither they nor I will try to escape.'

The young man was still translating his request when the man who had been searching Jacques approached the *fawjdar* and gave him what he had found.

With a hint of a sneer on his narrow features Darshan held

out his open hand. On his palm lay half a dozen bright new gold coins. Each bore the stamp of the Mogul's mint.

'The *fawjdar* asks,' Luis hurriedly translated, 'how your friend came by these gold rupees. This is a very large sum for a common sailor to possess.'

Hector felt the blood rush to his face. He remembered Jacques taking his chance to pilfer coins from the display of loot aboard *Ganj-i-Sawa'i* while the freebooters were quarrelling over the division of the spoil.

He was still groping for some sort of excuse to give the *fawjdar* when Vieira intervened smoothly. 'Luis, offer my congratulations to Darshan on his efficiency in carrying out his duties. The coins are proof of the unlawful activities of the *feringhees*. He must take them to Delhi to be used in evidence at their trial.'

Darshan listened to the translation impassively, his hand closed, and he slipped the coins into a pocket in his gown. 'I accept this man's word,' he said, pointing with his chin at Hector. 'He and his two friends will not be tied.'

Vieira glanced at Hector with a knowing look. Hector realized that he had seldom seen a bribe passed so smoothly.

FIFTEEN

THEY ASSEMBLED before sunrise next morning while the air was still pleasantly cool. Hector stood in the outer yard of the fortress with Jacques and Jezreel. He had already explained that they were being sent to Delhi to answer for what happened aboard *Ganj-i-Sawa'i* and they were watching Darshan's constables. The men carried oil lamps as they supervised the loading of three bullock carts. One vehicle was piled with tents, firewood, luggage and sacks of provisions. Another cart, lighter and smartly painted, was rigged with a canopy and was clearly intended to carry passengers. On the flatbed of the third cart sat a wooden cage like a giant chicken coop.

'No guesses as to who will be riding in that. I'd prefer to walk, however far it is,' commented Jacques.

'It should be six or seven weeks on the road,' said a youthful voice. Luis, a cotton satchel slung from a strap over his shoulder, came forward to join them. He had an eager look, full of cheerful anticipation.

'Pleased to be going to the capital?' Hector asked. He wanted to know a little more about the young man whom Vieira recommended so highly.

'Oh yes!' The young man smiled. 'I enjoy travel. There's always something new to see.'

'And have you travelled this particular route before?'

'Most of it is the same as the road between Delhi and Surat, and I've accompanied my father along it several times.'

'Is your father going to be in Delhi when we get there?'

'Maybe. He's been gone a long time, on a special mission for Aurangzeb.' There was a touch of pride in his voice though also a hint of sadness.

Hector looked more closely into the young man's face, saw again the resemblance and a suspicion began to harden in his mind. 'Your father isn't an artilleryman, by any chance, is he?'

Luis nodded, and this time the pride was evident. 'With the rank of *hazari*. He and Senhor Vieira have been good friends for many years, and a place was found for me on the deputy governor's staff while he was away on duty.'

Hector let out a slow breath. 'If his name is Jeronimo Tavares, then I've met your father. Aboard the *Ganj-i-Sawa'i*.'

Luis beamed. 'Senhor Vieira told me that you were on *Ganj-i-Sawa'i* when she was attacked by pirates as she was bringing pilgrims back from Mecca.'

Clearly Vieira had not told the young man about his father's terrible burns. Hector decided that speaking about them now would only distress the young man. Besides, it was not even certain that Tavares would have lived to reach Surat. It was better to change the subject.

'Will the lady who came ashore from *Pearl* be travelling with us to Delhi?' he asked.

Luis looked mildly shocked at the question. 'Oh no, sir! The lady's far too important to be travelling with us. She is a guest of the raja and he will make special arrangement for her safe return to her family.'

He stopped, and seemed to have remembered something. He reached into his satchel and handed Hector a small weighty object wrapped in an oiled cloth. 'Senhor Vieira asked me to give you this.'

Through the cloth Hector could feel the outline of a pocket

pistol. He presumed it was the twin of the one that Vieira had used aboard *Pearl*. Guns like that were very expensive and usually sold in pairs. 'I hope it won't be necessary to use this on our journey,' he said to Luis, half-joking.

The young man shook his head, his long black hair flopping from side to side. 'Senhor Vieira said you were to make a gift of it to the *omrah* when we reach Delhi.' He gave a shy grin as he added, 'In Hindustan it's a mistake to come empty-handed to a meeting.'

'Like those gold coins that the *fawjdar* received?'

'Exactly.'

'If we're to be six or seven weeks on our journey, I think it would be a good opportunity for you to instruct me in the local customs,' Hector told him. 'I can't afford to make too many errors when we reach Delhi.'

Luis's smile showed perfectly white teeth. 'I shall be pleased to help. Also to teach you to speak some Persian, as that is the preferred language among the *omrahs*.'

The last of the provisions had been loaded onto the carts, ropes tied and re-tied. Several of the *fawjdar*'s men went off through the stone archway that led into the main donjon. Hector presumed they had gone to fetch Gibson and the two sailors from *Pearl*.

'Don't know who does the most chewing, the cows or the carters,' observed Jacques. The harnessed bullocks stood patiently chewing the cud, the drool hanging in strings from their mouths. Their drivers squatted on the ground, their backs against the great wooden wheels. They too had their mouths full, their jaws moving, occasionally spitting out what looked like blood.

Gibson and the two sailors emerged, hobbled and their hands still tied in front of them. They did not glance in Hector's direction as the *fawjdar*'s men led them to the cage on the cart and helped them in, then the door was swung shut and padlocked. There was not enough room to stand, and the prisoners had to sit with their backs against the cage bars. Hector was reminded of the days he had spent cooped up in the cupboard on 'Exceeding Treasure', and felt sorry for them.

Luis was speaking again. 'Senhor Vieira has given me money to buy food and necessaries on the journey. Also he has arranged for spare clothes and other items to be included on the carts.'

'That's very kind of him,' said Hector. An hour earlier the deputy governor had said his farewell in private, with news that the fortress lookouts had watched *Pearl* weigh anchor the previous evening and disappear over the horizon. Hector could only conclude that Captain Mayes had given up on his ransom scheme and decided to go back to his more normal methods of piracy. Now he and his friends, and the three prisoners from *Pearl*, were the only ones whom the Mogul could hold to account for what had happened on *Ganj-i-Sawa'i*.

'Time to go,' muttered Jezreel. Darshan entered the courtyard, strode across to the cart for passengers and climbed into it. He made no attempt to invite Hector or his companions to join him. The driver flicked his whip and the bullocks began to move forward with their small, ponderous steps. The other two carts fell in behind and the little convoy creaked forward towards the gateway that led into Diu town. As he passed under its arch, Hector turned to take one last look at the huge fortress. High on the battlements was a small figure dark against the pink dawn sky. Deputy Governor Vieira raised an arm in a gesture of farewell.

*

THAT FIRST DAY on the road set the pattern of many, many days to follow. The little procession of three bullock carts crossed the town and entered on the sun-baked countryside that extended ahead of them as far as the early morning haze allowed them to see: a flat and arid scrubland alternating with small fields. The bullocks moved at their sedate amble and would not be hurried. The carts lurched and shuddered as they rolled over the ruts and bumps in the unmade surface of the roadway. The wheels squeaked and groaned as they turned on their axles. As the sun rose higher, Hector and his friends learned to walk off to one side to avoid the dust kicked up by hooves and wheels. If they felt like doing so, they hopped up on the tailgate of the baggage cart and rode, legs swinging in the air, or climbed up to join the driver on his seat. Darshan in his passenger cart continued to ignore them. His constables and at least a score of assorted attendants – water carriers, grooms, grass cutters – straggled along on foot in no sort of order, except for two men armed with spears who stayed close beside the prison cage. Every few miles they came to a roadside settlement of small mud-brick houses and halted briefly. Water was drawn from a well or from a storage pond, and given to the thirsty bullocks. Occasionally they met strings of four or five camels loaded with packs of trade goods or hauling two-wheeled carts, but the vast majority of other road users were on foot or accompanying bullock carts like their own. Everyone was moving at much the same slow, deliberate speed, pulling aside to give room when someone was coming in the opposite direction, rarely overtaking.

Shortly before midday, their little procession veered off the road toward a grove of trees and stopped in their shade. Once again the bullocks were given water and the drivers tossed a bundle of cut grass on the ground before each beast. Luis produced cold rice, sweet biscuits flavoured with aniseed and curdled milk and distributed the food to Hector and his friends, and also to the prisoners in the cage. Then everyone found a patch of shade, and dozed. When the worst of the day's heat had eased, they took to the road again, travelling until late in the afternoon when they halted for the night on an open patch of beaten earth beneath a great spreading tree in the centre of a village. The bullocks were unyoked and led away to be fed and watered, and the villagers came forward to sell fruit, eggs, vegetables and flat cakes of cow dung for the cooking fire. Soon the air was blue with smoke – for the cooks added green branches to the hearth – and the smell of their cooking hung over the encampment.

'He likes his comforts,' commented Jezreel. Darshan's servants had unloaded a tent from the baggage wagon and erected it on a choice spot at the edge of their camp. They were carrying into it a carpet, a bed, pillows and a thick mattress.

'He's brought along his own cook, too,' observed Jacques.

'Don't worry, sirs,' interrupted Luis earnestly. He had just returned from a foray into the village and brought back two metal pots, one large, one small. 'Senhor Vieira has provided you with a tent and blankets. Sometimes the nights will be chilly.'

He set the pots down on the ground. 'I've purchased *kicheri* and *dhal*, and can go back to get some toddy, if you want.'

Jezreel peered into the larger pot. 'Rice again, but at least it's hot this time, and someone has added vegetables. All that walking has made me hungry.' He looked around, searching for a plate.

'It will be easier if you use this, and your fingers,' Luis told him, handing him a large flat leaf. 'But please wait while I fetch a ladle from the baggage.'

'Onions, beans and some sort of spice,' noted Jacques as he sniffed the steam from the smaller pot.

Luis came back with the ladle and spooned out their portions. 'You must tell me what food you prefer,' he said. 'When things have settled down, I will employ a cook who will accompany us.'

'If he can produce anything as good as this, I'll not complain.' Jacques had taken his first mouthful. 'I'd like to know what spices were used.'

Luis glowed with pleasure. 'I'm glad it pleases you. Sometimes foreigners find the local cooking much too spicy.'

'Then they haven't had to live on stale ship's biscuit and scummy water,' said Jezreel, holding out his leaf plate for another helping.

'Leave enough for Gibson and the others,' Hector told him.

When they had finished eating, Luis carried what was left in the pots to where Gibson and the other two prisoners had been allowed out of their cage and were seated on the ground tethered to their wagon.

'I think I should have a word with Quartermaster Gibson,' said Hector getting to his feet. He had nothing in particular that he wanted to say to the man, but was feeling that a show of friendliness might not come amiss when the men from *Pearl* were enduring much harsher treatment.

'Come to gloat?' Gibson sneered, wiping his mouth with the back of his hand as Hector approached.

Hector shook his head. 'No, just to tell you what's happening.'

'Don't bother. We can look after ourselves.'

Hector told him anyway, the two sailors listening in, scowls on their faces. When he finished, he saw the gleam of revenge in Gibson's eyes.

'When we come up for trial,' the quartermaster informed him, 'me and my mates will make sure that you're found guilty as well.' He gave a deliberate belch in Hector's direction. 'Now clear off.'

Hector stood his ground. 'I can ask the man in charge that you are allowed to walk and don't have to ride in the cage,' he offered.

But Gibson was having none of it. 'Didn't you hear? Bugger off!' he snarled. 'I can see why *Fancy*'s quartermaster wanted to be rid of you. You're a right slimy bastard.'

Hector gave up and went back to join his friends who were putting up the small tent that Vieira had provided for them.

'What did Gibson have to say for himself?' asked Jezreel.

When Hector repeated the conversation, the ex-prize-fighter shrugged. 'If I were you, I wouldn't bother with him and those two blockheads. We should look out for ourselves.'

Sometime later when Luis went to collect the empty pots from Gibson and the two sailors, the young man returned, looking annoyed and upset.

'Hector, sir . . .' he began.

'Just call me Hector.'

'Hector,' the young man started again. 'Those men are very stupid.'

'What makes you say that?'

'They offered me money if I helped them escape.'

'And what did you reply?'

'I told them it was impossible. They have nowhere to run, they don't know the country and they would be caught immediately. In reply they swore at me, and one of them said that I was a dirty mongrel.'

'Don't let it worry you, Luis,' Hector assured him. 'Each day's travel will take us farther from the coast, and eventually they will realize that they have no chance whatever of getting free. Then they might be more reasonable.'

*

THEY WERE A WEEK into their journey when Hector noticed Darshan's constables acting strangely. It was just after the midday break, and the carts had starting moving again when their escort kept turning to look back down the road, then exchanging anxious glances. As far as Hector could tell, they were worried by a cloud of dust behind them and quickly getting nearer. Another party of travellers was moving faster and soon to overtake. Eventually one of the constables ran forward to speak with the *fawjdar* riding in his covered cart. Minutes later, the little convoy turned aside and, with some shoving and pushing, came to a halt several yards clear of the highway. All the other road users promptly followed their example and stood waiting. Even Darshan got down from his cart and took up his position a little ahead of his constables. They lined up, facing the roadway and forming a screen shielding Jacques, Jezreel and the other members of their party. Only Hector was left standing on his own. The dust cloud drew nearer and revealed itself to be a group of a dozen armed horsemen advancing at a slow trot. They were escorting two riding camels with tent-like structures on their backs, light cotton canopies striped in white, grey and red. Alongside the camels ran armed soldiers, their bare feet pounding on the road, javelins on their shoulders, red turbans wrapped around helmets of polished steel. Out of the corner of his eye Hector saw Darshan bend forward and place his hands on the ground in a gesture of respect. Taken by surprise, Hector was forced to step back when one of the runners in the armed escort shouted at him angrily. Moments later the leading camel drew level, and he looked up as a hand pulled back the side curtain of the canopy. A woman, veiled except for her eyes, was gazing down at him through a narrow gap. There was a shock of recognition. He was sure that the woman travelling in such grand style was the surviving lady-in-waiting to the Mogul's sister, whom he had last seen when setting her ashore in Diu.

The moment lasted for no more than a couple of seconds. Then the curtain flicked closed, and he was left standing in the cloud of dust as the entourage went on up the road.

He waited until the bullocks were once more on the move before he sought out Luis.

'That was the lady from *Pearl*, wasn't it?' he asked, falling in step beside him.

'She will be on her way to be reunited with her family in Delhi.' Luis's eyes sparkled with excitement. He appeared elated by the encounter with the Mogul aristocrat and her escort.

'I suppose she will describe to them how she was treated on *Ganj-i-Sawa'i*?'

Luis nodded. 'What she says in the *zenana*, the women's quarters, may decide what happens to you and your friends. Mogul women stay in the background but they have great influence over their menfolk.'

They were talking as much as possible in Persian, because since leaving Diu, Hector had been making a determined effort to learn the language of the Mogul court. He had a good ear for languages and was making rapid progress and needed only an occasional word of English to fill in the gaps in his vocabulary. Now, hearing the note of excited admiration in the young man's voice, it had occurred to him that Luis might have his own reasons for being so fluent in the language of the ruling class.

'Where did you learn to speak so many languages? Surely not from your father, Jeronimo?' he asked casually.

'He taught me to speak Portuguese and some English but I spent most of my childhood with my mother's family so my first language is Gujerati,' Luis answered. 'My father and mother were never married. My mother's people are Surati *banyans* – what you call merchants – and they did not approve of him as a *feringhee*, though they treated me as one of their own. They want me to go into business and insisted I learned to write and speak Arabic, which is an important language of trade. But my Persian – that I learned for myself so that one day I might be considered to be Mogul. My skin is light enough.'

Luis pulled his shoulders back as if he was in the presence of his mother's family and defying them. 'I don't want to be a merchant, sitting in a counting house. Instead I will make myself useful to an *omrah* so that he takes me into his household, perhaps as a soldier. From there I can advance through the ranks and become an officer.'

'But what has that got to do with the colour of your skin?'

'When we get to Delhi, you will observe that those who are considered to be Mogul have a lighter skin than the native peoples. In addition, I am prepared to convert to the religion of their Prophet.'

Hector carefully avoided a heap of camel dung in the road before saying, 'Your father suggested to me that I enter Aurangzeb's service, in his army or his navy. But he didn't mention that I would have to change religion.'

Luis gave him a solemn look. 'For you it is not the same. You would always be *feringhee*, a Frank, but I am born in Hindustan.'

'And what does your Surati family think of your plan?'

'They would prefer that if I am determined to enter Mogul service it should be as an adviser or a tax collector, something that lets me keep their religion. My family are Hindoo, and many Hindoos hold important positions, the *omrahs* depend upon them.' Luis made a disdainful face. 'But such people are still regarded as inferiors.'

He broke off, interrupted by a jingling sound as a man ran past them at a fast jog trot, a bag slung over his shoulder and small bells attached to his belt. He continued up the road without stopping. When Hector had first seen a *dak* runner, Luis had told him that they ran in ten-mile relays, carrying the letters and official correspondence that passed between the Mogul governors and the imperial administration. Despite the scorching heat of the open road, each time a *dak* runner overtook them, Hector felt a chill of fear at the thought of the evidence piling up against him. When *Ganj-i-Sawa'i* docked in Surat, the Mogul governor must have sent his report to Delhi about the pillage and rape aboard the ship. Doubtless further correspondence had gone back and forth as the other vessels of the hajj fleet straggled into harbour with similar tales of a pirate attack.

With effort, he pushed such thoughts out of his mind. What mattered now was to concentrate on becoming sufficiently fluent in Persian so he could speak in his own defence, and that of his two friends, when the time came for him to face Mogul justice.

NOVEMBER WAS DRAWING to a close when it became apparent that Darshan's little group was at last approaching Aurangzeb's capital. Their road merged with others coming from different provinces of Hindustan, and the amount of traffic steadily increased until there was a constant stream of travellers, going in both directions. Now, instead of camping out in the villages, the *fawjdar* brought them to stay overnight in large mud-walled compounds conveniently situated a day's travel apart. Each compound was arranged as a hollow square with workshops, food stalls, tea houses, storerooms and stables along the walls. The travellers' every need was catered for, at a price. Vendors sold ready-cooked food, carpenters offered to mend damaged carts, leather workers were ready to stitch broken harness and metalworkers were capable of everything from riveting a patch on a holed cauldron to fitting the rim to a cartwheel. Incoming travellers tethered their animals in the open space in the centre and parked their vehicles there. Wealthier visitors hired sleeping rooms but everyone else found a spot where they could settle down among their heaps of baggage. It reminded Hector of 'Exceeding Treasure' with the pilgrims all crowded together on the main deck, though a caravanserai was noisier and smelled far worse. There were donkeys braying and camels bubbling and groaning, while bullocks, mules and horses contributed to the all-pervading stink of the barnyard.

On their final morning on the road, the highway was so thronged with pedestrians, carts and animals funnelling in towards the city that the dust hung like a thin fog. Hector was curious to know about the people on the move, so Luis gave him a running commentary. He could tell a man's occupation and status with a single quick glance. That man swaggering along holding his sword in its fancy scabbard with brasswork decoration was a Rajput soldier. Trotting at his heels and carrying his leather shield was his servant. The prim figure dressed in white from the neat cotton cap to the full-length skirt-like garment that Luis called a *dhoti* was a scholar or a scribe. A skeletal creature naked except for a scrap of a loincloth was a holy man. His skin was covered in scabs and ash, and a tangle of long filthy hair hung to his knees. The fingernails of the hand which held his begging bowl had been allowed to grow to a four-inch spiral. There was no need to identify a Mogul. From time to time a palanquin moved at head level through the throng preceded by staff-wielding attendants who cleared a passage. Four or six strong men carried the Mogul reclining in his couch slung between two stout poles. On one side of the palanquin walked a man wafting the air with an enormous fan of peacock feathers, on the other side a water carrier held a jug in case his master needed to quench his thirst. Next to the water carrier was an attendant carrying a spittoon to catch the grandee's spit.

Hector was looking forward to entering the Great Mogul's capital. He imagined a city of broad avenues lined with the magnificent mansions of the *omrahs*. So he was disappointed when, passing through a down-at-heel district, Luis abruptly announced that they had reached their destination.

'This is where Senhor Vieira has arranged for you and your friends to stay.'

Hector looked about him in surprise. The small houses lining the road were built of mud brick. Washing was hung out to dry on their roofs. A few roadside stalls had displays of dust-covered fruit and vegetables. To his right was a high wall of brick and plaster with a single large gate, firmly closed.

Luis had run forward to tell the carters to stop. The vehicles slowed to a halt and Luis held a brief conversation with Darshan. When he returned it was to say that the *fawjdar* insisted on delivering Gibson and the two sailors to the common goal in Delhi.

'He's not pleased about letting you and Jacques and Jezreel stay here,' the young man explained. 'I had to tell him that *omrah* Nizamuddin is expecting you. Like many *omrahs* he prefers to live outside the city where it is less crowded.'

Darshan was sitting in his bullock cart with his arms crossed. The sour expression on his long face made his displeasure clear. When Hector took a step towards the cage on the cart, intending to speak to Gibson, the *fawjdar* gave a sharp order, and the bullock drivers plied their whips. Hector could only stand and watch as the little convoy lurched forward and was soon lost from view among the other road users.

'Good riddance. Let's hope that's the last we see of *Pearl*'s quartermaster,' Jezreel said quietly beside him.

Hector felt a light touch on his elbow. It was Luis. 'You and your friends should come inside.' He went across to the gate and knocked several times. When the gate was finally pulled open a crack, he spoke to whoever was inside, then turned and beckoned for the travellers to follow.

After the cramped heat and dust of the streets, it was like

stepping into an oasis. There were flowering shrubs in earthenware pots, fruiting trees and a broad immaculately tended lawn.
A network of shallow channels fed clear running water into a
central basin where a fountain played. A number of small pavilions stood among the trees. They had elegant arched doorways
and roofs of small turquoise and gold tiles like the scales of exotic
reptiles. Half-hidden behind a hedge with purple flowers was a
low, plain building that evidently contained the kitchen and quarters for servants.

'This is Nasir, the head steward,' Luis was saying. 'He will
bring you to your quarters and see that you are comfortable.'

Nasir was a tall, grave-looking man with a beautifully bar-
bered pure white beard and dressed in a dark yellow tunic. At a
dignified walk he led the new arrivals along a footpath paved
with slabs of marble to the far side of the garden, where he
showed them into one of the smaller pavilions. Its sidewalls were
made of open latticework so that any breeze could circulate.
Inside were cushions and low tables, and a fine silk carpet with a
pattern of flowers and leaves. The pavilion, the steward explained
in careful Persian that Hector was able to follow easily, was for
their exclusive use. Their baggage would be brought there shortly
and he would arrange for some sherbet to be served. There was a
small bathhouse to the rear of the pavilion. He apologized for the
short delay before the water basins were filled and towels provided, but he had not received notice of their arrival. The main
meal of the day would be delivered to the pavilion soon after
evening prayers. It was important that they let the cooks know if
there were any foods that they preferred or were forbidden.

'This is the life,' announced Jacques dropping down on a
cushion with a contented sigh after the head steward had bowed
himself out.

'I wonder where Luis has got to?' Jezreel asked. Their guide
had quietly slipped away.

'I expect he's finding out when our *omrah* will be back in
Delhi,' Hector told him. 'A lot is going to depend on this Niza-

muddin, and whether he's prepared to use his influence on our behalf.'

'In the meantime I'm going to practise being a Mogul and let the future take care of itself,' Jacques said, lying back and kicking off his shoes. 'I trust the staff know how to make a good lemon sherbet.'

Hector did not hear him. He was gazing through the doorway of the pavilion and thinking of Maria. He pictured her out in the garden beside the fountain where a rose bush was showing a mass of vivid scarlet blossoms. She was reaching out to select a flower and drawing it closer to sniff its perfume. When she turned and looked back towards him, her face was alive with contentment. With a sudden jolt of memory, the image brought back the dream they had shared of moving to Libertalia and starting a new life with a smallholding of their own. He felt a deep sadness at the way everything seemed to have gone against him. He could accept that Libertalia had probably been a fantasy all along, but the possibility of entering the service of the Great Mogul had been very real. He could have brought Maria and their child to Hindustan, to enjoy a good life together as a family. Instead, he had reached Delhi under suspicion of the robbery and rape of the Aurangzeb's subjects. If found guilty, he would suffer a brutal death. Nothing had turned out as he had intended.

SIXTEEN

'WE'RE IN LUCK. Today there's to be a combat of elephants in front of the emperor himself,' Luis announced brightly when he appeared in the door of the pavilion early the following morning. 'It's something you should see.'

'What about *omrah* Nizamuddin? When do we get to meet him?' Hector reminded him.

'I spent last night at the house of one of my father's friends, and he tells me that the *omrah* Nizamuddin is away inspecting his estates. He won't return for several days.'

Judging from the young man's cheerful expression, Hector guessed that Luis had still not been told about the terrible injuries that Tavares had suffered. News of what had happened to the artilleryman might not have reached Delhi during the two months they had been on the road but, just as likely, Tavares had died of his burns while still at sea.

'Any news about the enquiry into what happened on *Ganj-i-Sawa'i*?'

Luis made a dismissive gesture. 'It'll be weeks before any Mogul official gets round to interviewing you.'

'What about Gibson and the others?'

'The *fawjdar* will put them safely under lock and key. I doubt we'll see them again until much later.' He was shifting impatiently from foot to foot. 'Unless we hurry, we'll miss the fight, and a chance to see Aurangzeb himself.'

It took an hour of brisk walking to get from Nizamuddin's country home to where the elephant combat was to take place — an open sandy area directly under the looming east wall of Aurangzeb's palace-cum-fort, Lal Qila. The imperial citadel was everything that Hector had expected of 'the ruler of the world'. It was enormous. From where he stood, the towering rampart of great blocks of red sandstone was topped with extravagant domes perched on thin columns, watch towers and turrets. He could only imagine the splendours of what lay behind such flamboy-antly awe-inspiring defences.

'Up there is where Aurangzeb watches,' said Luis excitedly, pointing to an ornate wooden balcony projecting halfway up the wall of the fort. 'Today's combat will only begin once he is seated.'

They joined a crowd of onlookers gathered around the edge of the open ground. At some distance away were two very large elephants. Both animals were clearly in a bad temper, flapping their ears rapidly and shifting uneasily from foot to foot. From time to time one of them trumpeted, a shrill bellow of rage. Anklets of heavy iron chain led back to massive pegs buried deep in the ground tethering both animals safely apart. Their handlers, two groups of about a dozen men, stood off to one side; several of them carried spears.

'What's that low wall for?' Jezreel asked. A section of mud-brick wall, some six feet high and thirty paces long, had been built in the open space in front of the imperial viewing gallery.

'So that the fight takes place directly under the emperor's view.'

'And the towers?'

At each end of the wall was a square tower, on top of which several men could be seen holding long lances.

'The towers are refuges for the men on foot, a place for them to escape to if something goes wrong,' Luis told him.

'And what do we do if that happens?'

Luis flashed him a radiant smile. 'We run! The fight is for the emperor's pleasure. When there is a public spectacle like a military parade or an exhibition, viewing stands are erected for spectators. But not today.'

Jacques had been watching the elephant handlers. One of them ran forward, adjusted a thick rope girdle around the belly of one of the elephants, then darted clear.

'What's he doing?' asked Jacques.

'That'll be the elephant's mahout, his rider. He's getting his animal prepared.'

'He seems frightened of the brute.'

'Because his elephant is *mast* and very dangerous. He knows his animal better than he knows his own family. He'll have grown up with the elephant. They share their lives.'

'Are you saying that the animal is drunk?' Hector asked in surprise. He had learned that in Persian *mast* meant drunk.

'No, no. *Mast* is a temporary illness. Imagine you have a very bad toothache and the constant pain makes you want to lash out. That is what it is like for a bull elephant in the time of *mast*. He becomes mean and dangerous, even to his mahout. That is why *mast* elephants are chosen for the combat. If we could get closer, you would see that both elephants have a dark liquid running down the side of the head, from a hole behind the ear. That discharge is a sign that they are *mast*.'

'I'll take your word for it. I've no wish to come any closer,' muttered Jacques.

The young man chuckled. 'Don't worry, Jacques. Most of the elephants you will meet are females. They're the ones used for carrying loads and pulling the emperor's great cannon. Bull elephants are trained for war, to charge the enemy, gouge them with their tusks, stamp them into the ground.'

A general stir among the crowd, and a blast of trumpets followed by a roll of kettledrums announced that something was about to happen. Squinting up at the imperial viewing gallery,

Hector could make out men beginning to take up their positions. Even from a distance he could see that they were sumptuously dressed. There was the sheen of bright silks in the morning sunshine and the occasional sparkle of a turban ornament.

An outburst of outraged animal squeals brought his attention back down to the two elephants. Men on foot were poking at them with long lances, manoeuvring them into position, one animal to each end of the mud wall though on opposite sides of it. Their ankle chains were no longer attached to the ground pegs, but rattled and clanked as they trailed behind them. The beasts were growing increasingly furious, swaying and bellowing, sweeping their trunks from side to side. To his astonishment he saw that each animal carried two riders. His mahout sat on the beast's neck with his feet tucked in behind the angrily flapping ears. A second man was farther back, lying almost flat on the animal's spine and clinging to the girth rope that circled the animal's belly. Hector shivered in sympathy, wondering why the maddened animal did not reach back with its trunk, pluck off his mahout and fling him to the ground. Then he realized that both beasts were too intent on attacking the other. On a hidden signal they charged at one another, running forward with a curious stiff-legged gait. They met head to head though separated by the low wall, in a flurry of violent squeals and roars. They reached across the wall with their trunks, trying to pull their adversary close enough to gouge with their tusks. Over the clamour of grunts and bellows came thin cries of encouragement from their mahouts. They were urging on their beasts, kicking them behind the ears, jabbing the sharp points of iron goads into their necks.

For several minutes the two great creatures battled, their trunks entwined, twisting and heaving to gain advantage. They butted one another and lunged with their tusks. The contest seemed to have reached deadlock when, at a yell of command from his mahout, the larger of the two beasts disengaged. It backed away a few paces, rose on its hind legs and threw itself forward bodily, crashing down on the mud wall with its front feet. The top of the wall broke away in a cloud of dust. Seconds later the huge beast was scrambling over the obstacle. It closed with its foe, locked its trunk around its opponent's head, and twisted. Like an overpowered wrestler, the second elephant buckled. The front legs bent and it dropped on its front knees, sending its rider head over heels into the sand. Behind him his companion lost his grip on the rope girdle and fell to the ground. He disappeared among the legs of the victorious elephant as it pressed itself forward, gouging with its tusks, stamping with its huge feet, intent on killing its opponent.

Into this turmoil ran a dozen of the elephant handlers. They had firebrands tied to the ends of their spears which they waved in front of the victor, shouting to distract it and trying to force it to back off. Two men joined them, equipped with strings of lit firecrackers dangling from long poles. They held them close beneath the animal's head until the snap and flare of the fireworks had their effect. The great beast pivoted on its hind legs, and lumbered away, head swinging from side to side in fury and fear as the handlers, puny in size, ran behind trying to gather up the trailing leg chains. Moments later a gate in the wall of the fortress opened, and half a dozen more elephants came out at a run. Urged on by their mahouts, they caught up with the fleeing bull elephant and boxed it in, finally forcing it to a halt. Heavy straps were passed around the animal and secured, and it was slowly escorted away.

'That was magnificent, wasn't it?' asked Luis, his eyes shining. 'The emperor will reward the successful mahout handsomely.'

Hector exhaled deeply – he had not been aware that he had been holding his breath – and his eyes searched for the dismounted mahout. The man was being taken from the field in a makeshift litter while his defeated elephant was struggling to get back on its feet. All that remained of the beast's second rider was a shapeless lump lying on the sand. He looked up at the viewing balcony where Aurangzeb and his courtiers had watched the show. Already the Great Mogul and his courtiers had departed.

'I wouldn't mind having something cool to drink,' he said.

*

THEY FOLLOWED LUIS across the sand and in through a gate in Delhi's city wall. Once inside, Hector understood why *omrah* Nizamuddin preferred to have his residence elsewhere. Delhi's streets were narrow and cramped, hemmed in by the mould-streaked facades of buildings that rose on either side for three or four storeys. The air was stifling, with frequent whiffs of rotting matter mixing with the smells of charcoal cooking and incense. At every corner clusters of idlers gazed at passers-by and chatted amongst themselves, while sweepers, water carriers, night-soil porters trudged the alleys, rattling wooden clappers, clanging bells, and uttering long wailing cries as they tried to sell their services.

Fortunately, Luis knew his way and took them briskly through a succession of twists and turns until they came out on to a broad, straight avenue. 'This leads from the west gate of the city directly to the great square at the main entrance of Lal Qila. There we'll be able to find stalls offering every sort of food and drink,' he informed his companions.

The avenue was crowded with people dressed in an extraordinary variety of colours and styles. There were men in long flowing gowns and sandals, others in pantaloons under loose flapping shirts that reached down to their knees. A few were naked to the waist, barefoot and with nothing but a loincloth. Turbans ranged from tightly wound, neat bandages of bright scarlet to huge wheel-like arrangements that used yards of cloth and projected a hands span beyond the wearer's head. Beards could be long or neatly trimmed, snowy white or artificially black and oiled. Several were tinted with bright orange dye. The women favoured long shawls in pale yellow, white or lime green edged with broad stripes of indigo and violet. Chattering knowledgeably,

Luis identified Kashmiris, Biharis, Bengalis and men from the Deccan by the differences in their appearance and dress. 'Each and every one of them acknowledges the Great Mogul as their overlord and has come to his capital. Is he not the greatest lord on earth?' he boasted.

Eventually the avenue opened out into a large square in front of the principal entrance to Aurangzeb's palace, an immense barbican of red sandstone blocks three storeys high. Here the crowd thinned enough for Luis to point out lines of booths used by fortune tellers, astrologers, moneylenders, bankers and letter writers.

'Pay no attention to the hucksters,' he warned, shooing away a man blocking their path as he tried to sell them brightly coloured sweetmeats from a tray swarming with flies. 'They're rogues who will cheat anyone they think is a foreigner. I'm taking you to a place that serves drinks cooled with ice.'

'Ice in this heat?' asked Jezreel. Great patches of sweat soaked the underarms of his shirt, and his face was flushed.

'The imperial household has a regular supply of ice brought in straw-wrapped blocks from the mountains in the north, but not all of it reaches the palace . . . some of it melts on the way.'

Jacques had come to a dead stop. He was staring into the teeming crowd ahead of them with a look of utter disbelief. 'François Dufour, as I live and breathe,' he exclaimed, 'Dressed up like a pastry cook's disaster.'

Moving through the crowd was a figure in a costume so extravagant that it made the most exotic native costumes seem drab. A very tall, thin white man wore a three-quarter-length coat of sky blue taffeta with wide skirts that flared out over a triple layer of short, wide, frilly petticoats. Below them were exposed several inches of pink satin knee breeches, then white silk stockings and finally a pair of gleaming yellow shoes with three-inch heels that obliged their wearer to move with small, deliberate steps. Most bizarre of all was his wig. A cone of starched white curls rose at least a foot above his head and was decorated with tiny silver ribbons that glinted in the sun. For a moment Hector was reminded of the deputy governor of Diu in his ornate formal dress, though Pedro Vieira's costume would have looked restrained beside the stranger's finery.

Luis had followed Jacques's gaze. 'That's the Sieur de Tourville. Everyone in Delhi knows who he is: he advises several of the wealthiest *omrahs* on their purchases of gems and pearls. The rumour is that he may even be appointed as jeweller-in-chief to the Great Mogul himself.'

'No, he's not,' said Jacques firmly. 'He's François Dufour, the most devious fence in Paris.'

'I'm sorry, what do you mean "fence"?' Luis enquired.

'Someone who takes in stolen goods and sells them on discreetly,' Jacques told him. 'François Dufour gives you five per cent of what an item is really worth, even when he has someone lined up who will buy it from him for ten times as much, and no questions asked.'

Leaving Luis to wonder how he came by this information, Jacques shoved his way through the throng and tapped the tall man on the elbow. 'Well met, François. I didn't know you had joined the aristocracy,' he said in French.

The man turned and peered down. He wore a thick mask of white face powder. 'And who might you be, sir?' he demanded haughtily. He spoke in English but with a strong French accent.

'Jacques Bourdon, your former customer,' Jacques told him, switching to English.

Hector had caught up with the two men and watched Dufour hesitate for the briefest moment before answering in an affected drawl, 'Bourdon? I can't say that I remember that name.'

Jacques gave a derisive snort. 'Come on, François. What about your little office tucked away in a side street on the Île de la Cité? We met there often enough.'

Again the hesitation, longer this time, as Dufour calculated whether he should keep up his pretence of ignorance. By now several onlookers were staring at the two *feringhees*, wondering what was going on between them.

Dufour threw up an elegant hand in a gesture of mock surprise. 'Why, of course . . . I must apologize for not recognizing you sooner, Jacques. How are things in Paris? And our gracious monarch?'

'Haven't set foot in Paris for years, and I'm not likely to go back there.' Jacques touched a finger to the galley convict marks on his cheek.

Dufour's eyes flickered round the bystanders, now openly listening to the conversation. Hector doubted if any of them understood English, though clearly they were intrigued by the spectacle of the gorgeously dressed jeweller exchanging words with an unpretentious foreigner.

Dufour forced a smile. 'Why don't we step across to my place, and share a glass of wine? Catch up with news. I live close by.'

Jacques glanced at Hector seeking his approval. He nodded.

Together they accompanied Dufour as he picked his way carefully across the square and into the warren of narrow streets that lapped up against the walls of Lal Qila.

'This is a most auspicious encounter,' Luis whispered to Hector. 'The Sieur de Tourville is ranked among the most influential *feringhees* in all of Delhi. He may be able to assist when it comes to your trial.'

They arrived before one of the better-kept houses in the quarter, a tall, narrow building whose heavy door on to the street was protected by a watchman with a six-foot bamboo staff. Dufour muttered something to the guard who stood aside. A flight of stairs took them up to the first floor where Dufour groped for a key inside a petticoat pocket, unlocked another door and they found themselves in a large, high-ceilinged room. Slatted wooden shutters were closed to keep out the sun and left the air still and lifeless. All the furniture was European, with several chairs, a desk, a large settee and a sturdy iron safe in one corner.

'Welcome to my home,' said Dufour closing the door behind them and turning the key, locking them in. He reached up and detached his wig, revealing a shaved scalp prickled with beads of sweat. He placed the wig carefully on a wig stand, before letting out a great sigh and taking off his gaudy coat, which he folded neatly and set on one side. Finally he removed his shoes and put on a pair of low, flat slippers. Even without his three-inch heels, François Dufour stood a couple of inches over six feet tall.

'And who are your companions, Jacques?' he asked crossing to a table on which stood a heavy clay jug. He poured out five glasses of water to which he added a generous measure of red wine from a porcelain flagon with a graceful curved spout. Jacques introduced Hector and the others, and as Dufour handed each man his glass, he treated him to an appraising glance with sharp, deep set eyes that missed nothing.

'Here's to your health,' he said raising his own glass, 'and if you want it to continue, stick to Ganges river water mixed with wine from Shiraz, a safe combination. Just don't drink any of the muck that is offered to you in the bazaar.'

Indicating to his guests to be seated, he settled himself on a comfortable chair, stretched out his long legs in their silk stockings and when Jacques opened his mouth to speak, lifted a hand to stop him.

'Jacques, I know what you're going to ask. So first let me tell you that you see before you a gentleman of the bedchamber to his most august Majesty King Louis of France and also his former assistant keeper of the royal jewels, who now acts as his personal envoy to the Great Mogul in a private capacity.'

He looked around the faces of his guests and his voice now had a note of warning. 'I would be grateful if you would keep that in mind, for my own well-being and yours.'

He took another taste of his watered wine. 'Now let me put your curiosity at rest. I came to Delhi three years ago and have been living here ever since. For this happy change in my circumstances I have to thank a certain lady who attended what Jacques calls my "Paris office". She nearly brought disaster, but instead thrust me into this new and most agreeable career.'

He took a moment to run a finger round his neck band, loosening the lace cravat. 'The lady was of the nobility and married to a peer. She came late in the evening, uninvited and without her usual gaggle of attendants. She brought with her a collection of fine jewels for which she asked me to find a buyer. When she showed me the jewels – an exceptional collection of pearls and diamonds, including several unique pieces – I recognized them instantly. They were so valuable that even if I had made a ridiculously low offer for them –' and here he treated Jacques to a knowing glance – 'none of my trade acquaintances would be able to raise a sufficient sum to buy them from me.

'I was also aware that the collection was not the lady's property for her to sell. Of course, I should have declined to be involved. Instead I foolishly agreed to hold the jewels in safe keeping for a few days while I considered the matter.' He smiled ruefully to himself at the memory. 'The truth was that she was extraordinarily beautiful and I agreed to take in the jewels only because it meant I would see her again when she came to collect them. It was very naive of me.

'Within days,' he continued, 'the loss of so important a collection of gems was noticed by their rightful owner – a duke who held high ministerial office – and my beautiful lady was promptly placed under suspicion and taken in by the police for questioning. I knew that, under pressure, she would reveal where the jewels would be found, and that put me in an impossible position.'

He looked across at his audience; all four of them were listening closely.

'Have any of you heard of Jean-Baptiste Tavernier, by any chance?'

When no one answered, he got up and went across to his desk. Pulling open a drawer, he took out a book and held it up with a flourish. 'Published fifteen years ago at the request of the Sun King himself. Here, Tavernier tells of his six voyages to the Orient dealing in precious stones. He bought, sold, bartered and made exceptional profits. Among his clients were kings, rajas, princes, the Great Mogul himself. Every jeweller and gem merchant in Paris read his book with envy.'

He replaced the book and closed the drawer. 'For me, fearing any moment to hear the police hammering at my door, his book was an epiphany. I asked myself: why not pick up where Jean-Baptiste left off and use the beautiful lady's jewels as my initial stock in trade? I would follow in his footsteps, take the collection east where it was unknown, sell or barter it piece by piece and become another Tavernier.'

His smile of satisfaction swept around all four of his listeners as he returned to his chair, and sat down.

'So here I am: adviser and jewel expert at the court of the Great Mogul and confidant to a number of the most important *omrahs*.'

'Didn't the established gem dealers in Delhi resent your arrival?' Hector asked.

Dufour gave him a sly look. 'Of course. But I discovered that the chief among them had been less than honest with his principal client. He had passed off several flawed diamonds as being perfect. Jacques here will tell you that I have a good eye for the qualities of a gem.'

'And not above telling a poor thief that what he's stolen is defective or a fake made of hardened glass, when really it's a perfect stone,' Jacques observed sourly.

Dufour shrugged. 'Professional expertise. Besides, the native gem cutters of Hindustan can be clumsy. They make errors, ruin perfectly good stones, and I've been able to show them some new techniques in cutting and polishing.'

He cocked his head on one side and fixed Jacques with a steady gaze. 'And how about you, my friend? What brings you to Delhi with your companions?'

It took Jacques several minutes to explain what had happened since he, Hector and Jezreel had joined Avery's crew aboard

Fancy in Madagascar. When he described the attack on *Ganj-i-Sawa'i*, and Mayes's ill-judged attempt to extract a ransom for the woman he believed to be Aurangzeb's sister, Dufour shook his head in disbelief. 'I like the sound of Captain Avery. He showed brains as well as imagination and courage. But Mayes is an idiot. If Aurangzeb's people get their hands on him, something very unpleasant will happen to him.'

He paused to take a sip from his glass of wine and his voice took on a warning edge as he added, 'The same is true for anyone they consider to be an accomplice.'

'I have a supporting letter from the deputy governor of Diu,' Hector told him. 'It explains that my companions and I should not be held responsible for what happened on *Ganj-i-Sawa'i*. I'm to deliver it to *omrah* Nizamuddin and ask him to use his influence on our behalf. We're staying at his residence, waiting for his return.'

Dufour pulled a face. '*Omrah* Nizamuddin isn't going to be much help to you, I'm afraid.'

'But we were told that he is a friend to foreigners.'

'He is, and it's tripped him up. When Aurangzeb first heard what happened on *Ganj-i-Sawa'i*, he flew into a rage. Seldom has anyone seen him so angry. Normally he keeps his face expressionless. But I have it on very good authority from an *omrah* who was at the meeting of the council that Aurangzeb went pale with anger. Nizamuddin made the mistake of speaking up, suggesting that it would be wise to wait for confirmation of the assault. Aurangzeb took off his slipper and hurled it at Nizamuddin's head.'

Seeing his listeners were puzzled, he explained, 'To be beaten with a shoe or have one hurled at you is the greatest insult possible. Nizamuddin immediately bowed to the ground, uttered an abject apology and backed out of the council chamber. He has not been seen since, and is unlikely to return to Delhi until this whole affair has blown over.'

'And when will that be?' Hector asked.

'When Aurangzeb receives satisfaction from the English in Surat for what he considers a sacrilegious crime perpetrated by barbaric idolaters.'

Dufour crossed and uncrossed his long legs, smoothing the layers of petticoats to make himself more comfortable. When he spoke again, his voice had a lecturer's tone. 'In Mogul law the extended family is held to be responsible for the misdeeds of any of its members. The pirates who savagely attacked *Ganj-i-Sawa'i* were mostly from England or her colonies. So Aurangzeb expects their countrymen in Surat to make amends and to pay the penalty. He has ordered the cancellation of all permits for trade issued to English merchants. They will not be renewed until the English authorities have caught and punished those pirates responsible. Further, the English are to pay damages, a sum equivalent to the value of all the goods stolen from *Ganj-i-Sawa'i*. The money is to be handed over to the imperial treasury because the ship was the personal property of the Great Mogul, a fact that your greedy captain Mayes worked out for himself.'

There was complete silence in the room when Dufour finished speaking. Hector had seldom seen Jacques and Jezreel look so taken aback. There was a hint of tears in Luis's eyes and Hector guessed that the gem merchant's bleak assessment had put an end to the young man's hopes of ever achieving the status of a Mogul. 'So what do you suggest we do next?' he asked Dufour.

'For a start, retrieve your baggage from where you left it at Nizamuddin's and bring it here to this house. You're better off to cut any connection with him. The floor above this one is empty and I own the lease. You can move in while I take soundings with some of the *omrahs* that I know, find out if someone else might help your case.'

'That's very generous of you,' Hector mumbled.

Dufour gave him a look that was both sympathetic and pitying. 'If you live long enough, you'll discover that Delhi is a clannish place. Afghans, Uzbeks, Persians, Turks – each group sticks together. *Feringhees* do the same. If we didn't help one another we foreigners would be swallowed up by the whirlpool.'

*

THAT EVENING, after they had collected their meagre possessions and moved into Dufour's building, Hector sat down to compose a letter to Maria. He wanted to tell her where he was and that he was still thinking of their future. But he struggled to find the words to raise her spirits without misleading her. In his thoughts he could not avoid comparing himself with Dufour. They had both followed a vision of how to escape from their past, and start afresh in a foreign land. Libertalia had been his dream; Dufour had launched out in search of Tavernier's wealthy oriental clients to win their favour. Now Dufour was thriving and successful while he and his friends had lost control of their lives and were waiting to face Mogul justice.

After several attempts, he crumpled up the sheet of writing paper and threw it away.

SEVENTEEN

NOVEMBER TURNED TO DECEMBER and still they had no idea of what would happen to them. The days were pleasantly sunny and bright, but they were cold enough to require woollen clothing, and the nights were positively chilly. On some mornings a dense, clammy fog hung over the street as Luis left the house early to buy food from the market. The attack on *Ganj-i-Sawa'i* was common gossip in the city, and the market was a good place for him to pick up any rumours about what action Aurangzeb and his council were taking in response. But he heard nothing. Nor could Dufour learn anything at his meetings with *omrahs* who sought his advice when buying or selling jewellery. The gem dealer concluded that the pillage and rape aboard *Ganj-i-Sawa'i* was still too sensitive a subject with Aurangzeb for the Mogul nobles to discuss openly. In mid-January, when the silence continued, Jezreel suggested that perhaps their case had been forgotten and they should think about quietly slipping from Delhi, head to the coast and find a ship to take them beyond Aurangzeb's reach. Dufour was more cautious. He advised Hector to send Luis to the office of the Khan-i-Sama, the *omrah* in charge of the imperial household. The young man should buy information from the *omrah*'s staff using what remained from the money that Pedro Vieira had provided for their travel expenses. Luis returned from his errand to report that after taking the bribe, one of the Hindu clerks had told him that, far from being forgotten, the attack on *Ganj-i-Sawa'i* was under active consideration. Aurangzeb and his councillors were pressing the English merchants in Surat to respond to their demand for payment of damages and the punishment of the offenders. Hearing this, Dufour advised the three friends to be patient and stay on in the capital. If they tried to leave, they risked arrest and joining Quartermaster Gibson and the others in detention. He assured them that he was making so much money from his trade in precious stones that he could easily afford to keep them on as his guests.

In February everything changed. It was on a day when Dufour, with no appointments to meet with his *omrah* clients, decided to visit a friend of his, another Frenchman.

'Frederic has an unusual job – gunnery instructor with the *shutarnal*, the camel artillery. You'll find it interesting. Why don't you come along with me?' he suggested to Hector.

Hector immediately accepted the invitation, thinking of Tavares. There was still no news of the wounded artilleryman, and Luis remained ignorant of his father's injuries. If Tavares had died from his burns, Hector preferred to break the news to the young man himself. Dufour's friend was also a gunner in the Mogul forces, so he might have heard something.

'Could you advance Luis some more cash,' he asked the jeweller, 'this might be a good time to send him to speak again with his contact on the Khan-i-Sama's staff.'

Luis set out with five shiny new rupees in his money belt, and Hector and Dufour descended the stairs to the street.

'The camel brigade is quartered on the edge of town, and I don't intend to walk there,' Dufour explained, sending the doorkeeper to fetch a double palanquin. By his usual standards the Frenchman was dressed modestly: a tailored coat of maroon silk and a loosely wound turban of the same material, black satin breeches and patterned stockings. Nevertheless, his shoes had two-inch scarlet heels.

The palanquin arrived and was set down on the ground so they could climb in. The sudden tilt and sway as the eight bearers, grunting in unison, hoisted it on their shoulders, made Hector clutch the sides and brought a smile to Dufour's lips.

'It's much worse when a camel gets on its feet. If Frederic suggests you try riding one of his awkward beasts, don't accept the offer.'

Dufour was completely at ease, lying back, long legs outstretched as the palanquin men set off at a steady trot. 'Hector, you've never told me how you came to be in Madagascar with your friend at the start of your adventures.'

Hector was getting used to the motion of the palanquin, jogging and swaying at the same time. 'I had heard about a country called Libertalia close to Madagascar, a land with rich soil and a gentle climate where men make their own laws and there are no fences because all property is held in common. I intended to settle there with my wife.'

Dufour gave a cynical smile. 'Sounds like the Land of Cockayne, where the sky rains cheese and monks spank nuns on their bare white backsides.'

Hector had to suppress a grin. 'It was a countryman of yours, Captain Misson, who is said to have stolen a navy ship and sailed off to set up Libertalia. But I've never been able to track down Misson, and I've got to the point that I think he never existed.'

'You may be in luck. My friend Frederic learned his gunnery skills as an officer in the French navy. He may have heard of your Misson.'

It took them nearly an hour to reach the barracks where the camel brigade was quartered. From some distance away they heard the noise from the animal pens — an unhappy chorus of long-drawn-out groans and grumbles interrupted with angry roaring bellows as if the beasts were suffering from aching guts. The stench hit Hector as he got out of the palanquin: a smell of dung mixed with urine and sun-dried sweat. It occurred to him that on his journey to Delhi he had never seen a camel inside a caravanserai unless it was kept in a separate enclosure. Usually the creatures were tethered outside the walls. Now he knew the reason.

Dufour's friend Frederic was oblivious to the noise and smells. A stocky, square-headed man with farmer's hands and grimy fingers, he was wearing a worn quilted jacket over woollen trousers, and heavy leather boots. Standing at a workbench in the barnlike arsenal building, he was testing the firing operation of a huge musket, repeatedly pulling the lanyard so the hammer snapped forward, re-setting the trigger and then tugging the cord again.

The gunner looked up from his work and greeted Dufour with a broad smile. 'What brings such a magnificent creature down to the camel slums?' he asked.

'I thought my friend Hector would like to see how you use your toys.'

The artilleryman patted the barrel of the musket. 'The "wasp" – that's what the troops call it. Mounted on the back of the camel, it can give a bad sting.' He sighed. 'Or at least, that's what our Mogul masters would like to see.'

'You don't sound convinced,' Hector said. Stripped of its ornate brass fittings, the gun was a smaller version of the falconet fired over the dead pirate's grave in St Mary's.

'The theory's all right. Placed high up on a camel's hump, it can shoot over the heads of the enemy infantry and into their rear ranks. The trouble is that once it's fired, how do you reload the thing? It's a one-shot wonder.'

'Doesn't the camel get a fright?'

The gunner grinned. 'A terrified camel galloping through the infantry causes havoc. Effective if it heads into the enemy lines.'

Hector remembered the fireworks used to separate the fighting bull elephants. 'And what about the elephants? Do they panic as well?'

'Elephants can be trained to ignore gunfire ... so too can horses. But camels are jittery.'

The gunner wiped his hands on a length of cotton waste, and began escorting them towards the door of the armoury.

'Are you looking to take service with the Mogul?' he asked Hector.

'Hector was on *Ganj-i-Sawa'i* when she was attacked,' Dufour explained. 'He's waiting to be questioned about what happened.'

The gunner must have supposed that Hector was a member of the crew of the great ship. He let out a breathy whistle of surprise. 'I wonder if you know what happened to Jeronimo Tavares, a *hazari* with the big gun batteries? A friend of mine. He was posted to the ship, to manage her heavy armament.'

'I was going to ask you the same question,' Hector told him. 'Tavares was badly burned when one of the main cannon blew up. When I last saw him, he was barely alive and on *Ganj-i-Sawa'i* heading for Surat.'

'I hope he's all right,' said the Frenchman. 'Jeronimo's a good man, even though he's with the elephants. The big gun men tend to look down on the "wasps" – they complain of the noise and stink. As if elephants don't smell too!'

Later, during lunch with the artilleryman, Hector used the chance to ask him if he had ever met a Captain Misson when he was serving with the French navy.

'Misson . . . Misson . . .' the artilleryman said slowly. 'Don't think so. Knew a Lieutenant Masson, but he never made captain as far as I know. Do you have any more details?'

'He commanded a ship named *Victoire*.'

'Only *Victoire* I came across was a privateer, small sloop. Not a navy vessel. Mind you, it's a common enough name for a ship.'

'Perhaps that's why the name was chosen by whoever started this fantasy,' murmured Dufour, making it plain that he was still sceptical of the whole story. Hector decided to let the subject drop.

*

THEY GOT BACK TO Dufour's apartment in the city centre just as the brief Indian dusk was closing in, and the air was full of the smell of woodsmoke and the grating calls of crows searching for their roosts. Luis heard them climbing the stairs and met them on the landing in front of Dufour's rooms. He was shifting from foot to foot in his excitement. Hector could not tell whether the expression on his face showed anxiety or relief, or both.

'I've some news!' the young man announced eagerly.

'Then fetch the others,' said Dufour, unlocking the door to his rooms. 'So that everyone can hear what it is.'

Luis ran back up the stairs to fetch Jezreel and Jacques and when all of them were seated in Dufour's front room, he told them: 'Last week two English merchants arrived in Delhi from Surat. They came with an answer to Aurangzeb's demand for damages to be paid for the attack on *Ganj-i-Sawa'i.*'

'Do we know who these two men are?' asked Dufour.

'Yes indeed!' Luis was keen to show off his knowledge. 'From their descriptions I am sure that one of them is Mr Samuel Annesley. He's the East India Company's Chief Factor in Surat and leader of the English traders there. The other man is a member of his council, Mr Ephraim Bendall. They are both very important men.'

Dufour leaned forward. 'And did you manage to learn what answer they brought to Aurangzeb's demands?'

Luis shook his head. 'Only that they had a very long meeting with the wazir in charge of the government's finances. Rumour has it that they disputed the value that the wazir had placed on the stolen cargo from *Ganj-i-Sawa'i.* He told them that if they didn't pay the correct sum into the treasury, their trade in Surat would be shut down permanently and all English merchants expelled.'

Dufour looked across at Hector. 'So matters are coming to a head. Aurangzeb's people will pursue this matter until it is concluded.'

'There's more,' Luis hurried on. 'My contact on the Khan-i-Sama's staff mentioned that he was disappointed not to see the "infidel pirates", as he called them, put on public trial for attacking the Mogul's own ship. They're to appear before a *qadi* in the Lal Qila and it's to be a special closed sitting.'

A puzzled look appeared on Dufour's face. 'Aurangzeb himself holds open court when he listens to his people's grievances. I wonder what makes this case so different.'

'When's our trial to take place?' Jacques asked bluntly.

'Very soon,' Luis told him. 'According to my informant it will be while the two English merchants are still in Delhi.'

Jacques grimaced. 'That gives me an uncomfortable feeling that the verdict is already decided. Perhaps we should reconsider Jezreel's idea of slipping out of Delhi and making our escape.'

'Don't!' Dufour warned him sharply. 'If the three of you vanished, I'd be held responsible.'

'The authorities have no idea that we are staying with you,' Jezreel objected.

The gem dealer scowled at him. 'Whenever Luis goes to the marketplace, trying to pick up news about what is happening over *Ganj-i-Sawa'i*, you can be sure that others make a note of who he is and which house he comes from. As a matter of routine, that information has been passed on to the *kotwal*, the chief of the city police.'

The atmosphere in the room was becoming strained. To ease the tension, Hector spoke up. 'We stay where we are and go to trial,' he said. 'Then we'll produce the letter from Governor Vieira, and make our case that we gained nothing from the looting of *Ganj-i-Sawa'i*.'

But he was thinking of a reason why the trial was to be held out of public view: it was because Aurangzeb's sister had been aboard and the good reputation of the Great Mogul's family was involved.

*

MID-MORNING three days later the doorkeeper in front of Dufour's building sent up a small boy with a message that an official from the *kotwal*'s office was waiting in the street outside. Luis went down to speak with him and returned to say that Hector and Jezreel were summoned to the Lal Qila to appear before a *qadi*.

'And what about me?' asked Jacques.

'He said he's come to fetch only the Englishmen.'

Jacques was not to be put off. 'Then at least I ought to come along as a witness.'

Luis shook his head. 'A *qadi* doesn't need witnesses. He asks questions of the accused about the evidence against them, and then makes his judgement. I was told that I am to attend as an interpreter.'

With Governor Vieira's letter safe in an inside pocket Hector followed Luis and Jezreel down the stairs. The *kotwal*'s man wasn't the burly policeman he had expected, but a diffident elderly figure wearing a woollen blanket over his shoulders against the cold and holding a mace of polished wood tipped with silver. They followed him through the narrow streets and into the public square in front of the looming entrance to the Lal Qila. As usual the square was bustling with customers for its booths and shops, idlers, entertainers and pedlars. All of them quickly stood aside to leave a path as soon as they saw the *kotwal*'s mace. One or two hucksters turned their faces away so as not to be recognized. Two more policemen with silver-tipped staffs were waiting in front of the barbican. They flanked a gaunt, black-bearded foreigner dressed in ill-fitting, but clean, shirt and trousers. A light steel chain was looped between his wrists. It took Hector a moment to recognize *Pearl*'s quartermaster, Gibson.

'Where are the other two men from *Pearl*?' Hector asked, shocked. Gibson had lost so much weight that he was almost skeletal. His skin had a sickly pallor, and his eyes sunken in their sockets had a haunted look.

'Gaol fever,' he muttered, his hoarse voice just above a whisper. 'One's near death, and the other like to follow him. Too weak and sick to be brought here.'

With a stab of guilt, Hector realized that he had given no

thought to Gibson and his two fellow sailors since the day *fawjdar* Darshan had led them away from *omrah* Nizamuddin's house.

'We're to be questioned about what happened on *Ganj-i-Sa-wa'i*,' he told the quartermaster.

'About time too.' Gibson's voice was a little stronger but still strained. 'Been looking forward to it.'

There was something about this last remark which made Hector look more closely at *Pearl*'s quartermaster. This was a new, subdued Gibson. Three months in a Delhi goal had beaten the bully out of him. The previous bluster and aggression had gone. Yet there was still a flicker of defiance in his eyes.

A palace official, resplendent in a surcoat and matching turban of red and gold, detached himself from the group of soldiers guarding the entrance to the Lal Qila and came towards them. Evidently they were expected, for he exchanged a few words with the policemen, then indicated that they were to bring the *fering-hees* inside the palace complex. The covered passageway through the barbican was a miniature bazaar lit with scores of hanging oil lamps fitted with mirrors. There were racks of exotic furs, jewellery in glass-fronted cabinets and every imaginable fabric and colour: swags and bolts of expensive silk, velvet, damask, brocade and fine muslin. It was abundantly clear that those who lived or worked within the Lal Qila loved dressing up in finery and could afford high prices.

They emerged on the avenue leading to the centre of the imperial enclave. Every few yards a sweeper was wielding his broom, making sure that the roadway was spotless, and a small army of gardeners was tending flower beds – mostly marigolds. The large buildings that lined the avenue were made from the same red sandstone as the defensive ramparts. To his left Hector identified the nearest ones as barracks and stables for elephants and horses. Facing them across the avenue were buildings three and four storeys high and with balconies and balustrades. He was about to ask if they provided accommodation for favoured members of the Mogul's immense retinue when he was distracted by the sight of a court grandee strolling towards them. The *omrah* was robed in a frock coat of cherry pink and yellow, nipped in at the waist and flaring out in a skirt that reached to his knees. The material was so stiff with gold and silver embroidery that he seemed encased in precious metal. His tight leggings were of striped silk, and his slippers with their turned-up pointed toes were sewn with tiny pearls. A jewelled brooch was pinned to the front of his turban of heavy silk, and several ropes of larger pearls hung around his neck. More gems gleamed on his finger rings and on the handle and sheath of the ornamental sword hanging from a broad silk sash.

Tactfully their escort stepped aside and waited until the *omrah* had sauntered past with his entourage, before leading his little group through a double courtyard linked by an arcade. Luis sucked in his breath in mild alarm. Falling in step beside the young man, Hector asked quietly, 'Is something the matter?'

'We're going in the direction of the *zenana*, the women's quarters,' Luis whispered.

'How do you know?'

'My father sometimes brought me into the Lal Qila when visiting officers of the garrison. I was shown the Diwan-i-Am, the Great Hall, where Aurangzeb holds audiences for his people. I thought that's where we were being taken. But this is the way to the royal apartments and they are off-limits.'

They passed through an area where high walls blocked the view on either side until they came out on a broad grassy terrace that was the setting for a large, elegant pavilion. In contrast to the previous tones of red and pink sandstone, this building was the purest white marble. Delicate fretwork filled the upper parts of the five scalloped arches that formed the facade, and the slanting light of the wintry sun brought out the pearl-like lustre of the stone. Hector did not need anyone to tell him that this graceful construction had been designed to accommodate the womenfolk of the royal family.

By now, it was evident that the *kotwal*'s men shared Luis' disquiet at venturing so close to the *zenana*. They were exchanging worried looks and had slowed their pace, falling back several yards behind their guide. Their nervousness increased to open dismay as half a dozen heavily armed guards left their posts in front of the pavilion and came striding across the terrace to intercept them. The guards were squat and brawny and wore the red and gold that Hector now recognized as the colours of the Mogul's personal household. Shirts of chain mail reached to their thighs, and they were equipped with short curved swords and steel helmets. Some carried small circular shields of leather. Forming up in an aggressive line, they blocked the path and their leader growled a hostile warning in heavily accented Persian that no one was to go any farther. The pitch of the voice made Hector look more closely. The guard commander was a stocky woman. She had a broad flat Asiatic face, a yellowish-brown complexion and her deep-set eyes were such a dark brown under the rim of her helmet that they appeared black. A quick glance at her companions revealed that they too were women and equally formidable.

The palace official pointed towards a smaller building some distance away from the royal pavilion, and explained that he had instructions to take the visitors there. For several long moments the guard commander stared at him suspiciously, then gave a curt nod. When the little group moved forward, the guards kept pace with them, carefully shepherding them away from the pavilion.

'A platoon of those women on *Ganj-i-Sawa'i* instead of Turkish slave girls would have given Henry Avery a bloody nose,' Jezreel commented in a low voice.

'They're recruited in Mongolia,' Luis hissed. 'Specially chosen for their strength and trustworthiness.'

They had arrived at their destination and their guide brought them to a side entrance of the building. Instructing the *kotwal*'s men to stay back, he held open the door and indicated that the *feringhees* were to go inside. He did not follow them himself and closed the door behind them.

'What sort of place is this?' Jezreel asked, looking around. They were alone in a room, some ten paces across and lit by a skylight of multi-coloured glass panes. The walls were cheerfully painted with patterns of flowers and leaves. However, it was empty of furniture.

Hector positioned himself where he could keep a careful eye on Gibson. There was no way of knowing what the quarter-master might do now that he was alone in the company of men he detested. Even with his wrists chained, Gibson could turn violent. The quartermaster was ignoring the others, standing apart, with his head down and staring at the floor.

A sudden sound made them all jump. A strange wailing was coming from beyond large double doors on the far side of the room. Seconds later a buzzing drone, and then a sharp tapping sound beating out a rhythm joined the wailing.

'It's a band playing,' Luis explained. 'I think we're in a private theatre for the entertainment of the *zenana*. This must be the room where the performers wait their turn.'

Hector listened. He could detect the sounds of several stringed instruments as well as something very like a flute. There was also the chinking of small cymbals and the beating of different types of drums.

Jezreel pulled a face. 'Maybe this is how we'll be tortured.'

Luis glared at him. It was clear that he was very nervous. 'This is no time for jokes. If a *qadi* thinks you do not take him seriously, it'll go badly for us. He is both judge and jury, and there's no appeal against his decision.'

For perhaps ten minutes the music continued and soon after it ended, one of the double doors opened just wide enough for a good-looking young man wearing a red-and-gold turban to put his head into the room. It was evident that he was checking on their arrival. He seemed satisfied, for he immediately withdrew and closed the door.

'Are you sure this is part of the *zenana*?' Hector asked Luis. 'It doesn't make sense to have women guards stationed outside, and allow a man inside.'

'He'll be one of the palace eunuchs,' Luis told him. 'They're very popular with ladies.'

He broke off as both double doors were pulled open from the other side, and the same young man gestured that they were to remove their shoes and boots, before coming forward.

Barefoot, they filed past him into an audience hall that was the height of opulence. The walls were of white and brown veined marble inlaid with patterns of semi-precious stones. Scores of candles blazed in elaborate chandeliers that hung from a vaulted ceiling where the intricate plaster mouldings were picked out in gold leaf. Underfoot a single, huge carpet had a complicated repeated motif of birds, plants and flowers. It covered an area large enough to seat thirty or forty members of the audience. Here and there were low couches covered in silk brocade, and scattered around on the carpet were a number of plump velvet cushions. Evidently they had just been used as seats by women of the audience while they had been listening to the music. The air was still heavy with their perfume.

An older man, doubtless the *qadi*, was waiting for them. A simple gown of dark grey worn under a cloak of the same colour combined with his black turban to give him an austere appearance. Grey-bearded and unsmiling, he sat cross-legged on a rug at the front edge of a low platform that had provided the stage for the musicians. A tall screen of dark carved wood just behind him concealed the rest of the stage. Hector realized that the women of the *zenana* had been able to hear, but not see, the musicians.

The young eunuch lined them up to face the judge, then stepped up on the stage and disappeared behind the screen. They were alone in the room with the man who would decide their fate. For a full minute the *qadi* looked at them in silence, then reached into the pocket of his gown and produced a pair of spectacles. Placing them on his nose he leaned forward, selected a paper on a low folding bookstand in front of him and read aloud from it.

He had a strangely toneless voice and it took Hector a moment to understand that he was reciting a summary of the attack on *Ganj-i-Sawa'i* by English pirates. He spoke slowly, pausing between each sentence. Occasionally he looked up and waited for Luis to take his cue and translate for the benefit of Jezreel and Gibson. Listening, it was clear to Hector that the summary had been compiled from statements made by those who had survived the looting of the vessel. It made a grim story though there was no mention of the kidnap and attempt to ransom of Gaucharara Begum. Hector supposed that any reference to the imperial family in such sordid circumstances was unthinkable and prohibited.

Finishing, the *qadi* leaned back and asked if anyone disputed the account. Luis translated the question and as he did so, while the question was still hanging in the air, Hector knew what had been bothering him from the start: the *qadi* had not been giving his full attention to the men standing in front of him. He seemed distracted. With a shiver of apprehension Hector wondered if this meant the trial was a charade as Jacques had suspected; their sentence was already decided. He was still puzzling about this when he heard his name spoken. It was Luis, telling him that the *qadi* was waiting for an answer. Did he dispute the account of what had taken place aboard *Ganj-i-Sawa'i*?

Hector brought himself back to the present. 'Sir, I have a letter written by His Excellency the Deputy Governor of Diu about what happened on the vessel and afterwards.'

Wordlessly, the *qadi* held out a hand. Hector stepped forward and gave him the letter.

There was a long silence while the *qadi* read the contents, then he looked up and, addressing Hector in Persian, said, 'Why am I to believe the contents of this document? It states that you and two of your friends gave assistance to the victims of these barbaric events. This contradicts all the other evidence.'

'Can someone tell me what's going on!' interrupted an angry voice. It was Gibson. He had braced back his powerful shoulders and there was a contemptuous look on his face. With his wild black beard and glittering eyes, he looked a little mad.

In the shocked silence that followed, Luis could be heard explaining about Vieira's letter and its contents.

'Then translate this for me,' Gibson snarled at the young man, 'and get it right or I'll throttle you.' He gathered up the chain between his wrists with both hands and pulled it bar tight.

'Tell the old boy up on the stage that I was quartermaster of the *Pearl* when we took "Exceeding Treasure". I saw everything. As a ship's officer I tried to hold back that man,' he pointed with his chin at Hector, 'and his friend, but they were the first to help themselves to the women and plunder.'

In a shaky voice, Luis translated Gibson's outburst.

The *qadi* beckoned to Hector to approach and gave him back the letter. As Hector returned to his place, he met Gibson's eye. The quartermaster was relishing the moment. His former swagger had re-surfaced. He bared his teeth in a satisfied smile.

'Pity he didn't get gaol fever like the others,' Jezreel whispered to Hector.

The handsome young eunuch had appeared around the end of the screen. He came across the stage and knelt down beside the *qadi*. The two men conferred, their heads close together.

Hector nudged Jezreel to pay attention. The *qadi* was about to make an announcement.

'All three of you are pirates and infidels of the most depraved kind. Tomorrow, immediately after *fajr*, you will be taken outside the walls to the place of execution.'

The entire proceeding could not have taken more than ten minutes. Even before Luis had finished translating the verdict, the eunuch was on his way down from the stage, ready to usher them out. Gibson, as he brushed past Hector, gave him a vicious grin. 'I waited three months in a stinking gaol for my chance.'

EIGHTEEN

'BRIBE SOMEONE to cancel the sentence,' repeated Jacques stubbornly. After a wretched night, during which none of them had got much sleep, they were all back in Dufour's front room, bleary-eyed. Outside the open window, the sky was showing the first faint glow of daybreak and the conversation was now going round in circles.

'There's not a bribe in all the world that's large enough to change the *qadi*'s decision,' Hector told him yet again. He had lost count of the number of times his friend had made the same suggestion since he, Jezreel and Luis had got back to Dufour's home from the Lal Qila. They presumed that Quartermaster Gibson had been returned separately to spend his final hours in a cell.

'Jezreel and I both agree,' Hector reminded Jacques, 'that someone was hidden by the screen behind the *qadi*, someone who was watching and listening, making sure that the *qadi* reached the verdict they wanted.'

Jacques refused to give up. 'Then we must try to find out who it was, and appeal to that person to show mercy.'

'You wouldn't be able to get anywhere near them,' Dufour assured him wearily. 'The most likely candidates are Aurangzeb's sister, Gaucharara Begum, or her lady-in-waiting who survived being kidnapped by Mayes. Both are confined to the *zenana* while they're in Delhi. That's why Hector and Jezreel had to be brought there.'

'I still don't understand. Why wasn't I taken along as well?' Jacques insisted.

'Maybe because you're French,' Dufour told him patiently. 'It's all to do with Aurangzeb's perception of the attack on his ship. He and his wazirs want to put pressure on the English traders in Surat to pay damages. Putting a Frenchman to death doesn't achieve that.'

'And how will the sentence be carried out?' demanded Jezreel, a hard edge to his voice.

Dufour was silent a moment. 'It depends on the nature of the offence: for an ordinary criminal, death is by hanging. Those judged to have challenged the authority of the Great Mogul are thrown from the top of a cliff. I have also heard that snake poison is sometimes administered.'

Jacques had retreated into a morose silence, his face taut.

Hector could see that the death sentence imposed on his two friends had shaken the Frenchman. Jacques was now struggling to come to terms with the fact that of the three of them he would be the only one to survive.

'Jacques, I've got something I want you to do for me,' he said. He got to his feet and walked across to Jacques and tucked a folded sheet of paper into the front of his shirt. 'Take good care of it.'

'What is it?'

'A letter for Maria. I wrote it last night when I was unable to sleep. She'll read how sorry I am that I failed to make our dream of Libertalia come true. Give me your word that you'll deliver my letter in person.'

'Of course I'll do what you ask,' Jacques told him. 'But it could be a very long time before I get to meet her.'

'That doesn't matter. What's important to me is that you'll be with her when she reads my letter and you can answer her questions. If I know that, it will make it easier for me to endure whatever the Moguls are planning for Jezreel and me today.'

He held out the pocket pistol that Governor Vieira had provided as a bribe for *omrah* Nizamuddin. 'This is valuable. If neither you nor Jezreel have any objections, I'd like you to find someone to buy it for a good price. Use the money to buy a passage to Tenerife, where you'll find Maria. If there's any money left over, give it to her. She'll find it difficult having to raise a child on her own.'

Jacques took the pistol and laid it on the table beside him as the call to morning prayer came through the window. As the sound faded away, there was a knock on the door. It was one of the *kotwal*'s men rapping with his silver-headed staff.

Dufour and Jacques were grim-faced as the men and Luis accompanied Jezreel and Hector down into the street. The dawn was shrouded in heavy yellow-grey fog that left an unpleasant taste on the tongue so that the few passers-by they encountered had the ends of their turbans drawn across their mouths. Hector could see no more than a few paces in any direction, and he was glad of the padded jacket that Dufour had loaned him. Already numb from tiredness, he was finding it difficult to think straight. He stole a sideways glance at Jezreel. The big man was remarkably calm, almost indifferent. He wondered if Jezreel, in his days as a prize-fighter, had gone so often to the ring, perhaps to be badly injured there, that he had acquired the knack of closing his mind to what lay ahead.

They walked in silence, accompanied by five of the *kotwal*'s policemen. Crossing the main square, Hector expected that Gibson and the two sailors from *Pearl* would be added to their sombre little group. But the square was deserted except for a few shivering servants setting up the booths. Then they were passing through the narrow streets of a residential district until eventually they came to a postern gate in the city wall. Hector recognized it as the one they had used after they had watched the elephant fight and first entered Delhi.

Outside, the fog was equally dense and Hector quickened his step so he came level with Luis. 'When the *qadi* spoke about "the place of execution", was he talking about the open area where we watched the elephant fight?'

Luis would not meet his eye but stared ahead. 'I believe so,' he mumbled miserably.

Jezreel gave a short, bitter laugh. 'Well, we're not classed as state criminals, that's for sure. There's no cliff here from which we can be thrown. I wonder where Gibson is? He wouldn't want to miss our ending.'

They had gone some distance, angling to their left, when a dark shape loomed up through the fog. It was a scaffold of bamboo and planks. For an unsettling moment Hector thought it was some sort of gallows for a mass hanging. Then he made out that it was a makeshift viewing stand, its lower tier partially occupied by a small gathering of a dozen or so strangers. The *kotwal*'s men led them directly toward two men in the front rank who were dressed in clothes for a European winter – woollen trousers, warm coats, scarves and hats.

Pushing Hector and Jezreel forward, the senior *kotwal* official announced in Persian: 'These are the two English pirates that the Khan-i-Sama demands you punish, according to your custom.'

While Luis was translating into English, Hector studied the two foreigners. The one on the left seemed to be more senior. A big, beefy man in his early fifties, he had a broad, jowly face, a large bulbous nose and a ruddy complexion. He radiated self-confidence. His companion was much the same age but thinner and more thoughtful-looking. Hooded eyes in a long narrow face left the impression that he was someone who weighed his options carefully before reaching a decision.

The big man on the left nodded, and in a rich deep voice that matched his well-fed appearance, announced brusquely, 'I will see to it.' Turning to Hector and Jezreel, he asked. 'Your names?'

'Hector Lynch.'

'Jezreel Hall.'

'I take it that you were both members of the crew of *Fancy*, Captain Henry Avery, when it took the Mogul's vessel, *Ganj-i-Sawa'i*?'

'That is correct, though—' Hector began, but the big man cut him short with a wave of his hand.

'We'll go into that later. I am Samuel Annesley, in charge of the East India Company Factory in Surat. This is Mr Bendall, a member of the council. Both of you will be travelling to Surat with us. I will explain the details later.'

His glance strayed over Hector's shoulder to where Jacques stood talking quietly in French with Dufour whose extravagant clothing was hidden beneath a long winter cloak. 'And if these are your friends, they ought to join you in seeing justice done.'

Hector was confused. Two of the *kotwal*'s men had closed in on each side and were gripping him firmly by the elbows. Alarmed, he looked about him and saw that Jezreel was being treated in similar fashion. Moments later he was being bundled up past the first tier of the viewing stand and on to the upper level, where he was turned to face into the fog. Jezreel was set in place beside him. From below, Bendall looked back up at him with a wry smile that managed to be reassuring yet also contained a warning. 'Mr Lynch,' he called up, 'we kept the upper level, where the view is better, for you and your friend, though he is tall enough not to need it.'

Mystified Hector looked out over the heads of those in the front row. He had the impression that the fog was finally thinning, but very slowly. To his right was the brighter patch where the sun was beginning to show through. Somewhere ahead in the haze and as yet unseen would be the ramparts of Lal Qila and the balcony where Aurangzeb and his courtiers had watched the combat of the elephants. Very faintly he heard a sound that was vaguely familiar, a rhythmic thud and scrape. He was still trying to identify what it was when a rent in the fog briefly showed him the figure of two labourers with shovels, some fifty paces in front of him. They were digging a hole in the sand. Then the fog closed in again. He shuddered. He could only imagine that they were digging a grave.

Time passed, and he became aware of the growing impatience of those on the stand below him. There was a shuffling of feet, an occasional cough, an easing of shoulders. Only the *kotwal*'s men remained unmoving, impassively staring ahead of them. Hector supposed that they were the only ones who knew what would happen next. Gradually the fog dissolved and with it the visibility improved: at first as far as the mouth of the hole that had been dug and the small mound of gravelly sand heaped beside it like a molehill; then across the expanse of flat ground where, weeks earlier, he had watched the combat of the elephants. The mud-brick wall that had separated the fighting beasts was gone. It had been levelled, leaving no trace. Farther out to the sides a handful of idlers loitered where previously a crowd of spectators had stood in a great hollow square to watch the spectacle. The whole scene, Hector decided, had a forlorn and ominous look.

Finally the fog dispersed enough for him to make out the looming defences of the Lal Qila. A movement at the foot of the wall below and slightly to the left of the emperor's observation balcony drew his attention. A massive double gate that he remembered had been used for the elephants, opened just wide enough for a small procession to emerge on foot. It was led by four men carrying two stretchers. Behind them walked a number of guards in the imperial colours of red and gold led by an officer wearing a broad green sash. Hector had to squint into the diffused glare of early morning sun as he tried to make sense of what was happening at the rear of the little group. Two men whose plain shirts and loose trousers marked them out as ordinary workmen were supporting someone between them, their arms around his waist as they partly carried him, and partly guided his unsteady footsteps.

He heard Annesley pass a remark to his colleague in a loud, braying voice. 'It appears that the Moguls have had the decency to give him some poppy. I doubt the others are in a fit state to need it.'

That was when Hector recognized the heavy black beard and hulking shape of the man who was being helped forward. It was Quartermaster Gibson.

Slowly the procession made its way across the open ground towards the viewing stand. A few yards short of the earth mole-hill that marked the open hole, it came to a halt. Directed by the officer in charge of the guards the men who carried the stretchers moved off, one to each side, and laid their burdens on the ground some ten yards apart. By now Hector was in no doubt that the limp forms on the stretchers were the two sailors from *Pearl* who had been too ill to appear before the *qadi*. Next Gibson was brought towards the open hole in the ground. He was close enough for Hector to see that the quartermaster's head was lolling forward and his legs were buckling with each step. The men supporting him shuffled forward with great care, and took up their positions on each side of the open hole. From the strain on their faces it was evident that they were finding it difficult to support Gibson's weight as they shifted their grip from his waist to his arms. Then they attempted to lower him vertically into the ground. At the last moment Gibson's left foot caught on the edge of the hole and the leg bent back. There was an angry shout from the officer, and they had to hoist him up again. When he was clear, the officer gestured to one of his men who ran forward and knelt down beside the hole so he could clasp Gibson's legs together and guide them into the narrow opening. Finally, when his supporters released their grip, Gibson dropped upright to the full depth of the hole that had been dug for him. It left his head and neck above ground. He was facing towards the viewing stand, eyes closed, and his black beard brushing the sandy soil.

Hector's mouth had gone dry, and when he tried to swallow, his throat hurt. Deliberately he tried to empty his mind of all thought, trying to make it seem that the scene in front of him was something imaginary. When he shifted slightly as if to turn away, the *kotwal*'s men on each side of him tightened their grip, digging their nails into the soft flesh of his arms so that he was forced to concentrate and the pain brought him back to reality.

One of the labourers came forward with his spade and began to shovel the loose earth into the gaps around Gibson's body. 'They're going to bury him alive!' Jezreel burst out beside him.

When the labourer finished his work, he tamped down the earth all around Gibson's neck so that the quartermaster was wedged in place, able only to turn his head a few inches. To Hector's horror he saw Gibson's eyelids flutter.

By now the number of casual spectators had grown. They were still less than a hundred strong, looking on silently, apparently to satisfy their curiosity yet with an apathy that Hector found deeply unsettling. The workmen who had lowered Gibson into the ground moved off, followed by the stretcher bearers and the labourers with shovels. They began the long trudge back towards Lal Qila with the air of men whose work for the day was done. Only the liveried palace guards remained and they took up their position off to one side, and stood at ease. Hector could only imagine that they were there to prevent any last minute attempt to free the condemned men. If that was the case, their presence was a formality. Neither Gibson nor the two invalid sailors were capable of rescue.

For fully an hour everyone waited. The sun rose high enough to burn off the last of the fog, and Hector began to feel the sweat trickling down inside his padded jacket. Out of respect for the condemned, he felt that he should stay as motionless as possible. Annesley and Bendall unwound their woollen scarves and handed them to attendants. Dufour took off his cloak and folded it over his arm. Hector was glad to see that the Frenchman had chosen to dress in sombre colours, though his shirt front was a mass of flounces and frills.

Eventually, just when Hector was beginning to think that Jezreel had been correct and that Gibson's punishment was to be buried alive, a trumpet blared from the battlements of the fort. The great gate at the foot of the wall was opening. Out of the dark mouth of the entrance appeared an elephant, followed by two more. Each animal carried its mahout, riding high on its neck, while two attendants walked each side of the swinging trunk. As the animals advanced toward the viewing stand, Hector saw that they were fully as large as the great bull elephants that had been in combat. Each beast had a circle of small brass bells tied around the ankle of its front right leg, and with each step the little bells made a pleasant jingling sound which contrasted oddly with their look of ponderous menace. Each tusk had been cut off square close to the tip and reinforced with a steel band. It made a blunt weapon. In a nervous moment Hector looked for the dark line of discharge oozing down the side of their heads indicating that they were *mast*. There was nothing. He concluded that these were trained war elephants from Aurangzeb's stables and under perfect control of their riders.

With a jingle of their anklets, the three animals spread out and came to a halt a few yards short of where Gibson was entombed and the two sick sailors lay on their stretchers. They stood there, swaying silently from side to side, their broad ears flapping placidly.

The officer in charge of the guard stepped forward and called out a proclamation. In the silence that followed, Hector distinctly heard the gurgling rumble of elephant guts.

The officer took a couple of paces back and waved to the mahouts. In horrified fascination Hector looked on as the three mahouts kicked their heels into the soft area behind the great flapping ears. The three beasts lumbered forward with a soft jingling of ankle bells. Guided by the attendants on each side the two outer elephants came right up to the two sick sailors on the ground and paused. Then, with infinite delicacy they placed the left front foot beside the stretcher, before raising the right foot and holding it above the limp bundle of cloth.

The elephant in the centre, in front of Gibson, was distinctive. Larger than the others it had a large patch of pink skin on its forehead. Urged forward by its rider, it approached to within two yards of where Gibson's head protruded from the ground. There the great beast stopped. It reached out with its trunk and tested the air above the quartermaster's head. Its mahout kicked it twice behind the ears, but the elephant baulked. It refused to advance.

Sick to his stomach, Hector wondered if perhaps the execution would be cancelled. The mahout reached down between his legs and tugged out a small carpet on which he had been seated. He tossed it down to one of the attendants and called an instruction. The man caught the rug and went forward. Carefully he spread it over Gibson's head before returning to his position. The mahout produced a short iron staff with a hook and sharp point and he gave his mount a gentle prod behind its right ear.

This time the great beast stepped forward, and placed one foot on the carpet's fringe. The other foot it raised directly over the bump that was Gibson's head.

Meanwhile the two flanking elephants had grown restive. They had edged backward, and it was another few moments before their mahouts could manoeuvre them into position once again. Finally all three elephants were in position, in a line with their right front feet poised above their victims.

Hector took several deep breaths, trying to stay calm. He felt his gorge rising. The *kotwal*'s men on either side held him tight, so he was obliged to watch.

The moment stretched, and then the mahout in the centre glanced to his left and then to his right to make sure his colleagues were ready. In a high-pitched shout he called out, 'Hai!' and the three beasts brought down their right feet in unison with a majestic slow descent. Hector imagined he could hear a soft crushing sound.

For what seemed like an age, the three elephants stood there, pressing heavily down on their victims. Then the lead mahout called out 'Hai!' again, and the three animals lifted their right front feet clear, leaned back and with remarkable agility swung round, pivoting on their hind legs and began to walk back toward the fort, the anklet bells softly jingling.

Hector tore his eyes away from the grisly shapes left on the ground, and looked up toward the observation balcony used by Aurangzeb and his courtiers. It was deserted.

＊

HECTOR WAS GLAD that the *kotwal*'s men held him steady as they helped him and Jezreel down off the viewing stand and brought them around in front of Annesley and Bendall. Annesley was wiping beads of sweat from his forehead with a handkerchief and looking pale. Beside him, Bendall had his thin lips pressed tight together as he maintained his composure.

Out of the corner of his eye, Hector saw that the captain of the palace guard was conferring with the senior of the *kotwal*'s men. The policeman came over to where Annesley was standing and with Luis' help relayed a message: 'The *mansabdar* says that the two pirates, now that they have witnessed the power of Algemir's justice, are to collect their personal possessions. Afterwards I am to bring them to you and place them in your custody.'

'Please inform the captain that I intend to set out for Surat the day after tomorrow,' Annesley replied. His voice was slightly unsteady. Turning to Hector and Jezreel he told them, 'Aurangzeb's treasurer has demanded that we take the two of you to Surat and demonstrate to the foreign merchants how the English deal with pirates. I promised him we'll make an example of you. You should be grateful that a public hanging is more merciful than what we have just witnessed.'

During the long walk back to the city, Hector noticed Dufour was deep in thought. When they were nearly at the city wall, the gem dealer spoke up. 'There's something going on here that I don't fully understand.'

'It's clear enough to me,' Jezreel told him, 'they wanted to give Hector and me a bad fright, to make us think that we were due to be executed . . . and they succeeded.'

'But it's only a reprieve,' Hector pointed out. 'From what Annesley said, we'll be hung as pirates when he gets us to Surat.'

'That's what I'm trying to work out: what purpose does the delay serve?' Dufour said. He paused to adjust the frills of his shirt cuff. 'I've lived long enough in Delhi to know that it pays to look behind the scenes whenever the royal family is involved.'

'And you have a better idea who was behind the screen when we appeared before the *qadi*?'

The jeweller nodded. 'I'm certain now that it was the Begum Gaucharara, though her lady-in-waiting may also have been with her. The Begum would not have wanted to see you executed for piracy when your intervention meant she escaped Mayes' clutches.'

'But what about Jezreel and Jacques? How did the Begum know about them and that they weren't part of Mayes' kidnap plan?'

'Because I told her lady-in-waiting,' Luis interrupted in a quiet voice.

Hector swung round and stared at the young man. 'You told her?'

'She summoned me when we were getting ready to leave Diu fort and travel to Delhi. She wanted to know all about you and your friends. She asked why you had helped her mistress. I couldn't refuse to answer. She's a Mogul.' He gave an apologetic shrug.

'And you told her that Jacques was from France?'

'She wanted to know about the brand mark on his face. I know that GAL is a sign for someone who has served on the galleys of the King of France.'

Dufour looked pleased. 'Well, there you have it. Both the Begum and her lady-in-waiting concocted that scheme to make sure that all three of you didn't get stamped to pulp.'

'Then why have a trial at all?' Jacques asked.

'Because Aurangzeb demands a response to the attack on *Ganj-i-Sawa'i*. You'll remember that he was furious that his ship had been attacked and looted, and that pilgrims had been assaulted. As news of the execution spreads, people will know what happens to those who dare to steal from the Great Mogul, whether they are pirates or highway robbers.'

'Everyone will tremble at the wrath of Algemir,' Luis agreed. 'That is how the Moguls keep their power. They parade their great guns and their thousands of horsemen and – when it comes to exacting punishment – they make it . . .' He searched for the right word. 'A theatre.'

'You're right, Luis,' said Hector thoughtfully. 'Our so-called trial was also a piece of theatre, with spoken lines that had been composed with care. The *qadi* only said that we were to be taken to the place of execution. He did not say that we would be put to death.'

Dufour nodded in agreement. 'Yes, he'd been coached in what to say. Another reason why your trial was held in an annexe of the *zenana*.'

'But what will happen when Aurangzeb gets to hear that only three of the pirates have been put to death today?'

The gem dealer gave a thin smile. 'That's what's so clever about those ladies. I have no doubt that the *zenana* is already busy persuading the emperor that it is a master stroke to have the English merchants in Surat publicly hang two of their country-men. It shows that Mogul justice is merciless and wide-reaching. Meanwhile Jacques is safe because he's French, and three crushed English pirates are enough to satisfy Aurangzeb's immediate demands for retribution.'

'Do you think that Annesley and his colleague Bendall are somehow involved in all this?'

Dufour shook his head. 'No. It strikes me that they are being kept in the dark, and fully expect to hang you when you reach Surat.'

*

NOTHING MORE WAS SAID until they arrived back at Dufour's house, where the doorkeeper handed Luis a cloth-wrapped pack-age. 'He says that this was delivered earlier this morning from

Lal Qila. There was no message except that it is for the sailor *feringhee* who speaks Persian.'

'That must mean you, Hector,' said Dufour. 'We'll open it after we've had a chance to wash away the sights we saw today.'

In his rooms he went straight to the cupboard where he kept his flask of Shiraz wine and filled a generous glass for each person.

Hector sat down, feeling utterly drained. The relief that he and Jezreel had avoided execution had worn off. In its place was the worry about what would happen next. He looked across at Jacques, who had seated himself by the window and was staring morosely down into the street outside. 'Jacques, I know that you're thinking you should come to Surat with Jezreel and me. But I don't think that's a good idea even if Annesley would agree to it. He may well decide that three pirates on the gallows look better than two.'

'May I make a suggestion?' Dufour intervened. 'It's that Jacques stays on in Delhi as my assistant in the gem business.' He shot a sly glance at Jacques. 'As I recall Jacques has some experience in the handling of precious stones.'

'If you're asking me to prance around in petticoats, the answer's no,' Jacques snapped.

'You'd get used to it,' Dufour assured him. 'Having a *feringhee* as my assistant would increase my prestige among the *omrahs* who are my clients.'

Jacques scowled.

Hector got out of his chair and walked over to Jacques. Putting a hand on his friend's shoulder, he said quietly, 'You and I both know that we deluded ourselves when we thought of sailing to Libertalia and settling there. There's no such place and there never was. Instead, you now find yourself in a country where you could make yourself a good living, and be beyond the reach of French law. I think you should accept the offer.'

'I'd cut you in for five per cent of the profits, rising to ten per cent in the second year,' Dufour offered. 'The potential here is enormous. The *omrahs* love to buy and sell and exchange their jewels. For them it's a game that reinforces their self-esteem. Hindustan has some of the richest gemstone mines in the world, and they're playing with the loot from the treasuries of the smaller states they conquered, treasuries that took generations to assemble. I've seen diamond collections that you wouldn't believe – literally bags of gems. More often than not, the *omrahs* have no idea of the real value of what they have. Anyone who acts as a broker can make a fortune.'

Jezreel came to his support. 'Jacques, take this chance even if it means dressing up in a powdered wig and frock coat.'

Under pressure from his two friends, Jacques wavered. 'I'll think about it.' He reached inside his shirt and pulled out the letter that Hector had asked him to deliver to Maria. 'Whatever I decide, Hector, you must have this back. If I were to meet Maria, I won't know what to say to her.' He also held out the little pistol. 'And you might as well have this too as I will not be needing to buy my passage to Tenerife.'

Dufour broke the uncomfortable silence that followed by reminding Hector about the parcel that had been delivered for him.

Hector went across to the desk where it lay. The heavy cotton wrapping had been folded neatly, and then secured with a row of small stitches. He picked up the package and weighed it in his hand. It felt light and soft, and he had no idea what it might contain, or who had sent it to him.

'Go on, let's see what it is,' Jezreel urged.

Hector laid the parcel back on the desk and, with Dufour's letter knife, carefully cut the stitches. As the last stitch came free, the close-packed contents burst open so that he had to grab the first item before it slithered to the floor.

It was a length of watered silk shimmering gold and green, the ends fringed with gold. Hastily he gathered it together and held the material up for inspection. It measured six or seven yards.

'That's a turban length,' Dufour commented. He sounded surprised. 'What else is there?'

Hector set aside the silk and turned back to the opened parcel. There was a glint of brocade. Cautiously he pulled out a garment, a knee-length coat with wide skirts. Made from cloth of gold, it was magnificently embroidered with patterns of coloured thread.

'Try it on and see how it fits,' Jezreel suggested.

Hector slipped his arms through the sleeves, and turned to face his companions. Luis, sitting quietly in a corner, was looking on, spellbound.

'It makes you into a proper *omrah*,' Jezreel said.

There was one more item in the package – a wide sash of stiff yellow silk.

'Who would want to send me these clothes?' Hector asked, fingering the rich material. He recalled the expensive fabric in the shops at the entry to Lal Qila.

'A *serapha* – that's what you've been sent, Hector,' said Dufour and there was a note of awe in his voice. 'It's a rare honour, a symbolic gift bestowed by the Great Mogul or by his most important officers of state. A *serapha* is something Aurangzeb might choose to give to an ambassador from a friendly country or to a general returned from a successful campaign.'

'So what am I supposed to do with it?' Hector asked.

'If you were at court, you would wear your *serapha* so that everyone would know that you are high in the emperor's favour. However, as Aurangzeb probably thinks you have been crushed to death, I don't think Algemir is your secret admirer. You'd be wise if you put everything back in their wrapping and kept it safe with your other baggage.'

'What about selling them for cash?' Jezreel suggested. 'They should fetch a good sum. If Hector and I are going to be hauled off to Surat, we could at least repay you for some of the expenses you've had, looking after us in Delhi.'

Dufour sucked in his breath as if he had a twinge of toothache. 'Whatever you do, don't sell them! They'd be traced back to the person who sent them to you and that would cause deep offence. As you've been staying with me, I'd probably be thrown out of Delhi.'

Hector folded up the turban length and the sash and carefully put them to one side. As he was taking off the brocade coat, he felt something in a pocket. He fished out a black velvet purse tied with a drawstring. He unfastened the knot and tipped the contents into the palm of his hand. It was a bracelet, a triple circle of small, matched pearls. A memory stirred. He picked up the turban length again, raised the fabric to his nose and sniffed. There was a faint hint of sandalwood, and he knew he had been right. He had seen the bracelet in *Ganj-i-Sawa'i*'s cabin when he had conspired with the badly injured Tavares to misidentify Begum Gaucharara. He put the bracelet back into the purse and slipped it inside his shirt. Sometime in the future it would make a perfect gift for Maria if he and Jezreel were spared the death sentence that had been promised them. Twenty-four hours earlier he would not have dared to think of such a possibility, but the day's events had taught him that in Hindustan nothing was inevitable.

NINETEEN

ANNESLEY HAD HIRED four of the fastest hackeries – as he called the ox-drawn passenger vehicles – for his return to Surat. These were not the slow, plodding conveyances that Hector remembered from his journey between Diu and Delhi. They were smart lightweight carts pulled by specially trained oxen, their horns banded with rings of polished brass, which moved at a fast trot for hour after hour. Hector and Jezreel rode in one cart with Luis, who had so impressed Annesley with his skills as a translator and go-between that the English merchant had agreed that the young man could travel with them. They were given their meals separately, allotted their own room overnight in the caravanserais, and after Hector promised that neither he nor Jezreel would try to escape, the door was no longer locked.

As a result, the journey passed swiftly and by the last week of February they were passing through lush, fertile countryside very different from the dusty arid surroundings they had left behind in Delhi. Here the villages were set among groves of orange and lemon trees, and the fields were green with wheat, rice, and indigo. What struck Hector most was the industry of the people. Cotton was their main crop, and men, women and children seemed to be constantly busy spinning the yarn, weaving it into cloth, or dyeing the fabric in every shade and pattern of indigo blue.

'That's Surat calico,' Luis said to Hector as their little convoy rolled past bush after bush spread with great lengths of material for the printed patterns to dry in the sunshine. 'We're nearly at our destination.'

'How long before we get there?'

'No more than a couple of days.'

Hector glanced round to make sure that the cart in which Annesley and Bendall were riding together was some distance ahead. Now they were so close to Luis' family home in Surat, he felt he had to break silence and tell the young man the details of what really happened to his father aboard *Ganj-i-Sawa'i*. It would prepare him for what he might find there.

'Luis, I have to tell you something before we enter Surat,' he began hesitantly. 'It's about your father.'

The excitement that lit up Luis' large expressive eyes was childlike. 'Have you heard something?' he asked eagerly.

'No. Perhaps I should have told you earlier. It concerns the attack on *Ganj-i-Sawa'i*.'

Luis gave a slight frown of disappointment. 'Senhor Vieira told me that my father fought bravely.'

'He did. Very courageously. But . . .' and Hector hesitated. 'He was injured in the fight.'

'Badly injured?'

'Very badly.'

Luis let out a slow breath, his face now troubled. 'Please tell me. It is better that I know the truth.'

'One of the great guns blew up, and your father was caught in the blast. His face and upper body were severely burned.'

'You saw this?'

'Not the explosion itself, but later after the ship was captured. My friends and I tried to help your father as best we could. We treated the burns and a kindly passenger gave him some poppy to ease the pain.'

Several moments passed and then Luis asked in a small voice,

'Do you think he still lives? I have heard nothing from him in all these months.'

Hector chose his words carefully. 'With good treatment he should have survived. When I saw him again some days later, still on the ship, he was being well cared for, and *Ganj-i-Sawa'i* was headed for Surat.'

'But that was more than three months ago. Surely my father would have sent me a message.'

Hector did his best to sound encouraging. 'Maybe he did, but to Diu, thinking you were there. He was not to know that you had gone with us to Delhi.'

'I feared that something like this had happened,' Luis admitted wretchedly.

For a long time they sat in silence as the hackery continued down the road. Eventually Luis seemed to pull himself together, for he said, 'Hector, I suppose that you've noticed how Mr Annesley and Mr Bendall stay up late in the evenings, talking together. I've overheard snatches of their conversation, and they sounded very anxious.'

'Maybe they're fretting that Aurangzeb won't let them resume trading even after they've strung me and Jezreel up.'

'I think it is more complicated than that,' Luis told him. 'I believe they are worrying about what the directors of the East India Company in London will think about how they've handled this difficulty with the Great Mogul.'

'Annesley doesn't give me the impression of being someone who concerns himself with anything but his own interests.'

'That's what I mean,' said Luis. 'He and Bendall will have lodged a bond with the Company before they were appointed to their posts in Surat. The money is a surety against their good behaviour. To keep them honest and stop them from doing business on the side for their personal profit. If they've mishandled this business with Aurangzeb, their money could be forfeit.'

Hector glanced at his young companion. 'How do you know all this?'

Luis shrugged. 'It is common knowledge among the Indian merchants of Surat. They make jokes about it. They say that the only question to ask about a newly arrived *feringhee* merchant is whether he is clever enough to take a bribe, or stupid enough to be hoodwinked.'

*

SURAT SMELLED UNPLEASANT, even at a distance. Standing on the bank of the Tapti river and looking across at the town, Hector caught the whiff of river mud and human waste on the afternoon breeze that also had the salty tang of sea air. He could see a medium-sized castle flying the Mogul colours and a building that looked like the customs house. Several barnlike structures were probably warehouses. Farther downstream to his right were a number of shipyards. But Surat, at first sight, did not live up to its reputation as the great emporium of the Mogul empire. The town was an ugly sprawl of dingy low houses with roofs of thatch. Nor did it have a proper harbour, only a run-down waterfront of stone steps lapped by the dirty brown waters of the Tapti. Even the ships in the anchorage were not what he had expected. There were several dozens of them: small lighters, coasters, barges, but not a single ocean-going vessel.

Annesley was stamping up and down on the bank, gesticulating and shouting at the hackery drivers, urging them to hurry up and unload their carts before he deducted from their wages. That morning he and Bendall had changed into cream-coloured breeches with white shirts and cravats, and coats of dark blue broadcloth with a high stiff collar and a double row of gold buttons down the front. Hector supposed that these uniforms marked them as officials of the English East India Company.

'Come on now, Lynch. Don't keep me waiting!' Annesley bellowed. Hector slithered down the slippery bank, and joined Jezreel and Luis who were already on the ferry. As they were being rowed across the river Hector had a chance to speak quietly with Luis.

'Where are the foreign trading ships?' he asked.

'They'll be near the river mouth at an anchorage called Swally Hole. The Tapti is too shallow to be navigated safely, and Swally Hole has deep water and shelter behind a sandbar. It's only fifteen miles away by boat.'

'Shouldn't the customs house be located nearer those ships?'

'Officially the foreign vessels must off-load their cargo into smaller boats at Swally Hole and send it upriver for inspection at the Surat customs office.'

'That's an open invitation for smuggling.'

Luis grinned. 'Of course it is. But palms are greased and nothing is done to stop it.' He pointed at the castle. 'There you'll find Surat's governor, Sujat Khan. He's taking in so much money on the side that in a few years he will amass a fortune and retire.'

'Doesn't that raise suspicions in Delhi?'

The young man shrugged. 'The Khan-i-Sama will quietly auction off the vacant post to the highest bidder. He and his officials take the bid money and lodge most of it in the emperor's treasury. They are happy with the arrangement as it gives them less work to do. Afterwards if the new governor takes bribes to recover his investment, that's up to him.'

The ferry nuzzled up against the slime-covered steps of the landing place and was promptly surrounded by porters jostling as they clamoured for work. Annesley hired two of them to carry his and Bendall's luggage, leaving Hector and the others to shoulder their own bags. At the top of the steps they entered the maidan, the open space between the castle and the customs house. It served as a vast open-air market and was crammed with displays of trade goods – dried indigo paste in blocks, sacks of grain, black balls of opium heaped up like musket shot and hundreds upon hundreds of bales of cloth. These were stacked so tightly that Annesley had difficulty in picking a path between them. At one point, with Hector on his heels, he reached out, patted a bale and said over his shoulder, 'Half the world, from here to London, dresses in Surat calicoes and muslins. It's the foundation of our Company's trade.'

Conspicuous in his *feringhee* uniform, Annesley made a striking contrast to the Indian merchants transacting business. They wore plain white shirts, long unbleached dhotis and cheap sandals. If he had seen them in the streets of Delhi, Hector would have taken them to be minor shopkeepers or junior clerks. Yet a few of them undoubtedly knew Annesley and Bendall for they would put their hands together as the Englishmen walked past and give a gracious dip of the head. The courtesy was returned sometimes, but not always, with a curt nod.

'If Surat is such a good place for trade,' he commented to Luis, 'you'd have thought that the merchants would look a bit more prosperous.'

'Don't be deceived, Hector,' Luis said. 'Several of those *banyans* are wealthier than any *omrah* dressed in his fine silks and jewels. They are careful to make it appear that they are so poor they can scarcely put food on the table for their families. It is to avoid attracting the attention of their Mogul overlords who would then squeeze them for a share of their fortunes.'

He nodded in the direction of an impoverished-looking elderly trader in threadbare clothes who was picking over the contents of an opened bale. He had pulled out a length of the cloth and was fingering it with an expression of disdain on his gaunt face. 'You see that man there. He is one of the richest men in Surat. He and his cousins own a fleet of trading ships.'

Trailing behind Annesley into the town, Hector began to understand Surat's fame as a place of trade. It seemed that the entire population was engaged in constant buying or selling. In the meanest alleyways there was a pedlar every few yards with a tray of his goods hung around his neck and holding up samples, or he had a roll of embroidery balanced on his head and was dangling a strip of the fabric in the faces of passers-by. In the open doorways of shacks with bamboo walls plastered with cow dung, there were displays of brightly painted children's dolls, wood carvings and displays of furniture inlaid with mother of pearl. Everything was for sale.

Eventually they came into a street, broader and cleaner than most, dominated by a large, square-fronted building solidly made of brick. Iron bars in the small windows gave it a forbidding appearance. A loitering watchman spotted Annesley and his party and scurried off ahead of them so that by the time they reached the front entrance, an archway large enough to admit laden carts, the heavy double doors were being swung open.

'I'm calling an urgent meeting of the Council. Inform the cooks to serve dinner at sunset, sharp,' Annesley snapped at a flustered servant as he turned in under the arch.

Bendall dropped back a few paces and gave Hector a cold, unblinking look. 'Welcome to the Factory of the East India Company. Do I take it that you and your friend will not try to escape?'

Hector nodded, and the trader crooked a finger at a hovering servant. 'Show them to one of the empty storerooms and see that they get a meal,' he ordered. Turning back to Hector, he said, 'You will be sent for when required.'

Passing through a short passageway behind his guide, Hector emerged into an open courtyard. The main building through which he had just entered appeared to contain the offices of the Company. It was also where Annesley and Bendall had their lodgings, for he could see the porters carrying their bags inside. Beside it was a small chapel with whitewashed walls, a cross on its gable end and a sloping roof of reddish-brown tiles. Directly across the courtyard a cavernous building reminded him of Baldridge's warehouse in St Mary's. Workmen were using hand-carts to shift crates and bales under the gaze of an overseer with a tally sheet. The remaining sides of the courtyard were taken up with stables, sheds, kitchens and servants' quarters. Coming to a halt in front of what looked like a storeroom, his guide pulled open the door, and Hector peered inside. The room was bare of any furniture and the floor of beaten earth had been swept clean. Judging by the musty smell, it had recently been used for storing grain. Hector set his bag on the ground. 'I guess we slept in worse when we were on *Fancy*,' he said to Jezreel, 'and it's better than a prison cell.'

He turned to ask Luis if he could find someone to provide them with bedding. But the young man had vanished.

＊

NEXT MORNING Hector and Jezreel were out in the courtyard, seated on the ground with their backs against the storeroom wall and eating their breakfast of flat bread and fruit, when Luis reappeared. Hector presumed that he had gone off to find his family, but the stiff look on Luis' face made him wait for the young man to broach the subject first.

'Hector, I'm sorry that I disappeared like that yesterday evening,' Luis began.

'Don't worry about it. You're free to come and go. Annesley and Bendall are only concerned that Jezreel and I don't try to escape,' Hector reassured him and shifted aside to provide space. 'Sit down and have a bite to eat.'

'I set out intending to go to my family's house,' Luis admitted, accepting the peeled orange and piece of bread that Hector held out to him. 'But on the way I thought about what you told me had happened to my father on *Ganj-i-Sawa'i*. I decided that if he was still alive and perhaps badly scarred it would not be fair to burst in on him unexpectedly. I should give him time to prepare. It's been such a long time since I last saw him that another day would not matter.'

'So what did you do instead?'

'I returned to the maidan and sought out one of my childhood friends. He works as a sub-agent for an important *shroff*.'

Seeing Hector's puzzled expression, he explained. 'A *shroff* is a middleman. He acts between the trader and the producer. He locates products, negotiates prices and even lends out the money so a deal can be done. Every business transaction in Surat requires the services of a *shroff*.'

'You were talking about your boyhood friend,' Hector reminded him and began peeling another orange for himself.

'First he told me the good news that my father is indeed alive, though he shows marks of his wounds. I've asked my friend to get word to my father that I had returned to Surat and would call at the house later today.' He paused. 'But that is not all. While we were talking, a group of his colleagues joined us. All of them work at the maidan. Everyone has been waiting for Annesley and Bendall to get back from Delhi. They're anxious to learn what Annesley intends to do about Aurangzeb's demand for compensation for the loss of *Ganj-i-Sawa'i*'s cargo.'

'Why should that be important to the traders on the maidan?'

'Annesley and his Company colleagues borrowed heavily to buy this year's production of cotton cloth. They owe their *shroffs* a great deal of money. If they pay huge damages to Aurangzeb, they won't be able to meet their debts to the *shroffs*.'

Hector thought for a while. 'That explains why Annesley and Bendall were so agitated on the journey.'

Luis nodded. 'According to my friend, Annesley will be wriggling like a worm on a hook. He must find a way of either reducing the size of the compensation or delaying payment. If he doesn't, he won't be able to meet his debts in Surat and then no one in the maidan will do business with him or his associates.'

'And, in turn, that means this Factory will have to close down and it's the end of the English East India Company in the most profitable port in the Mogul empire,' Hector finished for him. 'Last night the lights burned very late over there in the company offices. Annesley and his colleagues must have stayed up trying to find a way out of the crisis.'

He looked up as he heard the sound of footsteps. Bendall, dressed in his formal costume, was approaching across the courtyard.

'Lynch, I've come to fetch you and Hall to the Council Chamber,' Bendall said in his flat voice.

Hector and Jezreel got to their feet, and Luis stood up to join them. 'Not you,' Bendall told the young man bluntly. 'This is to be a meeting behind closed doors.'

*

THE COUNCIL CHAMBER was a spacious room on the upper floor of the main building, its tall windows looking out on the central courtyard. As Hector stepped over the threshold, he had the impression that he had left Hindustan. Every item of furniture was imported. The long table in the centre of the room was made of dark oak and had heavy carved legs. Matching chairs were ranged down one side. Two sideboards, again of dark oak, stood against the whitewashed walls, and a pair of large canvases in gilt frames above them depicted scenes that were certainly not local. One was of a city under a grey sky and could have been London; the other was a sunny pastoral view where a herd of cows grazed a lush meadow beside a river lined with willow bushes. Prominent between the two paintings was a silk wall hanging embroidered with a coat of arms. From where he stood, Hector could make out a shield with three blue ships with silver sails, each with a red cross. The supporters on each side of the shield were snarling lions with fish's tails. It had to be the insignia of the English East India Company.

Five men sat on the far side of the table. Annesley as Chief Factor was clearly in charge, for he occupied the great chair in the middle. The men to left and right of him were strangers to Hector and all wore the Company uniform. They were regarding him and Jezreel with expressions that ranged between wary and disapproving.

Bendall closed the door, then walked across and took his place beside the others.

'Please be seated,' said Annesley. Hector had expected that Jezreel and he would be made to stand, but two empty chairs had been placed a couple of paces back from the table, facing towards the council.

Annesley waited until they had taken their seats before he

continued in a tight voice. 'Mr Lynch and Mr Hall, as you know, the *diwan* of the Great Mogul has directed that both of you are to be hung in public as a warning to all those who would think of engaging in piracy.'

He paused to run a finger round the inside of his high collar, then cleared his throat before continuing, 'At the same time the Great Mogul is demanding that the English merchants in Surat pay compensation for the piratical attack carried out by you and your gang.'

Out of the corner of his eye Hector saw that the trader seated at the end of the line, a fat balding man with red-blotched skin, was shifting uncomfortably in his chair, trying to scratch himself.

The Chief Factor picked up a sheet of paper lying on the desk in front of him and glanced at it. 'This is the inventory of the main items stolen by the pirates. It was compiled by the office of the wazir in charge of the imperial treasury. His officials place a value on each item. The total comes to over half a million gold *mohurs*, or approximately six tons of gold.'

That wazir of the treasury, Hector recalled, was Abdul Ghafar, uncle to Salima who had died in the attempt to rescue her from Mayes' ship. It was little wonder that he had issued such a punishing demand.

Annesley put down the paper and met Hector's eye. 'The Council admits no liability in this matter but has accepted with great reluctance that we have no choice but to make a payment.' His voice hardened. 'Nevertheless the Council considers the amount excessive.'

'Monstrously excessive,' added the fat merchant at the end of the table who had succeeded in satisfying his itch and was nodding sagely.

Annesley put his elbows on the table, steepled his fingers and stared at Hector. 'You have already admitted that you and Mr Hall were present when Henry Avery and his pirate gang looted the Great Mogul's vessel, *Ganj-i-Sawa'i*.'

'That is correct,' Hector replied. He was thinking furiously, wondering where the interrogation was heading. From the close attention being paid by the other members of the Council, there was something of great significance to be decided.

'It is the normal practice, is it not, that pirates make a public division of their stolen goods?' Annesley asked.

'That is correct, though as I told you earlier, neither Mr Hall nor I had any share.'

The Chief Factor made a dismissive gesture with his hand. 'That is of no consequence. You witnessed the division.'

'Both of us watched the sharing out of the loot, if that's what you mean. It is the custom among freebooters,' Hector admitted.

'Thieves at sea, you mean,' someone muttered farther down the table.

Annesley leaned back, apparently satisfied with the answers to his questions. 'This Council will contest the valuation that has been placed on the stolen goods.'

All of a sudden, Hector saw where Annesley's questions were leading. He decided it was time to take the initiative. 'You want Jezreel and me to revalue the goods that were lost? Is that the case?'

Annesley gave him a sharp look. 'You put it bluntly. It would mean that your execution would be postponed.'

'And what if our valuation agrees with that provided by the office of the wazir?'

'It would be in your interests to see that it doesn't,' Bendall interjected. There was an underlying note of menace in his voice.

Hector turned toward him. 'Surely you are not asking Jezreel and me to provide false accounting.'

'Call it an alternative appraisal of value,' said Annesley smoothly. 'That's entirely normal in any commercial transaction.'

Hector was not about to let his advantage slip. 'And if we do provide this alternative appraisal, then surely we merit more than a brief delay in our execution.'

When Annesley allowed himself a slight smile, Hector knew

that the Chief Factor was pleased that the interview was turning out as he intended.

'The Council has given this matter some thought,' Annesley was suave. 'The *diwan* intends your execution to be a warning to others of our countrymen. This is best achieved by having you hanged in public in London, not here. In London a far greater number of our countrymen would be on hand to heed the lesson that piracy leads only to death.'

Hector had to admire Annesley's ingenuity. He and Jezreel were being offered a long-term postponement of their execution if they cooperated in lowering the value of the loot taken from 'Exceeding Treasure'.

The Chief Factor gestured towards the sheet of paper on the table in front of him. 'You and your friend can go through the list, and prepare a more realistic inventory based on what you saw. All in strict confidence, of course.'

'How long have we got to make any changes?'

'A company ship, the *Maynard*, is now loading at Swally Hole with mixed cargo for London. Captain Phillips intends taking advantage of the north-east monsoon for a swift passage to the Cape. He sails the moment his lading is complete. If your work is done by then, you will be able to leave with her.'

Hector remembered Luis's description of Annesley and his associates wriggling like worms on a hook. He made up his mind to press home his advantage. 'If Jezreel and I are to agree to this arrangement, we have one condition.'

'Don't be so impudent!' burst out the fat man. He was so agitated that he began scratching himself again. 'You are in no position to make conditions.'

Annesley pointedly ignored him. 'What is it that you would want, Mr Lynch?'

Hector turned to Jezreel to consult him, but the faint grin on the big man's face told him that there was no need to seek his approval. 'If Mr Hall and I are to be sent to England on *Maynard* for execution, Captain Phillips must be instructed to call in at Tenerife in the Canaries to collect my wife and child.'

'You'll not long enjoy their company,' observed Bendall nastily.

Annesley shot Bendall a warning glance. 'That should be possible,' he said in a tone of calm finality.

As no one was making a move to see them out of the chamber, Hector got to his feet, and made for the door with Jezreel.

Once they were outside, Jezreel guffawed with pleasure and threw a brawny arm around Hector's shoulder. Giving him a congratulatory squeeze, Jezreel said, 'I went in there thinking we would be told the day on which we would be hanged, and we come out with a passage home and a free ticket for Maria.'

'We're not out of trouble yet,' Hector reminded him when he had recovered his breath. 'We set foot in England as self-confessed pirates and due to go to the gallows.'

*

HECTOR HAD EXPECTED that Luis would have left to go to visit his father so he was touched to see the young man waiting in the courtyard. Luis's anxiety was evident in the way he came hurrying across to intercept them the moment they emerged from the Company office.

'How did the meeting go?' he asked.

'Hector bamboozled them,' Jezreel assured him cheerfully.

'Annesley offered us a deal,' Hector explained. 'We're to help him scale down the compensation due to Aurangzeb for the looting of *Ganj-i-Sawa'i*.'

Luis frowned. 'How can you do that?'

Hector explained what had been agreed.

Luis pulled a face. 'Do you trust Annesley to keep his word?'

Hector shrugged. 'We've little choice.'

Luis brightened. 'Well at least that should mean you're no longer confined to this place.'

'Nothing was said about that, but I can't see anyone stopping us.'

'Then please come with me to meet my father. It would mean a lot to him if he could thank you personally for the help you gave him on *Ganj-i-Sawa'i*.'

'If you think that would be right . . .' Hector started to say but Luis was already heading towards the street.

TWENTY

THEY TOOK THE ROUTE of the previous day through the maze of alleyways until they came out again on the maidan. It was now mid-morning and with the sun beating down from a clear sky, the heat was oppressive. Yet the market was as busy as ever with suppliers, traders, middlemen, brokers and porters.

'My father's house is only a few minutes from here,' Luis said.

Hector caught him by the arm to slow his headlong rush. 'Why don't you go on ahead while Jezreel and I wait here? You should see your father alone, at least for the first few minutes; make sure he's ready to receive us. Then come back to fetch us.'

The young man hesitated for a moment, then agreed. 'I'll not be long,' he said and vanished into the crowd.

Hector and Jezreel strolled around the market to pass the time. A seller of indigo stood beside a chest packed with small square bricks of the powdered dye. His customer, a serious-looking *banyan* dressed in the usual humble shirt and dhoti, had picked out a sample brick and was crumbling it between his fingers. When he finished, he dusted off his hands, and made a comment to the merchant.

'What's he saying?' Jezreel asked.

'He's complaining that grains of sand have been mixed in

with the indigo powder to increase the weight, and also that the quality is poor,' Hector explained.

Jezreel laughed. 'A trick of the trade. You need to have your wits about you to do business here.'

Hector listened as the merchant, after pretending to be surprised, made an excuse. 'He is claiming that it's an oversight. The indigo blocks were set out to dry in the sun on a sandy surface, and the sand must have got in by mistake.'

Jezreel grunted in disbelief. 'A bare-faced lie. The rogue is trying to palm off shoddy goods.'

The attempt to cheat the customer made little difference. Unperturbed, the *banyan* started haggling with the seller. He was asking for a discount of forty per cent if he bought the entire chest.

They watched for a few moments before moving on, and Jezreel pointed out a trader overseeing his assistants as they checked a bale of calico that was on offer. They had slit open the bale and were pulling out the material yard by yard and carefully examining it for flaws.

Jezreel chuckled. 'Everyone here expects to have a swindle practised on them, Hector. We'll follow local custom when we tell our lies about the loot from *Ganj-i-Sawa'i*.'

LUIS HAD BEEN GONE for a little over half an hour when he returned to fetch them to a row of houses overlooking the waterfront. The buildings had an air of fading elegance. Each had a first-floor balcony with its ornately carved wooden balustrade, and a front door decorated with wrought-iron work. But the timber was weathered grey with age, and the paint had flaked away from the rusting metal. The street, Luis explained, was where the older families of foreign traders had established themselves in the days before the French, Dutch and English merchants. Most were the homes of the Portuguese, who had lived in Surat for generations. He stopped in front of a house a little more rundown than its neighbours, and pushed open the door. A dimly lit corridor led to the rear of the building from where came the sound of voices and the smell of cooking, spicy and rich. After the bright daylight outside, Hector's eyes had to adjust to the gloom as Luis led him and Jezreel up a flight of stairs, the worn treads creaking under their weight. At the head of the stairs Luis doubled back along the landing so that they entered a room facing out across the river. Blinds made of thin bamboo strips were lowered to block out the sun's glare from the windows, leaving the room in half-darkness.

Feeling a slight draught on his face, Hector glanced up. Suspended from the high ceiling was a length of carpet. It was swaying back and forth pulled by a cord, and acting as a fan, stirring the warm air. Directly beneath it someone lay full length in a reclining chair. Only when a husky voice with a Portuguese accent wheezed, 'Hector and Jezreel, welcome to my home,' did he recognize Jeronimo Tavares.

'Raise the blind a fraction, Luis, so I can greet my visitors properly,' said the artilleryman.

With the better light Hector could see that Tavares was dressed in a loose-fitting gown of lightweight material, open at the front to leave his chest bare. Yellow patches showed where the skin had begun to heal, but many areas were still very raw. On his head was a bonnet of white muslin like a nun's wimple. The side flaps covered his ears and the front projected far enough to shelter his forehead, leaving his face visible. Tavares was dreadfully disfigured. The fleshy part of his nose had been burned away, exposing the twin holes of his nostrils. The damaged skin around his mouth was like yellowed parchment and so tightly stretched that he could not close his lips fully and his teeth were bared. His eyes looked out from small red-rimmed holes. He had lost his eyelids.

He still managed a rictus of a lopsided smile.

'I apologize for my appearance, and please excuse the dark; my eyes cannot endure too much bright light.'

He made an effort to get up out of the chair, but eased back with a soft hiss of pain.

'I owe you my life, both of you,' the artilleryman continued. 'I'm only sorry that Jacques isn't here too. Then I can thank all three of those who treated my injuries. Without you I would not have survived.'

Hector waited for him to continue.

'My son tells me that you'll be leaving Surat in a few days. I didn't want you to go without repaying part of the debt I owe you.' He raised one hand to dab a scrap of soft cloth at his right eye. 'Luis worries that Annesley will hang you as soon as you've completed revaluing the goods stolen from "Exceeding Treasure". What Annesley did not tell you – and I'm sure it was a deliberate omission – is that he needs to keep you alive because your Captain Avery has vanished. *Fancy* was last seen at St Mary's in Madagascar when he called there to dispose of some of his loot. Nothing has been heard of him since, or his crew. That was a couple of months ago.'

Hector shifted uneasily on his feet. He could tell that Tavares was making a great effort to speak normally, pronouncing his words carefully between the ravaged lips.

'Naturally Avery is being hunted down,' Tavares said. 'Here in Surat there's a price on his head, and I've no doubt that an even greater reward is being offered in London. The problem is that no one knows very much about Captain Avery, what he looks like, or where he's likely to have gone to ground. He's a man of mystery, a phantom,' he paused meaningfully, 'except to those who sailed with him.'

Hector thought back to the day he had last seen Avery. It was the morning when he had transferred from *Fancy* and gone aboard Tew's *Amity* to pilot her out into the Straits of Alexander. So much had happened since then that he had given little thought to Long Ben. He remembered also that Avery, unlike Tew, had never been flamboyant or drawn attention to himself.

He had always kept in the background. Hector wondered if this had been Avery's deliberate policy all along.

'What about Captain Mayes and the crew of *Pearl*?' Jezreel asked.

Tavares' snort came out as a hollow whistling sound. 'There were reports of a foreign ship cruising off Goa, three local vessels plundered. But nothing's been heard in the last month. So if that was *Pearl*, Captain Mayes has headed home with his plunder.'

Luis had remained standing by the window. He came forward to pick up a water glass from a table and offer his father a drink. Tavares waved him away. 'Annesley will honour the deal he made. He'll want both of you in London so that his superiors, the directors of the East India Company, can extract from you any information that will help them catch Avery. It will also show them how astute he has been in reducing the amount of the reparations to be paid to Aurangzeb.'

Hector could see that Tavares was tiring. 'You should rest,' he said. 'Jezreel and I can come back another day.'

There was a slight movement of the bonnet as Tavares shook his head. 'I've left the most important to last. Hector, do you remember Manuj Dosi? He was on *Ganj-i-Sawa'i*.'

'The Surati merchant?' Hector's voice trailed off as he remembered Jacques describing how quartermaster Gibson had hacked off the finger of the rich merchant, forcing him to reveal where he had hidden his valuables.

Tavares confirmed his fears. 'Manuj Dosi is back in Surat, minus a finger. He'll be looking for revenge.'

'From the moment you set foot in Surat your presence has been maidan gossip,' Luis added. 'Manuj Dosi will know you are here.'

Tavares' anxiety showed in the way he raised his body and half-turned toward his visitors. 'Manuj Dosi is extremely dangerous. I beg of you, for your own safety, take every precaution while you are in Surat.'

In Hector's opinion, the artilleryman's fears were exaggerated but he could see that Tavares was genuinely apprehensive. 'Jezreel and I will be safe inside the East India Company premises. We've plenty to keep us occupied there.'

Tavares was insistent. 'Manuj Dosi has a very long reach. His cousin, Dayaram, is one of Annesley's *shroffs* and will know your every move. Be on your guard and take precautions, even inside the Factory.'

Hector smiled at the suggestion. 'Jezreel and I are pirates as far as the Chief Factor is concerned. He'll not allow us to wander around the Factory armed to the teeth.'

'What about that pistol that Vieira gave you?' Luis put in. 'It's small enough for you to keep hidden.'

'It's in my baggage.'

'With your permission, I'll bring it here after I've seen you safely back to the Factory. My father can check it over, and we'll find ball and powder. After that, please carry it with you at all times, and loaded.'

'I'll do that,' Hector agreed and, to change the subject, asked Tavares, 'What will you do when you are back on your feet?'

'My doctor promises that I'll be able to return to some sort of active life in another six months.' Tavares managed another painful smile. 'Luis has told me about the *serapha* you received from Her Highness Gaucharara Begum for what you did aboard *Ganj-i-Sawa'i*. I'll go to Delhi with Luis and ask for her help. Her influence should get me a job with an old friend of mine with the *shutarnal*. He'll appreciate having the services of someone to maintain his "wasps" and the camels won't mind what my face looks like.'

*

THE AIR IN THE SMALL ROOM off the Council Chamber had the sour, musty smell of spilled wine. Hector and Jezreel sat on empty crates that had once held straw-wrapped bottles from Bordeaux. In front of them, an empty barrel had been set on end to form a makeshift table. A single tiny window, high up in the thick wall, let in barely enough light for them to read the inventory of valuables that, according to Aurangzeb's treasurer, had been looted from *Ganj-i-Sawa'i*. It ran to five pages.

'It would help if we had some candles in here,' Jezreel grumbled.

'Annesley probably fears we'll set the place on fire, and the Council's stock of drink will go up in the blaze,' said Hector. He was only half-listening as he studied the first sheet of the inventory.

It was the day after their return from visiting Jeronimo Tavares when a visibly annoyed Annesley had told them that they were not to set foot outside the Factory again. 'I promised not to have you hanged while in Surat,' was how the Chief Factor had put it, reverting to his usual overbearing manner, 'but I said nothing about letting you roam free.'

Looking through items on the list from Delhi, Hector understood why the Chief Factor was so keen that he and Jezreel had no further contact outside the Factory walls.

'It would be an even worse tragedy for the councillors if the maidan traders got to know the contents of this list,' he observed to Jezreel. 'If they had any idea what enormous compensation Aurangzeb is demanding, they would shun Annesley, Bendall and the others.'

Jezreel reached forward, selected the next page of the inventory, and began to read out: 'Carpet from Isfahan, two strand necklace of rose pearls, six elephant teeth, one roll cloth of gold twenty-five cubits in length, one roll of the same material of twenty great cubits.' He looked up. 'What's the difference between an ordinary cubit and a great cubit?'

'I've no idea,' Hector admitted. 'But I'm sure a Surati *banyan* knows by the time he's six years old.'

He had found what he was looking for. 'Do you remember how much each crew member received when the quartermasters were sharing out the prize?'

Jezreel thought for a moment. 'Twenty coins each – fourteen gold and six silver. But there was a good pile of them left over when Dann spotted Gibson palming off the counterfeits on *Fancy*'s crew. Also there were a couple of chests on deck, still unopened.'

'An item here claims that *Ganj-i-Sawa'i* was carrying fifteen thousand *mohurs* in coin.' Hector made a quick calculation. 'If we only saw four or five thousand *mohurs* in coin – and that's being generous – it means Delhi is overstating by a factor of three.'

'Then this whole exercise is a farce. Why don't we simply divide all the values of the items on the list by three?'

'That's not what I've in mind,' Hector told him. 'Tell me this: what would Baldridge in St Mary's, or someone like him, pay for a necklace of sapphire and garnets brought to him by a free-booter, knowing that it was looted from the Great Mogul's own ship?'

'A quarter of the true value, if he's lucky; a fifth if it's some-thing that can be easily traced.'

'That's how we decide the value of jewelled daggers, ele-phants' teeth, silk brocades, and so forth: it's the price in gold that *Fancy*'s crew would get for them.'

'And how will Annesley justify such reductions when he starts negotiating with Aurangzeb's treasury?'

'I'm sure he'll call them "open market prices".'

Jezreel gave a snort of laughter. 'It's a pity that Jacques and Dufour aren't here. They'd have a much better idea of what things are worth.'

*

IN THE END, it took Hector and Jezreel most of the day to com-plete their calculations and when they added up the total it still came to over a ton in gold.

'*Fancy*'s company must be delighted,' said Jezreel, getting up and stretching. 'I wonder where they are now.'

'Scattered to the four winds, if they've any sense,' said

Hector. 'Avery will have got rid of the ship and advised her company to lie low.'

'With all that plunder to spend, they will not listen to him, the idiots.'

Both men knew it was true. Many of *Fancy*'s men would squander their money in a glorious spree, celebrating their luck. The moment they came ashore, there would be raucous drinking, wild extravagance and much boasting as they flaunted their new-found wealth. A swarm of spongers and toadies would descend upon them, as well as shady tavern owners, crooked gamblers, unscrupulous panderers and their whores. Within weeks, they would be penniless. Far worse, they would have attracted the attention of the authorities.

Jezreel rolled his head from side to side to ease his neck muscles. 'Long Ben's not going to survive for long with a price on his head. The net will be closing in on him as soon as the first members of his crew are arrested. They'll talk and the trail will lead to him eventually.'

'That's certainly possible,' Hector admitted. 'But I've a feeling that Avery has his own plans on how to give the authorities the slip.'

Jezreel gave him a quizzical glance. 'If Tavares is right and the London Directors of the East India Company ask us for information that might lead to his capture, do we cooperate?'

Hector thought carefully before he answered. 'Avery's different. He's not like Tew and certainly not like Mayes, nor those other freebooter captains who gathered at the Straits of Alexander. We'll just have to wait and see what is required of us.'

He was reluctant to admit to his friend that in some ways he retained his admiration for the astute way in which Avery had conducted his career as a freebooter.

Jezreel spread his hands in a gesture of apology. 'I know hardly anything about Avery. On *Fancy* he treated me the same as any other member of the ship's company, fair but strict. But he seemed to confide in you from time to time. So I'll go along with whatever you think best.'

Hector stifled a flicker of resentment. He remembered how it was Jezreel in St Mary's who had first put forward the idea of turning freebooter. Now the big man was shifting onto his shoulders the responsibility of deciding how best to avoid the consequences.

'Jezreel, it would help me to decide whether or not to cooperate with Annesley's superiors in London, if I knew what you would do in England if the choice was yours.'

The speed with which Jezreel answered told Hector that he had already thought about his future. 'I'd go to find my family in Sussex,' he replied instantly. 'I expect my parents have passed away, but I have a brother and two sisters. One or other of them could be living on the smallholding where we grew up. I'd see if I could settle down, get farm work.' He paused, and his eyes clouded over. 'But that will depend on the manslaughter charges against me.'

Hector made an effort to sound encouraging. 'Those charges have been gathering dust in a file for years, Jezreel. It's possible that the family of the dead man has given up trying to get you in front of the courts. And even if they do succeed, a good lawyer would argue that it was a genuine accident, as sometimes happens in a prize fight.'

'Good lawyers cost good money,' Jezreel answered glumly just as the door to their makeshift office opened and the Chief Factor came in.

Wordlessly, Hector handed him the revised list of values, and for a long time Annesley stood reading through the pages. Finally, he said, 'Add a line at the end to state that the values are based on first-hand observation; then both of you sign as witnesses. Tomorrow you can write out three fair copies. I'll provide you with enough paper and writing materials.'

Placing the list on the makeshift table along with the original inventory, he stood aside so they could leave the room, then he locked the door behind them. They were left to make their own way out of the building and back to the storeroom where they slept.

When the Chief Factor was out of earshot, Jezreel growled, 'Annesley's an ungrateful sod. He should get his bookkeepers to make those copies. We're not his secretaries.'

'He can't trust his local staff. They might leak the details of those lists to their merchant friends in Surat. As Luis said, there's a *shroff* working here who is related to Manuj Dosi.'

They had emerged into the courtyard as the Factory premises were being made secure for the night. Hector nodded towards the doormen sliding into place the thick wooden bar that would keep the heavy double gate shut until the morning. 'Perhaps we've got something to thank Annesley for; if Tavares is correct about Manuj Dosi being a danger, the Chief Factor is making it very difficult for him to get at us.'

*

AS IT TURNED OUT, Phillips of the *Maynard* was the sort of hard-driving captain who, having set a departure date, kept to it. Two days later Annesley informed Hector and Jezreel that he was sending them downriver aboard a lighter taking a consignment of cotton goods that had to reach Swally Hole before *Maynard* sailed. The lighter was already loading at the steps beside the maidan and would leave that same afternoon on the ebb tide.

It was Bendall who accompanied them to the waterfront. 'Here, you can make yourselves useful,' he said to Hector handing him a bamboo tube, some two feet long, both ends capped and sealed. 'Make sure you give this to Captain Phillips. It contains a copy of that list you prepared, for the Board of Directors in London to consider.'

Jezreel was already aboard the lighter so Hector turned and balanced his way along the narrow sagging gangplank. The vessel was a beamier version of the *thoni* that Vieira had used during the attempt to rescue Salima from *Pearl*. Most of the rowing benches had been removed to create a large open space amidships now tightly packed with bales of calico. A stubby mast was set well forward but there was no sign of a sail. Instead the two thwarts closest to the bows remained as rowing benches. Four oarsmen were already in position, waiting their orders from the helmsman who steered from a small decked area in the stern. He was a typical river man, lean and wiry, wearing only a loincloth and with a dirty cotton turban wound loosely about his head.

The craft was so crammed with cargo that the two passengers had no choice but to sit themselves on the bales of calico.

'Should be a lot more comfortable than riding an ox cart,' muttered Jezreel. He placed his rolled bundle of belongings behind him as a cushion so he could sit with his back against the edge of the helmsman's deck, facing forward. Hector sat down beside him while a teenage lad, the helmsman's son by the look of him, darted along the stone steps, casting off the mooring lines. The lighter began to drift out into the current and the youngster came scampering nimbly up the gangplank in time to turn and haul it aboard with the help of one of the oarsmen.

Scarcely had the *thoni* gathered way before there were shouts from the bank. It was Luis. He was thrusting his way between the traders and porters on the maidan, calling out and waving to attract their attention.

'Put back, please,' Hector asked, turning round to the helmsman and pointing at Luis. The boatman ignored him so he repeated himself more sharply, 'Put back!' When Luis reached the top of the steps he was some twenty yards away. The young man cupped his hands, and called out, 'I haven't said goodbye!' Then he held up a small package and shouted something in a language that the helmsman understood. After another moment's hesitation, he leaned on the tiller, and the lighter began to slant back towards the shore.

Luis kept pace, half-running, half-walking along the river bank. The ebb tide was beginning to run strongly, and the lighter was carried some distance downstream before it was close enough for him to take a flying leap across the gap.

'Luckily someone saw you leaving and sent word. I ran all the way,' he gasped, as he caught his breath.

'Another few minutes and we would not have been able to pick you up,' Hector told him. 'What did you shout to the helmsman that made him change his mind?'

Luis chuckled. 'I called out that I'd brought some *mithi keka* for you and the crew to enjoy on the trip to Swally Hole. I was counting on the fact that either he or his son has a sweet tooth.'

He passed across the package he had been carrying.

'What is it?' Hector enquired. The package was loosely covered in muslin.

'Take a look, but please handle it carefully.'

Hector unwound the cloth to expose a wheel-shaped cake, a foot across and an inch thick. The surface was studded with small nuts embedded in a glaze of honey, and there was an aroma of cinnamon mingled with unknown spices.

'*Bolo doce*, a local speciality of the Portuguese in Surat,' Luis explained. 'We eat it on feast days.'

He looked over Hector's shoulder at the helmsman for approval. The man was nodding appreciatively and grinning, while his son's eyes were bright with anticipation.

'I promised my father that I'd put the package into your hands personally, so it only remains to wish you a safe journey. Take good care of yourselves.' Luis embraced Jezreel, then Hector. Balancing on the gunwale, he launched himself into an ambitious leap that brought him most of the way to the bank, landing up to his waist in the swirling brown water with a great splash. Floundering his way on shore, he turned and waved goodbye.

Jezreel and Hector went back to where they had been sitting. Making himself comfortable, Hector carefully placed the package beside him. He would share out the *bolo doce* before they reached Swally Hole. As for the little pistol that Luis had wrapped inside the muslin, he would find the right moment to transfer the weapon to an inside pocket when no one was looking. *Maynard*'s captain would not be pleased that one of his passengers, a confessed pirate, had come aboard armed.

The current in the Tapti and the strong ebb tide made for rapid progress. The four oarsmen in the bow needed only to take an occasional pull with their blades to keep their vessel in midstream. Within minutes the lighter was level with the shipyards on the south bank. The rhythmic tap tap of hammers carried clearly though the shipwrights perched on the skeletons of the half-built vessels did not look up from their work. Then came the last outlying houses of Surat itself – a straggle of low, mean huts that petered out as the river widened and took a bend. Within another mile there was nothing on either bank but an impenetrable dark green wall above the tangled grey roots of mangrove swamps. Here the river was utterly deserted, with not even a fisherman in sight.

Hector had not realized how much he had missed travelling by water, with its gliding progress and the soothing gurgle of water sliding past a vessel's hull. The bales of calico underneath him made a comfortable mattress. He settled back and closed his eyes, appreciating the warmth of the sun on his face and the slight rocking of the boat beneath him. He was glad to be leaving Hindustan, though sorry to leave Jacques behind. His thoughts turned to the moment when he saw Maria again, and he began to rehearse in his mind what he should say to her.

Time passed, though he had no idea how long it was that he had been dozing. Something woke him. It was not Jezreel, for he could hear steady breathing beside him. The big man had also fallen asleep, an arm held across his face shielding his eyes from the sun. Hector raised his head. He had slid down until he was lying almost horizontal, his head on his bundle of possessions, his feet towards the lighter's bow. He began to sit up straight, squinting against the harsh glare of the sun off the surface of the river.

Something flashed across his vision, a split second of shadow.

The next instant a loop of cloth dropped past his mouth and nose, then clamped around his neck, and tightened. His hands flew up as he began to choke. He scrabbled with his fingers, trying to relieve the pressure of the noose. His head was hauled back, and he found himself staring up at the cloudless sky. Someone behind him was twisting the garrotte ever tighter. He felt his attacker press up behind him, smelled sweat and the sharp odour of curry on the man's breath. The helmsman was trying to throttle him. In desperation he threw himself to one side, wriggling and thrashing. He tried to call to Jezreel for help, but the cloth around his throat was so tight that no words came out. There was a roaring in his ears and he jerked forward abruptly, hoping to dislodge the man behind him. But the move had been anticipated. His attacker stayed clamped on his back. Ahead of him all four oarsmen had left their benches. One of them, a small man with a badly pockmarked face, was scrambling across the bales of cloth towards him and holding a short-bladed knife. The other three were advancing on Jezreel. Hector, both hands on the garrotte around his throat, was struggling to break free when the pockmarked attacker reached him and took hold of his left hand. He jerked it forward and pressed it down on the rough canvas surface of the bale beneath him. In a moment of awful clarity Hector knew what was happening: the man with the knife was about to cut off a finger. The realization produced a surge of panicked strength and he managed to snatch back his hand, then rolled away. With his one free hand he groped for Luis's *bolo doce*. His fingers brushed the stickiness of the cake and he fumbled for what lay beneath. The pain in his neck was becoming unbearable, and in a few seconds he would black out. Fortunately, the butt of the little pistol was toward him and fitted into the palm of his hand. He was pinioned so tightly that there was no way of taking aim or selecting his target. All he could do was bring his arm around his body, hold the little pistol under his armpit, press the muzzle against whoever was behind him and pull the trigger.

He barely heard the shot. Instantly the pressure on the garrotte eased, and the cloth slipped clear. He bent forward, gasping to draw air into his lungs. In front of him the knifeman was hesitating, disconcerted by the sudden turn of events. Hector lashed out with his foot and was lucky. The man had been crouching to do his work, and the kick connected with his pockmarked face, knocking him off balance. Hector twisted around. The helmsman was sitting on the stern deck, shocked and clutching his side. Blood was oozing between his fingers. His turban, his strangler's noose, was lying beside him. His son, alarmed and wide-eyed, was holding the tiller and keeping course in mid-river.

Hector turned his attention back to his knife-wielding attacker. Still short of breath, Hector knew he did not have the strength to take him on. He saw the knifeman glance warily toward the pistol in his hand. Hector raised the gun and took deliberate aim. Duped, his attacker edged backward, casting anxious glances to the other oarsmen for help. But Jezreel had them fully occupied. The ex-prize-fighter had picked up the gang plank. He gave a great intimidating roar and advanced across the cotton bales towards his three opponents. One man threw the knife he was carrying but missed. Then Jezreel was close enough to swing the gang plank in a great scything sweep that knocked the nearest man overboard. The other two retreated towards the bows, allowing Jezreel to come close enough to drop the gang plank and pick up an oar instead. Using it as a quarterstaff he clubbed one of his opponents to his knees, then rammed the other in the stomach with the butt end. Then he stood back, allowing time for both victims to abandon the vessel and jump into the river. A moment later, Hector's attacker followed their example.

'Now for the others,' Jezreel announced grimly. He stalked back toward the stern deck and glared menacingly at the helmsman's son. The youngster was frozen in place, gripping the tiller, his eyes stretched wide with fear. 'Clear off, you little turd,' Jezreel growled and made as if to use the oar as a club. The boy needed no further encouragement. He too jumped into the river and began to swim for shore. Setting the oar aside, Jezreel bent down and took the wounded helmsman by the shoulders. Then he casually dragged him to the edge of the boat, and threw him into the river.

'Incompetent bastards,' Jezreel commented, straightening up. He was completely calm. 'They waited until you had a loop round your throat. I was half awake by the time they got to me.'

'Manuj Dosi must have recruited them at short notice. They weren't professional killers,' Hector said. Without a helmsman, the lighter was spinning slowly on the surface of the river and had drifted close to the northern bank. If something wasn't done quickly, it would run aground. 'Take the helm for a moment and try to bring her back into mid-stream. I'll see if there's some sort of sail.'

After a few moments searching in the bows, he found a small, tattered sail wrapped around its spar. With Jezreel's help he hoisted on the stubby mast, and the two of them took turns, one steering, the other adjusting the set of the sail or rowing, while the last of the ebb brought the lighter down to Swally Hole.

TWENTY-ONE

FIVE MONTHS LATER, Hector stood at *Maynard*'s stern rail and felt his heart beat a little faster. Captain Phillips had brought his vessel within a cable's length of the shore and dropped anchor in seven fathoms. As the vessel swung head to wind and steadied, Hector caught a glimpse of red-tiled roofs and the bell tower of a church beyond the battlements of the two forts whose cannon commanded the roadstead. Rows of neat two-storey houses extended up the slope behind the little town, their whitewashed walls dazzling in the July sunshine. The sails of two windmills on the crest of a nearby hill were turning slowly as the onshore breeze picked up strength.

Santa Cruz of Tenerife was as sleepy-looking and peaceful as when he had said goodbye to Maria there two years ago. He remembered the sadness of that day. They had both known it would be hard to endure being apart, but they had believed the decision would lead to a better future. They told one another that the separation was only temporary and had talked about how it would be when Hector sent word that he had found a home for them in Libertalia. Neither of them had foreseen the emptiness of that dream.

From behind him, Phillips' croaking voice interrupted his thoughts: 'You have the rest of the day to locate your wife and child, and bring them aboard.' With an effort, Hector pushed aside his dread that Maria might have moved away or – worse – the birth of their child had gone wrong.

'If you're not back before dark, I'll inform the authorities that you're a convicted pirate and they'll bring you back in irons,' Phillips continued, before giving a wheezing cough.

When Hector had first laid eyes on *Maynard*'s captain, he had mistaken him for a sickly clerk. Phillips, though still in middle age, had lost most of his hair. He made the most of what was left of it by combing long strands over a bald, mottled scalp. Thin wrists emerged from the frayed cuffs of the sea coat, shiny with wear, and he shuffled rather than walked about the deck, frequently holding on to rigging for support. There was nothing to indicate that the stooped, frail-looking figure was a very competent mariner. He had brought his ship from Surat to the Canaries in near record time and without a single mishap.

'I give my word that I will return by dusk,' Hector promised. He was confident that he remembered correctly the house where he had left Maria with her cousins' family. If he was wrong, Santa Cruz was a small enough place, perhaps two or three thousand inhabitants at most, for him to make enquiries and track her down.

He cupped his hands and shouted in Spanish to a local boatman who was rowing out to *Maynard*, looking for a chance to earn a few coins. He needed to be brought on land, he called, and would be ready in a few minutes. He hurried down to the little cabin he shared with Jezreel, and sorted through his meagre bundle of belongings. He selected his only clean shirt and a coloured handkerchief to tie around his neck. He had no spare breeches so he pulled on a pair of *jamas*, the loose knee-length trousers of light cotton that he had acquired in Delhi. He took a moment to examine his face in the cracked mirror fixed to the bulkhead and wondered how much his appearance had changed since he last saw Maria. She would expect him to be tanned but even in the dim light of the windowless cabin, he could see flecks of grey in his hair and beard stubble. For a moment he considered wearing the gorgeously embroidered jacket that came with his *serapha*, but decided that it would create entirely the wrong impression. If he succeeded in finding Maria, he reminded himself, it was to tell her that their dream of Libertalia had come to nothing. He would be misleading her if he showed up dressed up in such finery when, in truth, he was being transported to London to face the charge of piracy.

The boatman eyed him with curiosity as he climbed down the rope ladder and settled himself in the stern. 'No one else coming ashore with you?' he asked.

'Just me. I must be back aboard by dusk so I may need you to bring me back out to the ship later.'

'A short visit, then?' The boatman was obviously keen to find out more about his passenger. He had noticed the resentful faces staring down from *Maynard*'s rail. Captain Phillips was allowing no one else to go ashore.

Hector was too on edge to want to get into a conversation, so said nothing.

'That's an English ship, isn't it?' said the boatman, settling to the oars and beginning to row.

When Hector did not respond, the boatman tried again. 'Don't recognize her. Sometimes we get Bristol vessels, coming to buy our Canary wine. I've a brother who has a fair amount ready for shipment if you're interested: good quality stuff, nice and sweet, with a fine colour – pale with just a hint of green.'

Hector gave up the attempt to ignore the man. 'The vessel's not here to buy wine. She's an East India Company ship, seven months out from India, bound for London.'

'Thought I recognized the flag,' said the boatman. 'How come you speak such good Spanish?'

'My mother was from Galicia,' Hector told him curtly.

'That accounts for the accent,' said the boatman. He took several pulls with the oars, before adding, 'If it's seven months you've been at sea, I know of a good tavern where there are some very obliging serving maids.'

Hector lost patience. 'I'm not looking for a tavern or for girls. I'm coming here to find my wife,' he snapped.

The boatman was so startled that he almost missed his stroke. 'Your wife! Who would she be?'

Hector scowled at him. 'That's none of your business.'

'Sorry if I gave offence.'

There was an uncomfortable silence until they were approaching the landing place at which point Hector decided that he had been unnecessarily rude. 'My wife's name is Maria. She has long dark hair and dark eyes.'

'We've a lot of Marias in Santa Cruz,' observed the boatman sulkily. He had not yet got over Hector's rebuff. 'Most of them have dark hair and dark eyes.'

'She's not from Santa Cruz,' Hector informed him. 'She's been staying here with her cousins. Her own people are from Andalucia, though we first met in Peru.'

Unexpectedly the boatman beamed. 'Then that must be Maria who lives at Alonso Fernandez's house on Calle San Cristobal. His people are from Andalucia originally.'

With a sudden surge of excitement Hector stared at him. 'You know my Maria?' he asked hopefully.

'She looked after my two young nephews when my sister was laid up with a bad bout of fever. Always generous with her time. A good woman.' He gave Hector a thoughtful look. 'She's got a little one of her own to look after now.' There was a tone of reproof in his voice.

'Boy or girl?' Hector blurted.

'You don't know?' This time it was definitely an accusation.

Hector felt he had to offer an explanation. 'I have to go to sea to earn my living. My last voyage turned out to be far longer than I anticipated.'

The boatman was regarding him with open distaste. 'Then you don't deserve her,' he grunted and spat over the side.

They turned into the narrow inlet that led to the town's landing place. Four or five men were gathered at the head of the slipway. Judging by the look of them, they included a port officer and a couple of customs men. There was also a militiaman armed with a musket. None of them appeared to be over-friendly and Hector sensed that his unannounced arrival had to be handled with tact.

With a final heave on his oars, the boatman sent the keel of his boat grinding up the slipway, and Hector climbed out into two inches of water. It was the first time he had set foot on land for seven months. The ground tilted and swayed beneath his feet.

'I would be grateful if I could be allowed to spend a few hours in Santa Cruz,' Hector explained to the circle of mistrustful faces.

'Why has your captain not contacted the authorities for permission to anchor in the roadstead?' demanded one of the reception committee. He was dressed in a uniform coat of dark green and though it was a warm day he had chosen to wear a wig. Hector guessed he was an official from the mayor's office, probably the port superintendent.

'Captain Phillips sets sail again this evening,' Hector replied in what he hoped was a suitably humble tone.

The official was openly hostile. 'Return to your ship, and tell the captain that he must depart immediately.'

'I need just an hour or so,' Hector pleaded.

The boatman, who had dragged his boat a few feet onto the slipway, sauntered over to join the group. 'He claims he's come to meet his wife.'

The official did not seem to have heard. Addressing Hector in loud, formal tones, he announced, 'You are refused permission to land. Further, if your captain does not leave within the next two hours, I will authorize the batteries to open fire.'

'Gonzalez, don't be so pompous,' said a woman's voice.

Hector's heart leaped. He spun round, almost falling. Walking briskly towards them was Maria. She was dressed in a pale blouse and long dark skirt, with a light scarf over her shoulders. She was almost exactly as he remembered her – poised and beautiful, the same light freckles, the dark eyes full of life and the same air of quiet competence. She was holding a toddler on her hip.

Gonzalez, the port official, blinked and stepped back. Maria strode past him, carefully set down the toddler on the ground, threw her arms around Hector and hugged him. Releasing her embrace she turned to face her audience and announced firmly, 'It's as he says: he's come to Santa Cruz to find his wife.'

In the stunned silence that followed, Hector stood transfixed. The breath seemed to have gone from his lungs. Then, feeling lightheaded and slightly dazed, he reached out and took Maria back into his arms. She leaned her head forward against his chest for a long moment, and he felt her warmth and the beating of her heart. He held her against him until, very gently, she pushed herself away from him, leaned down and picked up the toddler. Holding up the child in front of him, she said quietly, 'Isabel, meet your father.'

Hector found himself gazing into huge, dark eyes that regarded him gravely. His daughter had a tiny pert nose, smooth and flawless skin and her mother's trick of pausing for a moment while making up her mind. After several heartbeats the toddler treated him to a delighted smile, unhurried and genuine.

'I named her after my own grandmother,' Maria's voice came to him through a mist of happiness. 'I hope you approve.'

Hector was still at a loss for words. He had imagined this moment for so long, and feared that he was deluding himself. Yet the reality matched the dream. This was a moment in his life that he would never forget.

Someone cleared his throat noisily, and Hector looked up to see that the port official, Gonzalez, was flustered. His colleagues were looking on, slightly amused and waiting to see how he would handle the unexpected situation. 'Under the circumstances, Senhor . . .' began the official.

'Lynch, Hector Lynch,' Hector told him.

'Under the circumstances, Senhor Lynch, you are welcome in

Santa Cruz. We can regularize your documents later, when you have decided on how long you intend to stay.'

All of a sudden, Hector's delight at seeing Maria again was quenched by the bleak thought of what he had to explain to her.

'Thank you,' he said to the official. 'My wife and I would appreciate time together.'

With a few curious glances in their direction, the reception committee began to disperse.

Hector turned to the boatman. 'I'll need you to take me back out to the ship later, and will pay you then.'

He could not fail to notice the slight frown that passed across Maria's face as she overheard these words, and knew he had to tell her the truth as quickly as possible.

'Is there somewhere we can talk privately?' he asked her.

Her eyes flicked up to meet his, and then after the slightest pause, she said softly, 'Why don't we go back to my cousins' house, where I've been living. We can talk on the way.'

Side by side, they began to walk away from the landing slip. Between them little Isabel took unsteady steps, keeping balance by clutching a finger on the hand of each of her parents. The toddler's tight grip thrilled Hector. It made him feel even closer to Maria.

'How did you know to come down to the landing place?' he asked.

She gave him a sideways look, a slight smile on her lips. 'A watchman at one of the mills up behind the town reported an unknown ship making for the roadstead. Santa Cruz is a small place and word spread. Someone said that the vessel looked like an Indiaman. That's unusual. So I had this feeling that you might be aboard, or it carried a message for me. I decided to come down to the harbour.'

Hector allowed a long interval to pass while he thought how he might approach what he had to say. He waited until little Isabel had grown tired of walking, and Maria had picked her up. She placed the little girl on her hip, on the side away from him, so they could walk side by side, their shoulders occasionally brushing against one another. It created an intimacy between them, yet still he struggled to broach the subject of his past, and their future.

She seemed to appreciate his difficulty, and began to talk, lightly and easily. 'My cousins have been very kind. They are good people, and made me feel at home,' her voice dropped to hardly more than a whisper, 'but it has been such a long time.'

'Did you get my letter?' he asked. 'The one I wrote from St Mary's in Madagascar?'

She nodded.

'I tried several times to write after that, but it was never possible to know if you would get my letter.' He stopped, reluctant to sound as if he was making excuses.

She waited for him to go on, and Hector sensed that she already knew what he was about to say.

'When Jacques and I reached Madagascar, we couldn't find anyone to tell us exactly how we could get from there to Libertalia. There was only rumour and speculation.' He was choosing his words carefully. 'Then Jezreel showed up, and the three of us decided to join a company under a Captain Avery who was proposing to cruise in the Indian Ocean.'

'I've heard of Captain Avery,' she said quietly.

'Then you'll know he's a freebooter. His ship, *Fancy*, was powerful and seaworthy. I thought that *Fancy* might call in at Libertalia, wherever it was, and even if she didn't, my share of her prize would mean I had enough money for you and me, and the baby of course, to go wherever we wanted and make a new start.'

She was not looking at him as they walked, but concentrating instead on the cobbles beneath her feet.

'Go on,' she prompted.

He drew a breath. 'It didn't turn out well. We took a tremendous prize, but neither Jacques, Jezreel nor I shared in the booty. We finished up in Hindustan.'

There was another long pause. They had crossed the main town square and started up a narrow street that led up the hill. The slope was steep, and after months at sea Hector was beginning to feel the strain on his calf muscles. Maria seemed to be untroubled by the climb, even with the weight of the toddler on her hip.

'It turned out that Avery had plundered one of the Great Mogul's own ships, and we were lucky to be spared our lives when we were brought before an Indian judge.' A gruesome image of Quartermaster Gibson crushed under an elephant's foot came into his mind. 'Jacques has chosen to stay on in Hindustan while Jezreel and I were handed over to the English East India Company for punishment.'

The sun was directly overhead now, the air hot enough to keep most people off the street. Maria took a small length of cloth out of her pocket and placed it over the toddler's head to provide protection.

Suddenly all that Hector had wanted to say came out in a rush. He stopped, turned and pointed down into the harbour at *Maynard*. 'Jezreel's on that ship right now. When we get to London the East India merchants will question us about Avery and his piracy. We've agreed to cooperate. I've no idea what will happen afterwards. Very likely, we'll be executed as pirates.'

Maria transferred Isabel to her other hip. She retained her composure. 'Why has your ship called in at Santa Cruz, and why have you been allowed ashore?'

'Because I made it a condition that I would only help track down Avery if they let me see you . . . and my child, and you were able to come to London with me.'

He put both hands gently on Maria's shoulders and turned her so she faced him. Isabel, still sitting on Maria's hip, looked up at him and treated him to another of her heart-stirring smiles.

'Maybe that was a mistake,' he said huskily. 'Perhaps it would have been better if I had written to you to tell you all this, and not exposed you to this disaster. Then you could have chosen to go your own way, and put me behind you.'

She reached up with her free hand and touched him on the cheek. 'Hector, you've done the right thing. I prefer that we are together again, even if only for a few days or a few weeks. Anything else is unthinkable.'

Hector looked around, taking in the trim little houses, the surrounding hills and the sparkling blue waters of the bay, now stippled with whitecaps. 'Why would you want to exchange this quiet, pleasant place for an uncertain future in London? Would it not be better for Isabel to grow up here?'

Her eyes were brimming with tears. 'Here, hold Isabel for a moment,' she said, and passed him the toddler while she felt in her sleeve for a handkerchief. When she had dried her eyes, she looked up at him, and she was smiling.

'You can be such a fool, sometimes, Hector,' she said between sniffs. 'Of course I want to come with you, whatever happens in London. If I didn't, I would forever think what could have been.'

'Are you sure?' he asked, though he already knew her answer.

'Of course I am sure,' she said firmly. 'Now hand me back Isabel. You told the boatman that you would be going back to the ship later today. As Isabel and I are coming with you, there's no time to waste. We need to tell my cousins what is happening, and collect my things.'

He reached into his pocket and took out the pearl bracelet. 'This isn't booty. An old lady in India gave it to me to thank me for helping her at a dangerous time. I want you to have it.'

Maria took the bracelet from him and held it up so the sunlight brought out the luminous glow of the pearls.

'It's a wonderful gift, and I would dearly love to keep it,' she said, lifting the bracelet even higher as Isabel gave a crow of delight and tried to take it from her. 'But, with your agreement, I have a better use for it. My cousins are by no means rich. Yet they took me in, showed me every kindness and have never asked for anything in return. Now, so abruptly, I will be leaving them. This bracelet is my chance to show how much I value what they freely gave me.'

She looked at him, seeking his approval.

Of course he agreed. Maria's instinct for generosity was one of the many, many reasons to love her.

*

JEZREEL INSISTED on moving out of the little cabin and sleeping on *Maynard*'s deck. It was only right, he pointed out, that Hector, Maria and Isabel had their own accommodation as a family. Besides, it was no hardship for him to sleep under the stars. The July nights were short, and the temperature was mild. So while *Maynard* sailed north from Tenerife, Hector and Maria were able to enjoy some of the happiest hours of their lives together. Isabel charmed Captain Phillips enough for him to relax strict shipboard discipline and allow her parents to walk his quarterdeck by day, the toddler between them. At such times Hector found himself wishing that the voyage would go on for ever. The sunshine warm on his face, he would look up at the sails bellying in the following breeze, then close his eyes so he could better feel through the soles of his feet the gentle rocking motion as the ship ploughed forward through the sea. But when he opened his eyes again and looked about him, it was impossible to ignore the message of the cheerful faces and good spirits of the ship's company: every mile was bringing the ship nearer to her final destination.

Phillips kept a safe distance from any vessels they sighted. Hector overheard him remark to his first mate that, after successfully avoiding freebooters in the Indian Ocean, he had no intention of falling prey to home-based pirates.

So Hector was puzzled when, as *Maynard* entered the English Channel, Phillips ordered the helmsman to alter course and steer directly for a vessel approaching from the north-east. The stranger's sails had been visible for some time, and Phillips had been watching them intently through his spyglass. It was another two hours before the other vessel, a large merchantman, was close enough for Hector to make out the flag flying at her stern. The design was of nine red and white horizontal stripes and a red cross in the upper corner, the same as *Maynard*'s. She was another East India Company ship, outward bound.

The two vessels drew together until they were some thirty paces apart and backed their sails. For a few minutes they held their positions while the two captains had a brief exchange of information, shouting through their speaking trumpets above the creak of rigging as the two vessels rolled on the gentle swell, and the occasional slap of canvas.

Berkeley Castle was bound for Bombay and then for Swally Hole. Her captain wanted to know the latest news from Hindustan.

'Surat?' he shouted. 'I heard there was trouble with the Mogul governor.'

'All quiet now,' Phillips called back. 'Trading has resumed.'

'What about customs fees?'

'Unchanged from last year.'

Then came a question that caused Hector's stomach to give a lurch as he and Jezreel stood listening at the rail.

'Hear any reports of a freebooter vessel called *Fancy*?' asked the captain of *Berkeley Castle*. Phillips could not stop himself from flicking a sideways glance at his two passengers.

'You mean Avery's ship?' he called back.

'She's vanished, along with Avery and all his company. Leadenhall badly wants him caught and brought to justice.'

Jezreel leaned close to Hector. 'Leadenhall is the London street where the East India Company has its headquarters,' he said in a low voice.

'Heard nothing of him,' Phillips shouted across the gap.

'A pity. There's a five hundred pound reward on offer for information leading to his arrest.'

The breeze was causing the ships to drift, and the gap between them was widening. The conversation came to an end as the two captains wished one another a prosperous voyage before ordering their crews to make sail.

Phillips waited until *Maynard* was underway. Directing a sardonic smile towards Hector and Jezreel, he observed, 'Seems that the two of you will be very much in demand when we get to London.'

TWENTY-TWO

THE LAST DAY of July promised to be blisteringly hot as *Maynard* came up the Thames with the making tide. By eight in the morning a quivering heat haze had begun to form above the Poplar marsh when she picked up a mooring buoy in Blackwall Reach. A wherry came out with a searcher from the local revenue office to check her cargo. When he clambered out of the hold after finishing his inspection, he was gasping for air and his drunkard's face with its network of veins was flushed a bright red.

'Captain, these are my findings,' he said to Phillips, flapping his tally sheet in the air to dry off the sweat that had dripped from his forehead and was causing the ink to blur. 'I'll bring them to Customs House for the calculation of excise due. If you wish, you can accompany me into the city.'

Hector had been out on the main deck since first light, standing with Maria and Isabel at the rail and gazing at the passing shoreline as *Maynard* came upriver. It had been too hot and stuffy to stay in their cramped cabin.

'Come up here, Lynch!' Phillips called down.

Hector gave Maria's hand a reassuring squeeze, and made his way up to the quarterdeck.

'Lynch, I'm taking you and your colleague direct to Leadenhall. The Company can decide what to do with you.'

'What about my wife and child?' Hector asked. 'What happens to them while I'm away? When will I be back?'

Phillips turned his attention to where Maria was watching, Isabel on her hip. Seeing the captain looking in her direction, the toddler removed her thumb from her mouth and smiled up at him.

Phillips's expression softened. 'Your wife and child can stay aboard *Maynard* for now. The ship will be on this mooring for several days while we unload.'

'Thank you.' Hector's stomach knotted with anxiety at the thought of leaving Maria and Isabel and not knowing when he would return.

'The sooner you're off my hands, the better,' Phillips snapped, resuming his usual cold manner.

Hector had barely enough time to explain to Maria what was happening, before he and Jezreel were climbing down the ship's ladder to join Phillips and the sweaty searcher in the customs wherry. Three oarsmen rowed from the forward thwarts while their passengers sat facing one another on benches in the stern. As Hector settled into his place next to Jezreel, he could not help noticing the bamboo tube that protruded from a canvas satchel of ship's documents at Phillips's feet. Moments later the boat had cast off from *Maynard*, and the wherrymen were rowing up-river, keeping close to the north bank to take advantage of the slack water and counter-currents now that the tide had turned.

The Thames foreshore reeked. High-water mark was a swathe of rubbish where broken branches and rotten timbers lay jumbled together. The falling tide was leaving all manner of filth on the mud: raw sewage, shreds of rags and the bloated corpses of drowned animals. Their sodden, matted fur gave no clue as to their identity. Only by their size and shape could one guess whether the living creature had been a cat or a dog, or one of the sheep grazing the flood dyke. Buzzing clouds of flies rose and settled on the carrion, and seagulls tore and squabbled over fresh pickings. Occasionally one of the wherrymen gave an irritated grunt as his oar blade tangled with some nastiness floating in the river. When the boat passed an exceptionally foul object, the searcher covered his mouth and nose with his handkerchief. The rest of the time he used it to wipe the sweat rolling down his face.

Hector twisted round to look at the opposite bank a quarter of a mile distant. Here the view was very different. A magnificent parkland with tree-lined avenues and footpaths spread up the hillside behind the tiled roofs of a riverside village. At the foot of the slope the sunlight flashed from the glass windowpanes of a palatial mansion. On the summit of the hill stood a new-looking structure that could have been a defensive tower except there were no fortifications. The walls were of pinkish-red brick pierced by tall windows. Small turrets capped the corners of the roof. He was puzzling what purpose the building served when Phillips pointed up at it and asked the searcher if he knew when the 'king's astronomical observator' was due to publish his new star map for navigators. 'I've no idea, captain,' the man replied, 'I'm told that he just sits up there on his arse gazing at the sky. Refuses to tell anyone what he's learning.' The building on the hill, Hector concluded, was an observatory.

Their wherry was among a handful of vessels labouring upstream, following the curve of a great bend in the river. The majority of river users headed in the opposite direction. With little wind to fill their sails they were drifting with the current: crude rafts made of logs lashed together, coal barges and lighters, a sloop of war and merchant ships ranging in size from small hoys to a bulbous three-masted fluyt flying the red, white and blue of the flag of the Dutch Republic. A speeding shallop caught Hector's eye. Rowed by eight men in livery, it came weaving its way down through the slow-moving traffic, its sole passenger sitting in the stern under an awning with a gold fringe. Hector supposed that it was headed for the grand estate on the south bank.

Eventually the earth dyke on their right ended in a cluster of ramshackle cottages separated by plots of wasteland. They were scrubby forlorn little dwellings at the outermost fringe of the city. As the wherry progressed, the gaps between the houses disappeared until there was a continuous frontage of wharves, cranes, sheds, storehouses. Squeezed between them were the dingy run-down homes of dockworkers, sailors and labourers.

From time to time the oarsman nearest to Hector stopped rowing, produced a leather bottle and took several gulps. After a gassy belch, he passed the bottle on to his companions. Judging by the smell of the man's breath he was drinking beer.

During one of these pauses the customs searcher leaned forward and tapped Hector on the knee. It was evident that he had identified Hector as a newcomer to the capital.

'Know what we Londoners call that?' he asked, nodding towards a nearby dock.

In a gap between two moored barges was a light cargo crane with a rope and pulley, its arm projecting over the water. Hector could see nothing unusual about it. 'A hoist?' he suggested.

'A derrick!' The searcher grinned, showing bad teeth. 'It's for stretching the necks of those that the Admiralty Court condemns, pirates and the like. That's Execution Dock.' He settled back on his seat with an air of ghoulish triumph. 'Named after hangman Thomas Derrick in my great-grandfather's time.'

The wherry entered a final stretch of the river, and all at once Hector recognized the scene in the painting on the wall of the Company's council room in Surat. To his right was the massive bulk of a castle and up ahead the Thames was crammed with vessels. Some were riding at anchor waiting their turn at the quays. Others were rafted side by side in front of tall warehouses. Beyond the forest of their masts a row of houses apparently spanned the river itself. Beneath them was a glimpse of the pillars and arches of a bridge. The place was bustling with movement. Wagons were collecting and delivering their loads to the quays. Crates, sacks and barrels were being shifted between the ships and the warehouses. Dozens of small boats, painted red and green, hovered on the fringes, waiting for hire. The longest, busiest quay was dominated by a long, official-looking building that had the appearance of a customs house. They had reached London Pool, the head of navigation.

Their oarsmen swore and shouted insults, jostling and bumping other boats aside, as they forced a passage to the landing steps. They deposited their passengers ashore, and Hector and Jezreel followed Phillips and the customs searcher through the scrum of shirtless, sweating dockworkers stooped under sacks or pushing handcarts and wheelbarrows.

'Send the customs bill to East India House. They'll deal with it there,' Phillips told the searcher. Addressing Hector he said, 'Follow on close. I wouldn't want to have to tell your wife that I had lost you.'

Turning on his heel, he shouted, 'Chair!'

∗

IT WAS NOW mid-afternoon and a line of towering thunder-clouds was forming to the west of the city, though there was no immediate threat of a downpour. Nevertheless, the two burly men carrying Phillips in his sedan chair set off at such a brisk pace that Hector and Jezreel had to half-run, half-walk to keep up with them. Hector gave no thought to trying to escape. Phillips had reminded him that Maria and Isabel were hostages to their good behaviour.

An eddy of breeze brought another strong whiff of putrefaction. 'London stinks worse than Delhi,' he observed to his friend.

'That'll be the fish market at Billingsgate. I remember it from my prize-fighting days.'

Ahead of them the sedan men cut down a narrow alleyway, and there was a warning cry of 'By your leave!' as they trotted up behind a dawdling pedestrian. He must have moved aside too late for almost immediately came a shout of anger, followed by a string of oaths and a shout of, 'Have a care there, you brutes.'

Jezreel flashed a grin at Hector. 'Everyone in London is in a hurry.'

Judging by the twists and turns of their route, the sedan men were taking the shortest way to their destination. The streets they chose were barely wide enough for wheeled vehicles to pass one another. Anyone on foot had to avoid random scraps of rubbish and at the same time try not to step into the open central gutter. Scaffolding projected out into the road from half-built houses, and piles of cut stone, timber and sand provided further obstacles. It was evident that a building boom was in progress, and London was thriving. Yet as far as Hector could tell, the only people in the street were domestic servants on their errands, carriers making deliveries, labourers, costermongers and a number of ragged beggars.

'I don't see anyone who looks prosperous and rich, not like the *omrahs*,' Hector commented as they overtook a water carrier toiling along with small steps, his knees half-bent under his load. A wooden tub of water hung from each end of the yoke across his shoulders. Their contents occasionally slopped out on the roadway, leaving a trail of damp marks that rapidly evaporated in the sun.

'Everyone who can afford to do so has left the city and gone to their country houses,' Jezreel told him. 'They fear that bad air spreads fevers and disease.'

A strange-looking figure pressed himself against a wall to avoid being run down. Despite the heat he was dressed in three shabby coats, one on top of the other, and a stack of half a dozen hats was balanced on his head.

'That one should be in the madhouse.'

Jezreel laughed. 'He sells second-hand clothes. He's wearing his stock in trade.'

'I'd prefer to visit a tailor than to wear someone's cast-offs.'

'Most Londoners would agree with you, but they haven't the money. They love dressing up but they can't afford the prices. New cloth is expensive, so they make do with hand-me-downs.'

Which was why the East India Company shipped bales of Surat calico a third of the way round the world, Hector thought to himself. No wonder the merchants were desperate to appease the Great Mogul if cotton goods bought cheaply in Hindustan were being sold for a fat profit on the London market. A £500 reward for the capture of Henry Avery was a trifling outlay when they were also enriching themselves from the sale of silks, pepper and other luxury items. He jogged along behind the sedan chair, imagining how he would spend the reward. Split with Jezreel, the sum should be enough to keep him and his family in modest comfort while Isabel was growing up. If he invested the capital wisely there might even be enough to provide her with a dowry.

Sooner than he expected, the sedan turned out of a narrow passageway and on to the broader thoroughfare. Even if the sedan-chair carriers hadn't stopped and set down the chair, he would have known East India House among the other mansions. Thirty feet above the ground a large merchant ship sailed boldly across the front of the building. The vessel was the centrepiece of a brightly coloured tableau of prosperous foreign commerce. Two smaller ships floated on the same painted waves, heading over the horizon and into a pale blue sky. The building's parapet had been extended upward to accommodate the picture, and a pair of immense wooden dolphins, gilded and smiling, frolicked on the upper corners of the building. Presiding over this idealized scene was the carved statue of a man, three times life size. Wearing the working clothes of a seaman he stood feet apart, one hand on his hip, the other holding a walking stick, as he stared confidently ahead.

Hector craned back his head taking in the rest of the building's decoration. Between mullioned windows on the third floor was fixed a large shield with the royal coat of arms. A second shield on the floor below displayed the same company seal that he had seen behind Annesley's chair in the Council Chamber of Surat. Flanking this were more than a dozen smaller shields, extending across the width of the building. Some were still blank, awaiting their crests, others had coats of arms that he presumed belonged to major investors and officeholders of the Company. The overall effect was an unblushing statement of wealth and power.

Phillips had got out of the sedan chair and was paying off the carriers. 'I'm the captain of *Maynard*, newly arrived from Surat,' he informed a doorman in crimson livery. With a quick backward glance to check that Jezreel and Hector were on his heels, he led them inside India House.

The harsh glare of sunshine in the streets made the lobby seem very dark and gloomy. Daylight struggled to get past the iron bars that protected the small windows in the thick walls. Hector guessed that the ground floor of East India House was designed to discourage break-ins and burglars and to resist an angry mob. Fortunately the thickness of the walls also kept out the heat, and the large room was pleasantly cool.

'Wait here,' Phillips said, before crossing to a stairway in the far corner, and disappearing up to the next floor. Hector and Jezreel were left under the mistrustful oversight of two footmen stationed just inside the doorway.

They waited for more than an hour, seated on a bench and watching the day's business coming to an end. Junior clerks clattered up and down the stairs with folders and ledgers, and disappeared into back rooms apparently used for storage and archives. A few messengers called in at the street door with deliveries or to collect packages. The only person to give them more than a passing glance was a portly middle-aged fellow wearing a frothing full-length blond periwig. The coat of his lilac velvet suit was unbuttoned to display a brocade waistcoat stretched across an ample paunch. Stockings of the finest white silk showed off plump calves, and his jowly face spoke of good food and much drink. He exuded the air of someone comfortable with his own success and not afraid to show it. The attendants at the door sprang to attention as he came down the stairs and bowed him out into the street. Shortly afterwards the building began to empty as the company's employees left for their homes. Hector was beginning to think that he and Jezreel had been forgotten, when Phillips at last came down the stairs.

He was accompanied by a lean, trim man of about Hector's own age and height. Everything about him was an inconspicuous brown. The plain coat and breeches were the colour of dead leaves; his eyes were dark and slightly hooded; and the long loose hair that reached to his shoulders was mousey brown beginning to turn grey. The expression on his narrow face was watchful and reserved though there was a hint of purpose in his brisk stride as he came briskly across the lobby. Hector did not know what to make of him.

'These are the two men, Lynch and Hall,' Phillips informed his companion as Hector and Jezreel got to their feet. 'Both sailed with Avery and should be able to identify him.'

The newcomer was softly spoken but his voice held a firm edge. 'I will make sure that the company knows how helpful you have been, Captain.'

Phillips turned to Hector and Jezreel. 'Mr Lockwood has charge of you from now on. I must get back to my ship.'

'What about Maria and Isabel? What happens to them?' Hector demanded, alarmed by the note of finality in Phillips' voice.

'Don't worry, Mr Lynch,' intervened Lockwood. 'Captain Phillips has explained the situation to me. We have a short journey to make and, if all goes well, you will soon be reunited with your family.' He tilted his head slightly, assessing the two men standing in front of him. 'I'm hoping you'll introduce me to one of your old shipmates. If we start out now, we can use the last hours of daylight to make some distance from London.'

✳

TWO MATCHING ROANS stood between the shafts of the superb carriage waiting outside. Their coats shone with brushing, and their hooves gleamed with fresh oil. Fine lines of gold leaf picked out the flourishes of scrollwork on lacquered door panels, and the glossy black paint on the folding step looked as if no one had ever set foot there. 'Not mine,' said Lockwood noting Hector's reaction to the sight of such resplendent transport. 'Loaned by Sir Jeremiah, who you might have seen leaving earlier this evening. He's on the court of directors and tidying up this unfortunate misunderstanding with the Mogul.' He climbed into the carriage and settled himself facing the rear, then gestured at Hector and Jezreel to take their places opposite him. Padded upholstery of maroon calfskin gave off an aroma of wax and neat's-foot oil.

The carriage began to move at once, and over the noise of steel-shod wheel rims rolling on paving stone, Hector heard a shout. It was the doorman from East India House calling for a sedan chair for Phillips. It occurred to him that he should have asked *Maynard*'s captain to carry a message to Maria.

Lockwood was in a hurry, that was clear. The driver of the carriage was pushing his horses as fast as was safe, taking advantage of the fact that the streets were emptying now that it was late in the evening. Hector watched for any signs that would tell him more about the man who would now decide his fate, and Jezreel's. Lockwood had leaned back and his face was in shadow. Only when the carriage lurched, jolting him forward, could his features be seen clearly in the light slanting in through the carriage window. There was a severity in the set of his mouth, the thin lips pressed together, and his eyes, whenever Hector met his gaze, were hard and probing. His self-confident composure and the way he remained focused were unsettling. He reminded Hector of a predatory animal that would be merciless when it pounced. Lockwood, he concluded, would be a dangerous adversary.

Hector could tell that they had turned south and were heading back towards the river. The long-awaited thunderstorm broke as their carriage joined the line of vehicles and pedestrians queuing to use London Bridge. The rain suddenly drummed down on the roof of the carriage, and Hector felt sorry for the coachman and his assistant huddled in their capes. Before the carriage was returned to its owner, they would have to spend many hours restoring their vehicle's glossy sheen.

Their progress slowed to a crawl as they were funnelled across the bridge, and Lockwood, who had stayed silent until now, took out a notebook and pencil from an inside pocket of his sober coat.

'Tell me all about your days as a member of Avery's company,' he began.

Hector and Jezreel exchanged glances.

'It doesn't matter who speaks first,' Lockwood said. 'I need to know everything, however trivial, that will help me build up a picture of Henry Avery.'

'You'd better listen to Hector,' Jezreel told him. 'He got to know Avery much better than I did, helping him with navigation and the like.'

'But you would recognize Avery if you saw him?'

'Yes, of course.'

'Then give me a description.'

Jezreel shrugged. 'Middling height. Fair complexion. I think his eyes were grey. Didn't look like a seaman, though he was a good one, more like a shopkeeper.'

'Can you remember any of his particular habits?' Lockwood asked. 'Did he drink a lot? Smoke? Speak with a local accent that you could place?'

'Didn't drink much, and never smoked as I remember. His accent was from England, not from the colonies, that was certain. But from where I couldn't tell you.'

Jezreel lapsed into silence.

Hector had been staring out of the window, listening to what Jezreel was saying. The carriage had crossed London Bridge so slowly that he was able to look down through an occasional narrow gap between the houses on the bridge. Heavy raindrops pitted the surface of the river and sodden dockworkers were still handling cargo, trying to complete as many tasks as possible before their overseers called a halt. A group of older men had assembled in the lee of the customs house, trying to stay out of the rain until they came on duty – nightwatchmen whose job was to prevent pilfering of goods during the hours of darkness.

'Lynch, I'd be interested to hear what you have to add to Mr Hall's description of Henry Avery.' Lockwood's words broke into his thoughts.

Hector looked across at his questioner. He had managed to place Lockwood. 'You're a thief-taker, are you not, Mr Lockwood?'

A flicker of amusement appeared on Lockwood's face. 'That is correct, Lynch. Sir Jeremiah has instructed me to find and arrest those responsible for the attack on the Mogul's vessel, *Ganj-i-Sawa'i.*' He allowed himself a sardonic smile. 'I have his full authority, ample resources and the contract is open-ended. It continues until either Henry Avery is proved to be dead or he is in front of the Admiralty Court charged with piracy.'

'And you will collect the five hundred pounds reward?' Hector ventured.

Lockwood dismissed the suggestion with a grimace. 'You misjudge me. The five hundred pounds reward is something that I proposed to the Court of the Company, via Sir Jeremiah. I do not expect to claim it myself. It is a device to flush out the elusive commander of *Fancy* who, according to what I've heard, may have returned to this country.'

'So you have a network of informers.'

'Indeed I do. I regard them as greedy and untrustworthy, and they mingle mostly with the criminal fraternity of London. Avery does not belong to that class, and he could be anywhere. So the search for Avery requires a bait sufficiently large to get other fish to swim to the surface.'

The carriage was speeding up again as it left the bridge behind. It lurched and swayed, making writing impossible.

Lockwood paused to close his notebook and slip it back into his pocket. 'Of course the size of the reward also reflects the gravity of the offence he and his company committed.'

'Five hundred pounds should be enough to bring in all the information you need.'

Lockwood gave a dry laugh. 'You can't imagine the number of sightings of this notorious pirate that have been sent in. There will always be those liars and tricksters who hope to pick up easy money. Those are the ones who seek part payment in advance.'

'And not on this occasion?'

'Again, Lynch, you guess correctly. We are on our way to investigate a sighting that is rather more promising.' Lockwood treated Hector to a long, calculating stare. 'In any case this journey will not be a waste of my time if you improve on the rather vague description that Mr Hall has just provided of our quarry.'

Hector kept his face blank, hiding his own thoughts. He was certainly able to add to Jezreel's description of Henry Avery. But his instinct told him that he should not be too free with his knowledge. He had detected a ruthlessness in Lockwood, and that made him cautious. He should hoard a few nuggets of information and only use them if it was to his own advantage.

*

THEY SPENT THAT NIGHT at an inn five miles out of London, and were back on the road by the time the sun was lifting clear of the horizon. It promised to be another hot, dry summer's day, and the gangs of reapers were already walking to the wheat fields, ready to start work as soon as the dew dried off. Hector stared out of the window at the landscape, trying to read clues that would tell him where they were headed. They passed through a couple of small unidentifiable towns, and then they were in well-farmed, prosperous countryside. There were cherry and apple orchards, fields of beans and vegetables, solid-looking manor houses. Occasionally he caught sight of the distant glint of a broad river far away to the left. He suspected it might be the

Thames but he couldn't be certain, and he refrained from asking Jezreel. He did not want to speak with his friend with Lockwood listening. The carriage made rapid progress wherever the local landholder had maintained the road surface. During those level stretches Lockwood would again write his notes as he took Hector and Jezreel through their narratives of the months they had spent on *Fancy*. Where the road had been neglected, and the carriage lurched and wallowed over ruts still puddled from the thunderstorms of the previous evening, he leaned back and dozed. He volunteered no information about their destination, and it was the driver who eventually called, 'Coming up to Rochester, sir! I can hear the noon bells of the cathedral.'

Hector had heard the name before but could not remember where or when. He was searching his memory when the carriage driver pulled up his horses so that his assistant could get down and pay the toll for the long stone bridge at the entrance to the city. There was a sharp rap on the door and a voice called, 'Mr Lockwood!'

A small barrel-bodied man with a dark complexion and greasy hair was standing beside the coach. His short wooden staff tipped with metal reminded Hector of the *kotwal*'s in Delhi.

'I'm Tipstaff Bawmer, sir. I sent you word about Henry Avery.'

Lockwood swung open the carriage door. 'Then climb in, Mr Bawmer, and let us hear what you have to say.'

The tipstaff pulled himself into the carriage and squeezed in beside Hector. 'Avery's still at his house,' he declared. There was a note of suppressed elation in his voice. 'I've men watching him day and night. Knew him the moment your handbill arrived at the courthouse.'

A tipstaff made an ideal informer, Hector thought to himself as he listened to Bawmer's eager account. A tipstaff worked for the local magistrates and would be among the first to see official notices relating to legal matters. Lockwood must have printed up a circular offering the £500 reward and sent it out to as many courts as possible. Bawmer had chosen to contact Lockwood directly instead of informing the local magistrates about Avery's presence in Rochester. Doubtless he intended to claim the reward for himself.

'You are certain it is Avery?' Lockwood asked.

'No doubt of it, sir.' Bawmer was fidgeting with anticipation. He shifted the staff into the other hand so he could wipe a sweaty palm on the knee of his breeches. 'Showed up in Rochester a couple of months ago. Never short of ready money and pays in coin, usually gold.'

'What does he look like?'

'Medium height, brown as a berry from the foreign sun, light on his feet with that little sway in his walk so you know he's spent a long time on ships. And he uses foreign-sounding words. Must have picked them up when he was with foreign pirates.'

Lockwood was openly sceptical. 'That description could fit any mariner home after a lucky voyage. What makes you suspect that he's Avery?'

'Because he hides indoors most of the day, sir, and only goes out after dark or in bad weather when there's no one else about.' A crafty smile appeared on the tipstaff's face. 'That got his neighbours talking. He took them for fools.'

'And yet you know that he pays in gold coin. How's that?'

'My sister works at the tavern where Avery takes a drink of an evening. She says he prefers rum over our local cider, though it's five times the price.'

The thief-taker flicked a glance at Jezreel and raised an eyebrow. Hector remembered that Jezreel had said Avery was not a drinker. 'You say he goes to a tavern?' Lockwood asked the informer.

Bawmer sensed that he might have said something wrong, and hurried to cover his mistake. 'It's not often he goes out for a drink.'

Lockwood leaned back in his seat, implying that he saw no

point in asking any further questions. 'Well then, Tipstaff Bawmer, let's go and take this Avery.'

Bawmer glanced around him, taking in the luxurious carriage. 'He's a flighty one, this Avery . . .' he began apologetically.

'I don't intend to drive up to his front door,' Lockwood told him testily. 'Just bring us to within walking distance of where he lives. From there you and my two assistants can go on foot and bring him back to me.'

Hector was disconcerted to hear himself and Jezreel described as the thief-taker's assistants, but a warning look from Lockwood kept him silent.

The tipstaff leaned out of the carriage window and gave directions to the driver. The carriage rolled forward over the bridge, past the cathedral and along the high street. Bawmer called a halt when they reached a crossroads where a thick-set ox of a man stood waiting.

'I've enlisted the help of the constable,' Bawmer explained to Lockwood. 'He's put two men in the lane at the back of Avery's house. There's no chance he will escape.'

Hector and Jezreel followed the tipstaff out into the road. The carriage had stopped well short of a row of modest timber and thatch houses.

'Avery rents the fourth house along.' Bawmer dropped his voice to a whisper though they were well over a hundred yards away.

The houses were the sort occupied by tradesmen and skilled artisans. Each had its small fenced-in front garden and a tiny yard at the back. Behind them were water meadows where cattle grazed hock-deep in rich summer pasture. The river beyond the meadows provided an anchorage for three or four warships. Farther downstream was some sort of dockyard.

Hector was still racking his brains, trying to recall why the name of Rochester was familiar, when Bawmer and the constable beckoned him to follow them. The fourth house was so quiet that it looked uninhabited. Coming closer, he noticed that the upstairs curtains were drawn.

At the front door, Bawmer stood aside. 'You knock,' he said to Hector, making him wonder if the tipstaff feared the notorious pirate Avery might be violent.

Hector tapped on the door. There was no reply.

'Probably cleared out,' Jezreel murmured beside him. 'Can't imagine that Avery would let himself be taken so easily.'

Hector knocked again, more loudly. 'Anyone there?' he called. His voice came out tight and strangled. He did not relish the thought of delivering Avery into the hands of a man like Lockwood.

Again there was no reply, and he began to hope that perhaps the house was indeed empty, and that Avery had gone.

A third burst of knocking produced a response. He heard footsteps coming along the passageway, and a voice called, 'Hold hard there, cully. I'm on my way.'

With a sudden shock of recognition Hector knew the voice, and why Rochester was a familiar name.

There was the sound of a latch being lifted, and the door swung open to reveal the freckled face and curly reddish hair of John Dann, *Fancy*'s former coxswain, who had once told him that he had moved to Rochester to be near the navy yard.

Dann's blue eyes widened as he saw Jezreel and Hector. 'What are you two doing here, shipmates?' he exclaimed, startled. Then, with a look of alarm, he took a step back and tried to close the door. The burly constable shoved Hector aside and pushed Dann up against the wall. Dann was too stunned to twist away, and the constable slipped a pair of manacles over the coxswain's wrists. 'Someone who wants to speak with you, Captain Avery,' announced Bawmer triumphantly.

*

DANN'S INTERROGATION took place in a small private room overlooking the stable yard of the King's Head, Rochester's principal inn. The window was kept wide open to allow a little air to circulate and it carried the smells of hay and horse dung as well as a rhythmic clanking whenever someone worked the yard pump, filling buckets for the household and stables. Lockwood dismissed Bawmer contemptuously, and the disappointed tipstaff left the room grumbling that, by rights, he was due some part of the reward because he had promised money to the constable. Dann, still in manacles, sat on a hard upright chair facing Lockwood across a small table. Now and again he glanced toward Jezreel and Hector seated on a bench against the wall. His gaze was more reproachful than hostile.

'You were Henry Avery's coxswain?' The thief-taker placed his notebook open on the table in front of him.

'*Fancy*'s coxswain, not Avery's,' Dann corrected him. 'By vote of the ship's company.' He seemed resigned to his capture. His voice was flat.

'It's Henry Avery who interests me. Where did he take *Fancy* after looting the Mogul's ship?'

'To Bourbon.'

'Not to St Mary's? To do business with Mr Baldridge?'

The question made Hector sit up. He was surprised that Lockwood knew about a dealer in stolen goods based in Madagascar. Then he remembered Jezreel had mentioned Baldridge's name in passing while he was telling Lockwood about his time on *Fancy*. Hector did not recall Lockwood writing down the information at the time. It was a reminder that anything he said to Lockwood was liable to be put to use. He would have to guard his tongue whenever dealing with the thief-taker.

Dann shook his head. 'Avery had a low opinion of Baldridge. He had a bad reputation, and there was a rumour that he had fallen out with the native chiefs on the mainland. There was talk that St Mary's might be attacked.'

'So you made the division of the prize at Bourbon.'

'We shared out everything that could be divided easily: silver and gold coin, and the like. Some of the jewellery and other items had yet to find buyers.'

'Was anything kept back for Captain Mayes' company aboard *Pearl*? I'm told they took part in the attack, but left the scene without any of the prize.'

Dann swivelled his head and gave Jezreel and Hector a sour look that made it clear he knew where Lockwood had got his information. The thought occurred to Hector that this was exactly what the thief-taker intended.

The coxswain allowed himself a vengeful grin. 'We never saw those cheating bastards on *Pearl* again. Avery said he would not wait for them to show up. Made him twice as popular as before.'

'After the division of spoils, what then?' Lockwood prompted.

'Half our company, and all the foreigners – there were Danes and French and a couple of Dutchies – left the ship at Bourbon. There were about thirty of them on *Fancy*. They wanted to get back to their own countries, taking their prize with them.'

'But Avery remained in command?'

'We all thought he could do no wrong and *Fancy* was a lucky ship. Some wanted to continue with her cruise and get even richer. But Avery was having none of it. He insisted that we get well away from those seas and then go our separate ways.'

Two bluebottles had flown in through the open window and were buzzing loudly as they circled Dann's head of curly hair. Unable to move his manacled wrists, he ducked his head down into the collar of his shirt until they flew away. 'We were short-handed of course, a little more than a hundred men, and that was enough to manage *Fancy*. Long Ben had already thought it through, as usual. Worse luck.'

Lockwood pounced. 'Why worse luck?'

'He set course for the Caribbees, brought us to the Bahamas where he came to an arrangement with the governor. Seemed clever at the time . . . and so it was, for him.'

A resentful tone had crept into Dann's voice.

Lockwood turned over another page. 'So what happened in the Bahamas?'

'We spent several weeks ashore – though there is little enough to do in that godforsaken hole, however much chink is in your pocket. Governor took his bribe to look the other way, and we landed most of the prize. Then all of a sudden things turned nasty, and those of us who weren't arrested, cut our cables. We made a run for it.'

'Including Henry Avery?'

'He said he'd follow on. Me and half a dozen of my mates headed for New York, just as Long Ben suggested.' Dann gave a mirthless laugh. 'He gulled us. We trusted him with the rest of the prize that had not yet found buyers. He said he'd meet us in New York with the proceeds, and then we'd head home, in ones and twos.'

'And he never showed up,' Lockwood said softly.

'No sign of him. We waited a month. But the hunt was on for anyone from *Fancy*, and every day the risk increased of being picked up and questioned. I already had a fair amount of plunder so I took passage to Ireland and on to Liverpool. From there I came to Rochester.'

'And not a word from Avery since?'

'Nothing.' Dann glowered at Jezreel and Hector. 'I thought I was free and clear until those two showed up at my door.'

There was a long silence as Lockwood looked back through his notes. Finally, he said, 'In those weeks after Bourbon did Avery drop any hint of his own plans? Where he would go with his share of the prize? Think carefully, it could affect your own future.'

Dann gave a snort of frustration. 'He was always a close one, Long Ben. You never really knew what he had in mind.' He nodded in Hector's direction. 'You'd be better off asking him about Avery's way of thinking. They hit it off well enough.'

'Mr Lynch is doing his best,' Lockwood told him. 'Avery denied him and Mr Hall of any share of the prize from the

Mogul's ship. He abandoned both of them by sailing away, leaving them on *Pearl*.'

Hector had to admire Lockwood's guile. He had planted in Dann's mind the thought that two of Avery's victims were already helping in the hunt for Long Ben and, if he followed their example, he might escape the hangman.

Dann closed his eyes and sat for a while as he tried to think of any nuggets of information that might help his cause.

Finally he said, 'It was Long Ben who told us that anyone who planned on returning to England should go first to Ireland, then take a ship out of Dublin and land in either Liverpool or Bristol. He said it would confuse the trail. I recall thinking to myself that he had thought about it carefully, and maybe he would come with us.'

Lockwood closed his notebook and got to his feet. 'That will be all, Dann. I'm handing you over to the local magistrates to be held in Rochester Goal. What they decide to do with you is up to them.'

'What makes me different from these two?' Dann demanded in a sudden show of defiance. He jerked his head to where Hector and Jezreel sat on their bench. 'They had no profit from the Mogul's ship, but they were there when we took her.'

The look that Lockwood gave Dann was one of the coldest that Hector had ever seen. 'They still have work to do.'

TWENTY-THREE

'BRISTOL OR LIVERPOOL?' Lockwood asked. 'Come now, Lynch, if you know Henry Avery as well as coxswain Dann claimed, you must have an opinion.'

The thief-taker stood with his back to a window overlooking Leadenhall and the light fell directly in Hector's eyes. Three weeks had passed since the trip to Rochester and Hector was on the alert for the thief-taker's techniques. He recalled the cynical way Lockwood had used him and Jezreel as a device to squeeze Dann for every last drop of information.

Hector hoped that his face did not show his misgivings. During the journey back to London, Lockwood had made them an offer that was impossible for them to turn down: if they used their knowledge of Avery to assist him hunt *Fancy*'s captain, the thief-taker would keep their arrival in England secret from the authorities.

'Avery would have chosen to land at Bristol, if he returned to England,' Hector said carefully.

'Why Bristol?'

'Dann came in through Liverpool, and probably others from *Fancy*. Long Ben would not want to run the risk of encountering his former shipmates.'

'A chance meeting was hardly likely,' Lockwood objected.

'Avery repeatedly told his men to travel in small groups to avoid attracting attention. If Dann and his friends came through Liverpool, then Avery would have heeded his own advice and stayed clear, taking a different route.'

'That supposes that Avery kept track of Dann and his fellows on their way to England.'

Hector was not put off by Lockwood's unhelpful responses. 'One of the things I learned about *Fancy*'s captain was that he always let others take the first risk. If he intended coming back to England, Avery would have set it up so he followed Dann and his friends to Dublin, then waited there to see how they fared on the final crossing to England.'

Lockwood gave a grunt which could have been of approval or of frustration. He walked past Hector to where a tall long-case clock stood against the wall. Like the rest of the furniture, it was new and must have cost a great deal of money. The pale arabesques of the marquetry contrasted with the polished walnut of the main trunk. Hector guessed that the room was normally an office for the same Sir Jeremiah who had loaned Lockwood his opulent carriage for the trip to Rochester.

'I agree with you,' Lockwood said. 'Nevertheless, after listening to Dann I sent word to the magistrates in both Liverpool and Bristol to ask if there were any sightings of anyone matching Avery's vague description.' He pulled open the clock's door to inspect the mechanism of pendulum and weights. Watching him, Hector thought it was typical of the thief-taker that he had to keep himself busy, always seeking to find out more.

Lockwood waited for a dozen swings of the pendulum before he gently closed the clock door. 'So far I've heard nothing from either place, and each day makes it less likely that Avery will be found. I've delayed long enough.'

Hector waited, there was nothing he had to say. He was grateful for the three-week interval since Rochester. He had been able to collect Maria and Isabel from *Maynard* at Blackwall, and Lockwood had raised no objection when Jezreel suggested that they accompany him to Sussex when he went to seek out his own family. As it turned out, Jezreel's brothers and sister had prospered. They had expanded their smallholding and now owned or rented several adjacent farms. One of them had a cottage they were happy for Jezreel to occupy in return for help on the land. It was here that Hector had left Maria and Isabel when Lockwood sent word that he needed Hector in Leadenhall. The hunt for Avery had stalled.

'Sir Jeremiah has had no luck in Lombard Street either.' Lockwood had begun to prowl the room, stopping to examine various display ornaments, all of them costly. 'The magistrates had Dann's lodgings searched. They found a thousand pounds' worth of gold sequins and ten gold sovereigns sewn into a waistcoat. One presumes that Avery brought back much more, in bullion if not in coin.'

He selected the statuette of a dove, one of a pair carved from a green translucent stone, and held it up to the light to admire. 'If Avery reached London, he'd have to put his prize somewhere secure. His only choice is to use the goldsmith-bankers of Lombard Street. Sir Jeremiah has approached all his contacts among that fraternity. None of them has recently accepted a large amount of gold, least of all in foreign currency.' He put down the green dove, and allowed himself a cynical smile. 'Or they didn't admit doing so.'

The thief-taker moved across to a corner to inspect an ornamental globe on its mahogany stand. Large and showy, the globe was useless for practical navigation but it spoke of Sir Jeremiah's wealth and worldwide trade. 'Therefore, while I think Avery is in England, I don't believe he's in London, at least not yet.'

He gave the globe a gentle turn, so it spun on its axis. 'In theory Avery could still be anywhere,' he mused, 'but I have a hunch that he is here.' He stabbed his finger down so the globe stopping spinning. 'In Bristol where he first landed.'

He turned to Hector and asked, 'And you've just told me why?'

'Because he's waiting to learn whether any of his company, men like Dann, have been arrested by the authorities?'

Lockwood nodded. 'And that's why I'm sending you to Bristol, Lynch, to sniff around. See if you can pick up the trail of Long Ben.'

'I know nothing of Bristol. Never been to the place,' Hector protested.

'So you'll arrive there with fresh eyes. Get inside his head; imagine what he would have done when he disembarked the ship from Dublin.'

Hector had been expecting something like this ever since receiving Lockwood's summons. His heart sank. He wondered how long he would be away on this wild-goose chase. It could be months, and if Jezreel was with him, Maria and Isabel would be left on their own in Sussex . . .

The thief-taker must have read his thoughts, for Lockwood's next words shook him. 'Lynch, don't look so glum!' he snapped. 'Find Avery for me, and all charges of piracy against you will be dropped.'

Hector stared at Lockwood in open disbelief.

There was a touch of impatience in the thief-taker's voice. 'Ask yourself this, Lynch: who put up the five hundred pounds bounty?'

'The East India Company,' Hector said. 'That's what I heard.'

'The Company is supplying the money, but the Board of Trade decides who receives it. The Board is largely made up of ministers of the Crown and has exceptional powers.'

Hector waited for him to go on.

'The talk in the streets and taverns is always about the money, the five hundred pounds.' The thief-taker's voice dripped with contempt. 'That's what's in the big print of my handbills and posters. But the full government proclamation states, "any person or persons whose information leads to the arrest and conviction of Henry Avery will receive a pardon for all crimes of piracy while under his command".'

Lockwood allowed a short silence to pass, before he added softly: 'If you doubt me, Lynch, you can read it for yourself in the *London Gazette*. Find Avery for me, and I will recommend that all charges of piracy against you will be set aside.'

Hector's mind was whirling. 'And against Jezreel Hall too?'

'Of course. But Mr Hall doesn't go poking around Bristol with you. If Henry Avery is as alert and clever as his reputation says he is, and he hears that a large man with the look of a prize-fighter is asking questions about him, Long Ben will vanish again.'

For a moment Hector's guard was down as he thought about what Lockwood had said. He imagined the freedom of no longer living in the shadow of his questionable past. Yet something in Lockwood's manner struck him the wrong way. The thief-taker had returned to the spot where he could stand with his back to the light. It was impossible to read the expression in his eyes. Hector could only judge Lockwood's sincerity by his voice. His words carried an undertone that rang hollow.

THE JOURNEY FROM LONDON to Bristol was in a bone-shaking hackney coach that had no springs and was crammed with passengers. Hector spent the jolting hours trying to improve on Lockwood's instructions: he was to begin his search at Bristol docks. Lockwood had given him the money to bribe customs officials to show him their record books for ships arriving from Ireland. But Hector was sure that if Avery had indeed passed that way, those same officials had already taken the freebooter's money to make false entries. By the afternoon of the third day, when the coach drew up beside the High Cross in the centre of Bristol, he had still not come up with a better plan.

He stepped down into the street, stretched to ease his cramped muscles, and looked up at the sky. Fast-moving rain clouds were coming in from the west. He needed to find lodgings quickly. A fellow passenger had recommended a bookseller in Broad Street who rented out rooms above his shop, and he called up to the coach driver for directions.

'If you're going that way you can deliver this – his name's George Lewis.' The driver threw him down a flat package tied with twine. Shouldering his bag, Hector started walking. His first impression of Bristol was that it was just like London, only smaller. There was the same sense of hurry and bustle in the streets, the same air of making money while paying due respect to the Almighty. Huddles of prosperous-looking merchants stood talking business amongst themselves in a pillared arcade directly across from two churches on opposite corners of the central crossroads. The imposing building with a square tower and flag-pole, and larger than either church, had the look of Council Chambers.

Broad Street was lined with four-storey buildings with tim-ber-and-plaster fronts, and Hector had gone just a few steps along it when he realized the difference from London: there were no handcarts and wagons delivering goods, everything was being shifted on sleds. Even more surprising was the absence of a central gutter. Despite the warmth of the day, there was little smell. He could only conclude that the city drains were buried somewhere beneath his feet.

The bookseller's premises were much like its neighbours, tall and narrow, the upper floors projecting slightly. The door from the street opened into a long, low-ceilinged room that extended almost the full depth of the building. As Hector stepped inside, a tall, painfully thin man looked up from where he had been arranging volumes on a table at the back of the shop.

'Mr Lewis?' Hector enquired.

'How may I help you?'

Hector offered the package. 'This arrived with the London coach. The driver asked me to deliver it.'

'That'll be the latest *Gazette*. Thank you.' The bookseller took the parcel from him.

'Also I believe you rent out rooms?'

'Indeed I do.' The bookseller untied the parcel string and removed the wrapper, revealing a thin sheaf of printed pages.

'I'd like to rent a room for myself, for a week, perhaps longer.'

'I have a room available on the fourth floor. Three shillings a week. For meals you'll have to fend for yourself. The Three Crowns round the corner serves good food.'

'I'll take it,' Hector said. He watched the bookseller lick his thumb and count the sheets, twenty-one of them. 'You say that is the *Gazette*?'

'The *London Gazette*, printed two or three times a week and sent out to subscribers. The Council House receives a copy direct and the magistrates, and our two coffee houses of course. I have a list of private clients who like to keep abreast of affairs. A few of them will drop by to collect their copies during the afternoon. A lad will deliver the remainder to their homes this evening.'

'May I see a copy?'

'Of course.'

Hector took the newspaper. It was a single sheet, about seven inches by twelve, closely printed on both sides. 'Published by Authority' appeared below the title. The front page had a double column with various news items from England and abroad. He turned it over and found government notices, official proclamations, commercial information, and snippets of more lurid news: several fires, a report of a series of highway attacks on Hampstead Heath, cockfights, and a two-line account of the Tyburn hanging of a notorious criminal.

He handed back the page, and waited while the bookseller found the key to his room. After paying a week's rent in advance he climbed the stairs. His room was a garret with sloping ceiling but it was clean and dry. It had a bed, a cupboard and a chamber pot. He could hear the patter of raindrops on the tiles above him. Placing his bag on the bare floorboards he went across to the small window that looked out over Broad Street.

For a long time he stood staring across the wet roofs of Bristol, thinking.

*

NEXT MORNING when he came down the stairs on his way back to the Three Crowns where he had eaten supper, he found his landlord already in his shop.

'Good day, Mr Lewis, perhaps you can help me,' he began. 'Is there a glass grinder in Bristol?'

The bookseller put aside the book whose scuffed leather binding he had been examining with a critical eye. 'You'll find one in Tower Lane off the Pithay. A Mr Stephen Ormsby. I cannot tell you anything about the quality of his work as the council licensed him just last February. He would be your only choice.'

'Thank you. I'm sure I can find my way there.' His day had begun well, Hector decided as he went out into the street. If there was only one glass grinder in Bristol, that increased his chances of success.

Mr Stephen Ormsby's apprentice was taking down the shutters when Hector arrived. The glass grinder's front room, where Hector had to wait for half an hour, was sparsely equipped with a table, two chairs, an obviously second-hand four-foot telescope on a brass tripod and a glass-fronted cabinet with an array of spectacles. The door to the back room was closed. Hector imagined that was where the glass grinder kept his lathe and raw material. Stephen Ormsby, when he arrived, proved to be a pale-skinned, earnest man somewhere between thirty and forty years old, with an unremarkable face and a dry, reedy voice.

'How long have you been having trouble with your eyes?' he asked after apologizing for his lateness.

'For the past two years,' Hector lied. 'I notice it when reading charts.'

'You are a mariner, then?'

'My ship is in port, and I decided to take the chance to get some spectacles made. We're due to set sail in a few days' time, so they'll need to be ready as soon as you can manage.' Hector hoped that the spectacle maker would not ask the name of his vessel.

Ormsby had a nervous habit of toying with a button on the front of his coat, twisting it on its thread. 'That will depend on the difficulty of the work, and whether I have some blanks that are suitable.'

He despatched his apprentice into the back room to fetch his trials box and there followed half an hour of tests while the spectacle maker held up various sample lenses to Hector's eyes, and asked how they affected his vision.

Hector had to be careful in inventing his answers but finally the glass grinder reached his conclusion. 'You need very little magnification, Mr . . .'

'Lynch, Hector Lynch.'

'. . . And I can supply what is required from my existing stock of blanks, with minor adjustments. I can set the lenses either in a standard metal frame that grips the nose or a newer model with flat bars that extend back to the temples above the ears.'

Hector reached into his pocket and produced a sheet of paper which he spread out on the table. 'Here's a sketch of the spectacles used by a friend of mine, a fellow navigator I've sailed with. They were well suited for our type of work.' The drawing was of the spectacles that Hector had seen Avery use in Baldridge's office in St Mary's and later when *Fancy*'s captain was reading charts.

The glass grinder made a face. 'Very old-fashioned and rather clumsy, if I may say so.'

Hector tapped the drawing. 'The ribbon behind the head holds them in place when a vessel is being tossed about, and remember: we navigators must lean forward and look down when we consult our spread-out charts. The pinch-nose spectacles you propose would fall off.'

He sat back and allowed several seconds to pass in the faint hope that the glass grinder would announce that he had a client with very similar spectacles.

Instead Ormsby gave a resigned shrug. 'If that is what you prefer, Mr Lynch. But I'm afraid that means there will be a delay.' He took a closer look at Hector's sketch. 'I presume the lenses are held in leather surrounds.'

'That's right.'

'I can grind the lenses and have them ready for you in two days' time, and could have made metal frames here on the premises. But leatherwork is specialized and I'd have to find a skilled man, perhaps a glove maker who can do fine stitching.'

'How much longer would that take?'

'At least a week.'

'Then I'll wait,' Hector told him.

*

THE NEXT EDITION of the *Gazette* was due to reach Bristol after three days, and Hector spent them as a man of leisure. After breakfast he strolled down to the docks and chatted with port officials, then sauntered back up the High Street and paid the one penny entry fee at one of the city's two coffee houses. There he passed the rest of the morning. He took dinner in the Three Crowns, and afterwards he found himself a comfortable seat in the other coffee house. He positioned himself in a quiet corner where he could view the other customers, listened to their conversations as he sipped his coffee, and glanced through the copy of the *Gazette* brought by a servant. He neither saw nor heard anything about Henry Avery, nor had he expected to. Late in the afternoon, shortly before the bookseller closed for the day, he returned to his lodgings. If there were no customers in the shop, George Lewis was happy to discuss almost any topic, including local politics and the latest news from London. Little by little Hector managed to learn the identities of most of his clients with a subscription to the *Gazette*. He bought the names and addresses of the others on the list by slipping a few coins to the apprentice who made the deliveries.

The *Gazette*, Hector reasoned, might lead him to Avery. If

Long Ben was lying low in Bristol before making his next move, the *Gazette* was his only reliable source of information about the fate of *Fancy*'s crew. He would check each issue for reports of arrests and trials, as well as official government announcements. With so few copies of the *Gazette* available in Bristol, it was possible that Avery had joined the bookseller's subscription list. Hector accepted that this was unlikely, but he had to make sure.

So he was not unduly disappointed that the only person to take out a recent subscription to the *Gazette* was an elderly physician who had moved to Bristol for his retirement.

He was more optimistic about working with Stephen Ormsby's spectacles. As soon as they were ready, he carried them on his daily strolls around the docks. Choosing his moment, he showed them to port officials and dockworkers. He claimed to have picked them up on the quayside and would like to return them to their owner. No one recognized them.

With a greater expectation of success he tried the same approach in both coffee houses where he was now a familiar figure. But again he met with blank looks.

At the end of three weeks of fruitless enquiries, he had decided to abandon the search. He would wait for one more edition of the *Gazette* to be distributed, return to London and report to Lockwood that he had failed to find any trace of Avery. On the day of the *Gazette*'s delivery, he dawdled in the bookseller's shop watching George Lewis remove the sheaf of fresh newspapers from their wrapping. The bookseller followed his set routine. He licked his thumb and began counting the sheets. There should have been twenty-one, but that day there were twenty-two. Carefully the bookseller placed the extra copy on one side.

'What will you do with that one?' Hector asked.

'No point in sending it back. You're welcome to take it up to your room.'

'That's kind of you; I'll drop it back in the morning.'

'Put it behind the counter, out of sight. I would not want my regular subscribers thinking that anybody can read it gratis in the shop when they have to pay for their own copies.'

On an impulse Hector asked, 'What will you do with it afterwards?'

The bookseller was puzzled by the question. 'You mean, what happens to the old newspaper?'

'How long do you keep it?'

'Until the next edition comes out. Then my apprentice will put it with the other shop waste. A scavenger calls at the back door every day to collect old paper and rags.'

Hector felt a faint tremor of excitement. 'This scavenger, does he collect from other houses?'

'I suppose so. He has a permit from the city. The aldermen take pride in keeping Bristol clean of rubbish, as you will have noticed.'

'And is it always the same person?'

By now the bookseller was looking concerned. 'I hope you haven't mislaid something you wish you had kept, Mr Lynch. Perhaps thrown it away by accident? The maid who removes the chamber pot from your room is also instructed to dispose of any rubbish.'

'It was nothing very important. But where can I find this scavenger?'

'My housekeeper can tell you. I fear it would do you little good. The man makes his living by sorting his rubbish and selling anything of value.' Lewis offered an apologetic smile. 'Sometimes I think that my housekeeper feels sorry for him. She throws out old clothes that are perfectly good for another few months. Last week I saw one of my old shirts worn by a costermonger.'

*

THE SCAVENGER WAS a calculating ruffian with small, crafty eyes who dressed in a curious over-garment that had once been a lady's flowered gown but now served him as a loose, full-length tunic. Grime encrusted the cracked fingernails of the filthy hand he held out for Hector's coin.

'The Hot Well takes them regular, two pence a copy if not greasy or torn,' he told Hector, confirming that he picked out discarded copies of the *Gazette* from the rubbish he collected.

'What happens at the Hot Well?' Hector imagined it was some sort of low tavern.

'Poor folks could get themselves a free wash there, between tides, until the Council sold the lease. The new owners call it a "spa".' He pronounced the last word with a mocking accent.

'And why do they want old copies of the *Gazette*?'

The scavenger cackled. 'Probably use them as arse wipes. You can find out for yourself. Hot Well's just beyond Marsh Gate.'

Hot Well turned out to be a newly built sweat house and pump room. The doorman took Hector's sixpence before summoning an attendant who showed him into a changing room. The water for the pool, the attendant explained, was piped up from a hot spring exposed between tides on the riverbank.

'If you will leave your clothes here, I'll return to fetch you,' said the attendant, handing Hector a large cotton bath sheet. 'Have no fear, your property will be safe.'

Hector undressed, wrapped the sheet around him and allowed himself to be led down a corridor to the bathing room. There was a strong and unpleasant smell of sulphur.

The attendant prattled on. 'Full of minerals, and excellent for the skin. Most relaxing. And you'll have the place to yourself, except for one of our regulars.'

He pushed open the door and Hector found himself entering a chamber lit from above by glass panes in the domed roof. The warm air was foggy with steam. The water in the pool that took up most of the interior was a murky greenish brown. Seated in it, with his head leaning back on the tiled surround and his eyes closed, was Henry Avery.

Without quite knowing why, Hector felt drawn forward. He quietly descended the steps into the bath. The water came up to his thighs and was warm, rather than hot. He felt a slight tingling on the skin. He waded slowly over to Avery and sat down on the ledge beside him.

'Good day, Captain Avery,' he said.

For a moment Hector thought that Avery was asleep and had not heard him. Then, after several seconds had passed, Avery raised his head slowly and deliberately and turned to look Hector full in the face.

'Mr Benjamin Bridgeman to you, Lynch.'

Hector waited.

Long Ben remained as unruffled. He could have been talking to an acquaintance who had dropped by to see him. 'I always thought you were a sharp one.'

The presence of his former captain only an arm's length away had an effect on Hector that he had not anticipated. Instead of elation at his success in finding Avery, there was a confusing stab of regret. For weeks Avery had been his quarry, enigmatic and distant. Now *Fancy*'s former commander was real again, and exactly as Hector remembered: level-headed and unexcitable, someone who avoided confrontation and preferred to use intelligence rather than muscle. With sudden clarity, Hector saw that little separated Avery the freebooter from Lockwood the thief-taker. Both were clever and single-minded. Both kept in the background and deployed others to carry out their plans. The main difference was that Avery was outside the law, and Lockwood operated in its shadowy margins.

Avery sensed his indecision. 'If you're after the bounty, I'm sure we can come to some arrangement.'

He rose to his feet and went to the edge of the pool. Hector followed him into the changing room where they dried off on fresh sheets and dressed. Avery then led the way into an adjacent parlour. A tray of coffee had already been set out on a table.

'The service here is excellent as well as discreet,' Avery commented, waving Hector to take a seat. 'The pump room has only been open a few months and the proprietor is struggling to find customers. It suits both of us for me to rent lodgings from him.'

Avery's way of speaking had not changed. Hector recalled how persuasive Long Ben had been when addressing *Fancy's* company with that deep and husky voice, each sentence measured and deliberate. Listening to him, Hector found himself slipping back into the belief that Long Ben knew exactly what he was talking about.

Avery passed Hector a cup of coffee before pulling up a chair and sitting down. 'I'm curious to know how you tracked me down.'

'Through the *Gazette*.'

For a second Avery was thrown off stride. 'You put in an advertisement! Surely not.' Then he noticed Hector's glance flick towards a slightly crumpled copy of the *Gazette* lying on the table, thought for a moment, and laughed openly. 'And I took so much trouble to steer clear of the coffee houses.'

The laughter faded as he leaned forward. 'A bounty of five hundred pounds. If that's all that they think I'm worth, I beg to disagree.'

Avery's mood had changed. He was businesslike and serious.

'Twice the bounty, Lynch, in return for your silence. One thousand pounds in gold coin. To avoid attracting unwelcome attention, you would receive the money in instalments spread over, say, ten years.'

'How would the payments be made?' Hector heard himself say.

'I would give irrevocable instructions to a reputable goldsmith.'

An alarm sounded in the back of Hector's mind. 'The man who sent me to find you made enquiries. No one in Lombard Street has received large deposits of bullion in recent days.'

Long Ben gave a dismissive snort. 'I'm not so foolish as to have gone anywhere near Lombard Street. There's a goldsmith in a county town not too far from here who has more than enough of my coin in a strong room in his cellar.'

Hector was doing the sums in his head: fifty pounds a year was enough to keep a family in considerable comfort. With the money Avery was offering he and Maria could set up home wherever they chose, start some sort of business, buy a farm. His mind raced on.

'What about Jezreel?' he asked.

Avery waved his hand. 'Same amount for him. But paid from a different source . . . He can choose Dublin or New York or Amsterdam.'

Long Ben spread his risks and planned ahead, Hector remembered. Avery must have sent some of his prize to Amsterdam with the Dutchmen who returned from Bourbon when *Fancy*'s haul was first divided up.

He had to ask one question: 'That day on *Ganj-i-Sawa'i* when my two friends and I were forced to leave *Fancy* and go aboard *Pearl*, you gave me a nod, some sort of message. What did you mean by that?'

Avery paused before answering. 'I could not stop Hathaway from driving you and your two friends off *Fancy*. The company had elected him as quartermaster and that was his right. However, I wanted to reassure you that I would remedy the situation later if it was in my power.' He broke into a sudden smile. 'And it seems that is now the case. What do you say to my proposal?'

Hector sat quietly, his mind turning in slow circles. It came down to a choice between Avery's gold and Lockwood's offer of a pardon for him and Jezreel if he brought Long Ben to justice. He wondered if Lockwood knew of the earlier charges against him and his friends for piracy in the Caribbean. If he did, the thief-taker could just as easily revive those charges and send him and Jezreel to Execution Dock should the merchant grandees in India House later decide to appease the Great Mogul. He had little faith in Lockwood's justice. The laws had evolved to serve the interests of men like Sir Jeremiah.

He came to a decision. 'I accept your proposal, Captain, but with one condition.'

Avery's eyes narrowed. 'And what is that?'

Hector reached into his pocket and pulled out the spectacles on their ribbon. 'Find a glass grinder in another town and have him make you something more fashionable.'

ON THE DAY Hector got back to London, a gusty wind from the north carried the first hint of autumn rawness. Walking up Leadenhall he saw smoke streaming from the ornate fluted chimneys of East India House. In the lobby, where he had to wait, a large coal fire was burning in the hearth below the massive chimney breast. Every half-hour a servant came in to add another bucketful of fuel. Seated well away from the blaze Hector reflected that this was for the comfort of Company directors who had lived so long in the east that they felt the slightest chill. The footmen in their heavy livery coats of serge were taking turns to stand outside in the street.

HE STARED into the flames, going over in his mind what he would say to Lockwood, so lost in thought that he did not notice the thief-taker arrive. Only when he heard his name did he look up and see Lockwood standing right in front of him. The thief-taker had brought with him the bamboo tube that Annesley had sent from Surat.

He followed Lockwood up to Sir Jeremiah's office on the first floor, where it was evident that merchant had been spending more of his wealth, adding to his collection of ornaments. Now there was a ship model, four feet from bowsprit to rudder, precise in every minute detail, hull, sails, rigging, tiny brass deck cannon. The first glance gave Hector a jolt. He thought it was *Fancy*. A second look showed him the company flag at the masthead. He guessed it was a brand-new East Indiaman due to be launched from a dockyard on the Thames.

'Avery landed in Bristol,' he told Lockwood.

'How long ago was that?'

'Nearly three months, but he's moved on.'

'Where to?'

'I was unable to find out. The trail's gone cold.'

Lockwood went dangerously quiet. 'Let's start again, from the beginning. If Avery arrived in Bristol three months ago, he came to England ahead of Dann and the others from *Fancy*. What about your theory that he would wait in Dublin and watch to see how Dann and his shipmates got on?'

'He had a reason: he was looking for some Bristol men who had swindled him. Only they weren't from Bristol.'

Lockwood waited for him to go on.

'The rumour is that before Avery left the Caribbees, he bought half a share in a slave ship about to make her usual run home to Bristol. He stowed his prize aboard and sent her ahead, to bring his loot home on the quiet . . .'

Lockwood finished the sentence for him. 'And the ship never arrived.' There was a sour note of satisfaction in his voice. 'Much the same as what he did to Dann and the others. You'd have thought he knew better.'

'It wasn't even a Bristol ship.'

'And how did you learn all this?'

Hector produced the spectacles and held them up. 'With these. Avery uses an identical pair for reading. A few people remembered him.'

'Very astute of you.' Lockwood's approval was perfunctory. 'And did anyone you spoke to have any idea where he might have gone?'

'They lost interest in Avery when it became apparent that he was short of money.'

Lockwood began pacing up and down, the bamboo tube

tucked under his arm. 'What about you, Lynch? From your knowledge of Avery, where do you think he's gone?'

'Somewhere in the West Country. His accent is from those parts so maybe he was headed that way.'

Lockwood's head snapped round. 'A West Country accent? You never mentioned that to me before.'

Hector spread his hands in a gesture of apology. 'I didn't know before. This is my first time in England. I placed his accent only when I was talking with people in Bristol.'

The thief-taker's mouth had set in a grim line. 'To sum up: Avery is in England, short of funds and probably somewhere in the West Country.' He paused. 'And that leaves very little clue as to where to search for him.'

Which is what Avery wants you to believe, Hector thought to himself. Give him sufficient to keep his interest lukewarm, Long Ben had said, but not enough for him to follow up.

Lockwood resumed his pacing, toying with the bamboo tube, passing it from one hand to the other. 'So, Lynch, you don't qualify for the five hundred pounds bounty, nor a pardon. You haven't caught Avery and you haven't established that he's dead. Quite the opposite.'

The thief-taker paused in his stride and held up the bamboo like a baton. 'I brought this along to remind you of the inventory of the loot taken from the Great Mogul's ship, the list that you and your friend prepared and signed. The original is in the Company's files.'

He treated Hector to a cold professional smile. 'Sir Jeremiah and his fellow directors are extremely grateful. They have agreed to pay damages to the Great Mogul. Trade continues. Your list has saved them a great deal of money.'

Hector knew better than to allow his hopes to rise. He saw the gleam of malice that had appeared in Lockwood's dark eyes.

The thief-taker's smile vanished as his voice hardened. 'As far as I am concerned the inventory amounts to a confession of piracy by those who signed it. Any judge would agree.'

He paused, allowing the menace to hang in the air. 'However, I don't intend to turn you over to the authorities . . .'

Lockwood turned on his heel and walked over to the ship model. 'Every Company ship arrives home with another report of freebooters heading toward the Indian Ocean. More and more of them, all of them keen to follow in *Fancy*'s wake. Avery has set a bad example.'

He bent down and picked up one of the tiny brass cannon from the model's deck. Balancing it on the palm of his hand, he poked it with his finger to make the gun barrel move up and down. 'The directors are increasing the armament on all their ships so they can fight off any freebooter. But that's not their chief worry: they fear that if there's another freebooter attack on one of the Great Mogul's ships or a pilgrim convoy, it will put a final end to all commerce with Hindustan. They'll have wasted the compensation money.'

Carefully he replaced the miniature cannon on the deck. 'The directors and some of their friends in government have given a privateering commission to a speculator who says he can hunt down and hang the freebooters from their own yardarms. A thief-taker at sea, so to speak.'

He swung round to face Hector. 'I don't welcome competition in my line of work. I need to know what my rival is up to. I'm sure he'd value you as a member of his company.'

An awful sick sensation had been gathering in the pit of Hector's stomach. The future that he had planned for himself with Avery's help was slipping out of his grasp. He drew a deep breath and asked in as steady a voice as he could manage, 'This man, the thief-taker at sea as you call him, who is he?'

'A Scot who's been living in New York. He's come to London, bought a ship, the *Adventure Galley*, and set out on his mission. He's cocksure and impetuous, and that's his weakness. He's made a fool of himself once. If he does it again, I should be able to clip his wings.'

'What did he do?'

'Failed to salute the royal yacht when *Adventure Galley* was on her way down the Thames. The yacht reminded him of his duty with a signal gun. He should have lowered his topsail or dipped an ensign. Instead he let his men climb into the rigging, drop their trousers and slap their bare backsides. The idiot.' Lockwood gave a derisive snort. 'Farther downriver he comes upon some navy ships, and again fails to salute. This time he's stopped and boarded, and the navy makes him cool his heels, wasting a couple of weeks at anchor.'

'And where is he now?'

Lockwood moved across to where the ornamental globe stood in a corner and gave the globe a gentle quarter turn. 'He sailed to New York to pick up extra crew. Depending on his weather luck, he should now be somewhere in the middle of the South Atlantic.'

The thief-taker rotated the globe a few more inches. Hector found himself looking down at the familiar outline of Africa's southern cape.

'. . . headed for the Indian Ocean,' Lockwood continued silkily. 'So I'm going to arrange for you to travel on the next Company vessel leaving for Hindustan. The captain will call in at the Cape. There you're to jump ship. Pretend to be a runaway and boast about your time under Henry Avery's command. The moment you hear word of where *Adventure Galley* has got to, you make your way there. I've no doubt that you'll be welcomed into her company.'

A suspicion began to take shape in the back of Hector's mind. 'And what if the captain and crew turn rogue? Use *Adventure Galley* for piracy? There's nothing I could do to stop them.'

Lockwood stared at him with icy dispassion. 'Lynch, I don't expect you to try to dissuade the captain or his crew. All I want is for you to observe. Then when the time comes, and they are caught, I'll have a witness.'

Just like John Dann, Hector recalled.

'What about my wife and daughter? I've spent only a few weeks with them,' he protested.

Lockwood shrugged. 'Mr Hall can look after them. He stays here in England. The Indiaman won't be sailing for another ten days. You've time to get yourself to Sussex to say your farewells.'

The thief-taker had it all worked out, Hector thought bitterly. In a sudden surge of resentment he considered refusing this new assignment. But it took only a moment's reflection to make him realize that it would serve no purpose to antagonize Lockwood. The thief-taker was concerned only with his own interests. If thwarted, no doubt Lockwood would carry out his threat to alert the authorities that he and Jezreel had served with Avery and were back in England. They would be arrested and questioned. A thorough investigation would turn up their record of piracy in the Caribbean, and then he and Jezreel would be brought to public trial. Better that he stayed in Lockwood's shadow, his private agent, and safeguard his own private arrangement with Avery that guaranteed financial security for Maria and Isabelle. Whatever happened to him, his family would receive their annual payments from the funds that Long Ben had placed with his goldsmith-banker.

Lockwood was watching him closely and must have sensed something of Hector's inner turmoil. 'Lynch, if the captain and crew of *Adventure Galley* do turn pirate, you'll have the chance to wipe the slate clean. The person who turns King's evidence earns a pardon.'

Hector kept his face carefully blank. The role of spy for Lockwood was distasteful but it would not last for ever, and this time he was on the right side of the law.

There was one thing that he had failed to ask. 'This thief-taker at sea, what's his name?'

'Kidd, William Kidd.'

HISTORICAL NOTE

Henry Avery was 'King of Pirates' according to Daniel Defoe, who wrote *The Adventures of Robinson Crusoe*. Defoe also penned and published two fake letters allegedly written by Avery, giving a lengthy and wildly colourful account of his 'rambles and piracies'. There was no need for Defoe to invent. What we know about Avery's true story reveals a remarkable personality: intelligent, audacious and sly. He was persuasive and effective as a leader: notably in May 1694 when he was a prime mover in the mutiny that led to the theft of the royal warship renamed *Fancy*. Fifteen months later, he showed himself to be equally gifted as a fighting captain when he directed the successful assaults on *Fateh Muhammed* and *Ganj-i-Sawa'i*, one of the largest vessels afloat. His captain's share of the plunder brought him great riches, and he then showed a talent for clever management of his own success. In March 1696, posing as 'Captain Bridgeman', he brought *Fancy* to the Bahamas and disposed of the ship and what remained of the plunder to the corrupt governor. When the authorities offered a £500 bounty for his arrest, he vanished into a fog of misinformation. There is good reason to believe that he returned via Ireland to England. There, according to one rumour, he died a pauper unable to pay for his own coffin after being swindled by Bristol merchants. Alternatively, it is claimed that he lived as a very rich man under an assumed name. The one certainty is that he was never arrested or put on trial.

The looting of *Ganj-i-Sawa'i* caused a massive shock to the trade between England and India. This act of sacrilege against peaceful pilgrims outraged the devout Mogul Emperor, Aurangzeb Alamgir. English traders in Surat, the English East India Company's main trade port along with Bombay, were imprisoned for nine months as hostages. Reparations were angrily demanded. The East India Company put the value of the damages at £300,000 when dealing with the Moguls, but (in what amounted to a reversal of the under-valuation that Hector provides for the Company factor in Surat) looked for a £600,000 insurance claim in London. In the end, the furore died down when the foreign nations agreed to provide escort ships for the Indian hajj fleets.

Something is known of other characters who appear in *Freebooter*: Thomas Tew with the eight-gun sloop *Amity* had made an earlier piratical raid into the Indian Ocean before returning there and joining the ambush of the hajj fleet. He was killed, probably during the attack on *Fateh Muhammed*, when a cannon ball 'carried away the rim of Tew's belly'. William Mayes and the crew of *Pearl* made up for the disappointment of being denied loot from the hajj fleet. They took several Indian ships off the coast of India, and Mayes came back to New York with £7,000 in plunder. He returned to the Indian Ocean in 1699, again successfully. Thomas Wake died of disease at St Mary's. *Portsmouth Adventure* under Joseph Faro was wrecked in the Comoro Islands. Faro got himself to Réunion (Bourbon), where he was picked up by Henry Avery and accompanied him to the West Indies and then across the Atlantic to Ireland. Adam Baldridge, the dealer in stolen goods on St Mary's, double-crossed some of his Madagascan allies, and was forced to flee the island. He too finished up in New York, where he was interviewed by the authorities but not prosecuted. In the end, from Henry Avery's crew, only five were hung at Execution Dock, and not for acts of piracy, but for stealing *Fancy* when she was a navy ship with the intention of turning pirate. The chief witness for the Crown was John Dann. He received a pardon and went on to become a private banker-goldsmith in London. In a freakish twist of fate as strange as anything that Daniel Defoe invented, John Dann's bank failed when he fell victim to a swindler.